Praise for Sally Worbo

SALLY WORBOYES

Whitechapel Mary

CORONET BOOKS
Hodder & Stoughton

Copyright © 2001 by Sally Worboyes

First published in Great Britain in 2001 by Hodder and Stoughton
A division of Hodder Headline

The right of Sally Worboyes to be identified as the Author of the
Work has been asserted by her in accordance with the Copyright,
Designs and Patents Act 1988.

A Coronet paperback

2 4 6 8 10 9 7 5 3 1

A CIP Catalogue record of this book is available from the
British Library

ISBN 0 340 81892 1

Typeset by Palimpsest Book Production Limited,
Polmont, Stirlingshire
Printed and bound in Great Britain by
Mackays of Chatham plc, Chatham, Kent

Hodder and Stoughton
A division of Hodder Headline
338 Euston Road
London NW1 3BH

WHITECHAPEL MARY

For two Jewish, Whitechapel, men and their families
– John Pizer and Aaron Kosminski – wrongly accused
of the murders. John Pizer, a weak and frail man,
was a slipper-maker and trusted locally, before the
killings began. Although he was released after his
arrest, damage had been done and he was persecuted
and attacked in the streets. Aaron Kosminski, a small,
pathetic young man, lived with his sister and mother
and was of low intelligence. He would eat only bread
and drink only water. His sin was to make public his
low opinion of prostitutes.

ACKNOWLEDGEMENTS

My thanks as always to the supporting team at Hodders and especially to Faye Brewster, Sara Hulse and David Mitchell.

Chapter One

On a hot and humid day in August of 1888, Mary Dean, clutching the hand of her nine-year-old brother, Arthur, fought her way through the noisy street market in Bethnal Green. Her mission was to catch the greengrocer before his stall had been stripped bare. Old Martin Greenstreet was selling his root vegetables at a special price this Saturday and she didn't want to miss out.

Suddenly, in the midst of this busy place with the competing cries of pedlars, hawkers and barrow boys, the urgent call of a newspaper boy, as he threaded through the bustling crowd, chilled her. 'Faceless prowler of the night strikes again! Read all about it! Read all about it!'

The hushed voices of the market people as they turned to each other reflected the terror spreading through the lives of even the most resilient city dwellers. Quiet snatches of conversation gradually rose in volume until anger replaced fear. This latest victim had also been drawn from this small population and within the area. An area less than two square miles.

The barter interrupted, most were anxious to read the grizzly details as the boy went from one to the other rapidly selling his newspapers. Within minutes of the news being read, voices of the stallholders rang out once more. If they were to shift their goods they could not afford to let the shoppers drift away. 'Best spuds in the market, special price to warm ycr 'earts! Down a penny – spuds down a penny!'

'Mary, what does it mean?' said Arthur, petrified. '*Is* it a wild beast? *Did* a wild beast kill someone else?'

'Never mind for now, sweet'eart,' said Mary. 'Let's get in the queue or there'll be no vegetables left for us.' Smiling down bravely at her small brother, she disguised the fear sweeping through her. Glancing at the face of a woman reading the newspaper she stiffened. There was a look of horror on her face.

Pulling on his sister's sleeve, Arthur nodded towards a gaunt young man and spoke in a whisper. 'Daft Thomas is 'ere agen, with 'is Bible.'

'Turn away,' said Mary 'We don't wanna be linked with 'im. Look as if you 'aven't seen 'im, Arthur.'

Suppressing a grin, Arthur cupped his mouth. 'He's gonna do it agen. He's gonna read bits out of the Bible.' And so he was. In a world of his own and setting his wooden box down outside the Salmon and Ball public house, Thomas Cutbush ignored the commotion caused by the cries of the scruffy newsboy who was now scurrying away to fetch a fresh supply. The cryptic remarks directed at him from flushed beer-breathed customers coming out of the alehouse were futile. Thomas had his work to do and do it he would. He must try to deliver these people from sin.

Ma Cook's remarks as she tied string round a

bundle of second-hand clothing escaped him. The old Romany told her customers that the young man could preach until he was blue in the face, so long as he drew a crowd; and draw the crowd he did. The inhabitants of Bethnal Green had little else to laugh over. This corner of the East End with its dark unpleasant alleyways and overcrowded tenements left much to be desired. Most families lived in cramped conditions, and there was only just enough space in the rat-infested courts for a few donkey barrows and makeshift sheds for their beasts.

Before stepping on to his box, Thomas, with his hands clasped, looked reproachfully at a short, skinny character who endeavoured to hide his face under the peak of his cap. The dark-haired man threw him a filthy look as his eyes darted through the moving crowd. He was waiting for punters to come to bet on their fancied horses.

Deciding not to read him a lesson on the evil of gambling. Thomas opened his Bible but kept the message to himself, for the moment: *The man who wants to get rich quick will quickly fail.*

He then raised his eyes to the noisy scene of scruffy men and ragged women and other coarse females in huge feathered hats and cheap gaudy dresses; most of whom had already consumed too much alcohol, even though it was the early afternoon.

Inhaling slowly, Thomas raised his right arm. 'Young men listen to me, and never forget what I'm about to say: *Run* from her! Don't go *near* her house, lest you fall to her temptation and lose your honour!'

3

The robust laughter and quick asides from the crowd went above his head. 'Lest afterwards you groan in anguish and in shame, when syphilis consumes your body and you say, "Oh, if only I had listened!"'

The mocking jeers and laughter added to his determination. Wisdom shouts in the street for a hearing, he told himself. At least they were not ignoring him.

'Lest you say, "Oh if only I had not demanded my own way! Oh, why wouldn't I take advice? Why was I so stupid? For now I must face public disgrace!"'

'Good men – enjoy a good woman!' The grinning, leathery face of a stallholder who was counting apples into a paper bag, looked sideways at him.

Thomas reciprocated his remark with a wan smile. 'Drink from your own well, my son; be faithful and true to your wife.'

Tilting his hat forward, the man became sour-faced. 'Less of the *son*, old cock, you're still wet be'ind the ears.'

'Why delight yourself with prostitutes, embracing what isn't yours? God is closely watching you and He weighs carefully everything you do.'

Now it was the turn of the vendor's wife, a short rotund woman. 'You ain't saying my old man goes with other women by any chance?'

Gripping her shawl about her shoulders, she stepped closer, ''Cos if you are – them eyes of yours is gonna change colour any second!'

'You tell 'im, Martha!' bawled old Ma Cook. 'I'll bet four to one on 'im bein' a loony!'

Thomas turned the other cheek and smiled benignly. 'Spurn the careless kiss of a prostitute, stay far from her! Look straight ahead and watch your step—'

'You wanna watch your step, darlin'!' a prostitute yelled from the back of the crowd. 'Sayin' sich fings!'

'Shockin' talk'll see you in a dark place, you wicked boy!' screeched another.

'You leave 'im be!' A lank, elderly man pushed up a battered tall hat from his eyes. 'Listen and yer might learn a thing or two!'

'Go to hell!'

'Oh wot 'orrid langwidge!' cried an old dosser, as she snatched a handful of broken biscuits from an open tin on the cake stall and shoved them deep into the pocket of her long ragged coat. 'Shockin' it is.'

Thomas tilted his head to one side and pursed his lips. There seemed little point in continuing. His merry flock was fast turning into a mob. Abusive and foul language was taking over.

'Let me say this, before I leave you!' His voice was becoming drowned by the noise. Drawing breath he hollered for them to listen but they were talking among themselves again. 'Silence!' he bellowed, making this his final last-ditch attempt. It worked. His thunderous demand caught their attention and a guarded hush spread through the crowd.

'Take great care! Whores have had their throats slit!' He spoke slowly now, emphasising each word as he turned and pointed a finger at a gaggle of prostitutes in the crowd. 'Any one of you could be a victim!'

'Come on, Arthur,' said Mary Dean, 'we'll slip away

into the pie shop. There's going to be trouble.' And so there was. The fighting was spontaneous, as if the gathering had been waiting for those few inflammatory words. Sticks were ripped from packing cases behind the fruit cart and coshes appeared from under long jackets. A leg from an old kitchen chair appeared out of the blue. Anything that eager hands could find, they grabbed. The barrow boys were in like a flash and some of the market women took the opportunity to cat-fight with those streetgirls who were tarted up to the nines, hoping to lure away their spouses.

Bemused by the sight, Thomas stepped down from his box and lifted it with three fingers. He would slip quietly away. Shaking his head at one of the drunken women, a hand gripped him by the collar.

'Never-ending trouble, you lot!' A man smacked the back of Thomas's head with a long roll of twisted paper. 'Fink you're too good for the likes of us, do yer?' Another smack found his ear while a fist plunged into his stomach.

With the Bethnal Green police station just fifty yards away, two officers had arrived and quickly identified the instigator of the fracas. Saving Thomas from a heavier beating, one of them frog-marched him to the station while the other blew his whistle for assistance.

Locked in a cell, Thomas was content to recall the street pantomime. This had only been his second public address and he relished the response. Smiling, he drifted off into a light sleep.

Fortunately for Superintendent Charles Cutbush of Scotland Yard, a sergeant, who had escorted Thomas on a previous occasion, was on duty and realised who it was the constable had dragged in. Daft Thomas Cutbush, nephew to the Superintendent no less. A messenger was instantly instructed to take a hansom cab to Scotland Yard with a note for Thomas's uncle.

Returning in the same cab and giving the young messenger a silent response, Charles Cutbush cursed inwardly. This business of Thomas preaching was a new one.

Commanding instant respect as he entered the station, Cutbush was quickly ushered to the cell. 'I warn you, Thomas; this attention-seeking must stop before you land yourself in more trouble than I can get you out of!'

Lifting himself from the wooden bench, which might have been his bed for the night, Thomas smiled. 'God's work is never easy, Uncle. Would you have me ignore His calling because of this?'

'Keep your mouth shut and your head down when we walk from this building. Is that understood?'

'Of course.' He held his hands in front of him, locking his fingers in a devout fashion. 'You have your work to do.'

Striding through the tiny reception area of the station, Cutbush raised a hand to the officer at the desk. 'You can leave this one to me, Sergeant.'

Gazing after the two of them, the young officer remained straight-faced. The arm of the law was indeed long. It had stretched all the way from Scotland Yard and set free, without warning or reprimand, a young man who had caused a near riot on a busy market day.

Who was it, at a lecture given at Scotland Yard, he wondered, that had once said: Blood is not thicker than water, when it comes to criminal justice?

It had been an oppressive humid day, followed by a storm which had tailed off by evening, and now as the town hall clock struck the hour past midnight, Jacqueline Turner, the midwife, longed for her bed. She had just come from seeing to her neighbour, Mary Dean's mother, who was close to her time and in poor condition. Recently widowed, Mrs Dean had been slaving round the clock, piece-working for the shirt factory. Her saving grace was her daughter, Mary, who had grown from a sensitive child into a mature, hard working, lovely young woman who helped take care of little Arthur.

Having delivered three babies in the past eight hours had been more than enough for the midwife. Clutching her left side, she tried to ease the painful stitch which made it difficult for her to keep up with young Harriet Smith as she darted across a dark cobbled street. The nine-year-old spoke in short rapid sentences as she glanced over her shoulder at the midwife.

'Muvver said to tell you 'er waters broke over an hour ago.'

Undisturbed by this, Jacqueline focused on the small agile figure, who, with her grey shabby dress, kept merging in and out of the shadowy surroundings of

Nichol Street, which had no light to speak of. There were no gas fittings in this part of London's East End. The only light to see by was the moon and the occasional glow from sixpenny paraffin lamps hanging inside the houses in the alley leading to Black's buildings where the Smith family lived.

As she stepped into the dimly lit room, Jacqueline's heart sank. This was their only living space. An old kitchen table was covered with matchboxes spread out for drying, a good indication that Mrs Smith had been working until her pains had made it impossible to go on. There was a fireplace with a small oven at the side and a flat top on which a black kettle was simmering, two straw mattresses with blankets, an old chest of drawers made out of wooden tobacco cases and a coal cupboard with shelves over for storing food.

With his back to them, staring into the glowing embers, sat Mr Smith, in the one and only chair in the room. 'The missus ain't gonna give life to this one, Midwife. Do what you can to save my wife though. We've got these two to think of.' He nodded towards the smaller child huddled in the corner and jerked his thumb at Harriet. 'She's a bit on the young side to do a proper job of lookin' after us.'

Jacqueline placed her black bag on the worn piece of old carpet. 'How long is it since you ate anything, Mother?'

'What's that to you?' Mr Smith pulled back his bony shoulders and peered at her.

'She may need a douche.'

'No need,' murmured his wife, wincing in pain.

'Me and the kids 'ad a wedge of bread 'n' cheese. She wasn't up to eating.' His pride would not allow him to confess that he rarely found work, which meant they had to make do with just one meal a day, and that had been taken several hours ago and amounted to no more than a jug of penny-ha'penny leg of beef soup between the four of them, fetched by Harriet from the pudding shop.

As she lifted the thin grey blanket covering the woman, a sight she had not witnessed in all her twenty-four years as a midwife caused her to stiffen. Between the white legs dangled the tiny blue-mauve leg of the unborn child. A breach birth was difficult at the best of times. Grabbing a strong bandage from her bag she tied one end around the tiny foot and pushed the other end into the father's hand.

'Don't let go of it.' Her tone defied him to argue and even though he cursed under his breath, she could tell he was weaker in character than he liked to let on. Rolling up her sleeves, she poured water from the black kettle into a small, white enamel bowl and scrubbed her hands.

'Put the kettle back on Harriet and pour it into this basin when I tell you.'

Throwing the soapy water into the street, Jacqueline asked the Lord for His help. She was going to need it if she was to deliver this baby alive.

'Why hasn't the doctor been informed of this?' She directed her question at Harriet.

''E weren't in,' Harriet looked on the verge of tears.

'I went round twice but missed 'im both times. A neighbour told me where you lived.'

Jacqueline nodded and managed a smile; the child looked frightened to death. 'I could do with someone like you to run messages for me, Harriet.' She said this not only to lift the girl's spirits but to get on better terms with her father. An extra earned shilling would mean a decent meal on the table for this family.

As she wiped the perspiration from her patient's face, Jacqueline leaned over and whispered in her ear. 'It's going to be painful but between the two of us, we can deliver your baby. Have faith, be strong.' She pulled a small bottle of gin from her pocket and encouraged the woman to take a few sips.

With forceps and other implements laid out on her own clean towel, Jacqueline lifted the woman's knees and began her work. Slipping one hand inside the dilated womb, she eased the baby's other leg from its awkward position, encouraging Mrs Smith all the while.

'Pant, Mother, pant. *Don't* push.'

The woman did her best to follow instructions but the sudden intrusion from her midwife's hand inside set off the contractions again and as much as she willed herself not to, still she bore down. The noise in that small room reached a crescendo, as both children began to cry and Mr Smith hollered.

'Stop trying to save it, Midwife! We can make another kid any time but where'll I find someone to look after us?'

'Be quiet, man, and grab this other leg!' She felt like

calling him all manner of names but held her tongue for the sake of the children.

Begrudgingly, he did as ordered and cursed Jacqueline as she slipped both her hands inside the woman and cupped the baby's buttocks.

'A deep breath and then a gentle push, Mother. And stop when I say or you'll tear from front to back.'

Panting and pushing, the perspiration dripping from her, the poor woman did her best to follow instructions. '*Pant*, Mother, and then one good push!'

A determined cry from the mother as she bore down was rewarded by a sudden gush as the baby entered the world. The expression of gratitude in the woman's eyes touched the midwife.

Working at speed, Jacqueline cut the cord and then slapped the baby, bringing about his first piercing cry. She wrapped him in a piece of sheeting and laid him in Harriet's arms. 'You cuddle your brother while I see to your mother. He'll soon quieten down.' She turned to the shadowy drawn face of Mr Smith.

'Make your wife a strong cup of sweet tea, she deserves it.'

Looking across to little Harriet, the man jerked a thumb towards the kettle. 'Put the baby down and do as Midwife says.' He narrowed his eyes and stared back at Jacqueline. 'I wouldn't mind a drop of that gin m'self.'

Jacqueline scrubbed her hands. 'I'll call again tomorrow. Get as much rest as you can.' She had no intention of allowing the unshaven man near her liquor.

Making her way home through Wentworth Street, exhausted but proud of her achievements, it crossed Jacqueline's mind that maybe the scrap of a baby would have been better off had she not saved it. She had seen enough poverty in her time to know what kind of an upbringing he was in for.

Sighing at the futility of it all, Jacqueline turned her mind to her plans of emigrating to America. Her life savings, hidden away under her floorboards, had mounted up and there was enough to enable her to pay for the voyage with a little left over for lodgings. That she would find work as a midwife in America, she had no doubts whatsoever.

Apart from her adored nephew, Thomas Cutbush, there was nothing to keep her in England. She had disowned her demented sister, Thomas's mother, several years ago.

As she passed the entrance to George Yard, deep in thought as to the arrangements she would soon be making, a hideous scream and the echo of running feet as a market porter's heavy boots crashed against the cobblestones, made her blood run cold.

'Police! Murder!' His voice pierced the dark silence. 'It's 'orrible! Really 'orrible! Police!'

Within moments, the man was pulling the midwife from behind and begging her to go with him into George Yard Buildings.

'I do beg you with all my heart, madam. Please . . . please come with me!' His eyes were darting everywhere, terrified that a maniac was about to jump out of the darkness. With her heart beating rapidly, she followed the hysterical man, who was clearly in mortal fear of his own life.

The midwife could do no more than stare, horrified at the spread-eagled body of a woman lying in a dark pool of blood. Her throat had been slit and her mutilated body ripped apart, slashed in several places. Her eyes were open, showing the horror of what she had witnessed in the face of her murderer.

The sound of the porter's voice echoing through the backstreets as he ran off, filled Jacqueline's ears. He was succinctly reporting the nightmare scene in graphic detail for all to hear. The piercing, shrill sound of a policeman's whistle and more running footsteps caused the midwife to cower back into the shadows with only one thought in mind: to leave quickly. An urgent voice from somewhere inside was urging her, Get away, Jacqueline. Go home.

From her refuge she watched the arrival of the policeman, and waited for him and those following close behind to enter the forbidding tenement block, before she slipped away out of the yard, homeward bound.

Taking some comfort from the spasmodic gas lighting in Old Montague Street, she quickened her pace as more curious occupants came out to see what the commotion was about.

Sensing danger, her heart thumping with fear, Jacqueline glanced nervously in every direction, at every moving shadow. When she arrived at Osborne Street, she turned right, preferring the longer route home along the well-lit Whitechapel Road.

The familiar figure ahead caused her to sigh with some relief. It was her nephew, Thomas. Opening her mouth to call out she closed it again and slowed her pace. There was a pain in her chest now. Squinting in the dark she could see that he was in a hurry to leave the place that others were rushing towards.

Before she had time to compose herself and call out to him, he had turned the corner into the main road. Shaking her head, she continued on her way, thinking only of her nephew. That he should be roaming the backstreets at that time angered her. Although he was in his early twenties, she still saw him as a child.

What now puzzled her confused mind, was why Thomas should have been hurrying away. Maybe, like herself, his intuition was to escape from evil.

Once in Whitechapel Road, she peered both ways but there was no sign of him, he seemed to have vanished into the gloom.

1 September. There will be more drowned rats in the sewer. The rain is easing off but the gutter beneath my window is like a fast running stream. Such peculiar weather. Today the scorching September sunshine heated the paving stones to such a degree that it felt as if I were walking on hot ashes. Just a few hours and it will be dusk and later, after dark, the streets will be devoid of any decent folk. The air is heavy with fear and the quickening sound of footsteps is mixed with the slamming and bolting of doors. Inside the houses, there will be conjecture, vague suspicion and rough guesses as to what might be in tomorrow's newspapers. And I, too, wonder. Will there be another murder tonight?

Refusing to let her imagination run away and fill her mind with the vision of a maniac dressed in black, the midwife closed her diary and replaced her quill into the inkpot. Drawing the bedroom curtain she glanced down into the narrow street, catching sight of young Mary Dean who was stepping carefully round a large puddle on the pavement.

As she eased up the stiff sash window, the midwife made a mental note to speak to the rent man about the runners which were in need of repair.

'How's your mother, Mary?'

'Oh, Miss Turner!' Mary's hand flew to her breast. 'You gave me such a scare. She thinks it'll come next week!'

'Did you do as I asked and tell her to get more rest?'

'Course I did, but you know Mother. While the work's there she'll be up till past midnight sewing on shirt buttons!'

Jacqueline's mind flashed to the murders. 'Don't be out too late, Mary, there's a good girl. And if you can get someone to walk you home, so much the better.'

'Oh I'll be all right. It's the streetgirls he's out for.'

'We don't know that for sure, so be careful!' Returning Mary's farewell wave, she closed the window and watched as she disappeared into the steamy dusk and remembered vividly when she had brought Mary into the world. A bonny baby she was too – with a mop of reddish-brown hair. Now she was a young woman with the loveliest of smiles and twinkling blue eyes.

The word 'eyes' instantly brought back the nightmare

scene that Jacqueline had not been able to wipe from her mind. The look of terror in the eyes of the murdered prostitute, Martha Tabram, had caused her to wake in a dreadful sweat more than once.

With the smell of oxtail soup drifting up from the scullery, she remembered that the copper boiler needed stoking. 'No fire, no supper,' she murmured to herself as she heaved her frame down the narrow winding staircase.

Dropping peeled turnips and carrots into the pot, she leaned forward and allowed the sweet aroma of thyme to fill her nostrils. Her evening meal was something she looked forward to, especially when it had been simmering for hours. As she opened the tiny iron door of the boiler, her father's voice drifted into her thoughts: Only a spendthrift lets a furnace burn out. Thankfully, some of the coals were still glowing.

Once she had shovelled in more fuel, the midwife settled herself by the tiny fire in the front room. Her intention was to read until her meal was ready, but no matter how hard she tried to concentrate, she could not stop her mind from wandering to the murderer who had killed again and might be skulking in an archway or dark alley at that very moment.

She glanced at the faded green velvet fireside chair. Her father's chair. Her father – a private man who had always preferred the company of his small family to those outside. Her father who, unlike her demented mother, she had adored.

Allowing her thoughts to drift back to the past she recalled the times when he would carry her in one arm and her sister, Celestine, in the other. He would take them to the market to watch the cattle being penned after being driven all the way from Wanstead. The odour of the animals was something she would always remember. It was a smell she had warmed to from the very first time she had swept her tiny hand against the sweaty hide of a cow. Her sister had taunted her many times over her love for the beasts. During their childhood, she would often taunt and sing a ditty she had composed deliberately to rile Jacqueline during or soon after an argument between the two of them.

> So clever is my sister
> She writes her name so well,
> But what our farver doesn't know,
> Is what Jacqueline loves t'smell;
> A cow's arse!

'Your sister has a dark future. The poor child takes after your mother and no mistake.' This was something her father had murmured on several occasions. At the time, Jacqueline did not understand what he meant by it, but as the years unfolded his words were proved true. For in truth, both her mother and sister proved to be of unstable mind. Their personalities could change in an instant – from dull and moody to fits of rage *or* laughter. At least her sister had been blessed with beauty. With her long raven tresses and dark brown eyes, she did attract the most handsome of men. Her romances were varied and many, until she finally caught and married John Cutbush, a true gentleman, who earned a decent living as a clerk in one of the London banks.

Sadly, the modest house in Bancroft Road, Stepney, which he had purchased had to be sold off to pay his debts. Her mother and sister had spent all of his money on clothes and on drink and the family had had to move into rented accommodation. Soon after this, her brother-in-law passed away, a miserable and broken man.

'And who was to blame for his pains? I wonder . . .' murmured Jacqueline as she gazed into the fire, '. . . but then, it could have been worse. At least your son Thomas has me to watch over him should my sister ever throw him out.' She thanked the Lord that neither her mother nor sister, had ever seen fit to harm anyone. Nor had they been diagnosed insane. It was not uncommon to come across lunatics in this part of London and it was no wonder. In the backstreets, there had, for more than a century, been numerous overcrowded tenement houses inhabited by the most deprived and wretched people. The cramped conditions, the filth and poverty, were enough to send anyone out of their mind.

Emerging from her maudlin thoughts and distracted by the flickering of the gaslight, the midwife swept two pennies from the mantelpiece and pushed both into the gas meter. It wouldn't do for her to be cast into darkness while in this low mood. She thought again about her beloved nephew, Thomas, and wondered why he hadn't called in to see her, it wasn't like him. He never missed a day.

Scolding herself for having had a third gin, she went into the scullery to spoon herself some hot soup. Nearly drunk and not even close to bedtime – shame on you, Jacqueline. What if someone were to pound on the door right now, begging her to go to the aid of some poor soul who was in labour?

As she spooned the steaming oxtail soup into a bowl, her thoughts returned to young Mary Dean. She should really have stayed in and watched over her recently widowed mother and young brother. The family wasn't the midwife's responsibility after all, and yet here she was, worrying if Mrs Dean was all right.

Carefully carrying her supper, she walked unsteadily into the parlour and back to the fireside, wondering if it ever crossed any of her neighbours' minds that she too needed comforting, at times. If she had the build of a fragile woman, things might be different, but her square stocky frame had always given the wrong impression. From as far back as she could remember, Jacqueline Turner was viewed as a strong, independent woman who preferred her own company and never had the desire to marry.

Glancing across the room she gazed at her reflection in the large oval mirror on the wall. Hers was a square plain face, with narrow grey eyes and a nose which was too flat and merged into her ruddy cheeks. Her full lips would complement any other face but her own. And now, in her fifty-eighth year, the midwife had no illusions about finding a suitor. She was settled to living alone and couldn't imagine having someone else moving around her house as if he belonged.

Unfolding her newspaper she read the headlines for the umpteenth time: ANOTHER MURDER IN WHITECHAPEL! Reading through the article once more, she shuddered. Polly Nichols, this victim, just like her friend, Martha Tabram, had also walked the backstreets, luring men away from their duties and wives to have fourpenny-sex. Maybe the killer meant to sweep vile sin from the area? Make it a safer place for girls like Mary Dean who came from a decent family?

Whatever the reasons for the bloody deeds, at least the spreading prostitution had been brought to the attention of everyone. There was hope yet for her birthplace. Her father, were he still alive, would have seen the headlines as a step forward, she felt sure of it.

She closed the newspaper and ate her meal, aware of the unusual silence from the street. The cleansing was already taking effect. Families were together; the menfolk at home protecting their women.

Turning out of Whitehead Street into Cleveland Way, Mary Dean tried to push the midwife's words of warning from her. She would, after all, be returning after dark and fear could play terrible tricks on the mind. The spreading alarm of a maniac at large had gone haywire – thanks mainly to the press. There had been other murders in the past, so why were folk panicking now over prostitutes who risked their lives every night of the week? Playing with Satan's fire, as her mother would say, was inviting the flesh to be burned. It was a wonder more whores weren't murdered in dark alleyways.

Lifting the hem of her brown linsey frock and grey flannel petticoat to avoid it trailing in the rain water which had collected across the worn-down flagstones, she stepped carefully, not noticing the oncoming young man who rushed by and knocked against her.

'Sorry,' he said, turning and walking away awkwardly. 'Didn't think you were that close. Sorry.'

Mary straightened her reddish-brown straw hat and checked that the bow on the black velvet trim was still in place. 'That's all right, no 'arm done,' she said to the retreating figure. It was the midwife's daft nephew, Thomas Cutbush.

Casting her mind back, Mary remembered him when they were both children. He used to loiter in Whitehead Street while the others played. His mother often paid a visit to her sister, the midwife, Jacqueline Turner. The high pitch of her thin voice would produce a sensation in the turning when she threw abuse at the midwife or anyone who happened to pass by. What chance had the likes of Thomas, with a mother who sometimes behaved like a raving lunatic?

'Hello, Mary. Fancy seeing you agen?' A familiar voice broke into her thoughts. Tucking a few loose strands of hair into her high-fashioned bonnet, Lizzie Redmond threw back her head and laughed. 'Don't change much, do yer?'

'It can't be you . . . Lizzie Redmond?' Mary looked her friend up and down. 'Look at you all in satins and silks!'

A radiant smile on her face, Lizzie was pleased to see her old childhood friend. 'I saw you coming along and waited. You would 'ave walked straight by me, I reckon. In love, are yer?'

'Don't be daft.' Seeing how well-turned-out her friend was, Mary suddenly felt conscious of her own shabby, dark red ulster draped over her shoulders.

Waving on the hansom cab she had flagged down, Lizzie slipped her arm through Mary's and walked her towards a small coffee house, her silk and satin blue frock rustling with every step. 'So where was you off to then, Mary Dean?'

'A meeting. Annie Besant's giving a talk down the Mission Hall at seven o'clock.'

'She would! Fancies herself as a politician; what's she fighting for now?'

'Would there be much point in telling yer?'

'Not if it's boring.' Lizzie pushed her face close to Mary's and grinned. 'I'm really glad I saw yer . . . Mary Dean . . . my best friend for years.'

'By the look of your classy dress and feathered bonnet, Lizzie, you must be leading the high life. Hitched up to a toff, are yer?' Mary pushed through the swing-door into the coffee house and sniffed in the delicious aroma of cakes baking in the oven.

'Toffs don't marry the likes of us, Mary, they just like to bed us. Pay well though.'

Not that surprised at her friend's confession, Mary raised an eyebrow and smiled. 'You always said you'd make good use of that body of yours.'

'Sit yerself down,' said Lizzie and went to order the

coffee and jam tarts. Making her way back to the small round table by the window, she checked Mary's face to see if there was any hint of reprobation. There wasn't.

'Glad to see you're not shocked, Mary.'

'Each to their own.'

'It's not a bad life so long as you're picky about who yer clients are. And before you even fink of preaching remember that "Moral judgements are a curse to the deliverer more than to the whore". I read that in a journal.' She sipped her coffee and grinned. 'Not that *I'm* a whore.'

'D'yer know what you was blessed with, Lizzie Redmond . . . ? The gift of the gab.'

Lizzie leaned forward, cupping her coffee. 'We know husbands better than their wives know 'em. An' we know what they really like, an' we give it to 'em. Keeps 'em nice an' 'appy for when they get back home to their wives. They treat their servants all the better 'cos of us lot.'

'It's still whoring.'

'I told yer. I'm not a whore. I am a *courtesan*.' She raised her thick-shaped eyebrows, proudly.

Mary leaned back into her chair and laughed. 'You've got style, I grant you that. So where do you meet these rich geezers?'

'Ah ha! That's my business, find your own million-aires.'

'Come on you. Half a story's worse than none, as you full know.'

'All right, Virgin Mary. But keep it to yerself.'

Obviously Lizzie couldn't wait to tell her. She leaned forward and spoke in a quiet, mock posh voice. 'Mother is the proud owner of a ... House of Assignation.'

'A brothel?'

Lizzie drew in air and filled her lungs. 'Don't ever ...' she said, breathing out '... ever, let my muvver hear you call it that. It's worse than swearing.' Shamefaced, Lizzie dropped her theatrical act. 'My clients treat me with respect, Mary. One of 'em don't even touch me. He just likes to watch while I get undressed down to me drawers. Then all I 'ave to do is lay next to 'im on the bed and listen to 'is past. He was in a workhouse for most of 'is childhood.'

'If that's really true, you're more like one of them mind doctors then.'

'I am, yeah. You're *right*,' said Lizzie, brightening up again. 'An' I'll tell you summink else, the rich ones are obsessed with money. The more they've got, the more they've gotta 'ave. And as for the "arty" lot, well, let me tell yer . . .' Lizzie checked her surroundings for anyone ear-wigging and lowered her voice. 'Most, if not all, are on drugs.' She then whispered the word laudanum in Mary's ear.

'Even the famous ones. *Women* an' all.'

'Blimey,' sighed Mary, 'you see life all right, don't yer?'

Lizzie lifted her cup to her mouth and winked at Mary. 'I do, an' I love it.' She sipped her tea and leaned back. 'No reason why *you* couldn't do it.' She gave her friend the once over. 'You don't keep up wiv

25

fashion mind. Bustles are out.' She slipped one hand inside her silk pouch and withdrew a lovely gold-plated cigarette case. 'The gentry are very particular as to the way we dress.'

She narrowed her large green eyes and moved her face closer to Mary's. 'An' don't fink I don't 'ave to study. I do. Gentlemen don't like to fink we're ignorant.' Her cheeks were now flushed with passion for her work. 'Wit an' charm's at the top of the list and an interest in literature. Mention a character from a Dickens book an' they go stiff. That's the daft thing, they expect more from us than they do from their wives.' She drew on her cigarette and blew a perfect smoke ring. 'Mind you, we're not allowed to lose our cockney accent. Oh no. Mother's the only one allowed to talk posh. Don't ask me why.'

'Do any of 'em . . . fall for you?' asked Mary, wanting to know more.

'They say they do. Tell yer they love ya. It's all moonshine though, makes 'em feel better. I couldn't give a toss one way or the other.' She leaned back and became thoughtful.

'There's one special man, mind. He's a right tease.' She gazed out, a faraway look in her eyes. 'Makes me feel like a *real* woman and the only one for 'im. He knows that I know that there're others sizzling on the side, keeping their drawers warm.'

Having heard enough in one telling, Mary got ready to leave. She glanced at the clock on the wall. 'I don't wanna miss the talk, Lizzie . . .'

'Don't you wanna know who he is?'

'. . . and Mum's near 'er time, so—'

'You might bump into 'im as it 'appens. He's a mate of your socialist speaker. If he is there, you can't miss 'im. Soft Irish voice, tall with lovely red-gold hair and a beard that looks as if it's bin there for ever.

'From 'is face you'd fink he was full of courage, but really, underneath it all, he's quite shy.' She sat upright, drew on her cigarette and grinned. 'I'm 'is secret love. What's this meetin' about anyway?'

'We want more pay from Bryant and May.'

'That sounds like Besant. Anyway, you'll know where to come if you're skint.' She handed Mary a visiting card with the name of her mother's high-class brothel in bold capital letters. 'Don't let *anyone* see that.'

Studying the card, Mary was reminded of the recent murders. 'You're not worried about the maniac that's roaming the streets in the dark, looking for a whore to slash?'

'I am not a whore,' mouthed Lizzie.

'Ain't you even the least bit frightened?'

'Go on, clear off, or you'll miss all that fun.' Dropping her cigarette case into her purse, she raised her eyes to Mary's. 'I'm sorry about your dad. I read the obituary in the East London paper.'

'Thanks,' said Mary, casting her eyes down.

'Your mum must be missing 'is wages?'

'She is, Lizzie, yeah. Especially with another baby on the way. She was five months gone when Dad died. But Arthur's as pleased as punch, wants a baby brother to play with.'

Lizzie took Mary's hand and squeezed it gently. 'You don't 'ave to live scrimpin' and scrapin', Mary. Fink about what I said, my life's not as bad as all that. I wouldn't wanna change it now. Don't forget 'ow poor *my* mum was before she decided to use 'er looks and 'er brains. But that poor cow 'ad to go out on the streets night after night so she could save for a decent outfit, good enough for the toffs up West. She got a break wiv one of 'em. He set 'er up and he's still around, trying to get up the courage to leave 'is wife for 'er. He'll never do it and she knows that but blimey . . . 'as he ever turned her life round. That was ten years ago and he still comes to see 'er.'

'Does 'is wife know?'

'Course she don't! He's sort of well known in 'is own circle. Not a writer like my bloke.' She looked her friend in the eye. 'You could do it, Mary. You've got looks men die for and I know that mother'd—'

'Lizzie,' said Mary, interrupting her. 'I'm real 'appy for you, you look beautiful. But I would sooner go without an 'ot meal.'

'*You* would, yeah. But what about little Arthur and your mum and the baby when it comes?' She cupped Mary's sad face. 'No one would know. We keep everyfing under wraps. We 'ave to, for our sakes and to safeguard our gentlemen's reputations.'

'I don't blame you for what you do, Lizzie, *I* just couldn't, that's all.'

'Fair enough. I'm not short of a few quid so if you get stuck you know where to come. Promise me you won't let yer daft pride stop yer. Promise?'

'I promise.' Showing a hand, Mary bid her friend farewell and left the coffee shop, deep in her own thoughts: Don't think I wouldn't like to wear fine clothes too, Lizzie. Don't think it for one minute.

Taking a deep breath and pushing all thoughts of illicit money from her mind, Mary focused on the strike meeting, telling herself that if anyone could get more pay for the match girls, Annie Besant could. Her articles in the new journal, *The Link*, always hit the right chord.

Seeing the small groups of Bryant and May factory girls chatting and laughing, as they made their way along the Waste, evoked a feeling of camaraderie.

Arriving at the Mission Hall, she was pleased to see some of her workmates among the many other women who were there. Then, looking across the room to a small platform she caught sight of the speaker who lost no time in bringing the meeting to order.

Besant began with a quote from Victor Hugo: '"I will speak for the dumb. I will speak of the small to the great and the feeble to the strong. I will speak for all the despairing silent ones."'

Besant then went on to attack sweated labour, extortionate landlords, unhealthy workshops, child labour and prostitution. Ending her speech, she recited from one of her articles in *The Link* – White Slavery in London – in which she exposed the working conditions of the women in the factory.

During a refreshment break, and caught up in the excited talk of a strike, Mary found her thoughts drifting back to her friend, Lizzie. She imagined herself working with her. In shades of blue silk and satin, she would have made quite an impression.

Seizing an opportunity to approach the speaker, Mary wove her way through the crowded room. 'It's time someone came and helped us,' she said, reeling off the words before her courage melted away.

'I couldn't agree more,' said Besant, returning Mary's smile. 'But surely you're not a match girl?'

'I work in the office not the factory. I always read your articles and I was there on Bloody Sunday. I saw the way you stood up to the police, I don't know how you did it.'

'Full of spiritual pride, is the answer.' A tall, erect man placed a hand on the speaker's shoulder and raised an eyebrow at Mary. 'And do I not detect a similar look of defiance in your eyes?'

Embarrassed, Mary withdrew as Lizzie's words came flooding back. The tall Irishman had a mass of red hair and a beard to match. She had said nothing about his good looks and gleaming white teeth.

'Don't let the gentleman's audacious manner embarrass you. We don't want to feed his male conceit. He would have us believe he is shameless when in fact he works very hard for those causes he deems worthwhile.'

'I cannot seem to get it through to Mrs Besant, that I am no more than a mere loafer,' he raised his head and tilted his body back, a wide smile spreading across his face.

Picking up on the chemistry between them, Mary

thought it best to leave them to themselves. She thanked the speaker and excused herself.

'I shall look out for you during my talks,' Besant said earnestly.

'And does your name match your face?' said her gentleman friend.

'It's Mary. Mary Dean.'

Offering his hand, the man nodded approvingly. 'Bernard. Bernard Shaw.'

'I fear he is quite incorrigible.' Besant showed no hint of a smile.

'And none the worse for it,' he said, addressing his retort to Mary. He then raised his glass of milk and walked away, managing a show of humour by his long springy strides.

Turning into Whitehead Street, Mary was pleased with her eventful evening. First Lizzie telling her about her colourful life, then two intellectuals making her feel as if she was almost an equal. Was it because Besant was, after all, only an ordinary intelligent woman, and that she herself wasn't quite as insignificant as she had always thought?

Turning the key in the lock of the street door she couldn't help smiling about the secret she held. She could have so easily brought the flirtatious Shaw to heel had she whispered Lizzie's name in his ear.

As she closed the door behind her, she heard her mother calling her name. Struck by fear, she knew by her tone that something was wrong. Badly wrong.

She listened at the foot of the narrow stairs and

could hear Arthur, her young brother, crying in his bed. With a feeling of dread inside she went upstairs. Surely her mother hadn't gone into premature labour during the few hours she had been out?

Arriving at the doorway of her mother's bedroom she could do no more than gaze at her. She lay in a pool of dark red blood which had soaked into the bedclothes. Her face was so ashen it blended with the pillowslip and between her legs lay the lifeless body of Mary's stillborn sister.

'Take care of Arthur, Mary . . . and yourself.' Try as she might, her mother could not lift her hand more than an inch. 'I'm going to the light, Mary . . .'

Falling to her knees, Mary clasped her mother's white hand in hers and kissed the cold fingertips. 'Mummy . . . please . . . please don't faint, I'll fetch the midwife. Arthur can run for the doctor.' She looked into the colourless eyes which held no expression. 'Please don't die,' she cried, 'don't leave us . . .' The tears were pouring from her eyes. 'You'll be all right. I'll make you warm. I'll hold you till help comes.' The strange expression in her mother's eyes both frightened and calmed her. She seemed to be gazing somewhere beyond . . . Gazing at someone she recognised, but who wasn't really there. There was a hint of a smile on her face and she was trying to lift both her arms. 'Let me go, child. Let me go to her.'

'Who? Go to *who*?' Mary started to cry. 'Mummy, please . . .'

'I'm going to the light, Mary. Your grandmother's waiting.' Smiling weakly as the life and spirit began to leave her exhausted body, she whispered her daughter's name for the very last time before murmuring. 'Take care of Arthur . . . love 'im for all of us.'

And while Mary sat there staring at the marble-like face of her mother, frozen in time and silent, her brother watched from the doorway, shocked but mesmerised. 'Did she die?' Arthur said, his voice croaky and hardly like his own. 'Did Mummy die as well?'

Turning in slow motion, Mary looked blankly at him. 'I don't know, darling . . . we must get Mrs Turner. She might just be exhausted.' She pulled the blankets up over her mother and her stillborn sister's body and then brushed back her mother's hair from her white face and leant forward and kissed her forehead.

'We can't get the midwife, she's not there, I went and then came back. She's gone out. Daft Thomas was there. He could go and look for 'er.'

'No, I'll knock next door. She'll fetch the doctor.'

'She's gone to heaven, Mary,' said Arthur in a strange, calm voice. 'Mummy's gone to heaven.'

Turning round she saw that her little brother was shaking and was very pale. She lunged forward and caught him before his crumpled body hit the floor. The poor little waif had passed out.

Chapter Two

As Mary cut a thick slice of bread for her brother, she could feel his eyes on her face. Just two weeks after the family tragedy and most of the time spent crying, she was still unable to answer the question she had seen in his eyes. What is to become of us?

The money their mother had earned doing her piece-work, sewing buttons on to men's shirts, had just been sufficient to see the rent paid each week with some left over for gas, coal and food. Since their father had died, Mary had given over all of her wages which helped to clothe all three of them. Her mother had either bought their clothes from second-hand shops or made them herself. 'I don't care if I 'ave to go into Barnardo's, so long as I can come and see yer,' murmured Arthur, swallowing against the lump in his throat. He dipped his bread into the vegetable soup Mary had made from root vegetables and herbs. 'It's not a dirty place. I went up Stepney Causeway after school and 'ad a look in the doorway. It was all right.' Again he looked at her, hoping she might have a better solution.

Turning her face away from him she shook her head slowly. 'It won't come to that, Arthur.' If he could be so brave, then so could she. She would take in washing and make matchboxes at home. Age was on her side, keeping busy would at least stop her from thinking about her mother having been left alone when she needed her most. The least she could do now was to make certain that Arthur would always be with her, his welfare would be in her trust. He was her charge now and would always be so.

Once again, as so often had happened since meeting up with her old friend, Lizzie's words went through her mind. 'No reason why you couldn't be part of it, Mary . . . You don't 'ave to live like the poor . . . My life's not as bad as you might think.'

'We could move in with the midwife,' said Arthur, thinking for her. 'She's bin really kind to us.'

Mary sat down and placed a hand on his. 'Arthur, stop worrying. I'll think of something.'

'There ain't nuffink to fink about, I've tried. I don't wanna go into a workhouse, Mary.' His bottom lip curled under and his eyes filled with tears.

'Eat your supper now, there's a good boy. We'll talk about it later.' She said this knowing there really wasn't much to talk about. Unless she acted quickly, they would have to give up their home and be split up. She was going that very evening to see Lizzie.

'Rent man'll be round tomorrow.'

'I know, but Mr Allen's a decent man. He'll make excuses to the landlord for us. They'll give us a bit of time to sort ourselves out. You'll see.'

'So we won't 'ave to 'ide when he knocks then?'

'No, Arthur.' She forced a few spoonfuls of soup

down her. Food was the last thing on her mind right then, but she had to keep up her strength. If she were to fall ill her brother's fate would be out of her control.

'I'll have to go out for an hour after we've finished eating. Will you be all right by yerself or do you wanna go down Miss Turner's?'

'Go down Miss Turner's.'

'Good.' Mary leaned forward across the small table. 'But you're not to ask if we can move in with 'er. She's only got one bedroom and a boxroom. Anyway, Mum nor Dad would want us to scrounge off anyone.'

'I wouldn't wanna live there anyway,' he said, staring into his soup. 'Thomas gives me the willies. And he's always visitin' 'er.'

'He's all right, just a bit simple, that's all.'

'He's not simple, Mary, he's clever. He can read the Bible *and* books about medicine. He reads bits out to us kids when we're in the street, even when we're playing kickball. He should be in the loony-bin.'

'Arthur, honestly.' She said, mock scolding him, 'You mustn't say things like that. Finish that food and I'll take you down—'

'I can take meself.' He wiped his mouth on the sleeve of his shirt and scraped the legs of his chair on the scullery floor as he got up. 'Where you goin' anyway?'

'To see someone. A lady who needs some typewriting done in the evenings.'

'Oh. So we might be able to stop 'ere then?' He suddenly livened up.

She tousled his unkempt fair hair and smiled. 'Wild

'orses are gonna 'ave to drag us away from our home, Arthur, wild 'orses.'

'My teacher said I might get a job down the fruit market after school and Saturdays providing I don't fall behind in me lessons. He knows someone.'

'We'll see.' She picked up a brush from the sideboard and pushed it through his wiry hair. 'Don't forget to wash your 'ands and face before you go out.'

'You 'aven't got a typewriting machine?'

Mary laughed at the way his young mind worked overtime, *all* of the time. 'I won't need one. The lady's got one in 'er 'ouse. That's why I'd 'ave to go there to do the work. She runs 'er own little business.'

'Is she rich?' he said, pulling away from the wet face flannel she'd produced.

'She's got a few bob, yeah.'

'So I'll 'ave to get used to being on me own then?'

Mary closed her eyes and swallowed. Arthur could, with just a few words, bring her to tears. She winked at him and covered her grief. 'Not if I can 'elp it.' She tucked his shirt into his breeches and patted his bottom, hardly able to speak. 'You can always 'ave your friend Billy in or go over to 'is house. Or sit with Miss Turner.'

Picking up on her sorrow, he drew a quivering breath and managed a weak smile. 'She's gonna teach me to play cards. Her and Daft Thomas play all the time.'

'Well then, there we are, things are looking up already.' As much as she tried to control her emotions she simply could not. Without warning she began to weep.

Throwing his arms round her slim waist, Arthur told her they would be all right. But as brave as he tried to be, he burst into tears. 'I can't help it, Mary. I want Mummy. I want Mummy and Daddy.' He buried his face in the warm soft material of her frock and sobbed.

'You mustn't mind, Arthur, we're allowed to cry. We can cry for Mummy and the baby and for Daddy. But I promise you this, we will be laughing again, soon. We will, sweet'eart, I promise yer.'

'But it won't bring 'em back, will it, nuffing'll bring 'em back to us. They're not ever gonna come in the front door agen.' He pulled away from her and slumped down into the worn armchair. 'I should 'ave come and got you from the Mission Hall. Mummy was crying out loud . . .' he clenched his fists and squeezed his eyes shut tight. 'I should've got the *doctor*! I don't *want* her to be dead!'

'Nor do I Arthur, but she is and there's nothing we can do about it. But we're gonna be all right. I promised Mummy I would look after you, and she died with a smile on 'er face because she knew I *would*. She knew we'd be all right. She was *smiling*, Arthur, I promise you.'

'But what if *you* die?' he cried, looking pitifully into her face. His red-rimmed eyes held fear and misery. 'What will I do then?' he splayed his hands, showing no hope.

'Oh, no, not me. I'm gonna live to be very rich and

very old and so are you. And we'll never, never be separated. Cross my heart.' She held out her arms and pulled him up off the armchair and held him to her breast again. 'Now then. Let's give your face a spruce so no one'll know you've bin crying. We don't want people to take pity now, do we?'

Once she had smartened and comforted her adorable brother, Mary took him along to Jacqueline Turner's house. Arthur had given up on the idea of going by himself once they had stood on the doorstep of their house and seen Thomas going into his aunt's house.

'He's got them books agen,' Arthur murmured on the way. 'I 'ope he's not gonna read all that stuff out loud.'

'What stuff?' asked Mary, squeezing her brother's small hand and smiling down at him.

'From the Bible. All about wicked prostitutes.'

'Don't say that word, Arthur, it's not very nice.'

He looked up at her, puzzled. 'But everyone says it now, even teachers at school. They warn us not to go near any in case Jack the Ripper's in the shadows.'

Mary stopped in her tracks. 'Where'd you get that nonsense from? Who's bin filling your head with ideas like that? Jack the Ripper, indeed! Don't ever say such black things again, there ain't no such person!'

'There is. There's a bogeyman who's gonna cut us all up and his name's Jack the Ripper. He used to be Jack the Lad but then he grew up . . . you can ask anyone.'

Seeing the frightened look on his face, she broke into a smile. 'You silly thing, it's just daft talk, that's all.'

Arthur shrugged as he looked into her face. 'Is it?'
'Yes!'

Arriving at the midwife's door, Arthur pulled on her sleeve. 'Can't I come wiv you to the lady's 'ouse?'

'No. And in any case, I won't be that long, an hour, if that.'

Opening the door, Jacqueline Turner's look of surprise embarrassed Mary. It hadn't occurred to her that the woman might not want a charge to look after. 'I'm sorry to be a nuisance—'

Jacqueline raised a hand in protest. 'Come on in. I've had my tea and I was just going to make Thomas and myself some cocoa. You're more than welcome to join us.' She opened the door wide and stood aside.

Stepping directly into the small front room, Mary nodded at Thomas who sat huddled round the coal fire. 'The nights are drawing in already,' she said, 'and it's only September.' Mary was pleased that the room was a warm and cosy place for Arthur.

'It's been a good summer. With luck on our side, the winter won't be so harsh this year,' said Jacqueline. 'Thomas, move back from the fire, there's a good chap. We all want to benefit from the flames.'

'Sorry,' he looked from his aunt to Mary. 'Sorry, wasn't thinking. Cold outside. Damp.'

'It is. I won't stop for cocoa, Miss Turner. I've come to ask a favour. I wondered if you could keep an eye on Arthur till I get back. I shouldn't be gone long.'

'I can,' she said, ruffling his hair. 'He can help me and Thomas white-powder the cutlery. We aim to make the steel shine like silver.'

'And black the fire-irons. Black, spit and polish,' grinned Thomas. 'And the fender. So we can see the flames reflecting, eh Aunt?'

Jacqueline patted the faded green velvet armchair. 'Come on, curly-locks. Settle yourself here.'

'My hair's not curly,' Arthur looked far from pleased. Was she mad as well, like Thomas?

'Course it is,' she smiled, 'not a straight hair to be seen!'

'It's a joke, Arthur,' said Mary, wishing he wouldn't take everything everyone said so seriously and to heart.

Raising his eyebrows and sighing. Arthur dropped into the comfortable old chair and cupped his knees. 'You're not gonna read to us, Thomas, are yer?' He curled up one side of his top lip, hoping to get the message across.

'You should learn to read, my man,' said Thomas, pushing back his shoulders, assuming the authority befitting his twenty-two years. It wouldn't do to let a fledgling get away with showing no respect. After all, respect wasn't achieved with age as wisdom might be. It had to be earned. And earned it Thomas had. He knew that people shrank back when they saw him approaching, with his Bible under his arm.

Ignoring her nephew's sudden change of tone, Jacqueline Turner pulled a shawl about her shoulders. 'Where you off to then, Mary? Another of those political meetings?'

'Not tonight. I'm to see a lady about typewriting she wants done in the evenings.'

'Typewriting? Well, well, well.' She shook her head in wonder at Mary's determination. 'You're a clever girl and no mistake. But I knew that the minute I saw your eyes open. Well don't you worry about young Arthur. If I should get a call-out, he'll be safe with my nephew looking after him. They can keep each other company.'

'I'll teach the boy to read.' Thomas clasped his hands together and stuck out his chin. 'Ignorance is not bliss as so many like to believe.' Changing his pose and manner he turned to Arthur, 'Wouldn't you like to be a doctor when you grow up, young man?'

'Dunno.' Arthur eyed the medical book with suspicion and he was proved right. No sooner had he glanced from that to Thomas's face, a hand reached out and swept it from the small table. He tapped it with a fingernail. 'It's all in here. The entire workings of the human body. Inside, we are a complex, yet simple network of organs, each relying on the other.'

'That's enough of that, Thomas. You'll turn the boy's stomach.'

Pleased that Jacqueline had the situation under control, Mary gave her brother a hug and took her leave. 'You be a good boy, eh Arthur?' she called back over her shoulder before closing the street door behind her.

With Jacqueline in the scullery, warming milk for cocoa, Arthur had only Thomas for company. He looked round the room at the numerous pictures which were on the walls and sideboard. He could feel Thomas staring at him and the last thing he wanted to do was catch his eye. It mattered not, Thomas was going to preach come rain or high water.

'People think the abdomen is the stomach,' said Thomas, leaning his elbows on the arms of his chair and tilting his head to one side. 'The abdomen, young man, is the part of the body containing not only the stomach but bowels, intestines and other—'

'Pay no attention to him, Arthur, he always wanted to be a doctor.' Jacqueline placed the tray of cocoa on a small side table. 'We'll leave the polishing till another evening and play cards instead.'

Thomas gave her a sidelong glance, reached into his jacket pocket for his pipe and lit it in the cup of his hand. 'Rumour has it,' he said, with his pipe in the corner of his mouth, 'that the locals have nicknamed their murderer, Jack the Ripper. What have you to say about that, Arthur? What is the talk in the playground, mmm?'

'That's quite enough of that, thank you, Thomas. You'll scare the boy with such talk. Take no heed, Arthur. My nephew's mouth runs away with him at times,' she said, glowering at Thomas. 'It's bad enough we have to listen to your mother ranting and raving about all and nothing without you starting.' She sank back into her chair, fairly agitated.

'She's *your* sister, Aunt,' said Thomas, a smug look on his face as he drew on his pipe. 'Your flesh and blood.' He stretched his legs into the hearth and leaned back in his chair.

'No more she isn't. I cut our family ties once your father passed away, God rest his soul. I can't forgive

44

her for the way she drove that poor soul to his grave after the debtors' court. If she were normal I would wonder how she slept at night over it all. As it is, there is no way to fathom what goes on in her mind.'

'You don't mind me though, do you, Aunt?' The concern in his voice brought a level of normality back into the room. He spoke in a natural tone.

'Of course I don't mind you. You're my kin and I love you more than I love anyone and that's a fact. I sometimes wish you hadn't grown up and were still my little boy. Now, put a match to those candles to give us more light to play by.' She took a pack of playing cards from her apron pocket and shuffled them. 'And we'll have no more morbid talk this evening.'

'D'yer fink there will be any more? You know . . .' Arthur drew a finger across his neck to show a slit throat.

'Don't you worry yourself about such things, my lad,' said Thomas in a fatherly fashion. 'I should think he's proved his point by now. The whores will get themselves proper work and go to bed at a decent hour instead of walking the streets.'

'Pity you can't take a leaf out of that book you preach from,' Jacqueline mumbled. 'No good'll come of your nocturnal wanderings.'

'If I could sleep at night, I would. Mother keeps me awake with all her wailing. I would rather be living with you in this house.'

'No, Thomas, for the umpteenth time. This house is all I have for refuge after a tiring day. I shouldn't like anyone living in, I'm too used to my own company. Would that I could have your mother committed.'

'Please, Aunt Jacqueline . . .' said Thomas, unnerved by the remark. 'She doesn't break the law or lay a finger on a soul. I can hardly believe you would say such a thing.'

'Exactly. So stop exaggerating about her wailing or I shall think twice on leaving her be. Now then . . . what's it to be, whist?'

His little active mind working overtime, Arthur addressed Thomas. 'If you go out at night then you might 'ave seen Jack the Ripper and not known it was 'im.'

'Well, yes, that's true. And, for a lad of your age, you are quick off the mark. Wouldn't you say so, Aunt?' Jacqueline ignored him and shuffled the cards again while Thomas enjoyed the attention. Puffing at his pipe, as if deep in thought, he narrowed his eyes. 'He was too quick for me.'

'*You never did see 'im!*' Arthur's eyes were wide and his jaw had dropped.

'He was far too quick for me. Climbed a wall and dropped into the Board School in a flash. He was probably still hiding there when the cabman discovered the whore's body.'

'What did he look like? Was he all in black? Did he 'ave a sword? Did he—'

'He was wearing a top hat and long black silk cloak, and in his hand – from which blood was dripping – was a long shiny blade which the bright moon was using

46

for a mirror. The moon misses nothing, my boy . . . nothing.'

Hearing the midwife sigh, Arthur got in quickly before she stopped Thomas. 'What did you do then?' His own morbid curiosity had overcome his fear.

'Vanished into the night before anyone could cast aspersions. As if I would want to cut off her head.'

'*Was* 'er 'ead cut off, then?'

'Not quite,' he murmured, 'not quite.'

'That's enough, no more of this nonsense!' There was a sombre hush until Arthur's alarmed whisper broke the silence.

'My sister's out there . . .'

'She'll come to no harm!' snapped Jacqueline, and then softened her tone. 'Don't fret, Arthur, she'll keep to the main road and that's very well lit.'

'I didn't think your sister was a whore—'

'Thomas! How *could* you say such a thing? And in front of the boy. Never ending trouble is what you are, never ending!'

'I was merely easing the boy's worry, Aunt. Letting him know that he has nothing to fear because his sister is not a prostitute.'

Jacqueline began to deal the cards. 'We'll hear no more on it.' She ignored her nephew's low, tormenting snigger.

No one could have been more surprised than Mary as she stood in front of the big white house in Stepney Green. She had expected to find a run-down sleazy dwelling. Pushing the tall wrought iron gate open, she wondered if she had come to the right address. Hesitating before she drew the bell pull, she felt a wave of trepidation rush through her body as she questioned her sensibility. With her eyes shut tight she tried to be brave for Arthur.

'Who shall I say it is?' said Polly, the thirteen-year-old maid who wore a meticulous black dress and sparkling white apron.

'I've come to see Lizzie Redmond,' she said, feeling better at seeing the open honest face peering up at her. 'My name's—'

'Mary Dean,' the girl cut in. 'Come in and wait in the 'all and I'll see if she's free.'

Admiring the black and white marble floor and blue silk drapes at the elegant windows, Mary allowed her imagination to run away. She imagined herself sweeping up the wide staircase dressed in a fine gown. Hearing quiet laughter in the distance she began to relax; the place, if nothing else, had a light-hearted atmosphere and there was a lovely scent in the air.

'She'll see yer now. Follow me.' Polly led the way up to the second floor. 'I *fink* she's expecting yer tonight. It might 'ave bin tomorrer though or next week. You can never tell wiv that one, makes mistakes she does. Never informs me properly.'

'How did you know who I was?' said Mary.

'By your 'pearance.' She continued up the stairs keeping her back to Mary and reeled off her description. 'Dark red ulster, worse for wear, black crêpe bonnet wiv one red rose, black skirt, deep-mauve velvet bodice, a black silk skirt . . .' she stopped in her tracks. '. . . oh, I've already said that, 'aven't I?' Moving on, she continued, 'Well polished side-spring boots, twinkling blue eyes, red-brown 'air and a waist like a wasp. There . . . that completes the picture.'

Arriving at their destination, Polly stood beside white double-doors with bright shiny brass handles. 'I 'ave to be observant, it's rule number one.' She placed her hand on the big brass doorknob, winked at Mary and whispered, 'Welcome aboard.' She then pushed open the doors and announced the guest. 'Miss Mary Dean!'

'Yeah, all right, Polly, leave off with the theatricals.'

Poking her tongue out, Polly closed the doors, leaving the girls to themselves. 'I'm really glad you came, Mary,' said Lizzie, smiling broadly.

'I 'ad to, in the end. My mum died, so did the baby.'

'I know. I heard.' Her friend took her hand and led her to the deep, feather-cushioned gold settee. In her emerald green satin frock and dark blue silk petticoats, Lizzie resembled a sparkling jewel. 'I'm sorry about your troubles, honest. But I'm pleased as anythin' to see yer, I'll ask Lillian to give you the best clients. You'll bowl 'em over, I know it.'

'Lizzie, listen,' said Mary, lowering her eyes and wringing her hands. 'I'm still a virgin.'

'I know that, you daft cow. It's written all over yer.' She kicked off her shoes and flopped back into the feather cushions. 'My feet are killin' me. Bleedin' shoes are new and tight.'

Amused by Lizzie, Mary felt surprisingly at home

in these plush surroundings. 'I never expected anyfing like this, Lizzie.'

'Nothing cheap about what Mother does.'

'It's like another world.'

'This is one of the best rooms. They're not all this grand.'

'Who would 'ave thought it, eh? All of this in the middle of Stepney Green.'

'I don't s'pose you saw 'im then?'

Mary knew exactly who she was referring to. Smiling, she shrugged. 'I did as it just so 'appens. Strange chap with all that unruly hair on his face as well as his nut. Got lovely teeth, mind. And he's got personality, made me smile.'

Lizzie's eyes clouded over. 'I know, that's half the trouble. All the women fall for 'im, he's always at parties.'

'Do you see much of 'im?'

'Don't be daft, he's too busy.'

'And when you do, do yer . . . you know . . . ?'

'No, we don't. We did get in bed together once but I just laid there, scared stiff. Hard to believe, ain't it? Me with all my experience shy as you like with that one. He said I was tense. Tense? I was bloody rigid. Half an inch away from doing it we was. It never 'appened agen. You never mentioned my name, did yer?'

'Course not.' She gave Lizzie a sideways glance. 'You're gonna 'ave to do a lot of explaining, you know. I 'aven't got a clue what to do. I've not laid next to a man before.'

Laughing at her, Lizzie said, 'You just do what

comes naturally. That's what my mother told me. She was right an' all. There ain't no rules or instructions, Mary.'

The quiet rat-a-tat on the door silenced them. It was Lizzie's mother, Lillian. 'Your gentleman visitor's arrived, Elizabeth.' She looked from her daughter to Mary. 'How are you, Mary dear? It's been a very long time since I saw you.'

'I'm well, thank you.'

'Good. I'll take Mary to my rooms, Elizabeth, and ask Polly to show *your* gentleman up. I should touch up your lipstick. You look as if you've just eaten shortbread.'

Following Lillian Redmond down the staircase and along the corridor, Mary couldn't resist glancing at the tall refined man with a dark moustache who was handing over his black bowler hat, gloves and cloak to Polly. 'Is that Lizzie's visitor!' whispered Mary to Lillian.

'Hear nothing, see nothing, say nothing.' Lillian's tone made it very clear that she meant every word of it. Yes, thought Mary following the graceful woman into her rooms. This is another world. And I can't say I don't like it.

Her interview with Lillian over, Mary walked back home in a dreamlike state. She knew that this was a turning point in her life and she was very nervous of taking such a very big step. Becoming a courtesan, after all, was no less than becoming a prostitute. Pushing any thoughts of what her parents might think if they could see from where they might be, in heaven, she held on to her belief that was actually very real. If she didn't do this, Arthur would end up in a workhouse and she in a dingy room in a rough neighbourhood. There really was no choice and to be welcomed into Lillian Redmond's luxurious world was becoming more a privilege than a sin. And from what she had seen, Lizzie celebrated her way of life as if she were a glamorous actress in a West End theatre.

The worry that Mary was turning over in her mind was the return favour that Lizzie had obliged her to. A young woman who worked below stairs in the House of Assignation, a good pal of Lizzie's, had a close friend who was deep in trouble. This person, a young widow with a crippled son to look after, had been raped in the back and beyond of Stepney Green. She was pregnant. Having mentioned that her good neighbour, the midwife, was looking after Arthur, Mary had agreed on the spur of the moment to talk to Jacqueline Turner about Lizzie's 'friend of a friend's' predicament. Now, outside of Lizzie's world, it was a different thing altogether. She couldn't imagine how she would approach the midwife on the subject of . . . abortion.

Turning into Cleveland Way, she worried and rehearsed how she might broach the matter until she found she was on Miss Turner's doorstep.

'Well, if you're not a sight for sore eyes, Mary,' said Jacqueline Turner, 'these two would play cards all night if we were to let them.'

'What about draughts?' said Arthur, relieved that

his sister was safe but wanting to go on playing games. 'You said we'd play draughts after this 'and.'

'I did indeed but that was only if your sister hadn't returned by then.' She looked at Mary and smiled. 'It's throwing out time. I'm ready for my bed. It's not often I get an early night. The mothers are quiet tonight, thank the Lord.'

'I'm only too grateful to you Miss Turner for what you've done already. I would 'ave been that worried if I'd 'ave left Arthur by 'imself.'

'Well, yes, but I'm sorry to say that Thomas has been filling the boy's head with his morbid talk. I shouldn't be surprised if he has nightmares and will be climbing into your bed for comfort tonight.'

Thanking Jacqueline and Thomas, Mary urged Arthur towards the door. 'There was somefing I wanted to talk to you about, Miss Turner. Would it be all right if I came back once I've seen Arthur in bed and after Thomas 'as left?'

'Actually, Aunt,' said Thomas, 'I was thinking of staying over.'

'Oh, no! It's back to Kennington for you, my lad. I don't want your mother screaming the odds below my window in the small hours.'

'Well, you must do as you think fit, Aunt,' he said, looking disdainfully at her.

'Indeed.' Turning to Mary, she said, 'Of course you can call back round, later.'

Closing the door behind Mary, the midwife turned on her nephew. 'I sometimes fear for your mind, Thomas, I really do! All that talk earlier about seeing the dead woman. What if the boy spouts it in the playground? Another wild rumour will spread as quick as you like! What *were* you thinking?'

'I was merely trying to entertain the poor boy. Hasn't he just lost his mother?'

'Well just try and think of other ways in the future. Shocking talk. I don't ever want to hear the likes again. And another thing, why *were* you in the streets at such an hour? I saw you and have half a suspicion that you saw me. Why else would you be all but running along Osborne Street? You knew there would be hell to pay if I had of caught up with you.'

'And you worry over *my* mind, Aunt?'

'Idling your life away. Roaming the markets during the day when you should be working. How can you expect to sell encyclopaedias if you don't canvass!' She looked him straight in the eye. 'If *you've* been given the sack—'

'You were there?' said Thomas, ignoring all she had just said. 'You were in Osborne Street? At *that* time?'

Sitting down on the chair nearest to the fire, Jacqueline was exasperated by him. 'Thomas . . . I have to go out when I'm called. It's not something I would choose to do. And you knew full well that I was there, you were running away from me. No doubt you doubled back to George Yard, your morbid curiosity being stronger than fear.' She scooped up the playing cards from the table, her temper at pitch. 'Going around reading bits out of the Bible. You should think about what they are saying out there. Daft Thomas Cutbush. *Why* haven't you been *canvassing*?' She slammed the pack of cards down on to the table.

Sighing deliberately, Thomas shook his head slowly. 'I have. And it's not only the Bible I carry.' He picked up his medical book and offered it to her as if it were a presentation ceremony. 'I've been studying, Aunt. I thought you would be pleased. Studying and lecturing.'

Sinking her head back into a cushion, she closed her eyes. 'Of course I'm pleased with your studying but you must *try* and keep a job down. If anything were to happen to me I fear what might become of you if you have no profession to speak of.'

'I liked my work at the Tea Minories. You know I did and I was a good clerk. My reference stated that I was diligent and of good character.'

'I know . . . but that's why I don't want you to waste your life Bible bashing.'

'Well you can stop worrying, I'm not going to preach any more. Uncle Charles made me promise. I'm studying my medical books more and more.' He looked up, his watery eyes searching his aunt's face for a glimpse of respect. 'I could have been a doctor, Aunt Jacqueline. If things at home had been different. If my father had not—'

'I know, Thomas, I know.' She reached out and took his hand, squeezing it. 'Don't go upsetting yourself now.' This naive young man she had loved from birth could so easily break her heart.

'But I *am* upset, Aunt. Very, very upset. And if

I tell you this shocking thing you might very well understand why I've been preaching in the streets.'

Jacqueline narrowed her eyes as she looked into his troubled face. What now? she thought. What on earth can it be now? His expression was dire, his aura dark. 'What is it, nephew? Your mother?'

'No . . . it's . . . the whores.' He lifted his head slowly and swallowed. 'They gave me syphilis.'

A silence, to please him, followed as Jacqueline closed her eyes. Thomas's game of, *Is this true, isn't this true*, was getting too macabre for her liking. 'How so?' she said.

'They gave it to me,' he said, casting his eyes down again.

'Well, this is original, Thomas. So you've been with streetgirls – with whores. How much do they charge these days?'

'Please don't mock me, Aunt.' He covered his face with his hands. 'They let me do it free at first, when I was thirteen, for a bit of a laugh. then I started to earn a wage and had to pay full price. Fourpence for a—'

'Yes, all right, Thomas, enough, thank you.' Any feelings of comfort and security she had derived from her life as a midwife seemed to drain away when he was in this mood. Here was the only person in the world she loved, and he was telling her that he had been infected with the worst of diseases. Was it to have her sole attention or did he revel in his tormenting of her? 'Have you seen a doctor?' was all she could be bothered to say.

'No, I've looked it up in my medical book. Read

and reread . . . over and over. I've had the symptoms for six months. I expect to die from it.'

'And what are the symptoms?' He was beginning to amuse her with his fantasising.

'Sores on my private parts. Swollen glands in the groin. A skin rash and I get feverish. It cleared up soon after I first detected it but came back again. It comes and goes. I'm infected by those disgusting women and I can't wash it away.'

'Well you've certainly been studying your medical books, none can deny that. And do you hope for a cure or a remedy for relief? You should have told me this before now, Thomas, I shouldn't think you've much longer to live.'

'I'm disgusting, Aunt. Who would want to live with me?'

'If you're hoping to get my sympathy and have you here, you're wasting your time. In any case there must be a lovely girl out there somewhere . . . ?'

'I doubt I'll ever marry, women disgust me at times. Mary Dean is a fine young woman, I admit, but such innocent young things are few and far between. I'm a good man, Aunt Jacqueline. I do God's work.' He looked up from the floor to see that she had closed her eyes. 'God's work.' There was a long pause. 'I had it in mind that I was a bad child, a naughty boy. That the reason father died and left me was a kind of punishment for my badness. Mother was given to me as a punishment too . . .'

'Thomas, please . . .' Jacqueline lowered her head, her hand covering her brow.

'But not any more, I know better now.' He drew a long breath. 'I am an instrument of God, acting under His guidance. It's all part of His plan. God has wanted me all along to rid the world of whores so that we may all lead cleaner lives. I know that now.'

'Stop this minute, such *wicked* talk! You try and shock me and I'm in no mood for it tonight. I thought you had grown out of all of that, in truth I did.'

Kneeling before her, Thomas took her hands in his. 'Please, Aunt Jacqueline, please trust me, that's all I ask. I'm not trying to shock you this time, I promise.' He inhaled deeply. 'I've every reason to believe that He wants you to be part of this holy crusade too.'

'Thomas, how dare you! Have you completely lost your sense of morality? You blaspheme in my house and talk of such . . . such dark and humourless things.' She withdrew her hand from his. 'You've exhausted me and that's a fact. Exhausted me with your warped sense of humour if humour it be.' She looked away from him, close to breaking down in tears. 'Much more of this and I might suggest we take you to see a medical specialist.'

Thomas slumped in his chair, he shook his head, disappointed in her. 'And I thought you were listening. I really believed you were listening. You have so much to learn about the way of the world, Aunt, I fear for your innocence. I *did* go to a doctor, he gave me bad medicine, *on purpose*. He'd seen into my mind and wanted to stop my good work by poisoning me. I'm writing to certain people about that, lodging a complaint, we may well see him struck off.'

Jacqueline began to chuckle. In truth, with his peculiar sense of humour, he did brighten the dullest day at times. 'I swear you should be on the stage, Thomas, I swear it,' she said, wiping a tear from the corner of her eye.

'You were right to ask me why I was in Osborne Street, you know,' he said, sitting back in his chair, hands clasped. 'I *was* running away, but not from you. I'd never run away from you, Aunt Jacqueline. And yes, I did double back and watch with the small crowd of sightseers. I was studying them, for are they not worse for gloating?'

'Why didn't you run away from Whitechapel and back to Kennington? Why would any sensible person hang around the streets after committing a foul murder?' She sipped her gin. 'Your macabre story does not hold water, lad.' Resting her head back, she murmured, 'For such mercies may the Lord make us truly thankful.'

'I didn't say I had committed foul murder, Aunt.'

'Oh, so then all this talk about ridding the world of whores was not true? I can hardly believe it.' Now it was her turn to poke fun.

'You should know me better than that, I was merely teasing you. But I do wish you would not use the Lord's name, whenever you have ill-judged something I have said.' Pulling on his coat and hat he stood by the door and hovered for a brief time. His aunt, slumped wearily in her armchair, was ready for her bed. 'I hadn't meant to worry you, that was not my intention. I will not confide in you again, I promise.'

'Good, I'm relieved that you didn't kill those who made you ill.'

'If you had been listening to me closely, you would not feel quite so satisfied with yourself. Goodnight, Aunt.'

'Thomas, I take it you haven't spoken of this to anyone else?' She closed her eyes again and hoped he would say no. 'About the killings or the . . . syphilis.'

'Uncle Charles knows. Other than that, no.' He then left and shut the door behind him.

This time Jacqueline was stunned by her nephew's casual but graphic telling of something so terrible. Charles Cutbush had been listening to these ramblings? Never! He would have had his nephew certified on the spot for saying such things. She uncorked her bottle of gin and sipped what she considered to be her medication. Hearing Mary quietly call her name while tapping on the door caused her to be frustrated rather than angry at having to face someone else when she was in dire need to be alone.

'You're welcome to come in, Mary,' she said, opening the door, 'but I warn you, I'm on my last legs. You might be better off asking advice in the morning when I'm fresh. If it's advice you're after?'

'No,' said Mary, wishing again that she had never agreed to this. 'I've come to ask a very special favour, Miss Turner. It's a bit delicate.'

'Well don't look so worried,' she said closing the street door. 'Those who don't ask don't need. Sit yourself down while the fire's still in.'

'It's not for me self but a poor soul whose undergone

somefing really awful. It don't hardly bear talking about.'

'Well then why not leave it?' Jacqueline had had enough for one night.

'It's for a friend of a good friend of mine, someone I went to school with. This friend of my friend was raped and now she's pregnant and not even married or anything. Well, she was married but now she's a widow with a crippled boy to look after.'

Jacqueline felt her heart sink. As if she hadn't had enough for one night, her lovely neighbour, unless she was very much mistaken, was about to ask her to do something very much against her principles. 'I can see why you're rushing out your words, Mary. You're about to ask me to do the most wicked thing. I *deliver* life into this world, that's my calling.'

'I never said you'd do such a thing, Miss Turner, I just said I would ask you what . . . I just felt I couldn't turn my back . . .' Mary swallowed against her dry throat. 'I'm sorry. I should 'ave known you wouldn't like my mentioning it.'

'I don't, but now that it's been said we can't ignore it. A widow with a crippled son who has undergone the worst kind of nightmare – rape. If it's not a trumped up lie it's a worse fate than any poor soul deserves, *even* if the woman happened to be a common whore.' This double-edged response was deliberate, she eyed Mary's face for any reaction; there was none. Her innocent and honest expression had not been blighted one bit by a lie.

'How far gone is she?'

'My friend thinks she's about six weeks.'

'And you're certain this woman's not a common whore? That your friend isn't taking advantage of your good nature?'

'I'm sure she's not but' – she shrugged and looked concerned – 'I've never met her so . . .'

'I don't imagine you would have plucked up the courage to ask me such a thing if she wasn't a respectable woman – this friend of yours – who asked for a friend of hers.'

'I wouldn't, Miss Turner, no. Cross my heart and 'ope to die.' She crossed her fingers instead.

'And what does your friend's friend do for a living?'

'She's a charlady by all accounts. Scrubs the Town Hall and the Board School.' At least this is what Lizzie had told her.

'Well that's an honest enough occupation and hard work at that. Let me sleep on it. No promises mind – so don't hold me to anything. I'll turn it over in bed. That's all I'm saying for now.'

'Fanks, Miss Turner. An' I am sorry to 'ave troubled you so late at night.'

'Never mind. But tell me something . . .' Jacqueline looked into Mary's flushed face '. . . what are they saying at the match factory, about the murders?'

'Oh, just about everything and nuffing, Miss Turner. It's all they ever talk about. One of the girls reckons she was approached by a man wiv a black beard in a tall black 'at and black cloak. On 'er way 'ome from work. She swears he said: "You are about the same type of woman as the one that's bin murdered." Then he ran off laughin' an 'orrible laugh. She swears it was 'im and says she could 'ave bin the next victim.'

'Mmm,' Jacqueline narrowed her eyes. 'We're all getting het up over it, I dare say. It's a shocking affair. I don't recall anything like this ever happening before. But there, it's better not to think on it. Off you go, Mary, and push it from your mind. I'll watch from the street door until you're safe inside your house.'

'Thanks agen, Miss Turner. Goodnight.'

'Goodnight, Mary dear.'

Running along the gaslit street towards home, Mary wondered just how much gin her neighbour consumed. She had smelt it on her breath before, but tonight it was stronger and her speech seemed slightly slurred.

Turning the key in the street door, she heard Arthur call out, 'Is that you, Mary?'

'Of course it's me, silly! Turn over and go to sleep, there's a good boy. G'night! Sleep tight!'

'You coming up now!'

'Shortly! I'm just gonna 'ave a hot drink. Keep the oil lamp on if it makes you feel better. I'll turn it down low when I come up.'

Settling herself on a rug in front of the fire, Mary pulled her knees up to her chin and hugged her legs. Why the house sounded quieter tonight she couldn't say. Neither could she think why she should suddenly feel alone in the world with just a little brother to look after. Sipping her cocoa she glanced at the newspaper. The headline chilled her: ANOTHER HORRIBLE MURDER IN WHITECHAPEL!

Trying to be brave she read on: *This killing has created a painful sensation in the East End as a state of wild excitement borders on panic. No prostitute may think herself safe . . .'*

Having read enough to scare herself half to death she pushed the edition under a cushion and thought about all that the midwife had said. What if the girl in trouble was one of those working in Lillian's house? What if she was a courtesan? What if Miss Turner discovered it, if that were the case? She would most certainly lose a good neighbour and mother-figure. She decided to find out more the next evening, when she was expected back at the house.

Thinking again of the headlines on the newspaper under the cushion, she vowed to start the fire with it and tomorrow not to be drawn into any conversation to do with the murders. For tomorrow evening, she *herself* would be lowered to the ranks of a prostitute.

Chapter Three

With his back to the midwife, Superintendent Charles Cutbush gazed out of the window, feigning interest in the street below. 'I'm not saying that I'm sorry to see you, Miss Turner, but I would have preferred it should you have written to me in the first instance. I could have arranged to meet you somewhere, anywhere but here. Scotland Yard is hardly the place to take tea in the afternoon.'

'It wasn't easy for me, sir. I turned back twice before I took the plunge. It's an imposing building I must say.' Jacqueline wiped the perspiration from her palms with a handkerchief, willing herself to pluck up courage and mention Thomas. This unseemly visit was not only her first but would surely be her last. Cutbush, with his dour face and superior manner, was making it clear from the start that he did not welcome her presence.

'Luck or fate saw to it that I was at the front desk when you arrived. A few minutes later and you would have missed me. I was on my way out.'

An uneasy silence filled his room as Jacqueline summoned the courage to continue. She was now regretting this uncomfortable situation. Fear was creeping over her. If she dared to lay her cards on the table, another nightmare would begin. If she got out now without another word about her nephew, the lid would still be on Thomas's puzzling confession and she could discard it as pure fiction. Once and for all. 'Pure fiction.' The words etched across her brain. There was hardly anything pure about it.

'I wanted to have a word about my nephew.' The words were out before she could stop them. '*Our* nephew, Mr Cutbush.'

'Yes.' Cutbush fell silent again.

There was little doubt in her mind that if she and this intimidating man were not related due to an ill-matched marriage, between his brother and her sister, their paths would never have crossed. As it was, they rarely saw each other.

'I do wish you would sit down, Mr Cutbush. Try as ever I might, finding the right words is no simple matter and you don't make it any easier for me.'

Somewhat reluctantly, he sat behind his highly pol-ished mahogany desk and rearranged things on his already tidy worktop. 'I presume that something has happened to confirm that the lad is not quite as he should be at the moment.' He drew his fob watch from his waistcoat pocket and checked the time. From his expression, it was obvious that he wasn't going to give anything away and that Jacqueline was going to have to broach the subject first.

'Thomas was in a very strange mood last night, when he called on me.'

'Thomas is always in a strange mood, madam.'

'Yes, but this was quite different.' She breathed

66

deeply and stretched to her full height. 'Quite different . . . almost as if he were another person.'

'And that surprises you?' He raised an eyebrow, a ploy to make light of her concern.

'I found it distressing, sir.' She lowered her eyes. 'He means a lot to me.'

'I'm sure he does and that's all very well but—'

'He said some very disturbing things about the murders in Whitechapel. The whore killer.'

Shaking his head despairingly, Cutbush rapped his fingertips on the desk. 'As many people will. My patience on this subject is tried every day and all because of low-class streetwalkers from the wilderness of the slums, where each of the idle preys on the other.'

His pomposity was beginning to make her angry, but if she was to discover whether Thomas had told his uncle the same story he had told her, she had to remain calm and in control. This man could so easily accuse her of being just as excitable as her sister, which was something she had spent much of her life trying to avoid.

'Thomas believes in his sick mind that he is directed to kill prostitutes. There – it's been said and with great anguish I must tell you. I can't say how my heart grieves over this business, Mr Cutbush.' She pushed her shoulders back and composed herself. Above all else, she had to maintain her dignity.

'He's not the only one. Several lunatics have posted their letters of confession and if it's not too much of a disappointment, I would rather not continue with this

67

damaging and somewhat futile conversation.' His tone and agitated manner could mean one of two things. Either he was extremely busy or he knew more than he cared to admit.

'Mr Cutbush, if Thomas is not suffering from delusions then we may have a serious problem on our hands.' She was determined not to let his imperious act weaken her resolve.

'And what am *I* expected to deduce from his ramblings?'

'I cannot answer for you, sir, I'm sure. But he did say that he had confessed his deeds to you. I hardly believed it at first, naturally, but then, I've had the long-drawn-out night to think on it.'

Cutbush raised his chin and sighed. 'I assure you, madam, my nephew has not uttered a word of this to me. He knows better than to do so.'

'He contracted syphilis from a whore,' said Jacqueline, regretting the words as soon as they were out. 'Might he not just be capable of violence, brought on by revenge and a tormented mind?'

'What a dark imagination you have.' His eyes were filled with accusation. 'But there, what else are we to expect? How is your sister these days?'

'I wouldn't know, Mr Cutbush. You should ask your nephew. He shares the same roof with your late brother's wife after all said and done. He is the son from the ill-matched marriage, let's not forget.'

'Indeed. Now, I really must ask you to leave.'

'And that's all you have to say on this grave matter?'

'I do have more pressing things on my mind at the moment. The East End is in an uproar and the panic is spreading.' He sighed heavily. 'If I am to blame for anything, it is for providing an allowance for Thomas after he had lost employment. Without that support he would have had to find work. Idle hands make idle minds. I'm very fond of my nephew and I see enough of him to know that he lives most of the time in a world of make-believe. I tend not to take his fantasising quite as seriously as you appear to, forgive me if I appear to be insensitive.'

'Sir . . .' Jacqueline looked directly into his face '. . . I am familiar enough with my nephew to know when he is deeply troubled. I cannot say the same of you. We are not that well acquainted. But I will say this: I believe you are hiding something.'

His stern face was enough to wilt a rose. 'You are quite perceptive, madam. I have tried to *hide* my contempt. I would prefer not to have anything to do with Thomas's family – and being an intelligent woman, I'm sure you know why. But we are, unfortunately, linked by my nephew. Please do not use that ill-fated tie to try and work your way into my world. Now, if you would be so good as to leave this building without the look of someone with the troubles of the world on her shoulders, I should be grateful.'

'Don't trouble yourself, Mr Cutbush, I shall go out smiling. I am relieved to know that you believe our nephew to be innocent. I shall think no more of it.'

Moving towards the door, Jacqueline halted as he started to speak. Turning round, she was surprised to see that he bore a different expression. His face had relaxed into a mere hint of a smile. 'I would prefer it if this matter were not reported elsewhere. For all our sakes.'

'Rest assured, sir, it will go no further. Good day to you.'

With the door between them and in the privacy of his office, Cutbush pressed his hands against his face. It hadn't been easy lying to Jacqueline Turner. She was a good, hard-working woman and generous with her affections when it came to Thomas, his nephew. If only his late brother had married her instead of the crazed sister, things might have been different. He would have liked to have confided in the woman, pour out the miserable story in one sitting, explain how he had unwittingly compromised himself. But how could he be sure that Miss Turner would keep it to herself? How would any decent aunt react to learn that her only nephew was a pathological murderer. That it had started with a crime of passion which had taken a disastrous turn for the worse.

Cursing to himself, he rued the day he first heard the name Betty Millwood. The woman had been admitted to the Whitechapel Workhouse Infirmary in February that year suffering from numerous stab wounds to her legs and lower stomach. She had been discharged to the South Grove Workhouse where, after three weeks, she collapsed suddenly and died from her wounds.

Her end had been attributed to an ulceration of the lung, but a relative had insisted that the primary cause had been the stabbing and that there should be a police investigation. The family wanted justice.

When Cutbush's colleague and intimate friend, Chief Inspector James Swanson, had shown him the file on Betty Millwood, discreetly pointing to the name of the chief suspect, he should have told him there and then to arrest his nephew and have done with it. But the Chief Inspector had not wanted to make an arrest. The name Cutbush was not common but it would not take long for the press to make connections and track down his uncle to Scotland Yard itself. In their wisdom, three high-ranking officers had decided to close the file – destroy it. The report that went to the dead woman's family showed that Millwood had died from natural causes. And that should have been the end of it.

The officers believed that Thomas had attacked Millwood under stress, and that it was a crime of passion that would not be repeated. With his hitherto clean record, they believed that this simple-minded, heartbroken boy would not strike again. This convenient assessment, voiced at the time, suited all concerned, especially the three senior officers.

Cursing Charles Cutbush, Jacqueline broke one of her rules of not walking at speed. She had managed to contain herself many times during her working life, knowing how easily other people's problems could induce her to hurry and potentially shorten her life. The sound of her heels hitting against the flagstones echoed and with every step her anger grew. The one person whom she could hope to find as an ally, had rattled her to the bones.

Approaching Whitechapel she could hardly believe that she had walked in such a bad temper all the way from Scotland Yard without even stopping at a café for a light refreshment. Striding past Brady Street the stitch in her side worsened, and the sight of two of the lowest prostitutes, arm in arm, tormenting and teasing a sailor, made her blood boil. The face of her beloved nephew came to mind and she herself felt like venting her anger on the whores.

Turning into Whitehead Street, her heart sank at the sight of Mary Dean, who had arrived home from the Bryant and May match factory after her day's work, and was passing time with a neighbour. Her thoughts went back to the night before and all they had talked about.

'Miss Turner!' said Mary, pleased to see her. 'I was just gonna pop up to your house and see if you was in. I don't s'pose you've got a few minutes to spare me? I wondered if you'd 'ad time to think about what I was asking, Miss Turner,' said Mary, feeling as if she were about to be told off.

'No I haven't,' was Jacqueline's cold response. 'What with one thing and another.' She gave Mary a condoning look. 'I can see you're troubled, Mary, but I can't say I want to think about it. I wish you hadn't asked this of me to be truthful. I've enough to worry over at the present.'

'There's nuffing wrong, is there?' Mary tilted her head and studied Jacqueline's face.

'No.' She avoided Mary's probing eyes. 'Just a few too many expectant mothers at once, that's all.'

'You look as if a little catnap wouldn't go amiss.'

'I generally flag at this time. Now, what was it you wanted?'

'Well, I saw my friend at work and she said that 'er friend is worried sick. I said I'd asked you if you knew anyone but I never made any promises so—'

'She's wrong to be pressing you, as if you haven't got your share of troubles. You should never have entertained the idea.'

'I know and normally I wouldn't, but theirs is such a respectable family, her father's somefing to do with the Board School Committee and—'

'Where are the family from?'

'Forest Gate,' said Mary, speaking from the top of her head. She had to come up with a place that was far enough away so it would seem natural when she was going to offer up her own bedroom. If the midwife were to go to the woman's lodgings the truth might come out as to what her true occupation might be. 'I'd be happy for you to use my bedroom.'

'And we have your friend's word that no one else knows about this?'

Mary placed a hand on her heart. 'On my word of honour.' She crossed her fingers and made a silent plea: Don't let me down, Lizzie, please stay silent.

'And you haven't said where I live or how you know me?'

'No, I never said a word. Only that I would ask

someone I knew if they knew someone who might be able to help.'

'All right, Mary, I'll do it just this once but you mark my words now, I shall be vexed if you ask such a thing of me again. Get a message to the girl that I'll need to see her straight away. If she can be here by seven o'clock tomorrow evening, I'll see to it. If she can't make that appointment, I wash my hands of it.'

'Thanks, Miss Turner, you're doing good 'elping 'er out, honest you are. May God bless you in your work.'

May God bless you. Those words shouldn't have made Jacqueline feel any better but the way in which Mary had naively said them, had made a difference. Pushing the key into her front door, the midwife wondered if God would ever give His blessing to such a thing. Dropping exhausted into her armchair, she unlaced her boots and thought about her nephew.

'Oh, Thomas,' she murmured, 'what madness is it that seizes your simple mind, that you should make up such wicked stories?' She leaned back and tried to reason it out. Telling herself that she had been overly worried and that her nephew could not possibly be suffering from a split personality, she went into the scullery to prepare something to eat. Try as she might, she couldn't rid herself of painful memories, namely, the manic behaviour of her own mother and sister. 'And what of you, Jacqueline?' she said, unbuttoning her cape. 'Can it be possible that the same bad blood trickles through your veins?'

There was a loud knock at the door. Could this be

Mary Dean come to confirm arrangements for the following evening? She cursed inwardly. Wasn't it enough that she had to traipse through all weathers and at all times to attend her mothers? Now she was being pressurised into doing something for a complete stranger, something that she abhorred. She made up her mind to tell Mary that she had had a change of heart and wanted to hear no more about abortions. But it was not Mary on her doorstep.

'I won't ever kill again – cross my heart and hope to die.' It was Thomas.

Grabbing him by the arm, she pulled him inside and slammed the door shut. 'Do you want to see us both locked up?'

'It's all right, Aunt. God spoke to me in the night. He said that it was all right now and I may stop.'

'Don't you dare blaspheme in this house! Don't you dare!' She pushed Thomas down into an armchair and poured herself a gin. 'If you say another word about it I'll—'

'Those whores deserved to die, Aunt. So—'

'Stop! I'm warning you, Thomas.'

'You mustn't feel sorry for them, ever since I was twelve they tormented me. "Daft Thomas Cutbush can't cut the mustard."'

Jacqueline clenched her teeth and glared down at him. 'Tell me you are teasing, Thomas, tell me that none of them know your name.'

'Why shouldn't I have told them? I've known them since I was a small boy.'

'Yes,' she said, 'I suppose you must have, then.' Her

heart sank even further. All this had been going on while she thought of her nephew as an unworldly and shy boy who knew nothing about the low side of life.

'I'm feeling hungry, Aunt, may I cut myself some bread?'

'Of course, Thomas, as you wish.' She was too tired to pursue the matter.

'And some dripping?'

'Yes, it's in the larder in the blue and white dish.'

Listening to her nephew tinkering about in the scullery, she couldn't imagine him using his strength against anyone. He really was still a child. She felt foolish now for wasting Charles Cutbush's time. Thomas proffering to have killed the whores was a wild fantasy and so too, no doubt, was the venereal disease. 'There's a pitcher of milk by the yard door if you want to make some cocoa,' she said, wishing he were still a boy at school. She loved him so much it pained her to think that he might have been lonely all this time. Closing her eyes, she found herself relaxing into a light sleep, wondering what she would do without her gin.

'Here we are, Aunt, this should make you feel better.' Thomas handed her a small plate on which lay a thick slice of bread smothered in dripping. 'You don't eat enough, I swear it.'

Dragging herself from her fleeting dream where she and Thomas had been walking through the frost on a winter's night, she stretched and yawned.

'Would you like to spend Christmas with me this year, Thomas?' She spoke in a leisurely manner without really thinking.

'Indeed I would, Aunt,' he said, biting into his slice of bread. 'It's bedlam back there with mother and that crazy woman whom she should never have befriended.'

'They've been close friends for years, Thomas. Supporting each other.' Jacqueline tonged a few lumps of coal on to the glowing fire. 'I shall have to get it through your mother's scatterbrained head that I don't want her visiting at Christmas. Good will or not, she would only spoil things.'

'She doesn't wander far from home these days. Content to hang around the court shouting abuse at the neighbours.'

'I'm sure. Well then, now that you've agreed to stay over Christmas, I shall have to get in the fruit for the plum pudding and mince tarts.'

'I could do that for you, I could get all your shopping, Aunt Jacqueline. You know how much I love the markets.'

'I would sooner see you working in one of them, Thomas, really I would. Your mind needs to be occupied and that's a fact.'

'Is that how you see me now?' he said, seated and sipping his cocoa. 'A market porter? I was once a clerk, don't forget.'

'But you aren't any more and beggars can't be choosers. Learn that and you'll never be without a shilling.'

'I'm hoping Uncle Charles will fix me up within the offices at Scotland Yard. I shall ask him tomorrow.'

Jacqueline placed her half-eaten bread back on the

plate. 'I should bide your time if I were you. You're not in favour at the present. I went to see him today and he's not best pleased with you, nor me, I fancy.'

Thomas stared at her, sceptical. 'You went to see Uncle Charles?' He leaned towards her, his expression fixed. 'Behind my back? Why did you do that, Aunt?'

'Don't talk such rubbish, Thomas. Since when do I have to account for my movements? I was in the area, that's all.'

'You went to see him about me, didn't you?' He dropped back into his armchair. 'You were talking about me and I wasn't there to speak for myself. You and Uncle Charles, talking about me . . . just like everyone else.'

'Don't start all that over again, please, I'm tired of it. Folk have their own troubles to worry about. They've no time to waste on how to bring you down, even *if* they wanted to.'

He chuckled in his irritating way, shaking his head as if he couldn't believe her lack of intelligence. 'You're very trusting, Aunt.'

She collected her knitting from the sideboard. 'You lied to me, Thomas. Your Uncle Charles knew nothing about that wild story you told me last night. The fun and games of spinning such tales may mean little to you but it kept me from my sleep which I am in more need of as I get older, Thomas. I need my rest.'

Locking his fingers and cracking his knuckles he gazed up at the ceiling as if he were looking beyond this room. 'This is blacker than I first imagined. He denied my name in a flurry of lies.'

Jacqueline had had enough. She thumped her closed fist on the arm of her chair. 'I will not listen to this. If you must ramble then go on home!'

'Was there a gun in his office?' said Thomas, oblivious to what she had just said.

Try as she might, the midwife could hardly contain her sudden desire to laugh at him. 'If I didn't worry over you, Thomas, I swear I should advise you to go on stage. Why do you ask about guns?'

'I would be angry if he shot himself. He shouldn't have covered up for me the first time. I didn't ask him to, he did it of his own accord.'

Deciding that she should humour him and glean what she could while he was in this frame of mind, Jacqueline relaxed and softened her voice. 'Why did he scotch it the first time, do you think?'

'I'm his brother's son, his dead brother's son. He knows I mean well and he's an intelligent man, I only have to tell him something once.'

'And how long has he known that you are the famous Whitechapel murderer?' she could not resist goading him.

He leaned forward again and spoke very slowly as if she were a backward child. 'He-covered-up-the-first-attack.'

'I see. Well I apologise if I appear slow but it's been a tiring day.' She pulled a cushion from the small of her back and placed it behind her neck. 'Would you like to hear about the mothers I attended today?'

'Not really but if it pleases you . . .'

'Well, then, I'll just close my eyes. If I fall asleep it

will be from exhaustion and not bad manners.' She hoped she would doze off and he would become bored with his own absurd ramblings. 'Although I will say that I am fed up with hearing about those murders. It's on everyone's lips. Whitechapel is alive with sick-minded sightseers. It's all anyone can find to talk about.'

Her broad hints did nothing to stop him. Thomas, pleased to have an audience, albeit a tired old aunt, stood with his back to the fire, legs apart and assumed the pose of an orator. 'It was after a particularly bad bout of syphilis. I was out of discomfort but extremely angry.'

Jacqueline closed her eyes. Good Lord . . . the syphilis again.

'It was one of those fresh February afternoons when the air is icy-cold and yet the sun is in full glory. I was sick of trudging through the East End, canvassing for the Directory. Sick of being in the midst of the lowest types who live in dingy, cheap rooms: whores, thieves and pimps. Sabbath breakers.'

'Yes,' murmured Jacqueline, 'and I have to bring their offspring into the world.'

'I caught sight of Betty Millwood strolling through Whitechapel, as if she had no cares in the world. She was older than me, thirty-eight and a widow. We first met in the Prince Albert on the corner of Brushfield Street. She was sitting by herself looking miserable.

'"I am alone, young man," she said, "alone in a crowd. I want no part of Christmas." Now you will remember, Aunt, I told you it was February.' A warm smile spread across his face as he remembered. 'I soon cheered her. It wasn't long before she was out of that melancholy mood. She took me back to her lodgings in White's Row. One room, but it was clean. The sheets smelled of soap.'

Jacqueline was half listening and learning more about her nephew. Either he had at some time been to a prostitute's room or he really did have the imagination of a storyteller. She wondered if he was celibate or not. She still thought of him as her innocent child nephew.

'I filled her bucket from the yard tap and using soap washed her all over and, just to appear equal, I allowed her to wash me.'

That was enough for this God-abiding woman. 'Don't continue with your story, Thomas, there's a good lad. In truth, I think I've heard enough.'

He ignored this and continued to speak in a monotone. 'It was soon after the early signs of syphilis that I went to see my Betty again. I hadn't been with anyone since her. She was all I thought about, but she only shrugged when I told her about the symptoms. "You didn't catch it from me, sweet'eart," she said. "Try one of your other whores." I can't tell you how deeply that remark cut into me.

'I had my penknife with me when I saw her next, in Whitechapel. My favourite knife – the one with the bone handle. I left her bleeding and went home to ask God to help her die. He must have listened, because twenty-two days after I prayed for her, she passed away in the South Grove Workhouse in Mile End.'

Thomas paused and looked into Jacqueline's face. Now she *was* listening and worried. 'Do you see what I'm saying, Aunt? Twenty-two days. How old am I?'

'Twenty-two,' she murmured, 'yes, twenty-two.' She covered her face with her hands. Surely no one could make up such a story. 'Thomas please . . . please stop this.'

'She's better off dead, Aunt. The last thing she said before I ran off was, "Martha . . . Martha Tabram's got syphilis, not me."

'I had been with Tabram one week before I met Betty. So I would have passed it on to her. So you see, I had done her a service by giving her a quick end rather than a long painful drawn out one which *I* shall have to suffer. I had two good reasons for killing the whore, Nichols—'

Jacqueline put up her hand to stop him. 'No!' She pulled herself forward, ready to escape into the scullery and end it.

'But you can *stop* worrying, Aunt, my work in that field is *over*!'

She turned back and looked at him. He truly believed all he was saying. 'So women can walk without fear now, can they? The famous Whitechapel murderer is about to retire and Leather Apron will go to the gallows instead of you? In all my days I've never heard such trash.' She waited for him to break into a smile but instead he startled her by suddenly drawing a knife from the belt beneath his coat and stabbing the air with it, defying his imaginary foes to come anywhere near him.

'Stop this at *once*! Thomas, you're not amusing me!' She was more distressed by it than she let on.

In his own world, he continued to stab the air, punctuating his efforts with quiet laughter and then – stopping as suddenly as he had started – glared into the face of his imaginary victim.

Dropping his weapon, he lunged his arm forward and with his thumb outstretched, his fingers in a gripping position, he feigned to tighten his grip. Every facial expression, every gesture, was full of anguish and second by second his fervour was rising. Slowly forcing his imaginary prey to the ground, he squeezed for all he was worth, his jaw clenched, his body trembling. Then, bursting into tears, he stumbled towards his aunt and threw his arms about her soft warm body, falling to his knees. 'Help me, Aunt Jacqueline, please . . . please help me.'

'It's all right, Thomas, my boy,' she murmured in a trembling voice, patting his back. 'I'm here. I'll always be here for you . . . always.'

Dressed in her newly purchased outfit, Mary Dean admired herself in the tarnished full-length mirror on the door of her wardrobe. She had placed a down payment in a good second-hand shop close to Liverpool Street railway station and hoped to be able to pay off her debt quickly from the money she would earn as a hostess at Lillian Redmond's House of Assignation.

The dark green, stiff, silk skirt was smothered with horizontal bands and ruches, puffs and narrow-pleated frills and the matching green satin long-sleeved bodice was patterned with a red velvet pile and fancy buttons. Brushing the frilled, white lace cuffs and jabot with the tips of her fingers, she broke into a smile. 'All that's needed now,' she told herself, 'is to earn enough money to pay off the debt.'

Carefully placing her ostrich-feathered toque on her head, she tweaked the reddish brown wispy curls of her fringe until she was satisfied with her new look. 'This is the beginning of your new life, Mary,' she told herself, 'no backing out now.' With her black cape fastened at the neck and her embroidered silk handbag over her arm, she was ready to enter into Lizzie's world.

Standing back while Polly opened the door into Lillian Redmond's suite of rooms, Mary stopped herself from nervously laughing as she heard herself being announced by Polly: 'Miss Mary Dean, madam!' she spoke in a loud affected voice, trying desperately to cover her cockney accent.

Closing the door behind herself, Mary gazed at the dark red and gold interior. Lillian Redmond, with her long and frizzy red hair and dark blue crêpe gown looked lovely. Cascading from her shoulders and falling in folds was a matching delicate silk train. A braid of tiny pink flowers lay around her hips, clasped at the front with a small sapphire-blue glass buckle.

'Come and sit down, Mary dear. I just want to run over a few details on social etiquette.' Lillian smiled at her new protégée. 'Don't look so nervous, dear, it doesn't amount to much.' She lifted herself from the chaise longue in one sweeping move. 'Now, first things first. A glass of champagne.' She poured them each a drink. 'This was all new to *me* once, don't forget. I worked my fingers raw at one state in my young life – scrubbing floors and polishing copper from dawn until I dropped into my bed at night. But I watched, I listened, and I learned.

'Men are all the same underneath – rich or poor.' She handed Mary a glass of champagne and demonstrated the way in which to hold her glass and to raise it before sipping from the sparkling crystal. 'Here's to a new life. A better and worthy life for someone like yourself, born to a good family who, but for misfortune, would have mixed in circles of a higher station.'

'Bottoms up! said Mary innocently, flushed with excitement and not a little trepidation.

Easing herself back on to her chaise longue, Lillian looked admiringly at her protégée. 'You were just as pretty as a child. Your face and figure, my dear, will be your fortune, providing you treat both with respect.

'Now then, number one rule, never, under any circumstance, ask a client questions. You are here to listen and to comfort. You must never offer sex, wait until your guest makes an advance in that direction; sometimes they may not. Sometimes all they need is to be in these surroundings, in the company of a beautiful woman they do not have to answer to.

'And never, on any account, think of this place as a brothel. It's a House of Assignation – a place where lovers meet in secret. Always keep that in mind and you'll never be without respect for yourself or the other girls whom you will soon get to know. Try not to speak or mix with your fellow courtesans while you are here or outside. It causes more trouble than it is worth. Envy and gossip could be the ruin of us all. And . . . it goes without saying, that should you happen to see a client when you are outside—'

'I must ignore 'im,' said Mary, showing herself to be in the right frame of mind.

'Good girl. But of course you will do that gracefully, you simply do not address him or show any sign of recognition.'

'I take it that clients are just as discreet as they expect us t' be?' said Mary.

Lillian's face lit up. 'You couldn't have asked a better question. I think you are going to make an excellent courtesan, my dear.' She stood up, pleased. 'Your gentleman isn't due for another hour, so you'll have time to change and relax before he arrives.'

'Change?'

'You won't be disappointed.' Lillian pressed her finger on the bell-push. 'Elizabeth will be waiting there for you, she'll help you get ready.'

There was a tapping on the door. 'That will be Polly, she'll take you to your boudoir now. Oh and Mary, from now on you must always call me, Madam.'

Once outside of Lillian's rooms, Mary sighed with relief, especially when she saw Lizzie waiting at the foot of the staircase for her. Leaving Polly to herself she went to her friend and hugged her. 'Oh Lizzie, it's lovely 'ere. I don't know what t' say.'

Whispering into her ear, Lizzie said, 'Did you ask the midwife?'

'I did and she'll do it but we mustn't ever let on what you do for a living. But Lizzie, ain't you gonna ask how it went with your mother?'

'No need. What did the midwife say?'

'We must act quickly. I said tomorrow night at seven, at my 'ouse.' She clenched her friend's arm tightly. 'If she is a prostitute the midwife will be furious.'

Linking arms, Lizzie took her upstairs. Lifting her skirts she pulled a slip of paper from the pocket of her silk drawers. 'Here. This is the woman's name. Come on, let's get you out of them clothes and 'ave you looking your best.'

'Lizzie, I bought these especially to make an impression. They cost a lot and I've not even paid for 'em yet.'

'From a second-'and clothes shop, I s'pose? Come on. I've got some drink hidden away upstairs.' Lifting the hems of their skirts, deportment out of the window, the girls ran up the sweeping staircase to the room where Mary would entertain her very first gentleman.

'Now close your eyes,' said Lizzie, excited. 'An' don't open 'em until I say.'

'What's that lovely scent?' murmured Mary, her eyes shut tight.

'Roses for a rose,' she giggled. 'And dark red ones at that. Now then, open!'

Taking a deep breath, Mary slowly lifted her eyelids. At first she could do no more than simply gaze, mouth open. 'It's beau'iful . . . the wallpaper, Lizzie . . .'

She moved slowly round the room, trailing a finger along the walls. 'Real hand-printed wallpaper.' Her gaze moved to the soft sage and red design to the mahogany panelling beneath and then across the room to the long sash windows and the matching drapes. The thick pile carpet was royal blue, red and gold – a vibrant rich pattern which blended with the dark blue silk-brocade sofa and matching armchair.

She glanced at the four-poster bed – the focus of the room – from which hung drapes to match the red and green bedspread. In a dream, she allowed Lizzie to take her hand and lead her to a mirror-fronted wardrobe. Opening the doors, she said, 'Here . . . this is your introduction gown.' She drew the dark crimson and rich green gown from the wardrobe. 'The finest Genoa velvet madam is ever likely to have the pleasure of wearing.' She spoke in a mock posh voice.

'Oh, Lizzie,' murmured Mary, feeling the luxury of the soft material between her slender fingers. 'It must 'ave cost the earth.'

'Right. Strip down to your altogether,' said Lizzie, glowing with pride.

'I will not!'

'Well 'ow you gonna put all these fineries on then? On top of that lot? Get undressed and start with the silk underwear. Your drawers won't be good enough.'

'They're clean *and* paid for, Lizzie Redmond!'

'Course they are. Now just relax and let Lizzie sort you out. You'll be pleased, honest to God.' Apprehensive as to what she had let herself in for, Mary allowed her friend to remove her clothing until she was naked.

Gazing at the sight before her, Lizzie's expression showed wonderment. 'Stone me blind,' she whispered, 'you *are* beautiful. Mother was right. Just look at them tits; they'll have our gentlemen guests drooling.'

'Stop it and 'elp me on with the frock,' said Mary, blushing.

'Well all I can say is you are one lucky cow. You're gonna look like a different person time I'm finished wiv yer.'

'Just get on wiv it.' Mary caught a glimpse of herself in the mirror. 'I never 'ave me hair loose like this. I think I'd best put it up in a chignon.'

'You won't. Mother'd give me a dressing down if you did, I've got my orders to follow. She wants it flowing, Mary.' She stepped away and plucked a tiny red rosebud from the arrangement on a side table. 'The finishing touch,' she said, slipping it into Mary's lustrous dark red hair and securing it with a tiny tortoiseshell-comb.

Lowering the trailing gown over Mary's head and watching it slip down her curvy body, Lizzie let out a low whistle. 'Good job I'm not one of them lesbians,' she said, with a twinkle in her eye. 'You look like royalty an' all.' She admired her friend in the mirror. The loose-fitting, soft velvet gown with its kick-up at the shoulders looked as if it had been especially made and designed just for her.

Mary gazed down at her soft kid shoes. 'I feel as if I'm someone else, Lizzie.'

'I told yer. You're a royal princess now.' Taking her friend in her arms, she and Mary danced round the room as if music was playing. A soft tapping on the door brought a halt to their fun. 'That'll be Mother,' whispered Lizzie, 'come to give you the once over.'

The expression on Lillian's face showed that even she hadn't realised just how lovely her new recruit was. 'I'll be in my room if you need me,' said Lizzie taking her leave and winking at her friend as she went.

'Mary . . . may I introduce Sir Walter,' said Lillian.

'How do yer do, sir.' Mary gave a spontaneous hint of a curtsy and offered her hand believing he would shake it. Instead he lifted it to his mouth and kissed the bend of her fingers, fixing his eyes on hers. If hearts could leap, Mary's would have done just that. Here was a dream come true. Sir Walter, tall and distinguished, was also handsome with a warm smile. She felt something inside melting . . .

'I'll leave you to get acquainted,' said Lillian, unable to cover her pride. 'Do press the bell-push should you require any refreshments.' She withdrew, leaving the couple together in her loveliest of rooms.

The door closed, Mary could feel tension moving through her body. Alone with an aristocrat! She didn't quite know what to say or do. Not moving so much as a muscle she waited for him to say something. She had not long to wait. Mesmerised though he was with her beauty, he cleared his throat and spoke in a kind voice.

'Why don't I open that bottle of champagne? It might help us both relax.'

Mary unclenched her hands and nodded. Then finding her voice said, 'I'm sorry but I'm not used to being alone in . . . like this . . . with a gentle-man.'

'So I gather,' he said, uncorking the bottle. 'But you needn't fear, I'm not about to pounce on you. When Madam talked of her new protégée to a mutual friend he, quite unselfishly, talked me into coming here. So you see, Mary, we both are new to this school.' He refrained from telling her that Lillian had positively boasted of her new asset. A beautiful, untouched maiden in the East End of London joining a House of Assignation was a rare thing.

'My father was very strict,' she said, not really knowing why she had said it. 'I always had to be home by a certain time and wasn't allowed male friends. Well . . . not unless I brought 'em home first, before we walked out together . . .' She could feel the blood from her neck rise upwards and wished she could disappear into thin air. She had never felt so embarrassed in a situation before. 'He was over-protective, really . . .'

'That doesn't surprise me,' Sir Walter said, pouring the champagne, 'you are *very* beautiful, Mary. He was protecting you and rightly so.' He offered her a glass of champagne. 'You've no need to feel intimidated, you know. Just think of us as friends while we're in this private bit of heaven.' He could see that her hands were trembling. 'Perhaps I should put this glass on the table?'

'Yes, please,' said Mary, trying to relax.

He turned to her and took her hands in his. 'I've never met anyone so nervous, I don't eat young virgins for supper, you know.' Resisting the urge to draw her hands away from his, Mary lifted her chin and managed a faint smile.

'That's better. Your hands are warming now,' he said, gently massaging her fingers. 'I trust I am allowed to call you by your first name?'

'Course you are. You're allowed to do what you want.' She hadn't meant it to come out quite like that.

'If that were true,' he said, 'I should have kissed you when I first walked into this room. As it is, I fear I shall be leaving it without fulfilling that desire.'

'Oh,' said Mary, fearing the worse. 'If you do leave, I might be asked not to come back any more. I've got a little brother to take care of . . .' Why was she talking like this? Suddenly she felt very awkward and out of place and wished she was back home with Arthur.

'Join me in a toast and I promise to stay,' he said.

'I'm sorry I said that, I'm just not used to this. I'm not very good at it, am I?'

He picked up her glass for her and placed it in her hand. 'Now then, shall we toast our first meeting? Or Lillian's excellent taste?'

She clinked her glass against his. 'We'll toast the Queen.'

'To the Queen!' he said. 'To the Queen of England.'

A few seconds passed and Mary was aware of him studying her face. 'I'm not supposed to ask you questions so . . .'

'Ah, well then I shall take the lead. Why must you support your brother?'

'My mother was a widow and she died recently so

that left just me and Arthur. My work in the offices at Bryant and May won't be enough to pay the rent and such like, so . . .'

'Here you are?'

'That's right. But I'm not sorry I came. Madam has bin very kind to me.' She put the glass to her lips and almost finished her champagne before she began to cough. 'Oh, it's fizzier than the glass I 'ad in Madam's rooms.' Instead of being deeply embarrassed she found herself quietly giggling.

Sir Walter took the glass from her and placed both on the table. He then put a comforting arm round her shoulder. 'Look, Mary, I know this isn't easy for you . . . and really . . . that's why I shan't stay long.'

'That's all right. Your visit's wasted on me, you should 'ave gone to see Lizzie.'

'I *shall* leave. But before I go will you do just one thing for me? Will you look at me properly and see if you can manage a smile?'

'Course I can manage a smile,' she said, looking into his face and melting. 'Thanks for being so nice and kind.' Without thinking she brushed a kiss across his cheek. 'I 'ope I do see you agen.'

His face serious, he cupped her lovely face gently. 'We shall see.' His hazel eyes went from her face to her hair. He then kissed her lightly on the lips. 'Your pain will ease, Mary. I promise you, time does heal a weeping heart.'

Standing by the door, looking into her eyes, he took a deep breath. He knew he should say goodbye and wish her and her brother well but he wanted to see her again, just once more. Whether he would or not was something else. 'Goodbye, Mary,' he said quietly before leaving. This strange encounter had thrown him into an emotional unrest. This girl from a poor working-class background, who was offering herself, had managed in her own naive way to make him feel humble.

Falling over herself to get out of the gown and into her own clothes, Mary was filled with an urgency to get out of the house. She would go back to the second-hand shop the very next day and return the clothes, forfeiting the down payment. If not, she would keep them and use them when she walked the streets of Whitechapel where she belonged, as a low-class paid whore. If she and Arthur were to stay together in their family home then she had to find a way of making more money, one way or another. The sound of the door opening caused her to freeze. If Sir Walter was to walk back in and see her half-naked she would die of embarrassment.

'Well, Mary dear, you certainly made an impression.' It was Lillian Redmond. 'I'm to send you home in a prepaid cab and you're not to return until late Saturday afternoon. That's when Sir Walter would like to see you again.' She handed Mary an envelope and smiled. 'Your fee for what I can only imagine to have been an excellent performance. I've docked a guinea for your introduction clothes. Once you've cleared that small debt, they'll be yours to keep. Fifteen guineas should wipe the slate clean.'

'I can't afford that kind of money!' gasped Mary.

'You'll find three guineas in the envelope.'

'But all I did was give 'im a kiss on the cheek.'

'Well it's not always what you do, Mary, but the way you do it. He paid without so much as a hint of dissatisfaction. Well done.'

'Three guineas . . . and you've deducted your percentage as well?'

'Naturally. There'll be another envelope on Saturday. Although you might try to give Sir Walter a little more than just a kiss? Try not to take too long dressing, Sophia's due to use the room at nine-thirty. At least we shan't have to change the linen.'

Later, having collected her brother, and enjoying a mug of tea with him, Mary tucked him up in bed. 'Do you wanna spend tomorrow evening at Billy's as well, Arthur? Teach 'im how to play cards, the way Miss Turner and Thomas taught you?'

'Why, will you be typewritin' agen?'

'No, but someone's coming to see me. An old friend and I said she could stay overnight.'

'I don't wanna sleep over Billy's!'

'No, course not, silly. She'll sleep in my room and I'll come in wiv you. It'll be like old times, eh?'

'Why do I 'ave to go to Billy's at all then?'

'Well, it's manners really. The lady's not bin feeling very well and Miss Turner's coming in to have a look at her so—'

'Well then I'll go up 'er 'ouse and play cards with Daft Thomas. I like it at Miss Turner's. It's cosy and more like our 'ouse. And Thomas is all right, really; he makes me laugh.'

'We'll see. Wait till tomorrow comes, eh. Now then, some shut-eye, young feller!'

'Did you like the lady?' said Arthur sleepily. 'Was it all right?' He yawned, turned on his side and drew up his knees. 'Did she like your typewritin'?'

'It was good and yes she did. And she paid me a bit up front so we're gonna be all right, Arthur. There'll always be coal for the fire and food in the larder.'

Seeing that he was falling asleep, Mary kissed his cheek and tucked him in, promising that no matter what happened, his welfare would always come first. How could she think otherwise as she looked at him curled up in bed. 'I love you, Arthur,' she murmured, before turning down the oil lamp.

Chapter Four

Once Mary had changed the sheets on her bed and placed a small arrangement of flowers from her backyard on to the chest of drawers, she scanned the room for any dusty surfaces.

Satisfied that she had not forgotten anything, she laid a small clean towel over the jug and basin on the pine washstand to keep the water fresh.

Smoothing the twill bedspread she immediately thought of her mother, remembering when she had brought it home from the second-hand shop and boiled it in the copper until it was sparkling white. As her eyes wandered to the head of the iron bedstead and the faded scratched painting of birds, the stories which her father had created for her and Arthur, round that small scene, came flooding back.

The loud banging on the street door brought her back to reality sharply. The lady was early. It had just gone past a quarter to seven. When she opened the street door her smile disappeared. She was disappointed to see Miss Turner standing there and not the woman. She had hoped to have the lady comfortably in bed, ready and waiting when the midwife arrived.

'Arthur and young Billy are settling down to a game

of draughts, Mary. I've given Thomas instructions to see the lads home.' Jacqueline unbuttoned her cape and removed her hat. 'Is the woman here yet?'

'No, Miss Turner,' said Mary, 'but the room's spic and span.'

'Good, I'll go up then. Make sure there's plenty of water boiling in the copper, there's a good girl. Do you have a clean towel?'

'It's on the washstand, covering the jug of clean water.'

Leaving the room and going upstairs, Jacqueline looked over her shoulder at Mary. 'Do we know the woman's name yet?'

'No, I . . .' she took a deep breath and shrugged . . . 'I mislaid it. I had it written down somewhere.'

Shaking her head to show her displeasure, she went upstairs. 'Fetch her up as soon as she arrives, please!'

'Yes, Miss Turner. Would you like a cup of tea?'

'No, thank you, maybe afterwards. We'll see.'

Worried in case the woman had remembered the name of the street but not the number, Mary stood on the doorstep peering along the turning.

'The nights are certainly drawing in now,' the lamp-lighter said, arriving at the post outside Mary's door.

'That they are, Mr Armstrong. And foggy nights not far behind, eh?'

'Well, there's one chap who'll be thankful for it,' he said, making his way to the next lamppost. 'The Whitechapel murderer. He'll be having a field day as well as working at night!'

Mary felt a chill run through her. Why were people

taking it for granted that the maniac would strike again? Pulling her shawl about her shoulders, she stepped outside and strained her eyes against the half light, looking out for the Chapman woman.

'Come on, Dark Annie,' she murmured, surprising herself. The name which had been written in brackets on the screw of paper came back to her without her having to try and remember it. Dark Annie. Why dark? she wondered. Could it be that she's foreign? Or does it mean she's just mysterious?

Whatever the meaning, Mary was about to find out, for approaching from the end of the turning, passing through the glow of a streetlamp, appeared a woman, walking not too steadily. A stranger – it had to be her.

'Number firteen?' she said, arriving at Mary's house. 'Wot one is it?' Her speech was slurred and she reeked of gin.

'This is it,' murmured Mary. 'You're not Annie, are you?' She prayed that she would say no.

'That's right, cock.' She pushed her face up close as if she was doing her utmost to bring Mary's face into focus. 'Well ain't *you* pretty,' she said. 'Bit on the young side for this kind of work. Still so long as you gimme a good clear-out, eh?' She grinned, showing yellow teeth.

'You'd best come inside.' Mary hoped that none of her neighbours were watching from a window.

'Well we can 'ardly get on wiv it out 'ere, can we?' The woman cackled with laughter.

Grabbing the inebriate's arm, Mary pulled her inside

99

and shut the door, hoping they hadn't been spotted by a neighbour. Knowing that this woman was no more than one of the lowest streetwalkers, Mary cursed Lizzie. She couldn't believe her friend would trick her like this. She couldn't believe that Lizzie would know such a person.

'The midwife's upstairs, waiting for you. I'll tell 'er you've arrived.'

'Ooooh, ain't we posh for a backstreet gal, eh?'

'There's no need, Mary, I heard.' Jacqueline was standing at the top of the stairwell, her face taut, her eyes filled with anger.

'Well, well, well, if it ain't Turner the midwife. I sometimes wondered if you was entirely straight and respectible. Fancy you being a saviour, eh?' She turned to Mary and explained the pun, 'Save yer from gettin' too fat!' She patted her belly and cackled.

'Upstairs, if you please.' Jacqueline was not prepared to spend a second more than she had to in the company of this degenerate who had brought a putrid damp smell in with her. 'I'm pressed for time.'

Hanging on to the stair rail, Annie Chapman pulled herself up each step as if she were climbing a steep mountain. 'You wait till I tell the girls about this little find. And you ain't gonna charge me neiver. Get a kick out of looking up our fannies, I s'pose, eh, Midwife? One of *them*. Still, I ain' fussy, I've let more than one old lesbian 'ave a tuppeny touch.'

'I'm sorry, Miss Turner, I swear I didn't know. I *swear* it. I thought she was a good woman,' whispered Mary.

'Do you have a rubber sheet?'

'You're not gonna touch 'er, surely?'

'I have to now that she's here, otherwise she'll go out screaming the odds about both of us. The rubber?'

'It's in the drawer of the washstand.' Doing her utmost not to cry, Mary touched her neighbour's arm. 'You will forgive me for this—'

'No. You should have looked into it fully!' She pulled her arm away and went upstairs. Then, turning back she said, 'I'm not going to do what she expects. Your mother would turn in her grave just to think that such a woman had been in her house.'

'Shall I come up?'

'No, I'll have her out of here within minutes. You busy yourself in the scullery until we come down. The least said this evening the better.' Sighing loudly, Jacqueline made her way into Mary's bedroom where she found the whore sitting on a small chair, trying to unlace her boots.

'There's no need for that, Annie,' she said, trying to sound easy. The last thing she wanted was to rile this woman or antagonise her. Taking the rubber sheet from the drawer, the midwife shook it out and laid it on the floor. 'Leave everything on except your drawers, we don't want you catching a cold.'

'Can't I lay on the bed, Midwife? Be more comftable.'

'Best not, in case we stain it. It wouldn't be fair on the girl.'

'But I'm meant to be stopping the night, so I'll be slipping between them lovely clean sheets in any case. I 'spect she's put a rubber underneath.'

'First things first,' said the midwife, 'let's see what the problem is, shall we?' She looked from Chapman to the rubber square on the floor and waited. 'Slip your knickers off.'

'Leave off, Midwife. Wot would someone like me want with them, eh?' she chuckled. 'I 'aveta keep the door ajar, if you know what I mean.'

'Just lie on the floor then and open your legs.'

'Just as you wish,' Chapman grinned and then winked at her. 'I wiped me fanny with a damp cloth before I came out.'

'Very considerate,' said Jacqueline, using carbolic soap to scrub her hands in the china bowl.

Kneeling between the whore's legs, her chin up to avoid the sickly odour, Jacqueline began to feel her stomach. 'Strange,' she said thoughtfully, 'there is a swelling but the womb feels normal. How many weeks are you?'

'Gawd only knows. About seven or eight . . .'

'And how old did you say you were?' She pressed her hands into the woman's groin.

'I never said. About forty . . . ish, I should say.'

'Mmm. I should be very surprised if you were pregnant. But there, I could be wrong.' She slipped a hand inside the woman and made an excellent show of giving a full examination. Of course the whore was pregnant, Jacqueline knew that when she felt her stomach but that information would be kept to herself.

'No . . . No, there's no foetus growing in here.' She probed a bit more. 'This is typical of a woman in her change. The swelling is mostly water, you've been retaining water but that should right itself.'

Hauling herself up, Jacqueline plunged her hands back into the warm soapy water and scrubbed her nails. 'Think yourself lucky. A woman of your age wouldn't have found the after-pains of an abortion too easy to take.'

Leaning on her elbows, Chapman peered at the midwife. 'You saying I'm not in the club?'

'I am. You can go, you're in good condition for your age. You'll not see many more periods now. Perhaps one every three months or so until they fade altogether.'

'Well, well, Midwife. You 'ave taken me back. All that bleedin' worry for nuffink, eh? Wot a prat you must fink I am.'

'You're not the first to mistake the menopause for a late pregnancy. It happens all the time,' she lied.

'So I can go out on the game tonight then?' She grinned.

'Do what you have to, Annie. It's a free country.' All that Jacqueline wanted was to see the back of her.

'Well, I'm most grateful to yer, and I shall put some business your way for it.'

'Business?' Jacqueline knew what she meant but she was stalling for time, thinking ahead.

'Yeah. There's always some silly cow who's got 'erself in the club. They'll know where to come now, won't they?'

'Oh, no. I wouldn't have seen to you except it was

a favour for young Mary. I gather you're a friend of a friend?'

'Am I? Ah, well, it's a shame you couldn't do it for one or two of me mates. Still, now that we're personal like, you would see to one if they was in deepest trouble, wouldn't yer?' The tone of the whore's voice was very clear. This was a veiled threat of blackmail.

'Let's hope that the streetgirls are more careful than that. Prevention is better than cure.'

'Ah, but it don't take long, do it? You'd be able to fit one or two in now and again. Gawd luv us, I should know. I must 'ave got rid of at least a dozen in me time. Tried to do it meself once or twice. Made a right balls-up of it as well. Not that Sarah the Scrape made a better job of it. Don't know wot the girls are gonna do now that she's gawn. She only charged a shillin' as well.'

Back on her feet, Annie thanked Jacqueline and wished her good luck until the next time she saw her – another way of saying she would be back. On reaching the bedroom door, she turned and grinned, 'How's that nephew of yours, young Thomas?'

'He's very well, thank you.' Jacqueline answered matter-of-factly, hiding her true feelings. That this whore should know that she and Thomas were related bothered her. It bothered her a lot. 'What makes you ask?'

'Well . . . two of the girls 'ave got certain opinions about 'im.'

'Who wouldn't have?' Jacqueline forced a smile. 'He is a bit simple, should have been called Simon.' She tried to make light of it.

'Oh, I don't know about that—'

'Come on. What's the secret?'

'You promise not to say I ever told yer, Midwife?'

'On the boy's life,' she said, smiling benignly.

'Well, one of 'em reckons, and I must say she fairly convinces me sometimes, she reckons that Daft Thomas carries knives around wiv 'im. She says she wouldn't put it past 'im t' use 'em.'

'No, not Thomas. He carries a penknife, that's all, like lots of lads his age.'

'That's wot I said! I said the other tarts were right. They reckons it's a mad student from the London Medical School wot's doing the diabolical murders. But she said no and went as far as to—' The whore suddenly stopped.

'As to what, Annie?'

'I fink I've said too much already.' But she continued, 'She's 'ad 'is initials inked on to 'er body. TC. Silly bitch. She reckons she's gonna show 'im if he should turn up in daylight. So that if he is the one going round cutting us up, 'is initials are there for the law to see. If ever she should get done in, that is.'

Jacqueline felt as if she had been lashed across the face with the metal end of her mother's belt. She was shocked – shocked to the core. There had been talk of Thomas being the vile murderer . . . she couldn't believe it. 'Your friend has quite an imagination, Annie.'

'Well, I'll be seein' yer, Midwife,' she winked at her again with a sneer on her lips. 'Now that I knows where to find yer, I'll drop by for a chat and a cuppa, eh?

Tuppence for a feel, and for a tanner I'll sit on yer face.' She roared with laughter and didn't stop until she was downstairs and out of the house.

Dropping down on to the edge of Mary's bed, Jacqueline was stunned. Two prostitutes suspected Thomas and one had his initials inked into her arm? From now on she must encourage him to stay in at night, let him sleep on the floor by the fire, that would stop his night-time wanderings. But would it stop the rumour before it spread? And what of her own reputation? How long would it be before that was tarnished? Once word went through the filthy backstreets that she was an abortionist? And Chapman's insinuations that she was a lesbian – would that mud stick too?

'Wicked rumours bring people down,' she murmured. Wild speculation from whores who have too much time on their hands could cause damage. She would not waste any more time thinking about it, something had to be done . . . but what?

'Are you all right, Miss Turner?' called Mary from below stairs.

'I'm fine, Mary!' she called back. Fine? How could she be fine? The naive girl had also landed herself in trouble. More whores would follow Chapman to her door, of that there was no doubt.

'I could do with that cup of tea now.' Jacqueline uncorked her bottle of gin and felt better once the fiery liquid warmed her throat.

'The woman wasn't pregnant after all,' said Jacqueline as they sat drinking tea together. Best Mary didn't know too much, she thought to herself, she is young, unworldly and with much to learn about the human race.

'I'm really sorry. My friend was so sure she was a decent woman who had been raped.'

'Who is this friend?'

'Someone I went to school with,' she said, lowering her eyes. 'She was my best friend in the classroom.'

Jacqueline wasn't sure that Mary was telling the truth. 'You must be more careful, Mary. Be more choosy with regard to the company you keep. I should stick to your politics if I were you, you'll meet a better class of people.' Mary's poor judgement of character was worrying but at least she would have learned something from this experience.

'Yes, I shall be more careful from now on.'

'The woman who came here tonight is the lowest type.'

'I know, but when she left I felt sorry for her. I know she was laughing but she didn't 'ave anywhere to sleep tonight.' She shrugged and sighed. 'I gave her a sixpenny bit, I should 'ave given a bit more.'

'Is that a fact? Well I don't see how you can afford to give your hard-earned money away, Mary, especially not to someone like her. You won't earn that much extra with the typewriting and you'll need every penny if you are to keep young Arthur out of the work-house.'

'She made me feel guilty. At least *we've* got a roof over our 'eads.'

'Only just, Mary . . . unless I am mistaken.' She rose

from her chair, 'Well, I've two calls to make, I must be on my way. If Thomas hasn't brought those boys back by nine, I should go and fetch them. Once they start playing games they lose track of time.'

Seeing the midwife out, Mary apologised once more. 'I'm truly sorry, Miss Turner, it won't 'appen agen.'

'I should say not!' She bade her goodnight and left. Deeply concerned, Jacqueline weighed her choices. The whore was pregnant after all said and done and it wouldn't be long before she realised it and that she had been lied to. Of course Jacqueline could say that she had been mistaken, but streetgirls were canny. Chapman would work it out for herself that the midwife had avoided performing her abortion. To Jacqueline's mind there was no question that she would turn up again and cause a disturbance – it was inevitable.

In a few months' time she would be leaving for America but if Jacqueline was to see her name remain untarnished until then, she had to keep her wits about her. She had dedicated her life to her work as a midwife and she was not going to let a blackmailing whore ruin her good reputation.

Having made her second call, a fatigued Jacqueline turned into Brushfield Street scarcely believing her ears. The Spitalfields church clock striking the fifth hour came as a surprise. The two deliveries had been fairly straightforward births but she hadn't realised just how late it was. The night had flown by.

If the striking clock wasn't enough to stimulate her

senses, the sight ahead was. Annie Chapman was standing outside the small family run Italian café and Alberto, the congenial proprietor, dressed in black and sporting a dark beard and moustache, was leaning against the shopfront enjoying a cigarette. Jacqueline was not the only one who worked day and night. Several other people were already afoot and market porters were to-ing and fro-ing.

Swaying from side to side, Chapman, in her long black figured jacket, black skirt and boots looked little different from the rest of the whores dotted round in street doorways touting for trade. It was Chapman's familiar coarse voice that sent a chill down the midwife's spine.

'If I can't do a trick I shall 'ave to pawn me coat! I don't s'pose you want a fourp'nny one, Alberto? I've got a square of rubber you can wrap round it if you're worried you'll catch the clap!'

Jacqueline could not make out the Italian's answer, his voice was deep and quiet, his face earnest. He might have been cursing her or making arrangements. But whatever he said to Chapman it must have been amusing for it caused her to laugh raucously. 'But fourpence'll give me a bed for a few hours and I'm dead beat, Berto, almost washed out.' Dispensing with him she staggered off, her voice trailing after her. 'But I must pull meself together or I shall 'ave nowhere to sleep but under a sack!'

With no ulterior motive in mind other than a strange desire to follow her, Jacqueline smiled politely at Alberto as she passed. But he was not going to let her go so easily. He too had had an early morning tipple, or a late night one, depending if he had been to bed that night at all.

'Ah, Midwife! I was talking about you today. My wife, she say, Miss Turner eez the best. Our boy Max isa four-month-old yesterday!'

'The rest of the family are well, I hope?' she said, continuing on her way, hoping he would not drag her in for a coffee.

'*Magnifico!* And all thanks to you! Another emergency, no?' he called after her.

'Probably a false alarm, Alberto, but you never can tell. If I'm up to it I'll drop by afterwards.'

'*Eccellente!* Fora you, we are always here!'

Jacqueline showed a hand. 'You're a good man, Alberto, and your coffee is still the best!' Walking in Chapman's tracks, Jacqueline followed her into Commercial Street and along Wilkes Row. The intoxicated woman approached three market traders on their way to Spitalfields but each of the men rebuked her, receiving a stream of verbal abuse in return. By the time the prostitute neared Hanbury Street, the midwife had made up her mind to approach her and extract a little more information as to what else the streetgirls might be saying about Thomas.

'I thought that was you in front of me, Annie. Don't tell me you've walked the streets all night long?' said Jacqueline, arriving at her side.

'Oh it's you, Midwife. Yeah, I've bin trying to earn a few coppers. Nuffing wrong wiv that, is there?'

'I thought Mary Dean saw you all right. The girl

said she had given you sixpence, I must have a word with her.'

'So wot if she did give me a treat, wot's it to you?' She tucked her neckerchief under her coat collar. 'I'm saving it to put in the church plate on Sunday.'

'You look worn out,' said Jacqueline, taking a sixpenny-bit from her own pocket and offering it to Chapman. 'I'll walk with you towards your lodgings.'

'Fank you, Midwife. I've bin in that much pain since you probed my guts.' She took the small silver coin, lifted her skirt and slipped it into a purse tied around her waist.

'I could give you a pill if you like, to relieve the pain,' said Jacqueline.

'I still fink you was wrong, Midwife. If I ain't got a bun in the oven, I don't know what.'

'Maybe I was a bit hasty, I knew I had a long night ahead of me. Would you like me to feel your stomach again, I shan't give you an internal if you're sore.'

'Cheeky cow,' grinned Annie. 'You just want a sixpenny feel.' She chuckled to herself. 'For all your airs and graces you turn out to be a common old backstreet who fancies women. Come on, we'll go back to Dorset Street so you can give me the once over.' Her breath reeking of cheap gin, she slipped her arm though Jacqueline's and winked at her.

'Is that where you're lodging?' Casually, Jacqueline drew her arm away, pretending to straighten her hat.

'I will be now, won't I; now I've got a tanner to spend. I lodge there mostly, more's the pity. See that?' She turned one side of her face towards the lamplight so that the purple bump on her temple could be seen. 'Liza Cooper did that and all over a ha'penny worth o' bleedin' soap.'

Glancing at the bruise, Jacqueline said, 'I've got some lotion in my bag that should take the swelling down. Who's Liza Cooper?'

'Anuvver lodger. I chucked a ha'penny at 'er but the cold cow got all uppity and punched me. She never got off scot free though. Where's this lotion and pill then?'

'I don't think I should be seen by that woman, Annie. Let's keep this between ourselves. Cooper sounds like a pound of trouble. A private courtyard will do, it shouldn't take more than a couple of minutes.'

'Whatever you say, Midwife, whatever you say. I've only told one of the uvvers . . . about what you do, that is. I bumped into Cath'rin soon after I left you, I'll tell 'er to keep 'er mouth shut now you're one of mine. Don't look so bleedin' worried. Cath'rin won't blab if I tell 'er not to.'

'Catherine?' How many whores had she been talking to . . . ?

'Cath'rin Eddowes. Come on, we'll go to number twenty-nine,' said Annie, pulling at Jacqueline's arm, 'the front door's always open. We'll slip through to the backyard. It's pitch black out there so you can feel me fanny wivout that lot gettin' a free view.'

'Catherine Eddowes . . . that name rings a bell,' said Jacqueline, lying. 'What does she look like?'

'Skinny, five foot nuffin'. Dark 'air, brown eyes, wears a black straw bonnet. Got fur on 'er cuffs and collar, says it's mink but I say it's rat. The cow wears the skirt I was after, got to the rag 'n' bone man before I did. Dark green chintz with Michaelmas daisies. One of these days I'll 'ave it off 'er.'

Stopping outside 29 Hanbury Street, a three-storey house, originally built for weavers and now used as dwellings, Annie studied the exterior for any lights at the windows. The dreary property set in the midst of sinister buildings was dark and silent. 'We must be very quiet, Midwife.' Annie put a finger to her lips.

'She lodges in the same building as you, does she?' whispered Jacqueline, needing a little more information.

'Now and then . . . when she's got the money. Why? Fancy a rub wiv 'er as well, do yer?'

'No, I just had a feeling about the name that's all.'

'Yeah . . . well . . . maybe your Thomas mentioned it. She's the one who 'ad 'is initials inked on 'er arm.'

Jacqueline knew all she needed to know. Following Annie through the dank, dark passage to the rear, she felt her anger return. This whore had dared to mention her nephew again. Her heart pounding she knew what she had to do. Feeling her way in the half dark and treading carefully down some decrepit steps she gripped a rusty iron handrail.

Stopping suddenly on bare earth, and leaning against the close timber palings of a fence, Annie Chapman lifted her skirts. 'Be quick, Midwife, or me fanny'll freeze in this cold air.'

Staring into the whore's face, Jacqueline felt her throat tighten. Almost strangled with disgust and fury she glared into Chapman's eyes. This low, mucky, disease-spreading witch had tricked both Mary Dean and herself and it was filling her with rage. The thought of her beloved nephew's name being vilified by the lowest of the low caused her to lose all sense of right and wrong. Thrusting one hand forward she gripped Chapman's jaw. 'You disgusting child aborter. You're not fit to live on God's soil.' Clasping her other hand around Chapman's throat she squeezed and squeezed until her arm trembled under the strain. 'Your master waits in hell. Go to the devil, Chapman.' Squeezing with both hands now, she pushed her thumbs against the helpless woman's throat until her eyes bulged and the last short burst of putrid air escaped from her body.

Making no sound, the midwife lowered the lifeless body to the ground and listened for any noise from inside the dwelling. There was nothing but a deathly hush and a distant sound of a starving cat mewing. She snapped open her black bag and removed a six-inch knife. She then slashed the woman's throat, from one side to the other. Jerking back to avoid the blood, she turned her face away from the gaping wound as a message flew through her mind: Speed and skill, Jacqueline . . . speed and skill.

At arm's length she waited until most of the blood had stopped spurting out of the slashed neck. She then lifted the dead woman's skirts and threw them over her blood-splattered, white face. Then, with a sweep of her knife, she cut the white flesh of her belly and disembowelled the body, as a medical student might if the corpse were on a slab in the mortuary. The telltale pregnant womb was what she was after. No sign of a foetus must be found. Should it ever come out that Chapman *had* been to Mary Dean's house, the midwife's story would not hold water. She must make this killing look the mark of an insane incompetent medical student.

Her work finished, she wrapped the evidence – which could send her to the gallows – in her evening edition of the *Star* and placed it in her Gladstone bag, promising herself that she would see to it that the unformed child had a proper burial.

Before she left the corpse, Jacqueline pulled off the rings from her fingers to confuse the issue. She would make this look the work of a thief as well as a lunatic.

Later, with the early morning sun on her face, the midwife nodded at early risers as she made her way through Brick Lane feeling not remorse for the committed act, but sound that she had seen justice done. There was also a sense of freedom in her soul. The dark worry in the pit of her stomach had gone. It had taken long to save herself, Mary Dean and Thomas, from the worst kind of entrapment. Blackmail and slander, as far as she was concerned, went hand in hand. Now, at least the good name of her nephew would go unchallenged. Not that her work was finished. There was Catherine Eddowes to consider – Eddowes was the tarnished link. Rinsing her hands under a drinking fountain she splashed the cool water on to her face and felt the better for it. It had been the worst of all nights and this fresh, new day was most welcome. She embraced it.

'Mornin', Midwife!' The cheerful voice of a passer-by added to her sense of well-being.

'Good morning!' she returned. 'It looks as though we may expect a sunny September day!'

'I 'ope so, Midwife, I 'ope so!' The woman, carrying her large basket of matchboxes called back. 'Once these are delivered I shall be 'elpin' out on the fruit 'n' veg in the market. I could do wiv a bit of sunshine.'

Checking that her hands had been wiped clean enough and satisfied that the specks of blood on her cloak were excusable, Jacqueline, carrying her black bag, entered a café in Bethnal Green and ordered herself a cup of tea and two slices of toast and jam.

Seated in a corner, she lifted the cup to her mouth and tried to control the trembling which seemed to have taken hold of her hands. It would not do for her to appear distressed. Taking a leaf from her own book, she took long, deep breaths; the kind she taught her clients in their advanced stages of labour. Much to her relief, it worked, and after a second cup of tea, was able to let her mind wander. She speculated on what the press would make of this latest drama and what they would print in the midday editions.

Amused by the picture she had conjured in her mind of Charles Cutbush and his police colleagues, once it had reached their ears, she sipped her tea. Who would they target this time? she wondered, Which poor devil would be dragged in as a chief suspect? Not her, that she could be sure of. A midwife? Never. She was the last person anyone would suspect. Biting into her toast and blackberry jam, she realised how hungry she was and wondered why she felt so wide awake and alert, having missed out on a night's sleep. The adrenaline must still be coursing through her body.

Glancing across the room at the notorious Dove Lane boys who were leaving, she wondered how they might react if she were to give details of the deed she had just committed. One by one the gang filed out of the café, their caps pulled down to their ears, hands in their pockets, shoulders humped and jackets buttoned tight. They were doing their best to look tough and sinister.

Smiling, she watched them through the window as they lurched forward on their way to Spitalfields. Wiping condensation from the window, she caught sight of a familiar figure standing in a doorway across the lane. It was young Harriet Smith, looking the worse for wear, freezing and abandoned. She wondered what the poor child could be doing out there in the cold at such an early hour. Surely she wasn't up to mischief?

Calling Harriet from the shop doorway she could see that the girl was shivering. Dodging between a horse-driven cart and a cab, Harriet arrived grinning. ''Ello, Miss Turner.'

'Come in and warm yourself, Harriet. You look half frozen to death.' She turned to the woman behind the counter and ordered another mug of tea. Pushing a slice of toast and jam towards Harriet she told her to sit down.

'How is your baby brother faring?' she asked.

'He ain't, Midwife,' she said, sadly. ''E died. Muvver's milk dried up.'

'I'm so sorry to hear that, Harriet, but I can't say I'm really surprised. He was a weak little baby, my dear. I dare say he's better off.'

'He would 'ave only ended up in the work'ouse, Midwife,' said Harriet, bolting down her food. She hadn't eaten properly for days. 'That's where me mum and me little sister nearly went, but me aunt and uncle took 'em in. We got chucked out for not payin' rent.'

'And your father?'

'Dunno. He legged it agen.'

Jacqueline studied the girl, from the look of her filthy clothes and dirty hair, she had obviously been sleeping rough. 'And what about you?'

'I was dumped wiv a relative in the Old Jago, but I ran away. It's 'orrible there but I'm a lot warmer where I doss down now. Not far from the Old Jago but not *in* it.' She gulped half of her tea in one go.

'The Jago's not the best part of town,' said Jacqueline, 'I will say that. You probably are best out of it. So where *do* you doss down?'

'In the coalman's yard on straw, next to the 'orses. It's under cover and 'e gimme a blanket as well. Sometimes 'e pours 'ot tea on a dish of oats for me. I run errands for 'im.'

'And what about school?'

'Don't go no more. Ain't got nowhere to wash an' that, the soot dust gets in me 'air, so I can't go to school, can I, not looking disgusting?' She shrugged. 'I do sums though, for the coalman. He says I'm 'is bookkeeper and gives me a penny every day if 'e can.'

Wondering whether to leave the girl to her fate, Jacqueline fell silent and sipped her tea. After all, there were dozens of orphans and such like sleeping under tarpaulins in Spitalfields and Billingsgate markets, especially Spitalfields. The bruised and damaged fruit and vegetables from the gutter which had been discarded by costermongers were belly-filling.

'I was gonna go round your 'ouse. See if you still needed me to 'elp you out,' said Harriet, a look of hope in her dull eyes.

'There must be somewhere you can stay, Harriet?'

'Nar, there ain't. I'm all right though.'

'Maybe we should go and see Doctor Barnardo? He never turns a child away.'

'I could run messages fer free if you let me sleep on yer floor, next to the fire.'

'No, that wouldn't work. But you can come home with me now if you like. Have a bath and maybe stay over tonight. But only tonight mind, tomorrow we'll see if we can place you.'

'They'll only put me in the workhouse. I don't mind sleeping wiv the 'orses, they keeps me warm.'

'Well at least you'll be comfortable this night coming. We must take our leave now, child. My energy is running low,' said Jacqueline, heaving her frame out of the chair. 'Remind me to stop and buy a loaf of bread on the way.'

Walking hand in hand through the Bethnal Green Gardens, each enjoying the aroma of the warm fresh bread as it wafted from the bag, Jacqueline enjoyed her time in the sun. All the worries from yesterday seemed to have floated away now that she had, with very little effort, got rid of the blackmailer. She wondered if her time here was not only meant to bring new life into the world but to rid it of those who were like a rotten disease on an apple and spoiling what nature had intended.

'I wonder wot today's gonna bring?' said Harriet, her thoughts miles away.

Smiling down at the waif, Jacqueline imagined that the girl's mother had probably said that to her each morning to give her and the family hope. Even so, the words hit home. For now Jacqueline was also wondering how this day would end and what was happening right then in the back yard of number 29 Hanbury Street. In truth, she wanted to return and watch from a distance.

Now approaching 6.30 a.m. there was much activity in and around the lodging house where Annie Chapman had been murdered. Earlier, a cabman who rented a room in the attic had gone into the yard directly he'd come from stabling his horse and, while his wife was brewing tea, when he opened the back door, the sight that met his eyes had all but paralysed him. Once he had collected himself he stumbled into the street and managed to call out to some workmen. At first they shrugged off his cries for help but when he ranted as to what he had seen, they ran across the street to see for themselves.

Following him down the passage the men had stared at the corpse from the top of the yard steps until one of them boldly ventured down, stopping at a distance from the macabre spectacle. The full horror caused him to reel and almost pass out.

Once a policeman had been found and brought to the scene, he took possession of the yard.

The passage was soon jammed with spectators, but having received a ghoulish account of the grisly sight from one tenant, none were inclined to attempt to view the slaughtered prostitute.

Arriving at the top end of Whitehead Street, still holding Harriet's hand, the midwife encountered Mary Dean and her brother, Arthur.

'You're out early this morning, Mary. Going somewhere special?'

'We're off to the market to buy some new breeches for Arthur,' she said. 'Ain't it a lovely morning for it as well.'

'Are you now?' said Jacqueline, wondering where Mary had found the money. As she saw it, the orphans were living hand to mouth, with no money to spare for new clothes from the market.

'And who might this be?' said Mary, grinning at Harriet and avoiding the midwife's searching eyes.

'This is young Harriet Smith. She's homeless and we're going to find her somewhere to live tomorrow. Tonight she'll be staying with me.'

'Pleased to meet you, Harriet,' said Mary, taking an

instant liking to the ginger-headed girl. 'Where's your manners, Arthur, say hello.'

''Ello,' he mumbled, self-consciously.

'Wot's yer school like?' said Harriet, quick off the mark.

'Awright,' he said, keeping his eyes down.

'Do gels go there an' all?'

'Yeah. Worse luck.'

'I 'ave to go out for a few hours this afternoon, Harriet. Why don't you call in and play draughts with Arthur.' Mary felt her brother jerk her hand. 'It'll be company for 'im till I get back.'

'That's very thoughtful, Mary, I'll send her down. Off to do some more typewriting this afternoon, are you?'

'And a bit of bookkeeping as well, nothing complicated, bit of adding up, that's all. A few 'ours' work to pay for Arthur's breeches.'

The women bade farewell and went on their way and Mary felt better for not mentioning that Thomas had locked himself out the night before, after he'd seen Arthur home. She didn't want to tell tales out of school and she wasn't sure how Miss Turner might react to him having to sleep on Mary's settee. Any doubts she had had in the past about the young man had faded. Arthur had enjoyed his time playing cards with Thomas and after all, the midwife's nephew had done Mary a favour by watching over him for her.

''Ow old's Arfer then?' said Harriet to Jacqueline.

'Nine, I think . . .' Her thoughts were elsewhere . . .

on Mary. It was the first time she had seen the girl wearing lipstick and powder.

'Yeah, I s'pected I was older'n 'im. I'm nearly ten.'

Pushing the key into her front door, Jacqueline felt certain that Mary had lied to her about where she was going later that day. But why? She resolved to find out more.

'You've got a letter!' said Harriet as if it was a rare and wonderful thing.

Stooping to pick it up, Jacqueline recognised the handwriting on the folded piece of paper. It was from Thomas and read:

> *Dear Aunt,*
>   *I shut myself out last night. Miss Dean allowed me to wait in her house for you to come home but you never did and I fell asleep by her fire and she left me there till morning. I intend to look for respectable employment today. I'll start in the markets. I hope this pleases you. Your loving nephew, Thomas.*

'Well, that's something,' she murmured, 'at least his days will be filled.'

'Who's that then?' said Harriet.

'Never you mind.'

'Fire's out,' she said, picking up the poker and jabbing the ashes. 'I'll need some twists of paper if I'm to get this goin' agen.'

'First things first,' said Jacqueline. 'We'll fill the copper. It'll take a while to heat enough water for a bath.'

Filling a bucket from the outside tap, Jacqueline looked to the rear of the backyard where her father once grew root vegetables, it was just an overgrown patch now. She would bury the foetus there where it could rest in peace. She had thought of dropping the pathetic remains into the Cut where the slow but relentless current of the canal would carry it away to the Thames. Giving it a proper burial and grave in her father's small patch of garden seemed a more Christian thing to do. She would scatter some forget-me-not seeds on the earth over it.

'I've dun that,' said Harriet arriving into the yard. 'I've lit the fire. Wot else d'yer need doin'? I can spit 'n' press, peel vegt'balls, scrub floors, wash winders, make a pot of tea . . .'

'Tea sounds like a good idea. The kettle on the stove should be hot enough, it's been on there all night.'

'Right. Gimme that bleedin' bucket then. It's too 'eavy for an' old woman like you.'

'I'm not that old!' said the midwife, bemused by this funny creature. 'It's too heavy for *you.*'

'It ain't. I've carried twice as much,' she said, staggering inside with her load. Raising herself to full height, she could just manage to tip the water into the copper which was set into a brick edifice with a tiny fireplace below.

Standing in the scullery doorway, the midwife smiled at the straggly-haired, freckle-faced urchin. 'You won't be able to live here with me, Harriet. I've refused my own nephew, so I can hardly take you in.'

'I wouldn't wanna live wiv yer. I'll come in and

do, that's all. You can pay me wiv pies an' that so Mary won't 'ave to use her previshuns on me. I've got me 'eart set on living wiv 'er an' Arfer. I can be 'er 'ousemaid an' that. I wouldn't charge nuffink. I only wanna bed an' a bit of company.' She looked up at Jacqueline, squinting. 'You couldn't tell 'er 'ow good I am at wot I do round the 'ouse an' that, could yer?'

'I think she's got enough on her plate looking after herself and young Arthur.'

'I don't eat much.'

'No, I can see that. You're all skin and bone.' Jacqueline dropped down into her armchair, exhaustion finally catching up with her. 'I may well drop off to sleep while you make that tea, Harriet. If I should do so just leave me be.'

Kneeling on the floor, Harriet unlaced Jacqueline's boots and then sat back on her heels, hands on hips. 'I don't fink that's right. I fink you should go up t' bed right now. Tell me when to wake you up an' I'll fetch your tea then. You look all in.'

'You could be right,' said Jacqueline. 'I can hardly keep my eyes open.'

'Meanwhile I'll scrub yer boots. There's blood all over 'em. Good job I got the bleedin' fire goin', else I'd never get 'em dry once they're scrubbed. You never was this careless when you delivered muvver's baby, was yer? Looks like you've trod in it.'

'Yes,' said Jacqueline, thankful for her made-up alibi. 'It was a messy delivery but it all went well in the end.' Collecting her black bag which contained evidence that could see her on the end of a rope, she climbed the stairs slowly, ready for a much needed sleep.

'I've gotta propasishan to put to yer, Arfer,' said Harriet, as she and her new friend sat on his doorstep drinking lemon fizz. 'Summink for you to fink about.'

He stole a sideways glance at the peculiar girl and waited. 'Go on then.'

'Let me share your chamber an' I'll show you 'ow to do a really good click. I'll run errands for yer sister an' all 'stead of you 'aving to do it. An' I'll make the first pot of tea in the mornin'.'

'I ain't 'avin' a girl in my bedroom,' he said, looking away from her.

'We could shift the furniture. Put the cupboard an' drawers between the bed to make a wall.' She put the lip of the bottle to her mouth and finished her drink. 'I reckon I could 'elp yer wiv yer lessons an' all.'

'Wot's a click?'

'I'll tell yer once you've agreed to the propasishan. You'll 'ave to keep your trap shut about it mind. It ain't altogevver law abidin'.' She narrowed her eyes and peered at him. 'So wot d'yer reckon?'

'I thought you was gonna live wiv the midwife?'

'Nar, she won't want me there, she's got secrets that one. Dunno what they are yet, but I'll find out. She's all right though.'

'If you don't know what 'er secrets are – you don't know much, do yer?'

'More'n you do – kiss me arse if that ain't true. Wot time's your sister gettin' back 'ome?'

'Dunno. She's workin' for some rich woman.'

'I wouldn't like to be on me own at night like you are. Bit scary. Wot wiv that Ripper goin' about. He cuts up kids an' all, you know. Sells their insides to 'ospitals.'

'Anyone knows that. Not everyone knows 'is name though. It's Jack.'

'No it ain't. It's Pizer – Levver Apron. He's a Jew an' walks wivout bending 'is knees. Makes levver slippers and cuts people up wiv 'is levver knife. Bleedin' sharp an' all, it is.'

'Never 'eard of 'im.'

'Should 'ave done. He's bin slittin' froats for donkey's years.'

'No, it's definitely Jack an' he don't make slippers. He rips rags up so mothers can make mats wiv 'em. He wraps bits of body in some of the rags and chucks 'em in the Cut.'

'Wot bollocks you talk, Arfer. Come on. I'm starvin' 'ungry. Let's go up the midwife's an' cadge some bread 'n jam.'

Arthur caught sight of Thomas arriving and grinned. 'What does he look like runnin' along the street wiv 'is 'air all stickin' up. Prob'ly found somefing else in the Bible.'

'There's been another murder!' yelled Thomas as he ran past them. 'Another throat's been slit!'

'Well stop an' tell us, you barmy sod!' said Harriet.

Thomas stopped dead and turned to them. 'It was

in broad daylight. And no one did a thing! The mob's screaming for Leather Apron's blood!'

'They didn't catch 'im then?'

He looked down at the children as if he was seeing them for the first time. 'I trust your sister is safe inside, Arthur?'

'No, she's gone typewritin'. Did they catch 'im?'

'He got away, otherwise they would have torn him to pieces and what a tragedy that would have been. A tall dark devil has been spotted near the place of the murder, with blood soaked into his clothes and splashed on his face.'

'So it wasn't Levver Apron then?' Arthur said, looking slyly at Harriet. 'I knew he wasn't the Ripper.'

'This was the devil himself, up from hell, to continue the work.' He stared at Harriet and opened his Bible. 'The Scriptures say: "*The body is not meant for sexual immorality, but for the Lord, and the Lord for the body. Do you know that your bodies are members of Christ himself? Shall I then take the members of Christ and unite them with a prostitute? Never! Do you not know that he who unites himself with a prostitute is one with her body?*"' He snapped the good book shut and looked at them.

'Now read 'er a bit out of your medical book,' said Arthur, suppressing a grin.

'The body is not meant for sexual immorality,' repeated Thomas, emphasising each word. 'Remember that young lady, and you'll live a long and healthy life.'

'You ain't gonna last long goin' on like that. You'll

'ave a bleeding short and nasty end if you're not careful.'

Thomas did a quick about turn and strode purposefully towards the end of the turning to pass on his news to his Aunt Jacqueline.

'Bats in the belfry,' giggled Arthur.

'I fink I'm gonna like living dahn this street, Arfer,' said Harriet, watching Thomas striding away.

Just in from the backyard, having buried her secret, Jacqueline was scrubbing her hands when Thomas knocked on the door. She was in no mood for her nephew but recognised his knock and was ready to send him home if he was in any kind of mood which might upset her. She had had enough for one day.

'I expect you've heard the latest?' he said, hoping otherwise.

'No, but I'm sure you'll tell me. Did you get work in Spitalfields is what I should like to know, nephew?'

'I didn't try. Not once I heard the shocking news. I took a cab to Scotland Yard to see Uncle Charles. I thought that more important,' he said, unbuttoning his coat.

'I'm glad to see you've got money to throw at cabmen.'

Following Jacqueline into the scullery, Thomas deliberately sighed to convey his impatience. 'It was not wasted, Aunt. Uncle Charles was pleased with me. He's not going to stop my allowance after all, and he promises to speak with someone about work for me. I said I would do whatever he thought best.'

'And what have you done to earn his approval?' She

poured boiling water into the teapot, sure of what he was going to tell her.

'It's not so much what I have done, as what I did not do. I did not kill a prostitute at dawn.' He leaned on the scullery wall and folded his arms, thoughtfully. 'The look of relief on Uncle's face was quite gratifying.' He pursed his lips and sported a look of sympathy. 'Poor devil, he must have been worried sick.'

Carrying the teapot into the front room of the house, Jacqueline settled herself by the fire. 'Fetch in the milk and sugar, would you, Thomas, then you may be the town crier and give the news. What are they saying out there?'

'They are saying lots of things. I listened well and not only to the mob but to the newspaper reporters too.'

'I don't want the gruesome details, Thomas. Just tell me what they are saying for I guess from what you have said so far, that another murder has been committed. Fetch the milk and sugar first.'

'The man almost cut off her head. The belly had been ripped open and the intestines were hanging out of her stomach. A leg had been severed and thrown in the yard next door. And all you can think about is milk for the tea.'

'Cut off her leg? Well, well, well.' She enjoyed hearing the wild unsound stories. 'And your uncle thought that you might have done such a thing, surely not?'

'Haven't I always been the butt of other people's delusions?'

'But you managed to persuade him otherwise?'

'I didn't have to, I spent the night in Miss Dean's house. If you had read the note I put through your letter-box you would know that. I left just after six-thirty and Miss Dean saw me out herself. They say the whore was murdered sometime around six this morning and they have a good idea who did it.'

By the expression on his face, Jacqueline could see that he was enjoying himself. 'And who might that be?'

'Well now,' he leaned on one arm and cupped his mouth. 'There are two suspects at the moment. Leather Apron and a tall dark stranger, with a foreign accent, possibly an Italian. He was seen hanging around twenty-nine Hanbury Street – the scene of the crime.'

Jacqueline was surprised that Alberto should spring to mind. Surely he wasn't the type to go with streetgirls not when he had a beautiful wife at home? She jerked forward spilling some of her tea as a new thought struck her.

'I've shocked you, Aunt. I should have known you were taking this new murder too lightly. Dreadful business . . .' he said, relishing every moment. '. . . dreadful.'

'Thomas, I have to go out to see one of my mothers. It had slipped my mind but I shan't be gone for more than an hour or so.' She grabbed her hat and cloak from the stand. 'There's a piece of beef simmering on the stove. I've pared the vegetables. Just drop them into the pot for me, there's a good lad.' She pulled on her boots, thankful that Harriet had cleaned off the blood.

'Young Harriet's stopping overnight and—'

'Who?'

'The offspring of one of my mothers. She's been made homeless. I intend to find her refuge sometime tomorrow.'

'That wouldn't be the girl I saw sitting on young Arthur's doorstep, would it?'

'I should think it must have been.'

'Mmm. I can't say I'm overly pleased about that. I saw a look in that girl's eyes . . .'

'Don't talk such bosh! The poor urchin's ten years old and been turned out into the streets. I should think there *would* be a faraway look in her eyes.'

'I wouldn't have her in the house if it were up to me.'

'Yes, well, it takes one to know one,' mumbled Jacqueline under her breath. 'Don't let the fire burn down.'

Once outside, she pressed a hand against her face and swallowed air, bracing herself for the meeting she must conduct straight away. The consequences of getting rid of the blackmailing whore was now sinking in. If the police or the vigilantes found their way to Alberto, who fitted the description Thomas had just given, her name was bound to be mentioned as one of the last people to have seen Chapman alive.

Putting aside her usual frugality, she hailed a hansom cab at the top of Cleveland Way and instructed the man to set her down at Spitalfields Market, where she would have a few discreet words with Alberto at his café.

As she stepped down from the cab she could not help noticing the numerous groups as they huddled together discussing the latest murder.

'Miss Turner! What do you think of this new tragedy, it ees the worse so far, no?'

'Bring me a coffee, Alberto, there's a good man. You and I need to talk.'

'There ees something wrong, no?'

'Please fetch the coffee.' She looked round the café and saw a table for two.

'Can I offer you some cake, maybe a little—'

'No, thank you. I'm not really hungry.'

Settling herself on a chair in the corner of the café, Jacqueline wondered what might be her best approach. She didn't want to get into a drawn-out discussion. Just a few words and then be on her way. She felt distinctly uncomfortable in this area, with so many police in attendance, never mind the fleet of inquisitive journalists looking for someone who might have been one of the last to have seen Chapman alive.

'Here we are. A special Italian coffee for a special Engleesh lady.' He sat down opposite Jacqueline and smiled. 'So, you wish to speak to me?'

'Yes. Now, I don't wish to alarm you, Alberto, I just thought you should know that a man fitting your description was seen in the early hours, close to the place where the woman was murdered.' She put up a hand when she saw he was ready to protest his innocence.

'I'm not suggesting for one minute that it was you. But, just to be on the safe side, I don't think you should mention to the police or the newspapers that you spoke to the dead woman early this morning. The Yard are spoiling to make an arrest, to keep the press off their backs. Not to mention the public.'

'*I* spoke with her?'

'Yes, think back. She offered herself to you for fourpence.'

His jaw dropped slowly as his eyes widened. '*This* was her? This Annie Chapman they are talking about? It's no possible . . .'

'If I were in your shoes, I would keep quiet. For my part, I shall remain silent, I don't want them taking me in for questioning either. I don't have time for that sort of thing, besides, some of the mud is bound to stick.'

With a look of deep concern, he mumbled something in Italian. 'Miss Turner, what if somebody saw me talking with her? I must tella the truth. No?'

She leaned forward and lowered her voice to almost a whisper. 'You don't understand, my friend. Whoever saw her before she was murdered, will keep their mouths shut too, except maybe the other prostitutes. What have they to lose? Not their reputation, that's for sure.'

He nodded slowly. 'I understand what you say. Yes, I think it would be unwise to be mixed up in such a thing . . .'

'This *is* excellent coffee,' said the midwife, changing the subject.

With a glint in his eyes, Alberto leaned forward. 'Did you see anybody talking to this woman?'

'No. We went our separate ways at Shoreditch church. I take it you *haven't* spoken to anyone yet – about having seen her?'

'How could I? I didn't know that she was the murdered woman. As you can see, I have been very busy' – he leaned back in his chair – 'I see many people come and go. I don't remember seeing this prostitute this morning. No, she was not here.'

'Good. Me neither.' She smiled back at him. 'Now then, Alberto, you've customers to attend. Don't worry yourself over me, I shall be leaving soon and I expect you'll be extra busy today with all of this going on.'

'Business has never been so good,' he winked at her and walked away, happy to serve those filing into his café.

Looking out of the window, Jacqueline sighed with relief. At least one small worry had been settled and she managed to relax a little. Brushfield Street was packed with sightseers and the food vendors were doing a brisk trade. This for them was better than a Bank Holiday in Victoria Park.

Finishing her coffee, she began to feel drowsy through lack of sleep. You're not getting any younger, Jacqueline, she thought. You had better slow down or you'll not be fit to travel to America.' She wove her way between the crowded tables and left the café.

Controlling her sudden, macabre impulse to stroll past Hanbury Street to see what was happening, she made her way home through Whitechapel, hoping she would not have to be called out to attend a birth. A quiet evening in with young Harriet and Thomas was about as much as she could cope with.

Had Jacqueline gone to Hanbury Street she would have been surprised. It was a frenetic scene. Shops and businesses had been forced to close as hundreds of people blocked the street. Traders who did not live on the premises were furious that they were not allowed through. They would have had a field day. Cigar maker, cutler, ironmonger, hatter and a toymaker – all were desperate to open up shop.

The mounted police were kept busy, moving frequently into the crowd to disperse them. The surrounding streets were swarming with people who stood around in groups, discussing the gruesome details of the murder.

Sightseers had come from all over London and the difference in status was temporarily forgotten. The respectable, well-dressed citizens were only too pleased to hear firsthand reports from the poor, lower working-class folk.

As Arthur and Harriet made their way towards the midwife's house, Harriet stopped suddenly and grabbed Arthur's sleeve. 'I'm not goin' a step furver. Not while he's in there. You can go if you like. I'll wait on yer doorstep till Mary gets 'ome.'

'Why? Daft Thomas 's all right.'

'I fink it's that 'ouse. It's got secrets an' he makes it worse.'

'What d'yer mean – secrets?'

'Wot d'yer fink I bleedin' well mean? Fings 'ave

'appened in there. It's got dead people in the walls. I ain't goin' in.'

Giggling at the way she was pulling faces, Arthur said, 'What you gonna do tonight then? When you 'ave to sleep there?' He waved his arms and made horrible ghostly sounds.

'Bugger off, Arfer!' She backed away from him. 'Anyway, I'm not gonna sleep there. Not ever!' She turned on her heels and ran for all her life was worth.

Arthur called after her, but she had taken the corner of Whitehead Street without slowing down and disappeared. 'There ain't no such fing as ghosts . . . stupid girl,' murmured Arthur, sorry that she had gone. Dragging his feet, he walked slowly back home with his hands deep in his trouser pockets. Passing some girls who had formed a small circle he ignored their chanting.

'They'll capture Levver Apron now, if guilty
    you'll agree;
He'll have to meet a murderer's doom, and
    'ang upon a tree!'

'Girls are stupid an' useless,' he murmured, going into his house and slamming the door behind him. Throwing himself down into the armchair by the fire he stared into the glowing coals and rubbed his eyes. 'I don't care if you don't come back, ginger nut.' Then, against his strong principles, Arthur Dean, the tough nine-year-old, pulled up his knees, leaned on his folded arms and cried into the bend of his sleeve, remembering his baby sister and wishing she had lived. It wasn't fair and he was ready to say so – to anyone. Anyone at all. *If* anyone was there with him in that silent house which used to be filled with fun and laughter when his dad and mum were alive and everything was normal. 'The furniture's all we've got left,' he sobbed. 'Pictures an' furniture and bedclothes. Daddy's special chair and Mummy's laundry in the basket for ironing. But it's not Mummy's ironing any more it's Mary's but . . .' The sobbing turned to loud keening. This was the first time he had allowed himself to really cry out loud, and wish for his parents to come back.

Whether it was from the warmth of the fire or being on his own, Arthur began to feel drowsy. No matter how hard he tried, his eyelids would not stay open. Giving in, he snuggled his head into a cushion and drifted off.

Three loud knocks on the street door brought him out of his slumber sharply and almost caused him to fall off the armchair. Standing up, he stood very still and listened. Apart from the glow of the fire, there was no other light in the room. 'Who is it?' he said, trying to sound brave.

There was no answer, just more knocking. He tip-toed to the door. 'Who is it?' he said again, his voice quieter than he meant it to be. Still no reply. His heart pounding, he placed a hand on the latch, 'Who is *there*?' Then, acting like a brave soldier, something his father had told him to do many times, he gripped the brass doorknob, turned it slowly and then pulled his hand away. He would look through the letter-box instead. Bending down and pulling it up very carefully, he met with a pair of staring eyes.

'Open this bleedin' door!' It was Harriet.

'Why didn't you answer me?' snapped Arthur, pulling her inside by the sleeve of her coat. 'Deaf are yer?'

She slammed the door behind her. 'Yeah! But only in me left ear so don't take liberties!'

'Why'd you come back? Thought you'd gone fer good,' he murmured, sorry that she *was* deaf.

''Cos of the bleedin' murder – why d'yer fink? It's not safe in a stable *now*, is it? I might get done in as well. Don't want me bleedin' froat slit, do I?'

'I s'pose we'll 'aveta move the furniture then.' Arthur pushed himself on tiptoe and bolted the door for the first time in his life.

'Give us a match,' said Harriet.

'Wot for?'

'To light the bleedin' gas, wot else? It'll be gettin' dark afore long. An' where's yer up-to-bed candle?'

'In that corner cupboard wiv the matches.'

'Bleedin' daft place to keep 'em, innit? Come on. Get a move on. We'll get it all shipshape for when Mary gets back in. We'll s'prise 'er.'

Once she had lit the gas mantle and the candle, Harriet made her way up the narrow staircase. 'I'll 'aveta 'ave the bed next to the winda.'

'That's where I sleep! It's my bed. Even when Mary slept in 'ere, that was *my* bed!'

'You'll soon get used to it.'

'Nar, I'm not moving. Why should I?'

''Cos of me deaf ear! I won't be able to 'ear yer talking to me if I ain't got me good ear to yer! An' you'll always 'ave summink to wag about afore we get to sleep. Stands to reason.'

Arthur flopped down on to the edge of his bed. 'What if Mary says no? What if she don't want a lodger?'

'I'm not a lodger. I'm a live-in 'ousemaid.'

'What's Miss Turner gonna fink when you say you don't wanna kip there?'

'I won't bleedin' well say that, will I! I'll say I wanna sleep 'ere. There's a difference as it's a compliment to yer sister, not an insult to the midwife.'

'I dunno wot you're talking about half the time.'

'Not many kids do. I'm intelligent, that's why, I'll go far if I don't sink first.' She placed her hands on her hips. 'Right then, Arfer, let's make a start on this room. Wot we gonna shift first?'

'You can leave the beds where they are. I'll sleep in Mary's old one an' you can 'ave mine.'

'I ain't sleepin' in your bed. We'll switch 'em around. Boys 'ave willies an' they smell.'

Ignoring her crude comment, Arthur looked at the small wardrobe. 'We don't 'ave to move the cupboard. I can get undressed this side of it an' you can get dressed on the other side of it.'

Harriet pulled a face and stared at the wardrobe. 'I s'pose there's enough room to 'ide meself. I don't want you looking up me drawers.'

'Who'd wanna do that!' He grimaced and felt sick at the thought of it.

'Make sure I don't see your willy then, that's all.' She looked round the room. 'So wot shall we move then?'

The pair of them looked blank. 'We could swap chairs,' said Arthur.

'Yeah, that'd look good.' She moved one and Arthur moved one and the room looked no different.

'That's better,' said Harriet.

'Yeah. You can put yer clothes in the bottom drawer, it's empty.'

'Don't need no drawer. I'm wearing me clothes. I go abed in 'em.'

Arthur pulled a face. She couldn't mean it. 'Wot about yer nightshirt?'

'Tch. Come on. If we're gonna 'ave to butter up Mary, we'd best do some 'ousework an' that. An' we'll 'ave to 'ave a kettle on the go for a fresh pot of tea soon as she gets in.'

Following her down the staircase, Arthur caught a whiff of something he didn't like. 'Mary ain't gonna be back for a while. She's goin' typewritin' after work.'

'Well, we'll make a pot of tea for ourselves now in that case. I'll 'ave a rummage round in 'er cupboard, see wot I can find to cook. She'll 'preciate an 'ot meal. That's if she ain't bin done in.'

Having arrived at Lillian's house far too early, Mary had been met by an anxious Lizzie, who took her below stairs to Amelia Palmer, the char. Sitting at the scrubbed pine table in the servants' room, the three women had spoken non-stop about recent events.

'Nevertheless,' said Mary, having listened to all sorts of excuses, 'you should 'ave told me she was a common whore, I felt such a fool. I doubt my neighbour'll ever trust me agen.'

'Wot diff'rence do it make now?' said Amelia, wiping her eyes with the hem of her skirt. 'I've lost an old friend . . . and to meet with such a wicked end. It could be me laying on the mortuary slab. There but fer the grace of God go all of us.'

'I gave Annie Chapman sixpence when she left my 'ouse. She didn't 'ave to spend it on drink. She only needed sixpence for a bed.'

'Oh, *you* can be all bleedin' well high and mighty! Comin' the old madam. I know why you're 'ere don't forget.'

'Never mind all that,' said Lizzie, drawing on her clay pipe. 'Are you certain nobody else saw 'er goin' into your place, Mary.'

'The lamplighter was doing 'is rounds but he was further up the road and 'ad his back to us. There was nobody else in the street, I checked that as soon as I saw the sort of a person Annie Chapman was. Ours is a respectable turning.'

'Oh yeah? And is that why you turned 'er out bleedin' to death – out of respect?' snapped Amelia, the one who had started this ball rolling in the first place. 'I feel really bad over this. As if it was me who sent the poor cow like a lamb to the slaughter.'

'She wasn't bleedin',' said Mary, 'she wasn't even pregnant. She's in 'er change.'

'Well 'ow comes her womb's bin ripped out then? You certain your midwife didn't make a cock-up of the job? Wot if my mate Annie was in so much pain she cut her own bloody froat?'

'She was laughing when she left, couldn't wait to get back on the streets. Pleased that she wasn't in the club!' Mary hadn't much time for Amelia now that she'd met her. She was common and revelled in it – *deliberately* revelled in it. 'If the womb was taken out then it's obviously the work of a lunatic not a midwife!'

'Keep your voices down!' hissed Lizzie.

'She was fit enough when she left my house.' Mary lowered her eyes. 'I can't believe she's dead.'

'What must she 'ave gone through? It's gettin' worse. You'd think the police'd 'ave some real evidence by now. Supposed to be the pillar of the community, ain't they? Where are they, tell me that, eh?'

'I don't care where they are, Amelia, so long as they don't come poking their nose in round this place,' said Lizzie, offering her a draw of her pipe, which had in it her 'special' blend of tobacco today, since they were all so distraught.

Taking it from her, Amelia grinned. 'Yeah, they might close us down and wouldn't that upset some coppers. I see who comes and goes, don't you worry.' She took a long draw on the pipe and gave Lizzie a knowing look. 'Oh, yes, I see who comes and goes.'

'Never mind that,' said Lizzie, shooting her a look to kill. 'We give you regular work, Amelia, so you'd lose out as well. God knows what your old man'd say if he found out you was behind Annie going for an abortion. You set the thing up, don't forget. I bet he doesn't know you still mix with yer old mates.'

'No, he don't.' She gazed down at the floor, ashamed.

'And look at the risk *I* was taking, asking Mary to talk to 'er neighbour. Mother would go berserk if she found out. No, we must each keep our mouths shut and our wits about us,' said Lizzie, 'for all of our sakes.'

'They're bound to find their way to me,' said Amelia, sucking on the end of the pipe. 'I char for a Yiddish family near Annie's lodgings. I used to pop in and the others knew we were good mates. I even saw Annie last night.'

'Well there you are then,' said Mary, 'you must 'ave seen 'ow fit she was!'

'I was making double sure, gel. You could never be sure if Annie was speaking the trufe or wevver it was the drink talking. She 'ad her weaker side, I will say that, stayed out all 'ours. And I s'pose you could say she wa'n't that p'ticular as to 'ow she earned a living. But then who is?' She looked from Mary to Lizzie.

'Very industrious was my friend Annie. Unlucky that's all. She never 'ad the looks of you two so she 'ad no choice but to be a fourpenny-trick tart.' She pushed her hands into her face. 'What did she go through, Lizzie? What did that maniac make 'er suffer before she was cold? Did he rip her womb out while she was still alive?'

144

'Stop it, Amelia, we none of us know!' Lizzie tapped her pipe and emptied the ashes into the earth of a plant pot. 'Try and forget it.'

The door burst open suddenly to reveal a hot-faced Lillian. 'I don't know what you can be thinking, Lizzie, your client is waiting in your room!' She turned to Mary. 'And Sir Walter is waiting in *my* rooms!' She turned to the weeping Amelia. '*More* personal worries?'

'Amelia knew the murdered woman,' said Lizzie, 'she used to play with 'er when they were kids. We were just trying to console 'er, that's all.'

'Is this true?' Lillian's voice softened. 'Amelia . . . ?'

'Yes, madam.'

'I see. Well pour yourself a glass of sherry and get off home. Take a week off or at least until the police have finished with you. They will call on you, make no mistake. *If* you were that close.'

'We was quite friendly, madam. But only because we came from the same street and went to the same Sunday school and—'

'Yes, yes, yes. I know what you're saying, stay away for a week in any case.'

'What about her wages?' said Lizzie, looking at her mother appealingly.

'She'll be paid . . . with a little extra for silence.' She turned to Mary. 'Your guest is waiting in my suite. I shall send him up to your room with Polly. Do not keep him waiting a minute longer. Your lipstick needs attention and you might powder your nose. We're meant to cheer our clients not make them miserable.' With that she left the room, slamming the door behind her.

'What you gonna spend your silence money on then, Amy. You never know, Mother might give you a sovereign or two.' Lizzie knew how to make this girl smile.

'Silence money? Who's gonna take notice of the likes of me?'

'I saw the look on Mother's face, she don't miss a trick. All you 'ave to do is tell the newspapers where you work and they'll be 'ere in a flash an' we don't want that kind of attention.'

'I could give up scrubbin' and polishin',' said Amelia, smiling. 'An' then take a few more bribes from your muvver.'

'An' have one of the high mob hired to deal with you one night? Fancy a swim in the freezing cold river, do yer?' Lizzie had caught her like a mouse in a trap. She knew that once Amelia left the house her mind would have started to turn over and she would soon have come up with the idea of blackmail.

'I was jokin', Lizzie.' Amelia stood up, her face flushed. 'Tell yer muvver I'll pop back in tomorra for me wages.'

'No need. She'll want me to drop them in to you.' Lizzie pushed her face close to Amelia's. 'She won't want you around till you've bin questioned and they've lost interest. *If* you're questioned, that is. You might be gettin' money for old rope and a week off an' all. I'd settle for that if I was you, Amy. Don't forget you was the last one to see 'er alive, or nearly the last one. You could come under suspicion as well. Women 'ave bin known to commit murder, you know.'

'Shut up, Lizzie.' She pulled on her long faded coat. 'Well I shan't trouble trouble till trouble troubles me!' With that, Amelia left.

'You're gonna have to move like lightnin', Mary. You don't keep someone like Sir Walter waiting. And you'd best wipe that look off your face, we don't get paid to make 'em miserable – you 'eard what Mother said.'

'You can change mood so quickly, Lizzie. I'm still thinking about that poor woman an' what she must have gone through.'

'If you don't get upstairs, *you* might 'ave to walk Whitechapel looking for a cheap trick. You thought she was scum when you met 'er, stop acting like a saint and move yerself, remember you're one of us now. If my lover wasn't droppin' in later on, I'd go up and snatch Sir Walter from under yer feet.'

It was with mixed feelings that Mary climbed those stairs. She was nervous and with no champagne inside her this time, her confidence was on the low side. Arriving in her boudoir, she was relieved to find that she was alone. Quickly opening the drawer beneath the wardrobe she found freshly laundered silk lingerie. The quiet tapping on the door caused her heart to sink. 'Come in,' she said, her voice almost a whisper.

'I trust I'm not too early for you?' It was Sir Walter.

'I'm sorry,' she said, deeply embarrassed. 'I should never 'ave kept you waiting. And I'm not even ready for you.'

He closed the door, a genuine smile on his face. 'You look fine.'

'I'm s'posed to 'ave changed into the velvet gown by now. Madam would be furious if she knew.'

Sir Walter lifted Mary's hand and kissed her fingers, raising his eyes as before. 'No one need mind what happens between the time I arrive and the time I leave. Only me.'

'But you must mind. You don't pay to see me in these old clothes.'

'I might mind less if you were out of them.' He walked casually across the room. 'I see that our lazy young Polly has built a good fire for us this time.' He warmed his hands, rubbing them together. 'How is your brother?'

'Quite well, thank you.' She slipped her coat on to a hanger in the wardrobe and reached for a soft grey crêpe silk dressing gown. She would slip that on instead of the lovely dress.

'Would you mind very much turning yer back while I change?'

'Why not go behind the screen, isn't that what it's for?'

'I'd rather not.' To walk across the room carrying a flimsy dressing gown seemed cheap. 'I'm not a music-hall girl, don't forget.' She kicked off her boots and hid them under the blue sofa. 'It's a housecoat that Madam left for me to wear. I'll tell you when you can look.'

Finding it very touching that someone who was about to have sex for money could be so shy, he did as she asked and turned his back, but he could not avoid the ornate mirror above the fire. He lowered his eyes in case she should catch his reflection. 'Have you been in here since I last saw you?'

'No. Madam said I wasn't to come back until now.'

'Were you disappointed?'

'Course not. I've bin looking forward to the day though.' She folded her dress and underwear and placed them inside the wardrobe.

Checking herself in the full-length mirror, she was pleased with her appearance. The long soft trailing robe suited her more than the velvet gown. Easing the clips from her hair, she shook her head so that the long auburn locks tumbled down her back.

'You can look now,' she said, sounding more like a happy child than a woman about to lose her virginity.

He had seen her reflection, but when he turned to see her in the flesh, resembling a beautiful oil painting, he once again felt humble in this beautiful, innocent, woman's company.

'I'll put the velvet gown on if you want,' said Mary, believing him to be let down.

His face set, he walked towards her slowly and cupped her face. 'You really are quite beautiful, Mary.' He touched her lips with a finger and gazed into her eyes. 'Sapphires,' he whispered before kissing her on the mouth.

Aroused by his gentle warmth, she slipped her slender arms around his broad shoulders and moved against his body as he kissed her again, this time with passion. He took her hand and led her to the bed.

Kissing her face and neck as if this was not only the first time for them but the last, he said, huskily, 'I'm going to disrobe now, Mary. It doesn't mean that we have to make love; if you like, we can simply lie next to each other.'

Turning on to her front while he went behind the screen, Mary swept her finger across a trailing leaf on the patterned eiderdown, and enjoyed the moment. She felt as if she had not a care in the world and belonged in that room and on that bed, waiting for her lover. Feeling his warm hand on her shoulder, she turned and looked into his face. In his eyes there was a question: Did she want him as much as he wanted her? Her answer, as she held his gaze, was to slowly unfasten the tiny satin buttons which ran the full length of her silk negligée, until the cream, silky fabric slipped apart, showing her firm round breasts.

Seated on the edge of the bed, he looked from her lovely face across her body and down to her legs. Trailing a finger from her soft round shoulder and between her breasts he spread his fingers through the thick reddish-black hair between her legs. Then, cupping and caressing her breasts, he lowered his head and filled his mouth, sucking and kissing until her nipples grew erect and so sensitive that they tingled to the point of hurting – but the pain was exquisite.

Slowly moving his hand down once more he slipped his fingers between her soft and fleshy moist lips, and she could not stop herself from opening up to him. Filled with longing he kissed every part of her body. Moaning with untold desire she began to squirm and turn: she needed him inside her. As he eased his weight upon her she wanted him to crush and hurt her and she was not disappointed as he thrust deeper and deeper inside. Moving rhythmically together, his deep moans added to the intoxicating ecstasy as they reached a climax which was beyond her wildest dreams.

Their bodies were as one as they slowly descended from their ecstatic pleasure. Gently caressing her, he laid his head on the pillow and gazed up at the ceiling, tormented that he could be in love with this beautiful woman.

'I have never felt like this before,' said Mary, her head resting on his broad shoulder. 'I've never bin this happy, ever.'

Disturbed by a sudden spasm which went through his body, Sir Walter swung his long legs off the bed and drew the black silk robe from the screen and slipped it on. After pouring himself a glass of champagne, he moved slowly round the room as if he were a stalking panther, and finally came to rest on the padded bedroom chair.

'Why're you sitting over there, is it time for you to leave?'

'I can see you better from here. Are you bleeding?'

'I don't fink so – p'raps a little – but I do know all about that, Lizzie told me. It's nothing to worry 'bout.'

'Did I hurt you?'

She couldn't help smiling . . . she felt so good – so happy. 'You did, but it was a very nice hurt, thank you.'

He laughed quietly at her adolescent sense of humour. 'Well I'm pleased to hear that.'

'Am I s'posed to get dressed now?'

'No. We'll enjoy this champagne together and then I fancy we may be peckish. I may ring for some light refreshments. Are you hungry, Mary?'

'Starving I am. I should 'ave 'ad my tea before I came out but I was all at sixes and sevens.'

Smiling, he slipped off his robe and joined her on the bed and side by side they lay there, happy to do nothing but just that. 'I've never quite known anything like this,' he said, talking more to himself than to her. 'Never in my entire life have I met someone like you.'

'Well you wouldn't do, would yer? We come from different worlds. Very different worlds.'

'Oh, I don't know, is it in the blood or in the birthplace?'

'Bit of both I should think.'

He turned his head and peered into her face. 'You know what I'm talking about?'

'Of course I do. We may live in the poorest part of London and we may not be educated but we do have brains and common sense. If I was born to your parents and you was born to mine . . . that's what you're thinking about . . . ain't it?'

'And should two people like us, have a child . . .'

'It would be a posh cockney.'

Laughing aloud, he rolled over and hugged her. 'We have to be so careful,' he said, looking into her eyes.

'Of what?'

'Pain. Because I for one cannot take any more.'

Studying his face, Mary was puzzled. He had everything a man could wish for and yet in his eyes she sensed alarm. Fear and grief. 'What is it? Have you lost someone you loved?'

'No, nothing like that. Don't let's spoil a beautiful evening, Mary Dean. Kiss me. Kiss me as you have never kissed before.'

'I already have. But I'll do it agen, if it please you, sir.'

'Stop teasing me,' he said, loving every minute.

'I will if you stop being so serious. All that talk about pain . . . it's the sort of thing I'm trying to forget.'

'Yes, you're right,' he said, stroking her hair. 'I'm sure you've had enough to last you a lifetime. I saw that the first time I set eyes on you.'

'Yeah, I 'ave, but I fink that's all behind me now. Me and Arthur are gonna be all right. So no one has to feel sorry for us. I don't ever want people to 'ave to take pity on me and my brother.'

Chapter Five

Seeing the lights of a hansom cab as the cabman drove his horse towards her, Mary was relieved to see that it was slowing down and coming to a halt. She wanted to be home with Arthur as soon as possible and could easily afford the fare. What she hadn't expected and was the furthest thing from her mind, was to see Mr Shaw climb down from the carriage. Paying the driver, he spoke to Mary over his shoulder.

'The cabman has seen you. He'll not fly away.'

'Thank you, sir. It's good to meet with you again.'

Instructing the driver to wait, Shaw took Mary to one side and peered into her face, a vague recollection in his eyes. 'Do I know you?'

'We met at the Mission Hall, sir. Mrs Besant was giving a lecture.' She offered her hand. 'It's Mary Dean. I work in the offices of Bryant and May.'

He looked from her to the House of Assignation and a frown appeared on his forehead. 'And you come here in the evenings and weekends.'

She shrugged and managed a smile. 'We must live the best way we can, sir.'

'Indeed. I take it you know the other girls?'

'Only Lizzie. I'm new. She's looking forward to your visit.'

'Ah. So you have not only seen me in the company of Mrs Besant but . . .'

'Don't worry, Mr Shaw. My lips are sealed. Lizzie is a good friend of mine. She told no one else.'

'Indeed. I wonder . . . would you be so good as to give Miss Redmond a message. I came to deliver it myself but I am in rather a hurry. Would you tell her that my visit would have had to be fleeting in any case and that I was here to say goodbye. I am to go abroad . . . for rather a long spell.'

'Begging your pardon, sir, but shouldn't you tell her yerself?'

'Better she despises me for it.' He tipped his hat and climbed aboard the cab, ordering the driver to move on.

Furious with him for not offering her the cab she stamped her foot. How dare he treat women like this. And what of poor Lizzie, waiting inside for him? She was at sixes and sevens as what to do for the best. She really didn't want to be the one to break the news.

'Mary!' Polly's voice was easily recognised. She rushed forward, her cheeks flushed. 'Madam told me to give you this. She said you're to read it and give an answer which must be a straight yes or no.'

Opening the notelet and still fuming over Shaw, Mary read it and could hardly take it in. It read: *Sir Walter has requested that he may have you exclusively to himself. I'm not happy about this but he will insist. Do you agree?*

'Tell Madam I said yes.'

'Blimey,' said Polly, 'didn't take much working out then, did it?'

'Is Lizzie with anyone?'

'Nar. She's waiting for 'er Prince, en't she? Daft if you ask me. You should see wot he looks like.' She rolled her eyes. 'Why, 'ave ya got a message for 'er?'

'No. No, I just wondered, that was all. Night, Polly,' she said, walking away.

'You're not gonna walk through the streets by yerself are yer? There's bin another murder, you know!'

'I'll be all right. Just a few minutes an' I'll be on the Mile End Road where it's well lit.'

'Madam won't be very 'appy about this! Wot if you get done in?'

Continuing on her way, Mary had other things to think about. She had just let her friend down and let her down badly. She should have hidden her face from Bernard Shaw and kept her mouth shut, it was obvious to her now as to why he should take off like that. Lizzie had said that he was her *secret* love. She recalled one of her mother's sayings: A secret between three people could be kept but only if two of them are dead.

Mary cursed aloud, not caring if a passer-by should hear. Lizzie hadn't held her tongue as she should have and Mary had just given her away. She had blown away any trust that Shaw had placed in Lizzie's of keeping their affair a tight secret. Shaw's words came flooding back to her. 'Better that she should despise me.' He was right about that at least. Maybe he had come to end their liaison and given a good reason for it. Lizzie would then have been left with a sense of unrequited love due to no fault of the man himself.

As she arrived in the Mile End Road, Mary glanced behind her at the dark cobbled street from whence she came and shuddered. With her thoughts flying the way they had been, the dangerous short journey had passed quickly. Polly had been right to be concerned. With a maniac at large and in the vicinity, she should not take any chances. Not now, now that she was a prostitute.

Frightened for her safety, she flagged down a cab. Apart from the terror rising from the pit of her stomach, she wanted to get back to Arthur. Harriet might well have returned to the midwife's house and he could be sitting by himself, half scared to death. Guilty now that she had revelled in her work and not thought about anyone else, she was urgent to get home.

Relieved to be in her own surroundings, Mary waived the driver's concern at her asking to be dropped at the end of Cleveland Way. She had walked down her narrow turning in the dark a thousand times and no harm had come to her yet. With her eyes cast to the ground her thoughts were with Walter and the note that Polly had given to her. She pushed a hand deep into her coat pocket and felt the folded piece of paper. She would read it again once she was safe inside.

With a strong desire to be off the streets and aware of shadows in the dusk and the quiet, she stepped up her pace. The voice of the midwife coming from the shadows caused her to draw breath. 'I trust your employer is paying you enough to warrant taking a cab, Mary?'

'Oh, Miss Turner!' she said, a hand on her pounding heart. 'You gave me such a shock.' She leaned against a wall by the lamppost and tried to compose herself. 'Frightened me half to death.'

'Save your pennies and your pounds shall look after themselves.' The midwife was beginning to sound like her nephew. Mary felt herself shudder at the inflection in her neighbour's voice. 'My employer paid for the ride.' She lied not only to cover herself but because she was now scared of the midwife who seemed unlike her old self.

'You wouldn't be telling me lies now, would you, Mary?'

'No, why would I have to do such a fing, Miss Turner?'

'I should be very upset if you were being led down the wrong pathway. I would feel as if I had let your parents down by not keeping a keener eye on you.'

Presenting a smile of sorts, her heart still pounding, Mary overly reassured her. 'Oh I'd never be led astray, not when I've got my Arthur to think of. My employer was concerned for me as well. That's why she paid for the cab. She'll dock it from me pay once I've got on me feet. Once they've caught 'im we can all walk free in the dark agen, can't we?'

'That's true, Mary. Indeed. We're all on edge over the horror, let's hope they catch him soon. Now I must be on my way, I've four calls to make. You've a surprise waiting at home.' With that the midwife walked away, her heavy footstep's echoing in the empty street.

Arriving at her door, Mary glanced up the turning at the midwife before she turned the corner. Her stocky body, draped in a dark cape and skirts looked sinister as she passed beneath the dim yellow glow of the gas lamp. Her midwife's hat looked like something a shabby genteel might sport. A shiver ran down her spine. Why was she seeing her neighbour in this different light?

Resolving to leave her fears at the front door, she went inside and was relieved to see that Harriet was keeping Arthur company and not Thomas. 'What's all this I hear . . . a surprise in store for me, the midwife said?' She was amused at the way Harriet was standing to attention like a maid-in-waiting.

'I've got everyfing ready. The bacon's chopped ready for frying up and so's the cabbage. I'm making a nice bubble and squeak for supper. The taters are on the boil.'

'That's very good of you, Harriet. What's brought this about?' said Mary, glancing at the room. 'You've 'ad a change round, Arthur . . .'

'I did that an' all, made it a bit more cosy like.'

'Well it looks lovely,' said Mary, thinking she would change it back to the way it was in a week or so.

'You'd best tell Mary about the surprise,' said Arthur, keeping his eyes fixed on the floor.

'I'm gonna be your live-in maid! You won't 'ave to pay me. Arfer don't mind if I share 'is room and I'm gonna teach 'im a fing or two, about learnin' an' that.' She brushed the end of her watery nostrils with the sleeve of her cardigan and sniffed. 'I'll make a start on the supper then, shall I? I've put a clean cloth on the table.'

'So I see. And what about you, Arthur? Speak up now 'cos this girl is with us for a while by the sounds of it . . . if we agree to it.'

'I don't care wot she does.' He screwed his face and narrowed his eyes. 'She talks a lot but makes a good cup of tea. Don't know about 'er cooking though.'

Mary had to smile. The longer the gap grew since their father had passed away the more her little brother came out with one of his sayings. 'Well, we'll see 'ow things turn out, eh?'

'I don't care one way or the uvver.' He studied the draughtboard and made a move. 'You missed one, Rat-face,' he grinned.

'Don't call 'er that, Arthur. It's not nice.'

'She calls me Artful.'

'D'yer like pepper on yer cabbage, Mary?'

'Just a bit.'

'Wot about vinegar?'

'No, I can't say I've ever 'ad vinegar on cabbage . . .'

'Good. Nor 'ave I, jes thought I'd best ask. You being posher than me. Take the weight off yer feet an' I'll fetch you a cuppa tea.'

Settled in the armchair by the fire, her stockinged feet in the hearth, Mary spoke quietly to Arthur. 'You are all right about Harriet lodging with us, 'cos if not—'

'I don't care,' he said, interrupting her. 'It's up to you.'

'She would be company for you, when I'm out typewriting.'

'She's deaf anyway,' he said, counting how many black draughts he had on the board. 'So she can't sleep rough. She wouldn't 'ear Jack the Ripper creep up.'

'Arthur?'

'Wot?'

'Look at me.'

He looked from the games board to her, squinting. 'Wot?'

'Will yer be glad if she stops?'

A suppressed smile spread across his freckled face. 'Yeah, she makes me laugh.'

'Me as well. If the gingerbread man 'ad a daughter, she'd be it.'

Arthur covered his mouth and giggled. 'She never brushes 'er 'air. It looks like orange knitting wool after Mummy pulled one of your woollies out for the yarn. *And . . .*' he looked over his shoulder, leaned forward, whispering, '. . . she pongs.' He pinched his nose, 'Pheeew.'

'She can't 'elp it. It's her clothes. We can soon get them washed.'

'We don't really 'ave to whisper. She's deaf as a doorknob.' He switched a black draught for a white one.

'I'm not bleedin' well deaf! And don't cheat, I saw wot you jes did!'

'I never said you was bleedin' well deaf.'

'Don't change the subject!' She handed Mary her tea. 'It's only me left ear.'

'Oh well, that's not so bad, eh?'

'Wot?'

'I said . . . that's not so bad!'

'You don't 'aveta shout, Mary. It's only me left ear.'

Sipping her tea, Mary was determined to keep a straight face. This skinny ginger girl who had come into their lives had peculiar old-fashioned mannerisms. Standing there, leaning forward with her hands on hips and the teacloth draped over her shoulder, she bore the look of a wise old woman in charge. 'Wot d'yer fink of that then?'

'It's lovely, Harriet. A smashing cup of tea.'

'Miss Turner might 'ave a remedy for 'er deaf ear,' said Arthur, his attention still on the draught-board.

Harriet shrugged at Mary, 'I never thought of that. A bleedin' nurse, ain't she? Course she'd 'ave summink for it. I'll go an' see 'er tomorra.'

'She got rid of my warts,' said Arthur, showing his hands. 'See? – all gone.'

'How'd she do that then?'

'Lemon peel soaked in vinegar, on every day for two 'ours till they drop off.'

'D'yer know wot I fink,' said Harriet, folding her arms. 'I fink she's a witch. An' that Thomas is a wizard. Puts the bleedin' willies up me an' I don't mind sayin' so.'

Laughing at her, Arthur said, 'She wouldn't go down Miss Turner's 'ouse 'cos Thomas was in there.'

Ignoring him, she turned up her nose and then

turned to Mary. 'You'll git chilblains puttin' yer feet near 'ot coals. Bleedin' painful they are, an' all.'

'You ain't got chilblains, an' all, 'ave yer?' said Arthur, enjoying the torment.

'Wot?'

'You ain't got chilblains as well as bein' deaf?'

'I ain't deaf! An' I ain't got no chilblains!'

'This is definitely the best cup of tea I've tasted, Harriet. Just right,' said Mary, throwing Arthur a look of warning.

'Fanks. I'll go an' see to the bubble and squeak.' Giving Arthur a clip round the ear, Harriet left the room.

'D'yer think that Thomas *is* a wizard?' said Arthur, pretending he hadn't felt the sting.

'Don't be so daft. Harriet's got a vivid imagination, that's all.' Leaning back in her chair she closed her eyes and thought about her knight. He was to be her only client and Lillian had agreed to it. She relived their time together and couldn't believe that it would last. Hearing the call of the paperboy outside, she rose from her chair and took her coat off the hook. 'I'm just gonna buy the evening edition, Arthur. Give Harriet a hand if she needs it – there's a good boy.'

Hearing the door shut behind Mary, Harriet arrived from the scullery. 'Where she bleedin' well gone? This is nearly ready.'

'Gettin' a newspaper.'

'Good. I thought she'd 'ave fetched one in wiv 'er. Too much on 'er mind, I s'pose.'

'Wot good's it to you. You can't read.'

'Course I can!' she said, peering at the board game. 'It's about time you could, an' all! School ain't done you much good, 'as it? I learned meself from buses and billboards.'

'I can read.'

'Not as good as I can, I bet.' She jumped a draught over three of Arthur's. 'That's wot 'appens when you try and cheat.' She tossed back her matted hair and returned to her cooking.

'I bet Ginger Nut, who fell in the cut, was 'er bruvver,' he mumbled.

'I 'eard that!'

Later, once Harriet and Arthur had eaten and gone to bed, Mary enjoyed a quiet time by herself, in front of the coal fire. She hadn't looked at the newspaper while the children were up but hidden it under her cushion. The headlines were too gruesome and she knew they would be interested. She read the front page:

WHERE IS LEATHER APRON NOW?

Midnight horror. The ghoulish fiend who creeps about Whitechapel after midnight, spreading terror among women, wielding his sharp leather-knife is still at large. The Jewish slipper-maker having abandoned his trade for reasons unknown, now takes pleasure in bullying prostitutes at night. We learn from various sightings, that he is approximately 5ft 8 inches in height and wears a dark cap. He is gaunt and somewhat ungainly. His beard is rough and he has a sinister expression, his small staring eyes are said to fill the women with terror. 'He parts his lips and grins in a most loathsome manner,' said a local woman. 'Anybody who meets him face to face knows it,' said another. 'He never looks anyone in the eye.'

However, police inform us that they are looking for a man who entered the passage, in which the murder was committed, with a prostitute. Aged in his fifties, height 5ft 7 inches, he wears a dark cloak down to the ground and a dark hat and carries a large black bag.

'I saw him previous to this, on the night Tabram was murdered; he was crossing London Bridge,' said another informant. 'He was going into Southwark, his head pulled into his coat collar which was turned up about his neck. He walked very quickly. Yes, you could even say that he was running, almost. Looking about him all the time, checking the shadows before he arrived at them. That was him all right. He was not a dark fellow though. Very pale skin, yes, pale and scrawny but full of menace. He looked very evil. Small piercing eyes and a horrible grin. Horrible it was.'

The East End of London has become panic-stricken. Crowds of people parade the thoroughfare, aimless and frightened; anger and indignation is prevalent. With blind fury a mob will turn upon anyone they fancy to blame for the tragedy.

There is one aspect of these disturbances which is particularly sinister. The indignant community has become anti-Semitic. Crowds assembling in the streets are beginning to threaten and abuse Jews.

It is repeatedly being asserted that no Englishman could have committed such a horrible crime as that of Hanbury Street and that it must have, therefore, been done by a Jew.

'It is so easy to aggravate the mind when it is startled by hideous crime. There may soon be murders from panic to add to the murders from lust of blood,' remarked a gentleman from the Jewish community. 'We are living in very dangerous times.'

Glancing across the room at her street door, Mary checked that she had remembered to bolt it. Feeling worse for reading the article, she was ready for her bed where she would feel safer.

Vowing never to walk too far in the dark again, she couldn't help worrying for the safety of her brother and for Harriet. A person who could commit such atrocities was obviously insane and as far as Mary was concerned such a creature should not be given any leeway as to what they might or might not do next. She wondered how the midwife dared to walk through the backstreets in the early hours of the morning. Maybe this was one of the reasons why she had been in a dark mood earlier? Miss Turner, unlike most women, had no choice but to go out when called upon, no matter what time of day or night.

Throwing salt on to the burning coals so that they would burn more slowly during the night, she listened at the bottom of the stairwell, hoping that both Arthur and Harriet had settled down to sleep. She could hear them talking to each other and their tone was soft and friendly.

Pleased that Arthur had company and that they were getting on together, she went into the scullery and tonged a few more lumps of coal into the range beneath the copper boiler. There was nothing she hated more than to start a fire first thing in the morning in order to boil water for the porridge.

Reminding herself to give Harriet's hair a good wash and brush the next evening, once she was home and fed after her office work at Bryant and May's, she checked to see if the stone jar of hair-wash needed replenishing. There was enough in there for the three of them and the mix of rosemary, almond oil and liquid soap had not lost its lovely scent. Opening a tiny worn cardboard box, she looked to see if the family black tar soap and nit comb were still there – just in case they should be needed. Putting out the small oil lamp, she went upstairs to bed carrying her lit candle, ready for her pillow and sleep.

In Arthur's bedroom all was quiet but once Mary closed her own bedroom door behind her, Harriet began whispering again. She was relishing her new experience of lying in a proper bed, albeit small. Having a bed all to herself was a new experience. 'Are you awake, Arfer?'

'Wot d'yer want?'

'You ain't asleep then?'

'No.'

'Do we 'ave ta go out in the yard if we need the lav?'

'No. There's a chamberpot under yer bed.' He went quiet and then said, 'You're not gonna go now, are yer?'

'Never said I was, did I?'

'I never said you did.' The sudden piercing shrill cries from two cats in the yard quietened both of them.

'Arfer?'

'Wot?'

'Do ya miss yer muvver and farver?'

'No.' He turned over, his back to the wardrobe between the two beds and closed his eyes. Of course he missed them. He missed them badly, especially the bedtime stories and warm cuddles.

'Wot, never?'

'Only sometimes.'

'I miss my muvver and my little sister,' murmured Harriet. 'My farver was awright, sometimes, when he wasn't wild or blind drunk. When he got 'is wages he was awright then. I never got the belt on pay-day – got a bag of chips instead. D'yer wanna come wiv me to see my muvver and sister?'

'If you want.'

'We could go by omnibus. Have ta do a click first mind. So's I can take 'em some toffee.'

Arthur curled his toes, as he did when annoyed with himself. She was talking about a click again and he still wasn't sure what she meant by it. He wasn't going to ask again. He would find out from Alfie Fairbairn the next day, at school. Fairbairn knew everything. He knew more words that weren't in the books than anyone. Even more than Teddy Greyburn.

Relieved that Harriet had gone quiet, Arthur closed his eyes and looked forward to the next morning when she would bring him a cup of tea in bed. This had been her promise. Drifting off to sleep he realised that he hadn't said the alphabet. Wishing to be as clever as Harriet he ran it through his mind without any problem and then fell asleep.

The sound of a tap running drifted into his dreams and caused him to wake up again. He wondered if there could possibly be someone in the backyard, stealing water from the tap. Or worse still, was it Jack the Ripper, washing blood from his hands? Not daring to move a muscle, Arthur whispered Harriet's name.

'Wot?' She let out a long high-pitched fart and continued to piddle in the pot.

'Was that a fart?' he said, only half awake.

'Wot if it was? Wherever you may be always let yer wind go free.'

'Are you sitting on the pot?'

'What if I am?' She stopped piddling and farted again. 'D'you wanna go?'

'No,' he said, pushing his face into the pillow to muffle his laughter. Yes, he was happy to have this funny new friend sharing his room.

'You know what?' said Harriet, climbing back into bed. 'I nicked a newspaper today 'cos I needed to crap.'

'Wot, out in the street? You did your toilet . . . out in the *street*?' Arthur could hardly believe this.

'Well I ain't gonna do it in the middle of a bleedin' shop, was I? Any'ow, I tore the back page off ready to wipe me arse and read the front one while I was crapping. The description of the Ripper could 'ave bin Daft Thomas. Wot d'yer reckon?'

'Did you do it into a tin can or summink?'

'No. In the gutter. You sits on the paving kerb and you do it in the gutter. Ain't you ever done that?'

'No, never. I wouldn't either. That's got nuffink to do with a click, 'as it?'

'Course not.' She said no more but simply pulled the blanket over her face and within seconds was fast asleep, leaving Arthur wide awake and wondering about the kind of lives different people led.

In the next room, with the gas mantle turned down to very low, Mary lay awake listening for any outside noises. She had never known the streets to be so quiet. Conscious of her own beating heart, she turned the gas mantle out and tried to settle down. She couldn't really believe there would be another killing. With so many police forces hunting the killer, there had to be an arrest soon. The puzzling thing was, if they believed Leather Apron to be the killer, why wasn't he behind bars?

'Thomas . . . how many times have I asked you not to come here?' Superintendent Charles Cutbush slammed a drawer shut and rose from his desk. 'High ranking officers are due in ten minutes and I am supposed to have my notes ready for presentation. Say what you have to and take your leave. I give you five minutes.'

'I had to come, Uncle. I'm very worried. Quite

disturbed actually.' Thomas sat down, crossed his legs and looked ponderously at the floor.

'Get on with it,' snapped Cutbush, turning his back on his nephew and looking out of the window. A meeting to discuss the Whitechapel murders had been arranged to take place in his office in no less than fifteen minutes' time. If this were not the case, he would have enjoyed more time with his nephew. He had seen a change in the lad which had given him some relief. He no longer ranted about prostitutes and their damnation. He had thrown himself into his work and seemed changed for the better. Yes, he was thankful that Thomas's dangerous moods had been just another of his passing phases. This time, the change in him looked more promising.

'I think I should have your full attention, Uncle.'

'Quite so, but I must look out for Sir Charles Warren, who, in case you had forgotten, happens to be Commissioner of the Metropolitan Police. If I should see his coach arrive, I shall ask you to leave instantly. Say what you have to, lad, and be quick about it.'

'I can see you are agitated so I shall come to the point. During my time spent canvassing today, in Stepney Green and not Whitechapel, having followed your good advice—'

'To the point, Thomas. To the point.'

'I saw things that displeased me and I'm sure if you knew what was going on there, you would want to put a stop to it straight away.'

Cutbush sighed, fearing the worst. His nephew was slipping back into his odd fantasy world. 'Put a stop to what?'

'The running of a whore-house, in broad daylight, with various policemen walking past every so often, oblivious to what is under their nose.'

Livid at what he was hearing, Cutbush turned to face his nephew. 'How long were you standing there for God's sake?'

'Longer than I would have preferred, but duty called. Since the police on the beat showed no interest whatsoever, I made notes of my own.'

Composing himself, the superintendent smiled benignly. 'My dear nephew, there are a hundred more brothels in the East End. Were we to interfere we would have many, many more prostitutes on the streets, inviting *trouble*. I'm sure you take my meaning?'

'I do, but this was no ordinary whore-house. The gentlemen I saw coming and going were far from ordinary. Most sported a top hat or a bowler.' Thomas showed the flat of his hand when Cutbush opened his mouth to stop him. 'I know you have a lot on your mind at present, Uncle, but I feel it would be perilous not to heed my warning. There is more, I fear.'

'Oh, get on with it!'

'One of the gentlemen going into the house of sin, was an officer from this very building. As yet, I cannot give a name, but I have seen him here on my previous visits.'

The slamming of his uncle's fist on the desk, startled him. The sheer fury in his eyes caused him to be more concerned. Was he about to protest too fearsomely? Had he himself been to visit the house of sin? 'You must understand, Uncle, I am not here to make accusations.'

'I am not interested in anything else you have to say and I must insist you take your leave immediately. You have wasted enough of my time and the clock runs on! I advise you to mind your business and stop playing at being a sleuth!'

Undaunted, Thomas proceeded to describe the officer as if he were reading from his notes. There was no need, Cutbush knew exactly who did and did not visit Lillian Redmond's house. 'Time's up, my boy!' he said, his back to his nephew once again. 'The police coach has drawn up. I shall speak with you in good time, at my home. I do not want you to come here again, in fact I forbid it. Is that understood?'

'But Uncle, if we are to clean up the East End . . .'

'Enough, I said!'

'. . . there must be no more cover-ups.'

Cutbush stormed across the room and opened his door wide. 'Keep away from places which do not concern nor welcome your intrusion.'

Rising from his chair, Thomas slowly shook his head. 'What I have told you was just the surface. There is more.' He stood in front of and very close to his uncle. 'I followed one of the women. A very attractive prostitute who was obviously not without means. She wore medium quality cloth, Uncle, not cheap and dirty clothes. And do you know to which place she led me? To the very lodging rooms of Amelia Palmer.'

'The name strikes no chord with me. Now—'

'I do read the newspapers, Uncle,' said Thomas, grinning. 'The woman has been interviewed by a reporter. She was Annie Chapman's closest friend and she was one of the last persons to see her alive.'

'And what does that tell us?' said Cutbush, keeping an eye on the staircase and an ear out for the sound of the Commissioner's voice.

'Not a great deal in itself . . . but I posed as a reporter and paid four shillings for her story. She wanted five but—'

'You did what!'

'Annie Chapman' – Thomas fastened the top button of his coat, enjoying his deliberate pause – 'was pregnant. Good day, Uncle. I hope your meeting goes well.'

Leaving his uncle thunderstruck, Thomas walked to the top of the staircase and stood aside, touching the peak of his newly acquired deerstalker, as the officials passed him on their way up to his uncle's chamber. Having recognised Sir Robert Anderson, head of CID, Thomas knew he had his man. All he needed now was to discover his name.

As the officials filed into the office, Cutbush shook each by the hand and when he came to Sir Robert he had a quiet word in his ear. Leaving the others to remove their outer clothing, the two men slipped outside the door and into the wide passage. Speaking in a low urgent whisper, Cutbush told him he must be brief. 'You have been seen going into the house in Stepney Green. There's more to it. We shall have to close it down until things blow over. Will you have a quiet word or shall I go through official channels?'

'Leave it with me. You are certain of this?'

'Yes. It must be executed as soon as possible, today in fact. Let us talk after this meeting.'

Walking boldly into his office, Cutbush said, 'I have asked that refreshments be brought in, should the meeting go on till late. Hopefully that may not be the case and we shall come to a satisfactory conclusion sooner than—'

'Never mind *hope*, Superintendent,' Sir Charles Warren cut in. He was not a man to mince words. 'The press are flaunting our failures and demanding a result. The sooner we see Pizer behind bars the better. I trust you have new evidence to convict him? One more Whitechapel murder and we shall *all* have to resign.' His face was stern and his manner showed no weakening or tolerance.

'He is a slippery customer, Commissioner,' smiled Cutbush, 'if you will excuse the pun?' he was attempting to lighten the atmosphere.

'This is no time for witticism, sir. We are close to having a riot on our hands. The people of the East End are in a very black mood. A very black mood indeed. And I cannot say I blame them.' He slammed his briefcase down on to a side table.

'No one ever sees the murderer, sir,' reasoned

Sir Robert Anderson. 'They all cry out for Leather Apron's blood but none have actually seen the slipper-maker in the area round the time of the murder. This is the problem.'

'Yes, and it's a rather stale one. Have you anything *new* to tell me?'

Sir Robert took his notebook from his waistcoat pocket and begun to read: 'Insane. Has a great hatred of women, especially of prostitutes, and has strong homicidal tendencies—'

'Confound it, man! This is not evidence!'

'From *my* notes, Sir Charles, you will glean that I am convinced the man is guilty and that we should make an arrest and put an end to the matter,' said Cutbush, helping out his friend and colleague who looked to be a touch deflated.

'But is there any fresh *evidence*?' barked Sir Charles, slamming his fist on the desk top. 'What of Ostrog the Russian? Or the Polish Jew, Kosminski? Or your damned nephew, Charles? Where was he *this* time when Chapman was killed?'

'Sitting with a small boy, sir, while the lad's sister, Mary Dean, a secretary at Bryant and May, was at a political meeting at the Mission Hall. My nephew fell asleep by the fire and the good woman left him there, having placed a blanket over him. She woke the next morning at six o clock, as usual, and soon after that, Thomas left.'

'I trust this Mary Dean is a respectable woman?'

'Indeed she is. Both her parents passed away this year and she, alone, is bringing up her brother. She keeps a very proper house in Whitehead Street, off Cleveland Way.'

'So he has a watertight alibi. That's something. I take it he's been under your close eye since the Millwood affair?'

'Yes, Sir Charles. The lad is repentant and deeply regrets his fit of anger. Anger which I may say we might all have felt under the circumstances.'

'Stuff and nonsense,' the Commissioner gave Cutbush a look of admonishment. 'Talk like that could bring us all down.'

'Indeed. I apologise. But to answer your question, Thomas is now the placid young man he was before the disastrous love-affair. He sees the error of his way.'

'Make damn sure he stays in that frame of mind and keep him away from reporters. If it should leak that you and your colleagues saw fit to conceal damning facts, the newspapers would make short work of it. Scotland Yard would be brought down, make no mistake.'

'As far as Ostrog is concerned,' said Anderson, wishing to turn the attention away from Cutbush who was obviously deeply embarrassed and under stress, beads of sweat from his forehead were now trickling down the side of his face, 'Ostrog is a dangerous man, who rules the criminal world – he is a very strong suspect.

'I am convinced that he, Kosminski, and Pizer, should receive our concentrated efforts. Every movement should be followed. If we execute this plan, we can either expect no more killings, or catch one of them red-handed.'

'Are you telling me you want us to deploy *more* of our officers? You'll have the entire Met force in Whitechapel at this rate.' He stood up and shook his head, angrily. 'Scandalous. We've got the best officers in London on the case and we still cannot nail this lunatic.

'I trust none of you know more than you're letting on?' He looked from Cutbush to Anderson and then Swanson. 'We're sitting on a political time bomb, gentlemen. Spare no one, but not at the expense of my department . . . nor Scotland Yard.'

With his hand on the doorknob, he turned to them. 'I'm not suggesting you break tradition and tell tales out of school, but we *must* have a conviction and soon!' He glared at Cutbush. 'Send your nephew abroad if needs be.' The Commissioner having taken his leave, the men relaxed into silence, each with their own thoughts. Cutbush pondered on Sir Charles's remarks.

Once the officers settled down to read out their scant information, a discussion took place between the three of them. At times it became heated when theories clashed. In the end, each of them had to admit that they were no closer to finding evidence which furthered the case. During this arduous seminar, Cutbush had become increasingly quiet and detached from the exchanges of opinion. He was struggling with his own dilemma. How could he possibly divulge the most serious information he held: that his nephew had *not* stopped after the attack on Betty Millwood but had gone on to murder the second victim, Martha Tabram and then Polly Nichols? And yet, to withhold these vital facts was not allowing them to move forward since they were under the impression that they were dealing with one murderer and not two, as was clearly the case.

'Are you unwell, Cutbush?' Chief Inspector Swanson asked.

'Unwell?' he gazed vacantly back at him.

'The colour seems to have drained from your face, my man. Here . . .' Swanson poured water from a jug into a glass and handed it to his colleague.

'I think a drop of brandy might help,' said Anderson, taking a silver flask from his hip pocket.

'Gentlemen, I don't think I can take much more,' murmured Cutbush. 'I feel as if I am in the very depth of a dark whirlpool. Or on a downward spiral with no chance of saving myself.' He covered his face with his hands. 'I'm sorry, my friends. I am truly most dreadfully sorry, but I simply must unburden myself or I too shall go insane.' He wiped his eyes with his hands and sighed almost with relief. 'Insane, like my wretched nephew.'

The room fell silent once more and Swanson and Anderson could do no more than simply look at each other in fear of what might come next. Such words from the superintendent, whose appearance had rapidly deteriorated to that of a broken man, was not something to be taken lightly by any means.

'Thomas had nothing to do with the Annie Chapman murder,' said Cutbush, his voice no more than a whisper.

'We know that, you old fool,' chuckled Sir Robert, embarrassed for his colleague and friend of old.

'But I believe he was responsible for not just Millwood, but Tabram and Nichols.' Avoiding their eyes, he looked upwards and drew breath. 'Gentlemen, there is more than one murderer involved in the Whitechapel killings.'

'Charles, you can't be serious?' said Anderson.

His lips pressed hard together and face full of anguish, he nodded slowly. 'I wish I could tell you I was joshing. You have no idea what I have been going through these past months. Thomas is the son of my beloved late brother, as you know, and I love him as if he were my own son. I cannot entertain the thought of him hanging from the gallows.' He pulled his handkerchief from his top pocket and covered his eyes, soaking up embarrassing tears.

'I have nightmares of him hanging from the noose. I simply cannot bear the thought of it.' Heaving with despair, unable to control his trembling, he continued to weep. 'The poor boy had such a dreadful upbringing with that woman . . . his mother. I wish to God I had taken him from her when my brother died . . . when Thomas was no more that four years of age.'

Stunned by his admission, the officers were speechless and could do nothing but watch as he released his pent-up agony and grief. 'I'm sorry to have loaded this upon your shoulders but you are the only friends I dare mention this to.'

'I think you might have told us of this a little sooner,

Cutbush,' said Swanson. 'It would have saved us going up blind alleys.'

'I didn't want to believe it. I truly thought that my nephew was in one of his dark fantasy moods, seeking attention again. But now, I believe he might well be very seriously ill.'

'And you believe he will strike again?' Swanson did nothing to hide the anger in his voice.

'No, I do not. I give you my word. My only regret is that I allowed myself to bury my head in the sand up until now at least.' He looked from one to the other, 'What if it should come out?'

'How so?' Swanson delivered his question with a touch of threat, daring Cutbush to suggest that his nephew may wish to come clean in order to off-load his guilt.

'Thomas has put it behind him, and if his past behaviour pattern is anything to go by, he will begin to treat his crime lightly. Soon he may become proud of what he has done and begin to boast from that confounded soapbox.'

'There are enough murderers out there,' Anderson cut in. 'That one should hang for a killing he did not do, makes no odds.' He turned to Swanson. 'We have got to find this other lunatic who murdered Chapman. He may as well hang for a sheep than a lamb. He will be our serial killer. If we can apprehend him with sufficient evidence of guilt, no jury will believe that he was not responsible for the others.'

Anderson reached across the desk and clasped Cutbush's hands. 'You have done us a service, my friend, and it was brave of you to speak out. We can now study this recent murder and not look for a pattern with regard to the others. We can waive the mark in trade left after the previous killings. We have closed ranks before and I see no reason why that should change now.'

'Thank you. You are most generous.' His composure regained, Cutbush heaved a sigh of relief. 'In truth, I was in fear of losing my own mind. I could no longer carry this heavy burden.'

'What of Sir Charles,' said Swanson, 'must we break this to him?'

'No, I beg you.' Cutbush raised an eyebrow. 'I sometimes wonder if the man has a sixth sense. Cast your minds back to his words as he was leaving this meeting. And make no mistake, gentlemen, his eyes were fixed on mine when he delivered his message.'

'Telling you to send your nephew abroad if needs be . . .'

'Yes, but the message before that was weightier, I believe. Cast your minds back and remember the look on his face when he said, "We're sitting on a political time bomb, gentlemen. Spare no one, but not at the expense of my department. Nor Scotland Yard."'

'I see what you mean,' said Swanson, 'he has his suspicions but would rather we did not recognise his part in it? What say you, Robert?'

'I think that would be exactly what the Commissioner would want.' Sir Robert Anderson's face gave nothing away but the message in his eyes, meant only for Swanson, was received with no more than a flicker in acknowledgement. The message read: You and I shall speak privately on this matter.

'Then so be it, gentlemen,' said Swanson. 'We are behind closed doors. For my part, I am ready to swear that what we have learned here this day, will go no further.'

'But,' said Sir Robert, 'there is something you must do for us, Cutbush. You must take a week or so away from here. Somewhere quiet where you may grow strong again. The police home in Brighton is yet to be finished and I imagine it will be some time before it is available. I suggest the small seaside home in Hastings. What do you say?'

Cutbush eased back in his chair and sighed heavily. 'What a relief that would be. But I must be here surely, to keep my nephew in line. He presently has taken on the role of amateur sleuth.'

'Well then,' said Anderson, 'what if he were to accompany you? It would serve a dual purpose, if you see what I mean?' He was trying to press home his point regarding the business of the discreet closing of the house in Stepney Green. 'The fresh sea air would do the lad a power of good, don't you think?'

'Yes. I see what you're getting at.' It would be easier to deal with the business of the brothel if Thomas were out of the way. With the lad in his present mood he would most likely want to keep a vigil on the place, to see who came and went.

'I am overdue for leave,' said Cutbush, relieved that the suggestion had been made. 'A week away from London right now sounds like bliss, I confess.

A sensitive time to withdraw, I know, but I cannot give my best under the circumstances.'

'Well then it is settled. Now then, I don't know about you gentlemen but a drop of brandy right now would not go amiss. Personally, I think we deserve it, no matter what derogatory reports the editors see fit to print in their rags. To hell with them.'

The meeting over, Sir Robert Anderson, the head of CID, and Chief Inspector James Swanson, walked down the staircase together. 'We must do something about his nephew,' said Anderson, 'and we must lose no time. Do you agree?'

'Indeed. But what *are* we to do?'

'Have him certified and silence his tongue. Will you be at home this evening?'

'I shall make it my business.'

'Good man. Shall we say nine on the hour?'

Swanson gave a curt nod of agreement and left the building, on his way to Bucks Row in Whitechapel. He was to meet with yet another woman who had written in to say she knew something which might help with the investigations. Every lead had to be followed. Reports were flooding in daily and any one of them might just lead them to the man responsible for this latest murder.

It was true that people saw the maniac in every dark place. In Brick Lane, two innocent passers-by had been attacked by a mob suspecting them simply because they were strangers out in the dark. In the Prince Albert public house, the landlady had let her imagination get the better of her when a stranger stopped for a quick pint of ale. His rough appearance and startling look in his eyes had frightened her. When the poor man left she had had him followed.

Outside Scotland Yard, Sir Robert could waste no time in making his way to the house in Stepney Green. Hailing a cab he asked the cabman to set him down on the Mile End Road where he would walk through to Beaumont Square. Arriving at the gate of Lillian's house, he looked discreetly about himself for Thomas Cutbush and was taken aback to see him behaving in a more professional manner than he had envisaged.

Sitting on a park bench inside the small public gardens, he stood out no more than any of the others who were there, idly passing time. Thomas was reading a book and smoking his pipe. The position he had chosen gave him an excellent view of the entrance to the imposing white house. Losing no time he approached the fool.

'I had a feeling you might be here, young man.' Sir Robert spoke in a deliberate, exasperated manner. 'Your uncle has spoken with me. I cannot say that the team working on this case is going to be pleased should I have to report back that you are hindering the course of police investigations. I have made good progress in attaining almost enough information to prove whether the residence is being improperly used.'

'Ah,' said Thomas, closing his book. 'This does throw a new light on things. I was deeply worried when I observed you entering the whore-house, Sir Robert. Quite perturbed.' He all but patted the head of CID on the shoulder. 'You see,' he said, 'I have detected your identity already. You must have a quiet word with the officer on the desk at Scotland Yard. I fear he is not as tongue-tied as he should be.'

'Quite. Now then, Thomas, it would please me if you were to leave now and go about your business. And we'll say no more on it.'

'Do you think that's wise, Sir Robert? I do have a new lead. It would be a pity to let it go, wouldn't you say?' He fixed a smile.

'You are *not* a policeman, Thomas.' Sir Robert was making it very clear that his patience was being stretched to the limit.

'Granted. But did Uncle Charles tell you what I found out? About Annie Chapman, recently murdered?' He narrowed his eyes and stuck his chin forward. 'I trust he did not withhold this information from you.'

Sir Robert stretched himself to full height and looked Thomas in the eye. 'Off you go then, dear boy. Be a good lad and leave this sordid business to the Yard.'

'She was pregnant – Annie Chapman – did he tell you that?'

'No and rightly so. We do not waste time on street gossip.' He checked his gold pocket watch. 'I do not want to have to *insist* you leave.'

'It would account for the murderer ripping out her womb, would it not? Maybe a gentleman of great importance had made her with child, have you thought of that?'

Having heard enough for one day, Sir Robert would have no more of his time wasted. 'I insist you leave immediately. And that you do not return. I shall instruct the officers who patrol this street to turn you away should they see you. Developing rumours does not help the course of justice!'

Rising slowly from the bench, Thomas looked into his tormentor's face and smiled. '*Qui tacet consentire videtur.*' He raised an eyebrow. 'He who is silent seems to consent.'

'I know what it means. But I warn you . . .'

'I hope to be joining the Grand Lodge very soon, Sir Robert.'

'That, sir, is none of my business.' He scowled at the young man who had turned away from him.

Watching Thomas leave the gardens, his books under his arm, his head held high, he questioned not only himself but his colleagues. How could they have let things get so shockingly out of hand? There went a young man who had murdered three women in the most horrific manner and had the entire country in a state of panic and fear, and they were leaving him to roam the streets! The thought which had gone through his mind so many times that day returned. They should never have covered up the first time when Thomas killed a prostitute out of passion. If they had realised then that they were weaving a dangerous web they would have acted differently. Shame lay on each of their shoulders. In their positions they should have realised the possible consequences. But then, who in their right mind would have imagined that more murders would follow and in such a short space of time and all of the victims, whores from the same area? Crimes of passion were no rare thing and at the time it seemed far the better thing to cover it up than to lay open Scotland Yard to ridicule. After all, Thomas's uncle, Superintendent Charles Cutbush, was a public figure and fair game when it came to newspaper reporters hungry to point the finger at the law. To have it made public that Cutbush's nephew was a murderer, crime of passion or not, would have certainly forced a resignation, never mind the bad publicity.

The full severity of the situation was sinking in. This one seemingly harmless idiot had placed not only Sir Robert and his colleagues in jeopardy but the integrity of the entire police force was at risk. If the scandal were ever to become open knowledge, public confidence in law and order would plummet. It was little wonder that Cutbush had broken down.

And what of the Commissioner, Sir Charles Warren? If he really believed that Cutbush's nephew not only attacked Betty Millwood but might be behind the other murders, was he not carrying the heaviest of burdens? Closing ranks is one thing, but this was potentially explosive.

Still preoccupied, Sir Robert could remember little of walking out of the garden square and across the narrow cobbled street towards Lillian's house. He was not looking forward to delivering the bad news; he knocked on the front door briskly.

'Would you kindly summon Mrs Redmond, Polly,' he said, his face serious. 'I should like a brief word.' He stepped inside the grand entrance hall.

'Yes, sir. Will you wait in the library?' said Polly, her best voice forward.

'Thank you.' He removed his top hat and followed Polly into the small panelled room. Glancing at shelves lined with books, he thought how sorry he would be to see this place close down. It had served him and many of his colleagues and comrades so well in the past. An oasis in the midst of a mad world.

'Robert,' said Lillian, happy to see him. 'How are you, my dear?' She closed the door behind her and studied his face. 'You look dreadful.'

'I feel dreadful, my dear,' he said, opening his arms to her. 'If only I could stay locked away in here for ever.'

'If only you meant that,' she said, running her fingers through his hair. 'If I believed you would spend the rest of your life with me, I would sell up and move out to the country without giving it another thought. But then . . . you know that.'

'I could do with a drink, Lillian,' he said, wearily.

'I can see that. Trouble at work or at home?' She poured him a brandy from the cut glass decanter.

'Worse. I think we had better sit down,' he said, taking the glass from her.

'I prefer to be on my feet when I receive bad news. Go on, Robert, get if off your chest. No matter how bad it may seem there is always a silver lining, don't forget.' She imagined that he had heard about her employee being the best friend of the latest victim. 'What's happened?'

'Lillian, my dear sweet woman, you are going to have to close your doors for a few months.'

Smiling at him, she flicked the air with her slender fingers. 'Don't be so melodramatic, darling. You've got yourself stewed over something and nothing, no doubt. Close my house – I don't think so.' She raised an eyebrow. 'Unless you are going to get a divorce?'

Dropping into the small sofa he found it very hard to amuse her. 'Some damned idiot has been observing the house. An amateur sleuth who informed one of my colleagues that this is a whore-house and that he has the names of high-ranking gentlemen who have been coming and going.'

'Is that all? Honestly, Robert, sometimes I wonder if it might be the time for you to take early retirement, worrying over such a thing. It's a wonder I've managed to fend off the snoops for this long. Give me his name and I shall throw money at him. It never fails. You've played into his hands; it's blackmail, short and sweet.' She shook her head at him slowly, 'You old worrier.'

'I wish it were that simple.'

'It will be. I was brought up in the backstreet slums, don't forget. I know how human nature works, remember my background is my fortune not my face.'

'It's not that simple, Lillian. You *will* have to close down.' Blunt and to the point was the only way he was going to get her to take him seriously. 'For a few months, that's all. Six at the most, until this business with the Whitechapel murderer is cleared up. It's bringing all sorts of would-be detectives out of the woodwork.'

'Robert, I can ill-afford to do that. To pay for all this grandeur I must have a good regular income. If I close it will have to be for good. And if this *is* real then I need to be convinced of it, then I shall go to see an estate agent. I would have little trouble finding a purchaser for this house and I'm sure I would find something suitable in another part of London. Maybe North London.'

Looking round the room, Robert sighed. 'It's a lovely house. I wouldn't mind it myself.'

'Is that an offer?' Her question was double-edged.

'Hardly, my dear. The purchasing of a brothel would not go down too well, I fear.'

'I wish you wouldn't call it that, Robert. It's a—'

'Yes, yes,' he said, interrupting her. 'I know. I know. I've a lot on my mind at present, you'll have to make allowances, Lillian.'

'I can see that,' she said, pushing her fingers through his hair. 'Why not come to my suite and tell me all about it?'

'I think not. The mood I find myself in would only depress you. I know how much this place means.'

'You could never depress me, my dear. I miss you between visits. I really do.'

'Me too.' He looked beyond her smile to see a concerned lover who thought more of him by far than his wife ever did or could. 'You look adorable, and I am in need of comfort. I would love to come with you to your rooms and forget all else. But you know that.'

'Of course I do. You make it all sound so final. The end of this house doesn't have to mean the end of us. I shan't move so far away.'

'No. No, it doesn't mean that. You're too much part of my life now.'

'How long do I have before I must close the shutters?' She walked to the window and glanced outside.

'Only a week; the idiot sleuth is going away for that length of time, to the seaside. Or at least we hope so. He's meant to go with his uncle . . .' He stopped short. It would not do to mention Charles Cutbush as being a relative. Too much would have to be explained if he did pique Lillian's curiosity. She was an intelligent woman and would have the whole story out of him in no time.

'That should be enough time for word to circulate,' said Lillian, too wrapped in her own thoughts to care where the sleuth – idiot or not – was going. 'As you know, I never ask my guests to leave an address so—'

'I shall see to it that those in my field know. You can depend on it.'

Lillian smiled at him. 'Your coming here personally and probably at some risk means a great deal. I don't think I would have accepted it from anyone else. But I shall move swiftly.' She studied his face. 'Robert, I don't think you're listening.'

He squeezed her arm tenderly. 'If only,' he said, 'if only.'

Understanding his meaning, she cast her eyes down. 'Once you've retired perhaps? One is never too old to start a new life, you know. Now then, I think it's time for you to leave.'

'And you wouldn't mind?'

'No. I don't think there would be any point in us being alone and intimate. Your mind is elsewhere and loaded with worry.' She kissed him lightly on the mouth. 'Come and see me once this is all over.'

'It's been seven years since we first met . . .'

'I know. And in seven years' time it will be fourteen. On your way now before I change my mind and lock us both in here.'

Uneasy and still troubled over the whole sordid business Sir Robert headed for a favoured restaurant where he would work out a plan. Wondering why he had not had a romp in bed with Lillian, which would have made him feel better, he cursed Thomas Cutbush upon whom he laid the blame. Given the opportunity he would shoot the insane imbecile himself and rid the world of one more demon.

With his seductress, Lillian, back in his thoughts, he found himself smiling. With Thomas Cutbush out of the way the house in Stepney Green would no longer be under threat of exposure and Lillian would not have to close down. Surprising himself, Sir Robert was actually enjoying the thought of getting rid of the menace, one way or another. The more he thought about it, the more he warmed to the idea.

Chapter Six

Sitting by the fireside with her nephew, the midwife had no choice but to listen to him as he read from the day's newspaper. Too tired to plead for him to think of something more cheerful, she rested back her head and closed her eyes, fancying he was reading from a book of fiction.

'At eight o'clock last night,' read Thomas, 'the Scotland Yard authorities had come to a definite conclusion as to the description of the murderer of at least two of the hapless women found dead in the East End, and the following is the official telegram despatched to every station throughout the metropolis and suburbs: Commercial Street, 8.20 p.m. Description of a man wanted, who entered passage of the house at which the murder was committed of a prostitute, at 2.00 a.m. the 8th. Aged thirty-seven, height 5ft 7in., rather dark, beard and moustache; dress: short dark jacket, dark vest and trousers, black scarf and black felt hat; spoke with a foreign accent.'

Passing the newspaper to his aunt, Thomas shook his head slowly. 'They're stabbing in the dark. And to think that Sir Robert ordered *me* out of a public garden. They are all fools, Aunt. This country is run by a bunch of dimwits.' Stretching his legs and crossing his feet, he gazed thoughtfully at the ceiling. 'Can you imagine their reaction if I were to write an article? Telling them some of the things that I have found out? Giving them a very good idea of what happened and why. There's more to it than meets the eye, this Annie Chapman took a secret to her grave. I would love to see it printed in the next edition, maybe I should write to the editor and spell it out in plain English?'

'And you are able to do that, Thomas, are you?' said Jacqueline, slightly amused by his mannerism.

'You must make up your own mind over that, Aunt, I have said what I have said. Make of it what you will. Of course I should like to know who is responsible for this recent murder, it's by far the most interesting. I have a feeling he is *not* self-educated and from a family of standing. The tree of knowledge bears a variety of fruits.'

'Why don't you warm the milk for some cocoa,' said the midwife, scanning through the newspaper.

'I should like to shake his hand. This man who cleanses the streets of whores. Congratulate him on his fine work and perhaps exchange ideas.' Having no response from his aunt other than a bored sigh, he recited from memory from the Bible. 'For the lips of a prostitute are as sweet as honey and smooth flattery is her stock in trade, but afterwards only a bitter conscience is left, sharp as a double-edged sword. She leads you down to death and hell. For she does not know the path to life. She staggers down a crooked trail and doesn't even realise where it leads.'

Staring at her nephew from over the top of her newspaper, Jacqueline said, 'Did I hear you correctly, Thomas, you mentioned Sir Robert. Do you mean Sir Robert of Scotland Yard?'

'Indeed. We've been working on a case together and I am sworn to secrecy.'

'But you said he sent you packing, ordered you away from the gardens?'

'It shouldn't surprise you. I am, after all, a mere student of law and journalism and self-taught at that. He was embarrassed that I had discovered important evidence which he and his colleagues had missed.'

He stretched his arms with no obvious intention of rising to warm the milk for cocoa. 'Omniscience is power. I have the omniscient view and they do not. What a different place Whitechapel would be in the future if this cleansing had not begun.'

'Tell me about Sir Robert and your meeting in the park. Do you think he was following you?' For all her experience of people and especially of her nephew, she could make not head nor tail of his mood.

'Innocent children chant something in the street,' he said, ignoring her question. 'Children chant and the British newspapers print it. What *is* to become of this great country? I feel obliged to accompany you, Aunt, when you sail off to America.'

Irritated by him, Jacqueline said, 'Your uncle came here asking questions, you know, before he left for the seaside. He wanted to confirm that you were in Mary Dean's house when you said you were.'

'And that surprised you? The man has little faith.

I told him I did *not* commit that particular crime and yet still he comes here for a clandestine meeting with you. How could you entertain him so, Aunt? I can see now, he is in need of a rest. The sea air will do him good. He wanted me to join him, you know. I said I might follow up in a few days.'

'Entertain him? Was I supposed to leave him on the doorstep?' She folded her newspaper and stood up. 'He left here a lot less worried than when he arrived, I might say.'

Thomas continued to gaze into the fire. 'He worries me, Aunt, I will confess that much. Both he and his colleague, Sir Robert, were given crucial information and they chose to ignore it. I told them that Annie Chapman was pregnant and they did not believe me.'

Feigning interest in the hot coals, she stabbed at them with the iron poker, her mind working overtime. How could Thomas know that? Even the police doctors hadn't realised it, otherwise it would have been reported in the newspapers. 'And what makes you think she was pregnant?'

'I don't *think* it, Aunt, I know.' Lighting his pipe he continued, 'I did well in my role as a journalist.' Again there was a pause as he drew on his pipe. 'I have given it a lot of thought and I believe I know the answer. Would you like to hear my reasoning on it?'

'Go on, then,' said the midwife, sitting down again, her mind working overtime.

'Yes, I believe I know the answer. It was very likely an important gentleman who made Annie Chapman with child, probably a high-ranking aristocrat. Some of the newspapers are saying this latest murder has the mark of a professional physician, an expert who knew exactly how to extricate a womb. It could have been the Queen's physician himself. But I would have thought that anyone associated with the Royal family would read the good book on a regular basis. He should have drunk from his own well and been faithful to his wife and not fornicated with women of the streets. It's an insult to all of us, Aunt Jacqueline, to *all* the Queen's subjects.'

'I couldn't agree more, Thomas, but I think you should mark every bit of the Bible. A little knowledge is a dangerous thing, all said and done.' She decided to go along with him.

'How so?' said Thomas, patronising her.

'Do not judge thy neighbour? I agree, it was a most wicked act to commit, but you must not cast the first stone. That you have been given this information must surely mean that you are to keep it to yourself?'

'You may well have a point, Aunt. I was led to the woman who gave me this tip-off. Yes, I can see that now.' He nodded very slowly and mumbled something she could not quite hear. He then raised his eyes to hers. 'You must swear on the Bible, Aunt, that you will not repeat what I have told you today.'

'If you feel that necessary, Thomas, then I shall. But will you at least tell me the informant's name? I feel I should know it before I swear on the good book.'

'It was Annie Chapman's closest friend, Amelia Palmer. She is working below stairs in a dishonest house. A whore-house, right in the centre of Stepney Green, if you can believe that. A short cab drive away.' Thomas leaned forward sucking his pipe and began his story as to how it had all come about. And the midwife was all ears. Once he had finished his drawn-out tale, he sat back in his armchair and waited, but his aunt was speechless.

'I did ask you to keep an eye on Miss Mary Dean, but as usual, you took no heed. I sometimes wonder—'

'What has Mary Dean to do with this?' snapped Jacqueline.

'She is one of them. One of the courtesans, as they like to call themselves. In my book they are prostitutes of the worst kind.'

'I think this has gone far enough, my lad,' said Jacqueline, 'I will not listen to such things in my house. You make me so very cross at times, Thomas, really you do. Mary Dean a prostitute? How could you!'

'A woman I followed,' he spoke in his slow condescending tone, 'came out of the big gates and was dressed in very fine clothes. She was *not* from below stairs.'

'And this woman was Mary?'

'Please, Aunt, I did not say that. Let me finish my story.'

'Go on but keep to the point, I am getting tired of this.'

'The woman is Miss Dean's closest friend. I have seen them walking together, arm in arm, and going into the milliner's at Whitechapel. The bonnets in this particular shop are not cheap and are mostly to attract the wealthy tourists. I have also seen the young woman entering Miss Dean's house, on social visits. I miss nothing, Aunt, because I *am* a good detective but, *why* must people always do their utmost to stop me, stupid men like Sir Robert Anderson?' His accusing eyes bore into her.

'You have to have special training for these professions, Thomas. No one is out to stop you.'

Sighing loudly as was his wont, he spoke in a tired tone. 'You really do have a lot to learn about people, Aunt Jacqueline. What would you have me do about Miss Dean?'

'Nothing! It's none of our business who she keeps company with. And she is not a prostitute. And I insist you do not mention this to me again or to those children whom she entrusts to your care. Do you mark me, Thomas? I stand very firm on this. Very firm indeed!'

'I can see you're upset, Aunt,' he said, the tone to shrink a violet still in his voice. 'I should not have slurred your young friend. I apologise. I shall purge it from my mind and not allow it to change my opinion of her. I too think she is a fine young lady who would make a very good wife.' He clasped his hands together now preoccupied with his thoughts.

His expression amused her, he was obviously taking his thoughts on her very seriously. 'Well that's a good conclusion to all this dark talk. I'll make our cocoa and then you must be on your way, Thomas. I have no calls to make this night and I am ready for bed.'

In the scullery, Jacqueline gripped the edge of the small scrubbed table as everything sank in. Such revelations within the hour: Mary Dean, Annie Chapman, the House of Assignation. She uncorked her bottle of gin and felt for the first time in her life that the tide was perhaps against her. Exposure was becoming too close for comfort. She must think and she must think fast. She had no regrets about killing Annie Chapman whatsoever. Something had happened to her. Predestination was forcing a change in her very soul. Almost as if it were written. As if she was not, after all, in control of her own destiny.

Her thoughts going way beyond her sensibility she began to think like her nephew: *Maybe we are simply the instruments of God? Here only to cultivate this earthly world as He wishes us to.*

Coming into the scullery, Thomas said, 'Has Miss Dean been seeing anyone, Aunt? That you know of?'

'What do you mean, seeing anyone?' She knew exactly the way his mind was working.

'Does she have an admirer?' Sometimes his patience with his old aunt stretched thin.

'I couldn't say. I don't recall any gentlemen friends. Why do you ask?'

'I think it may be in her best interest, if I were to escort her to the theatre occasionally. What say you to that, Aunt Jacqueline?'

Jacqueline poured warm milk into the two cups. 'You are a gallant boy, Thomas,' she said. *Quite mad too*, she thought. 'It's a free country, after all, so you're at liberty to walk out with whoever will have you. But

I doubt it would advance any feelings she might hold for you, should you read to her – from the Bible.'

'Oh dear.' He put a hand against his forehead. 'I wish you would stop treating me like a child. I was not thinking of courting Miss Dean. I had only her welfare at heart. I have my work to do. I do not have time to waste on romantic notions.'

'Work?' she said following him in to the parlour with their cocoa.

'As an investigative journalist. I don't think that God would be best pleased if I were to waste this acquired talent. It would be a sin to be lackadaisical when I have been given a gift.'

'True. But you can't blame your silly old aunt for wanting the best for her nephew. And you did murmur that she would make a good wife. I must have misread your intentions.'

'Doesn't everyone, Aunt?' he said, sipping his cocoa. 'But I am now used to it. We are what we are.'

'Indeed,' she said, 'indeed we are.'

While Thomas was considering where he might escort Miss Dean, Mary was comforting Lizzie over the affairs of the heart. Her wonderful Mister Shaw had left without a word and she was heartbroken. With Arthur and Harriet asleep in their beds, the girls huddled round the fire in Mary's front room.

'I s'pose you're wondering if Sir Walter's gonna dish out the same dose of grief as my lovely Bernard?'

'I never imagined he'd be any different, Lizzie. We're from different worlds. I just wish I never fell in love with 'im, that's all. I didn't reckon on it hurting this much.' Mary turned her face away from Lizzie's because her friend was actually smiling at her. Did she think her a fool?

'I'm to tell you to come tomorrow evening at eight,' said Lizzie.

'Please, Lizzie . . . don't. Making fun of it might be all right in a month or so . . . but not now. Not yet. I'm really down over it.'

'I'm not 'aving you on, Mary. Walter's gonna be there so it's up to you.'

'Honestly?'

'Cross me heart and hope never to die. Now then . . . d'yer know what I reckon we need? We need a treat? Let's go to the music 'all at the end of the week. The Empire on Friday night – what d'yer say? We'll 'ave ourselves a real good time.'

'Why not? We'll take Arthur and Harriet as well.'

'Good. That's settled then. Now . . . I'd best be off.'

Standing with her friend on the doorstep, Mary said, 'You sure you'll be all right out there, Lizzie? You can stop the night and share my bed if you like.'

'Nar. I'll be safe enough. Walk down the middle of the road and scream blue murder should I see so much as a movement in the shadows or a—' Grabbing Mary's arm, Lizzie spun around as she heard footsteps in the dark. 'Who's that?' she snapped.

'Thomas Cutbush,' came the haughty return. 'On my way home.' Arriving by their sides he looked from one to the other. 'I hardly think this is wise, ladies.

It's late and it's dark. Most women are behind locked doors by now.'

'Well I don't know you but what luck, eh? You can walk me to the main road, Mr Cutbush,' said Lizzie.

'Allow me,' he said, offering his arm. Then turning to Mary he said, 'I'll wait until I've heard your bolts thrown, Miss Dean.' He spoke in a manner to imply they were closer than mere neighbours.

'Thanks, Thomas,' she said. Bidding them both goodnight, Mary closed the door and Thomas waited until he heard her lock up.

'How lovely to meet a gentleman,' said Lizzie, slipping her arm though his.

'And how long have you known Mary Dean?' he said, deliberately slowing down their pace.

'Since we were little. Best friends at school, we was.'

'And out of school?'

'Never saw that much of 'er. Sometimes we'd be in the park gardens at the same time and sometimes she came back to our 'ouse for a cup of tea. But at school we was always linking arms. Best friends. What about you?'

'I've known her nearly all my life,' he said, as if they were already promised to each other. 'Spent most of my childhood in Whitehead Street, watching the other children playing together. The boys in the street seemed rather dim – as most boys will.'

Stopping at the billboard outside the music hall, Lizzie said, 'Me and Mary are gonna come 'ere on Friday night. The bill looks good. I love magicians and a bit of singing, don't you?'

'Not particularly. I prefer to read quietly and smoke my pipe. Watching bawdy women and cheap entertainers is not my cup of tea, I'm afraid.'

'It's good fun, you daft sod. Meet me and Mary 'ere at seven this coming Friday night and see for yerself. You shouldn't knock what you don't know, Thomas Cutbush.'

'Well perhaps I might. Providing you promise not to mind should I leave before the end of the programme.'

'That sounds fair enough,' she said, her attention drawn to a hansom cab pulling up. 'An' don't be late, will yer?' she said, running towards her ride home.

Passing the usual haunts where he knew that streetwalkers preyed on their victims, Thomas felt a degree of self-satisfaction. The area was quiet and deserted. A lighter spring in his step, he continued on his way towards Tower Bridge and Kennington proud to have stimulated another crusader into action. This latest slaying of a whore was the mark of a like-minded man. An educated man. A man with moral fibre prepared to put himself at risk in order to cleanse the streets of the lowest type of disease-spreading females. His only disgruntlement was that he could not enjoy a smoke with his Uncle Charles and discuss the matter intellectually. He felt sure they could learn from each other. His thoughts turned to his mother and her companion and he wondered what kind of a mood they might be in tonight. In their presence, he dare not even mention that he had been to his Aunt Jacqueline's house for fear of retribution. He hoped that he might be able to slip into his own small room with just a mild burst of abuse coming from the mouths of one or both hags. More likely was the possibility of him being subjected to interrogation over a cold supper. One could never tell. But he was used to it by now. He had long since lost the yearning for her affections and the release was most welcome. It gave him *some* small comfort when she *was* in a motherly mood but no more than that. Sadly, time and rebuke had deadened his love for her.

Passing a middle-aged Jewish man, Thomas nodded, bidding him good evening. It seemed unjust that public opinion had turned against the Jews since the killings began. This was not something he imagined would happen. To his mind, they did practise unfamiliar religious ceremonies and observed a biblical code which he regarded as suspicious but the Jews were decent law-abiding people. He wished that the local community could be more tolerant and less bigoted and consider things intelligently. Hadn't any of them read that the Israelites had a revulsion for blood?

Shaking his head, he wondered what he might do to help the plight of the Jews. He could, of course, go along to the synagogue and talk to them about keeping a low profile for the time being. He might even suggest they slaughter their meat without the ritual of swiftly slitting the throat of a beast. He couldn't see why they should not heed his advice – at least until the pressure was off. He decided then and there to have words with Rabbi Zeid. He felt sure that the worried man must be desperate to discuss the Jewish problem. So deep in thought was Thomas that he hadn't realised he had been talking to himself and that the two men who passed him were not enjoying a private joke but snickering at him.

The angry tide of pent-up anti-Semitic feelings must not be allowed to continue, thought Thomas, scolding himself for not having considered this problem before when the resentment and the threat of violence had been but simmering. *I must act quickly if calm is to be restored.*

Hoping he would not be approached by streetgirls, he walked on. He really was in no mood for the girls. His thoughts turned to Mary Dean's friend. It had been pure chance that she had invited him to the music hall. It would now give him the chance to observe the two of them. To see if the prostitute *had* led Mary astray, as he suspected. It would be refreshing to prove his Aunt Jacqueline wrong and himself right.

Returning to the streets of Whitechapel the following day, Thomas mingled with the various groups of agitated locals as they propounded opinions as to the guilt, or otherwise, of the latest suspect of the murders. Young urchins were chanting their own verse as they skipped around a news placard or played clap-hands.

> 'Boys and girls are out to play,
> They've taken Levver Apron away,
> He's a foreigner, he's a Yid,
> In Annie's blood he slipped and skid.

Now the streetgirls are crying for joy,
They're going to hang that *naughty* boy!'

'Leather Apron,' sighed Thomas, 'a mere slipper-maker.' What could the police be thinking? He was as unlikely a candidate as the brainwashed children. He looked again at the headline and imagined his own name there.

The crowd, who had been arriving from Leman Street police station, having caught a glimpse of the accused, Pizer, were going into the alehouse to soak up more of the atmosphere and the beer. Going into the alehouse himself, he smiled as a short, thickset man of the worst type, told his story.

'Yus, they've got their man awright! Saw 'im wiv me own two eyes! 'Orrible look on 'is face; evil it wus. Like the devil 'imself. The dried blood was still beneaf 'is fingernails. Bloomin' great scar across 'is face and dahn 'is arm. Piercin' black eyes an' all. Looked right froo yer! Cursin' an' aswearin' 'e wus! Swearin' froo 'is clenched teef. All in black. Yus. 'Cept for 'is shirt. That wus as white as the bleedin' snow at Christmas . . . wiv dried blood all dahn the front!

'"Why did yer do it?" I says to 'im. Yus, ladies and gents, I talked right into 'is face. "Answer me that," I says. "Give it me straight." An' that's when it 'appened.'

The story stevedore emptied his glass and licked his lips. 'Me froat's gawn dry from the thought of it.' Another pint of ale was placed in his outstretched hand as the eager audience hung on to his every word.

'First orf, I wasn't dead certain he was gonna 'urt

me, but then he moved that quick. Flashed a bloomin' dagger in me face. This long it wus.' He drew his left hand away from his right which held the beer mug. He showed a space of at least twelve inches. 'But fank Gawd for that flash copper, Thick. He put up 'is arm in the nick of time. The knife ripped right froo 'is sleeve to the bone. Yus, I owes me life to Sergeant Thick.' He took another slurp of his ale.

'Wot did Levver Apron say, Rat-ears? Did 'e talk to yer?'

'Yus 'e did. He snarled at me worse than a mad dog foaming at the mouf! "I weel catch you when I am free. I weel cut up your body . . . into little pieces and feed it to the pigs!"'

Gasps from the spellbound crowd fuelled his imagination. 'Oh yus! Yus it's 'im awright. And I've got to pray for me life shud 'e ever escape. I'll be a goner. Yus.' He hung his head and kept them waiting. 'I 'ad to speak out. You follow? Yus. I did it fer all decent blokes wot fears fer their missus and daughters.'

Turning away, Thomas despaired at the human race into which he had been born. How could they be so ghoulish? Why were they so desperate to hear every detail – fictitious or otherwise?'

'Thomas, my boy!' the voice of Sir Robert Anderson startled him. Irritated to be called a boy by this man, he pressed his lips together, looked Anderson in the eye, and waited.

'I was hoping I might bump into you.' Sir Robert took Thomas by the arm and led him to a quieter spot, outside the railway station. 'You mentioned something when we met in the garden square. I wondered if you were serious in your request?'

Inhaling slowly, showing a bored face, he said, '*What* request?'

Sir Robert checked his surroundings and lowered his voice. 'Joining the Lodge?'

'Why do you ask – have you a plan to prevent that too?' said Thomas.

'Good heavens, no. We need astute young men like yourself. You're a smart chap. A quick brain – just like your uncle.'

'You've changed your tune somewhat, Sir Robert,' said Thomas, peering into his eyes, searching his soul.

Sir Robert leaned forward and spoke into his ear. 'Had a lot on my mind. But you were stepping out of line and upsetting those from a higher station than mine. If you get my drift?'

'You were carrying out orders,' said Thomas, matter-of-factly. He then offered a handshake and Sir Robert obliged, hoping none of his colleagues were within sight. 'I am to meet with a Fellow this very evening. At his home. Why not join us for drinks. You'll need more than one recommendation.'

'I do realise that, Sir Robert. I have done my homework.' The superior tone exuded from him and was galling to say the least.

'Excellent. Good man. What do you say, then, eh?'

'I say let bygones be bygones, Sir Robert. Where and when shall I meet you?'

Sir Robert pulled a slip of paper from his pocket. 'Here we are. Memorise this and then tear it into small pieces, there's a good chap. Don't want any of this lot finding it and turning up.' He squeezed Thomas's arm and left, weaving his way through the robust crowd.

Smiling, Thomas was indeed happy. So much so, when talking to himself, as was his habit, he raised his voice from the usual whisper, not caring who heard. 'Well, well, well. It would seem the authorities are not quite as foolish as they would appear. Sir Robert Anderson has at last seen that he has not been dealing with a simpleton.' He glanced at the address, memorised it and then dutifully popped it into his mouth and chewed it to pulp. Spitting it on to the flagstones, he continued on his way towards Stepney Green to carry out his canvassing.

Chapter Seven

Waiting outside the music hall with Lizzie, Harriet and Arthur, Mary was preoccupied with Sir Walter and their time together at Lillian's house the previous evening. He had looked sad on parting, having heard that Lillian was to close down the House of Assignation. Yet he had said nothing to her about them seeing each other again.

'If Thomas is not 'ere in five minutes, Mary, we're going in!'

Lizzie's voice brought her back to the present. 'It wasn't my idea to invite 'im, Lizzie. He'll be a damp squib, make no mistake.'

'I 'ope he bleedin' well don't turn up,' said Harriet. 'Funny sort of bloke if you asks me.' She peered through the glass doors of the music hall. 'Look at that, Arfer. Two staircases. Bit posh, innit?' She pressed her nose against the glass. 'Look at the tarts who're goin' in though. They ain't posh.'

'I know,' said Arthur. 'So it don't matter that you never brush your 'air.'

'Don't intend to brush it niever. Mary made it nice in the week. I ain't gonna spoil it, am I now?'

'Move along there, if you please!' the uniformed

attendant waved a hand behind Harriet's head.

'Move yerself along. Bleedin' cheek! We're gettin' proper tickets to go in there!'

'Buy your tickets or move along. The show begins in five minutes.'

'Come on,' said Mary, 'Thomas won't turn up. This is not 'is cup of tea. I don't know why you bothered.'

Passing through the vestibule of the Empire, Harriet was wonder-struck. She looked from the ornate mirrors to the glass lamps all around the walls and then up at the domed ceiling. 'It's blooming lovely,' she said. 'All red and gold like a palace.' She turned, grinning, to Arthur. 'This is a right bleedin' treat this is!' She then took the stairs two at a time.

Once they had settled down and got used to the noise from the tawdry audience, Lizzie's face lit up. She was reading the programme. 'We're in for a treat all right. They've added another act.' She read it aloud. 'Billy Green and Sophie Blue will perform their very own mimed version of The Ripper in Action!'

'That should be a lark,' said Mary, watching a woman in the stalls stepping up on to the bench. Her voice loud and shrill wasn't quite drowned by the excited noise of the collected audience. 'They've set Levver Apron free!' she yelled. 'He's out there now! Lurking in some dark passage. They couldn't nail the filthy swine!'

A deathly hush spread through the music hall. 'Ignore it,' said Lizzie, 'there're always loud-mouths down there.'

'That's right! They don't believe he's their man! Jack

the Ripper's still out there! Roaming the streets and laughing at us!'

'Shut yer bleeding gob!' came the voice of another loud-mouth. 'The man's locked up. Sit dahn or piss off!'

A sudden boom of drums as the house lights went down stopped a fight breaking out. A brightly dressed juggler backed on to the stage, throwing and catching not only three balls but a baton too. In his red and black costume he looked exactly like the drawing on the poster outside. The cut-glass buttons on his fitted tunic were twinkling like stars in the gaslight.

'Put a bit of life into it!' yelled the first heckler.

'What? Wouldn't your missus let you stroke 'er pussy before you come out?' yelled another. They quickly forgot the scaremonger in the audience as the hall filled with laughter and suggestions flew as to what the performer might juggle next.

Having never been inside a music hall, Harriet wasn't used to the raunchy crowd. Standing up, she leaned over the balcony and showed a fist. 'Shut yer bleedin' gobs! We paid good money to come in 'ere!' No one took a blind bit of notice. And when the juggler dropped his baton, there was more heckling from the crowd.

'Mind ya don't drop your balls an' all!' came the shrill voice from a large woman who sat below and in shot of Harriet. Leaning forward as far as she dare, she began to draw saliva and then spat at the woman below, catching the centre of her flower-decked black bonnet.

'Harriet!' Mary was not best pleased.

'She shouldn't be so bleeding wicked! He's doin' 'is best, ain't he?' She glared at the rude woman below who was now whistling between two fingers. 'You old trollop!' she yelled and spat at her again.

'Harriet. Stop it!'

'Shut up, Mary,' said Lizzie enjoying herself. 'Everyone shouts at each other. Wouldn't be an East End music hall elsewhere.'

Arriving on stage hoping to save the poor conjurer from mouldy fruit, Daisy May, a regular singer at the hall, was there to stop the taunting.

'Well, well, well . . . if that didn't get you all going, eh?' She slapped her knee and roared with laughter. 'I says to our juggling giant before he perambulated this stage . . .' she showed the flat of her hand to quieten her audience '. . . I says to 'im, "I'm sure you can 'andle your balls, juggler, but what about yer baton?"'

The audience was with her straight away. Laughing and whistling they cheered her on. 'And do you know what, ladies and gentlemen – and the Queen, if she's in – he looks at me with not a trace of a smile and he says, "As a matter of fact, I do know where there's a policeman's truncheon, but it needs a bit of a polish. You couldn't give it a little rub for me, Daisy, could yer, luv?' Laughter filled the hall. Laughter, whistling and cheering. Daisy waited for them to quieten down.

'Now then,' she said, 'don't you fink a good sport like that deserves a bit more respect from us at the Empire?'

'Never mind that, Daisy, did you oblige the poor codger?'

'No, I told him straight! I spoke in my very best voice, sir. I said, "Me name is Daisy May but that don't mean Daisy will!"' Allowing them a few seconds to laugh, she got in quick before they took charge of the show. 'Now then, as part of this little act of our friend the juggler, I am to sing you a ditty which he will juggle his balls to.' She turned to the performer and winked. 'Ready?' He was. Tilting her hips in her own particular way, Daisy began to sing:

'Whoever it was, that said life was dull,
Had no imagination in the skull,
O, dearie, dearie, dearie me
What kind of man would that man be?
I can liven four men's tickers
With just a flash of me naughty knick – ers!'

Seeing the juggler was keeping good time with her, she gave him another wink and quickened the pace.

'I've got red ones, blue ones, black ones too,
And if you're good, I'll show them to you.
Yes I can liven four men's tickers,
With just a flash of me red satin knickers.'

She waved a hand encouraging the audience to join in. Mary, who was singing along with Harriet, who was in top voice, saw Arthur giggling behind his hand and looking a little flushed. He jabbed the air with his thumb to let them know what was going on behind them. Lizzie was on her feet, singing and lifting her skirts and petticoats high enough to give a flash of her drawers.

Two hours later Mary and Lizzie walked arm in arm out of the music hall. Harriet and Arthur followed close behind. Daisy May had, as usual, managed to get the audience singing along with her. In all, she had sung six songs. The other acts were good but she was the favourite by far. Laughing and chatting the small party came into the fresh air only to hear the voice of a thin distraught woman who was scurrying past. 'They've let 'im out, they've released the Ripper! A woman's not safe, get yerselves 'ome, girls! We shall be murdered if we're not be'ind locked doors!'

'Oh God . . .' said Lizzie, 'it must be true then.'

'You'd best stop with us tonight, Lizzie. You don't wanna go 'ome by yourself,' said Mary, her eyes darting everywhere. 'He could be hiding in any dark corner.'

'I can't do that, Mother'd be worried sick. The news will 'ave reached 'er by now.'

'We'll see you into a hansom cab, don't you worry. Then me and these two'll run for all we're worth. Blooming Thomas Cutbush! If he'd turned up like he said he would, you'd 'ave 'ad him to walk back with you.'

It was past midnight when Mary finally doused her bedside candle. It had been an exciting evening but had ended with women, young and old alike, fearing for their lives – again. Lying in the dark, Mary could not get rid of the worry inside. The midwife was on her mind. The midwife and her nephew Thomas, but she wasn't sure why. Pulling herself up in bed she relit the candle. Her mind went back to the early days when Jacqueline Turner's sister, Celestine, would visit and cause a commotion in the street. The women were often talked of in a derogatory fashion among other neighbours and it was taken for granted at the time that there was insanity in the family. Thomas was simply referred to as 'Daft Thomas'. Mary recalled snatches of conversation between her own mother and father. Her mother saying how rumours and gossip should not only be ignored but put down. Her father on the other hand had insisted that there was no smoke without fire. Questions came into Mary's mind as she sat propped up against her pillow. Why was the midwife such a loner? Her only visitor was Thomas. No one could deny that Miss Turner's work was her life but to have not one friend or neighbour dropping in for a cup of tea and a chat seemed odd. Especially in Whitehead Street which was a close community.

Mary wondered if there was more than met the eye when it came to Thomas and his maiden aunt. Then, telling herself not to be foolish, she plumped her pillow and sank her head into it. She would leave her candle this night to burn itself out.

Chapter Eight

'What the dickens are we to tell Cutbush on his return?' Sir Robert Anderson spoke in a quiet, grave voice.

'Surely, Robert, you had considered this before now?' Dr Browning shifted his position to enable Thomas's drooping head to rest on his shoulder. The driver of the hansom cab seemed to have no consideration for his fares. He had taken the narrow turn out of a back street with unnecessary speed.

'He's not due back from leave until next Monday; I'll think on it.' He would like to have said that this plan had taken up most of his time but feared that awkward questions might be raised. It had been tricky enough trying to persuade the man to change his mind and not take his nephew with him to Hastings. Sir Robert closed his eyes and sighed inwardly. The sooner this lad was committed to the lunatic asylum the better.

'I shouldn't over worry,' said the doctor, 'Cutbush is quite aware of the state of mind of his own nephew. We must tell him that this poor chap lost all sense of right and wrong during a heated argument between the three of us. Lay the blame at my feet if you must. Say I disapproved of him joining the Lodge, that I felt he was too young and a little too reckless.' He gazed out of the cab window. 'Say what you bloody well like. As far as I'm concerned we are about to place this young man where you should have had him committed to, months ago.'

'I couldn't agree more,' said Sir Robert, 'with hindsight.'

'A man of your calibre should not depend on hindsight, sir.' It was an honest if not cutting remark and it had hit home.

'None of us are perfect, Dr Browning.'

'You can damn well say that again! To let it go this far was inviting the worst kind of trouble. You, Swanson and Cutbush may well feel ashamed of yourselves. You are a disgrace to Scotland Yard.'

Anderson remained silent for most of the journey onwards. His travelling companion had angered him. To his mind, the only wrong that he and Swanson had done was to agree on the Millwood affair. And they had only covered things up because the attack had been from passion and the woman had only sustained a few cuts. The fact that she died later from infection in the wound was down to her decrepit state of being. He still held firm to the belief that it would have been unfair on Cutbush to have him resign because of this unfortunate family connection. Neither Cutbush, Swanson nor himself could have had any idea at the time that the maniac slumped against him in the cab right then, would have repeated his diabolical deed.

The sooner Thomas Cutbush was locked away, in a catatonic state, the better. Drugged and incapable of intelligible speech he would no longer be a threat. Three men's reputations were at stake and Anderson had no intention of allowing a raving lunatic to ruin their careers. He knew that when Cutbush returned he would agree that his nephew posed too much of a threat. The risks were too great and Thomas was the cause – he had to be removed. At least this way his nephew would not face the gallows.

The sound of low moaning coming from the semi-conscious Thomas alarmed Anderson. 'Do you not think a little more chloroform?' he whispered to his companion.

'Perhaps. We shall see what state he is in once we are there.' Dr Browning was making it clear that he wanted no more conversation.

'Pray, do not trouble yourself, Dr Browning. I shall explain this away with ease. I have a feeling that Charles Cutbush may well be relieved. At least the killings will stop now.'

'I thought you said that Thomas did not commit the most recent crime, sir?'

'I was merely passing on his uncle's opinion on the matter. I cannot say that I was convinced.'

'Let us hope your instincts are right, Sir Robert. There must be an end to this dreadful business.'

Relaxing for ten minutes before turning her Christmas pudding mixture into a basin, Jacqueline Turner was surprised when her clock on the mantelshelf struck four. This Saturday afternoon seemed to have slipped away and she had three visits to make. She had been thinking about America and the superior class of women she would be attending. Not whores, that was for sure. Correspondence from her distant cousin assured her of that. Her thoughts turned to Mary Dean. She hoped that the young woman, whom she had helped her mother to nurse through childhood ailments, had not turned to a life of prostitution. Again, Annie Chapman the lowest of whores came to mind. She had left a turmoil in her wake. Amelia Palmer being the biggest problem. This girl knew far too much and could possibly be her downfall.

Suddenly, loud banging on the front door startled Jacqueline. Opening it, she was surprised to see Charles Cutbush on the doorstep once again.

'Please forgive me, Miss Turner,' he said, 'I should have written but this visit is quite impromptu.' He looked furtively along the street.

'I was rather hoping it might be Thomas,' she said, closing the door behind him. 'I haven't seen much of him. Nothing in fact for almost a week. I take it he didn't join you on your break?'

Placing his top hat on the side table, he turned to Jacqueline and looked directly into her face. 'No. I think you should sit down, madam.'

'And why should I do that, Mr Cutbush?' If he was there to give her bad news, she would rather be on her feet. 'I trust there hasn't been an accident. You sport the look of a worried man.'

'No. Thomas is alive. But not, I am sorry to say, in good health.'

'I see.' She felt a wave of nausea. 'I can't say I'm too

surprised.' She presumed it was the syphilis. 'Please sit down, Mr Cutbush. I was just about to take afternoon tea, will you join me?'

'Thank you, yes.'

'Thomas must be quite sick or you wouldn't have taken the trouble to call.' She handed him his tea. 'Please help yourself to milk and sugar.'

'Something happened while I was away,' he said, settling himself on the settee. 'A short holiday by the sea was the order of the day.'

'I'm sure it was. And while you were away, Thomas was taken ill, is that what you are here to tell me, sir?'

'You are a woman of substance, Miss Turner. If only . . .' he said, losing concentration on the matter in hand.

'It had been this sister and not the other that your brother took for a wife?'

'Indeed. You read my every thought, madam.'

'No, Mr Cutbush. You regard me too highly. Your brother said the same thing and on more than one occasion. I fear the brain will never rule the heart. My sister had beauty, there's no disputing that.'

Embarrassed, Charles felt awkward. 'Looks are not everything and besides which, you were in every way as attractive as your sister in those early days when we were all a little more carefree.'

'Please tell me, Charles, where is my nephew? Just give me that piece of information and then I shall leave you to tell me the rest, in your own time. I must know where he is because my mind is conjuring up the worst kind of pictures.'

'Yes. Yes, of course.' The man looked wretched and almost broken. 'Thomas is in the Lambeth Infirmary.'

Placing her cup and saucer on the table to prevent it from falling from her hands, Jacqueline took a deep breath. 'Please go on.'

'Our nephew wanted to join the Lodge. I must say this came as a surprise to me. I don't recall him ever talking of this. And . . . as you know, once Thomas has a new thought he will not stop airing it. Had he mentioned this new interest to you?'

'No, I can't say that he did. But please get to the point. Why has my nephew been taken into an infirmary?'

'A colleague of mine, Sir Robert Anderson, was keeping an eye on Thomas while I was away.'

'Anderson?' She looked directly into her brother-in-law's face.

'You know Sir Robert?'

Composing herself, she straightened her back. 'Only what I read in the newspapers. He sounds like a good officer of the law.' For the moment she would keep to herself the fact that she knew he had been marking Thomas.

'Indeed.' Cutbush cleared his throat. 'From what I gather, Sir Robert invited Thomas along to meet another Mason. He and Sir Robert were to recommend Thomas. This other Mason thought Thomas too young and a row broke out. Apparently, our nephew's reaction went from anger to outright rage. He smashed one or two pieces of Dr Browning's furniture, I fear. There was no choice but for the doctor to restrain and sedate him.

'Sir Robert and Dr Browning took him to the infirmary by hansom cab, for a thorough examination. The medical staff there recommended that he should be detained in a secure ward.'

'I see.' Jacqueline was not best pleased. 'This tale may have fooled you, Charles, but it does not get past me. I do not believe that Thomas would behave in such a way and I do not believe he would have been invited to join the Masons. There is more to it and I cannot believe you are not of the same mind.'

'Yes, I did accept all that I was told, I see no reason to believe otherwise, but you think differently?'

'Indeed.' Jacqueline was livid. 'Those men had no right to commit my nephew to a lunatic asylum.' She avoided his sorry eyes. 'Have you been allowed to see him?'

'I paid a visit as soon as I heard.'

'And?'

Cutbush looked away as his eyes filled with tears. He held up a hand to show that he needed a few seconds to compose himself.

'I have some brandy in my medicine chest. May I offer you a drop?'

'I would appreciate that, madam, yes.' He wiped his eyes and mumbled quietly, 'May God forgive me.' He shook his head gravely. 'I was offhand when you came to see me about Thomas. It would have helped, I am sure of it, had we discussed the problem together. I expect that is why you took the trouble to come and see me in the first place. I apologise for my behaviour.'

Jacqueline handed him the brandy. 'You had a lot on your mind, no doubt.'

Sinking into the settee, he closed his eyes, giving Jacqueline the opportunity to study his face. 'How was he when you left him, Charles?' she asked.

'I shall tell you directly, just give me a moment, please.'

'Was he restricted?'

'If you mean, did they put him in a straitjacket, I believe not. When I saw him he was heavily sedated. The spirit seemed to have gone from him – quite deflated he was though somewhat content in his own private world.'

'He should never be in such a place, poor lad, I find it very hard to take. It's not easy to think of my nephew, whom I love dearly, to be in such a place.' She pursed her lips and gazed into the fire. 'No. He shouldn't be in there.'

'I wish to God I could have as much faith as you, Jacqueline. I wish I could believe it. My heart tells me one thing and my mind tells me something else. I fear our nephew is not improving as I had hoped.'

'Why not say what you think, sir; you believe Thomas to be insane, don't you?'

'No. No, I will not have that.'

'I'm relieved to hear it. No good will come from locking him away, of this I am sure. I am quite capable of looking after him myself.' She caught Cutbush's eye. 'He wasn't responsible for the last murder, I can tell you that for certain.'

'My dear sister-in-law, what difference does it make? He has murdered others, has he not?' The strain showing on his face, Cutbush sighed. 'I fear that if we stir things up at the infirmary and try to get him out, we may be taking a risk. The press are always close by these days, no doubt one or two of them have followed me here. My colleagues are shadowed constantly.'

'Tell me something,' said Jacqueline. 'Does Sir Robert Anderson by any chance know as much as we do? You know, the bizarre confession that Thomas made to you and I? Do you think he might also have mentioned it to your colleague?'

'I don't know. *I* told him nothing.' He was lying and the very fact that he averted his eyes was proof enough. 'They may have deduced it for themselves, of course.'

Jacqueline looked purposefully at the clock on the mantelshelf. 'My thoughts entirely.'

'Well, we each have our work to attend to. I expect you'll want to visit Thomas?' He stood up, ready to leave. 'Believe me, he is in the best place, you know.'

'On this we had best agree to differ. I know him too well and I know that he would be best off here with me until at least he recovers from this latest upset.'

Once Charles Cutbush had left, Jacqueline clenched her fists and cursed him. Tears of frustration and anger coursed down her cheeks and she thrust her leg forward and kicked a small footstool across the room. There was not a shred of doubt in her mind. Her brother-in-law and his colleagues had conspired to have Thomas locked away – to protect themselves and Scotland Yard.

'You may think you have me fooled,' she said, sitting by the fireside and looking into the flames, 'and I shall go along with it. But I have not done yet.' Resolute that she would clear his name and obliterate all doubt of him having killed Annie Chapman, she planned her next move. If Sir Robert and his Masonic partners in crime thought they had seen the last of the killings by having her nephew locked away, they were very much mistaken.

Sitting at her small bureau by the bedroom window, she began to feel more positive. Her mind was set. She knew what she had to do. Opening a drawer in the bureau, she took out a slim black book which had belonged to her father. This had been given to him some years before he died when he himself had toyed with the idea of becoming a Mason. She remembered the chapter that she had read at the time and which had shocked her. It had a ritualistic element to it. This, she decided, would be the pattern she would follow when carrying out her second execution. Catherine Eddowes' mutilation would have a Masonic hallmark. She opened her writing slope and withdrew a plain sheet of paper. Considering the content and tone of the letter she was to write, she dipped her quill into the red ink pot and began.

Dear Boss, I keep on hearing the police have caught me but they wont fix me just yet. Leaning back in her chair she smiled to herself and wondered what her father would have thought had he seen this opening line. He had always been strict when it came to grammar. Continuing, she wrote, *I have laughed when they look so clever and talk about being on the right track. That joke about Leather Apron gave me real fits. I am down on whores and I shan't quit ripping them till I do get buckled.'*

She covered the notepaper with her blotter and went to pour herself a gin. She would finish the note later. With Annie Chapman still on her mind, the midwife could not help thinking of Mary Dean and how she had brought trouble to her door. To fathom how this lovely girl had got herself involved with such low people seemed impossible. She wondered if, for the sake of Mary's good parents whose life had been cut short, she ought to try and save the girl from embracing such company and being drawn into the low life. She would think on it.

Meanwhile, a few doors away, in Mary's small front room, she and Lizzie had been discussing the murders over a cup of tea. 'Listen to this bit,' said Lizzie, reading the latest edition: '"The veil had been drawn aside that covered up the hideous condition in which thousands of our fellow creatures live, in this, the very heart of the wealthiest city in the world. Deplorable misery, gross crime and unspeakable vice – mixed and matted together – lie just off the main roads that lead through the industrial quarters of the metropolis . . ."'

'Industrial quarters of the metropolis?' said Mary, smiling. 'We're important all of a sudden.'

'Shush,' said Lizzie, eager to continue her reading aloud: '"Parts of our great capital are honeycombed with cells, hidden from the light of day where men are brutalised, women are demonised and children brought into this world only to be inoculated with corruption, reared in terror, and trained in sin, till punishment and sin overtake them. Amid such gross surroundings, who can be good? Who can rise to anything better?"'

'Blooming cheek! That reporter should come and take a look around the East End himself. Living in gross surroundings? What about the People's Palace; Trinity Square; and Bethnal Green Museum opened by the Prince and Princess of Wales no less! And we've got some lovely churches and parks.'

'He's referring to the backstreets, Mary. Aldgate and Bethnal Green . . . Russian Lane.'

'Well there are places we wouldn't go after dark, I grant you. But that don't mean all of the East End. And we've got one of the finest and most famous hospitals. And, after all, the rich and famous love to come in to visit, don't they?' She smiled at Lizzie, 'Artists, writers . . .'

'Mmm. Bernard Shaw for instance. He came all right, but soon went, didn't he, once he thought he might be caught out. Unless he 'ad enough material.'

'Material?'

'For a book or a play or something. I don't know. But I reckon he was studying me. He said that's mostly why he liked to come to our neck of the woods. To study the real and earthy people.'

'They're all the same,' said Mary, downcast. 'I really believed Sir Walter when he said all those nice things to me. Then he gets a whiff of scandal at your mother's place and he's off without a word. If I could just see 'im once more I'd—'

'Oh not agen, Mary! Every time I see you he comes into the conversation. He's gone – they've both gone. We'll just have ter forget about 'em. They just trifled with our feelings and our fannies now and then when they had a day off. All men are the same, if you ask me.'

Mary was gripped with laughter. Lizzie could be very funny at times, crude or not. 'I can just imagine us 'avin' tea in the tearooms with the pair of 'em and you coming out with that. Can you imagine their faces?' She started to laugh.

'I can an' all,' said Lizzie, enjoying it. 'Especially if I said it nice and loud.'

Once they had both got over their fit of the giggles, Mary leaned back in her chair, shaking her head. 'It really hurt at first. Not knowing why he never came back or got in touch. P'raps he's gone abroad?'

'Might 'ave done. Come on, I fancy a stroll along Whitechapel. We'll treat ourselves to coffee and a cake in the tearooms. But no stopping to gaze in shop windows. I can't even afford to buy a bonnet now.'

'Don't exaggerate, Lizzie, you're not skint. Just out of work for a few weeks.'

'I'm not so certain. The clients 'ave vanished into thin air, will we ever see 'em agen?'

'They'll be back once this 'as all blown over. Your

muvver won't 'ave to uproot, I'll wager you sixpence on that. It stands to reason that decent men won't come into the East End right now, not with a copper on every corner.'

Lizzie gazed into the embers of the fire. 'Will they ever catch 'im, Mary? Will they ever catch the devil?'

'Yeah, they're bound to. Come on, enough of this, let's go out.'

Arms linked, Mary and Lizzie headed along Cleveland Way towards the tearooms. 'By the way, what's 'appened to Daft Thomas? I've not seen 'im wandering along Whitehead Street for a while preaching from his Bible.'

'I don't know,' said Mary, 'and the midwife's been a bit strange lately. Looks at me differently. I think she might 'ave guessed where I got my bit of extra cash from to buy Arthur's new breeches and now knows it wasn't from typewriting.'

'Give me the creeps, the pair of 'em,' said Lizzie sitting down at a small table.

'First time I've 'eard you say that. And it was you who invited Thomas to the music hall, don't forget.'

'Yeah, well, that was then and this is now. I've changed my mind about 'im.'

'Well just so long as you don't say such things in front of the midwife. Thomas means everything to 'er. He's all she's got 'cept for Thomas's mum, her insane sister, Celestine.'

Lizzie placed her cup back on its saucer and raised her face to look into her friend's eyes. 'Insane sister?'

'Seems that it runs in the family, Miss Turner's mother was mad too.'

'You might 'ave said before now. To think I sent Annie Chapman to see the midwife.'

'I never said that the midwife was mad. She's the *white* sheep of the family. Everyone down our street respects 'er, and she looks out for Thomas. If she'd 'ave known the sort of woman I was arranging for 'er to see at my place that night she would never 'ave agreed to it. Neither would I, come to that. You could 'ave got me into a lot of trouble, Lizzie.'

'How was I to know she was a streetwalker? I took my friend at 'er word. She said she was a decent woman. Anyway, enough of that. What's done is done. This is a lovely cup of coffee.'

'It is,' said Mary, 'but it's not that excellent. What's put that daft smile on yer face?'

'Turn your 'ead *very* slowly and take a look at the headlines on the gentleman's newspaper. The one sitting directly behind yer.'

Doing so, Mary read the leading headline: SHOULD BE CAGED IN AN ASYLUM? *Strong evidence that Aaron Kosminski is the Ripper?* Leaning forward to have an easier read of smaller print, Mary was startled if not to say shocked when the top of the newspaper was flicked down to show the reader's face. It was Sir Walter. 'I've finished with this for now,' he said, 'you may borrow it if you wish. Should you be in here this time tomorrow you may return it.' With that, he stood up, took his bowler from the hat stand and left. Mesmerised, Mary watched him through the window of the tearooms as he strode away.

'Crafty devil,' murmured Lizzie, smiling. 'He's bin looking for yer. Someone, like Sir Walter, don't frequent a coffee 'ouse in Whitechapel. I wonder 'ow many times he's bin in, hoping to catch sight of you?'

'Don't be daft,' said Mary, blushing. 'This is a respectable tearoom. Why wouldn't he come in occasionally?'

'Tch. You might be good at typewriting, Mary, but you're hopeless when it comes to folk. He's bin coming 'ere on the off-chance of seeing you come in or stroll by.'

Mary leaned forward, pushing her face close to Lizzie's. 'All he had to do was ask your mother where I lived.'

'He did. She wouldn't give it to 'im. She's got more business sense than that. Oh stop looking at me like that, Mary. You're not the only one. Most of the gentlemen 'ave asked where they can reach their women. They're missing their tricks on the side.'

'Lizzie, please!'

'And so am I, to be honest with yer. Living like a flippin' nun ain't no fun. If Mother catches so much as a whiff of men's hair lotion on me, she'd go potty. I've never bin allowed to see anyone outside 'er world in case I degrade myself. Mustn't go with anyone unless the surroundings are classy.'

'But she couldn't possibly think Sir Walter's—'

'Oh use your loaf, Mary! She ain't gonna risk losing one of 'er girls. Business is business. If Walter wants you so badly, he's gonna 'ave to wait until Mother's found somewhere else or opened up again once things 'ave improved. Once they've hung the Jew for the murders.'

'Your mother don't own me, Lizzie.'

'Oh yes she does. You 'aven't earned your advance yet.'

'What advance?'

'The beautiful dress, underwear, shoes – purchased especially for you. None of the girls can wear them now, Mary. Not once *you've* donned 'em.'

'And if I don't pay up?'

'You won't work again. Not unless you wanna join the streetgirls.'

Mary slumped back in her chair. 'You never told me about this. I've never bin in debt in my life and nor 'ad me mum or dad. You've tricked me.'

Lizzie laughed quietly at her friend. 'I'm just telling you the way it is. You've 'ad it blooming easy, that's your trouble. One of the best gentlemen who've crossed our threshold asks to 'ave you exclusively to 'imself? Lucky cow. He left 'ere a bit sharpish, though. What was it he whispered to yer?'

'He never whispered it. He always talks quietly.'

'Fair enough. Now give us that paper. Let's see if the dozy buggers 'ave got the right bloke this time.' Reading the latest news she left Mary to her daydreams.

'Poor devil,' murmured Lizzie, having read the article. 'If they ain't using 'im as a scapegoat my name's not Lizzie Redmond. Listen to this: "*Sir Robert*

Anderson"' – she raised an eyebrow and grinned – 'Mother's lover, no less . . . "Sir Robert Anderson, head of CID, told a member of the press that both he and Chief Inspector Swanson are convinced they have found the Whitechapel murderer, and once this man is secured in an infirmary, they feel certain the killings will cease. Kosminski, a Polish Jew, is said to strongly resemble the individual seen by a City constable near Mitre Square."

'Well they've got that wrong for a start. That's the Met's patch. City police wouldn't 'ave no right being there,' said Lizzie. She read on, '"The case against this shabby genteel . . ." Shabby genteel? Tch. He's from a poor Jewish immigrant family. His mother and sister 'elp out in the 'airdresser's. They ain't got two sticks to rub together. Aaron walks about like a bag of rags. Clean rags, but rags all the same. They're stitching the poor bastard up just to get an arrest.'

'Read some more,' said Mary, intrigued by Lizzie's interpretation of the way things were.

'"The case against Kosminski looks strong if we are to believe the authorities. 'We are tantalisingly close to ending this nightmare,' said Chief Inspector Swanson. 'During my absence abroad,' added Sir Robert Anderson, 'a house to house search was carried out, investigating the case of every man in the district whose circumstances were such that he could come and go and get rid of his bloodstains in secret. And the conclusion we came to was that the murderer is a low-class Jew, for it is a remarkable fact that people of that class in the East End will

238

not give up one of their number to Gentile justice.'"'

Folding the paper, Lizzie slumped back in her chair. 'I've gone cold. If they don't lock 'im away the mob will lynch him. Poor devil. He's trapped.'

'And these are the men who are running this country,' said Mary. 'Is that the end of it?'

'That's all there is. Poor sod. He can't be a day over twenty-two and walks about rambling to 'imself acting like a ten- or eleven-year-old at times. Won't eat anyfing else but bread and only drinks water from the tap. He can't weigh much more'n seven stone, Mary. My 'eart goes out to 'im. It really does. Those swines'll trump up enough evidence to hang him, you'll see.'

'He might only go to gaol,' said Mary. 'He might—'

'He'll die in gaol. Make no mistake. They'll skin 'im alive.'

'Mind you, there is another rumour spreading through the streets,' said Mary, trying to lighten their mood.

'Collar and cuffs Clarence,' you mean, 'the dozy Duke. The Royal Ripper. They say the Queen knows and can't stop 'im.'

'Gone soft in the 'ead,' said Mary. 'And they reckon there's a skeleton lurking in the cupboard. Her beloved son Eddie's bin a naughty boy!'

'And that's why we must 'ave a scapegoat – to protect the Royal family. Will you come back tomorrow then? To give Sir Walter 'is newspaper back?'

'I thought you never 'eard what he said?'

'I was teasing you, Mary, just teasing you. Will you then?'

Going quiet and feeling sad without really knowing why, Mary shrugged. 'Who knows what tomorrow will bring? *I* might 'ave been murdered.'

After a couple of gins and a spate of deep thinking as to what she might write in her letter, the midwife with quill poised continued . . .

Grand work the last job was. I gave the lady no time to squeal. How can they catch me now? I love my work and want to start again. You will soon hear of me with my funny little games. I saved some of the proper red stuff in a ginger beer bottle from the last job to write with but it went thick like glue and I cant use it. Red ink is fit enough I hope, ha! ha! The next job I do I shall clip the ladys ears off and send to the police officers just for jolly wouldn't you. Keep this letter back till I do a bit more work then give it out straight. My knife's so nice and sharp I want to get to work right away if I get a chance. Good luck.

Yours truly Jack the Ripper.

Smiling to herself, Jacqueline wondered what her father would say had he seen this work. Not one comma in sight. Yes, he would have been furious had she shown him anything similar when she was a girl. He had been very strict when it came to punctuation and grammar.

Undeterred, she folded the letter and slipped it into a plain envelope. Her original intention had been to post it direct to Scotland Yard, but careful, second thoughts had brought a change of mind. She would send it where it would be printed for the world to see. Using the same untidy handwriting she addressed it to The Boss, Central News Office, London City.

Pleased that she had refrained from the temptation of leaving a clue to make it look like this was the work of a Mason, she sealed the envelope. She imagined this is what a member of the Lodge would do. Make it look as if the letter was from a semi-literate and not a Mason. In her next correspondence, she would make a deliberate blunder, to the detriment of that secret society.

All that was left now was for her to remember, in detail, the description of the whore Catherine Eddowes that she had wheedled out of Annie Chapman. She would then concentrate her efforts on securing the release of Thomas.

Chapter Nine

In the communal kitchen of Mr Cooney's board-ing house in Fashion Street, Spitalfields, Catherine Eddowes was cooking breakfast for herself and her lover, John Kelly, while the proprietor sat at the table resting his elbows and admiring her.

'I reckon me and John should 'ave bin born gypsies,' she said. 'We're like a couple of bleeding Romanies, tramping round the countryside. Fruit-picking, hay-making, hop-picking. We've done the lot so 'elp me we 'ave.'

'P'raps there *is* a bit of Romany in yer blood, Chic,' said Cooney, smiling and winking at her.

'John'll 'av your guts if he catches you calling me that. You're not funny. Pass me them eggs.'

'Awright, only when we're on the bed then, eh?' he murmured mischievously. 'Or when John ain't wivin earshot.'

'You never know when anyone's in earshot so keep yer voice dahn.'

'So where'd the cash come from then, Chic? For this little slap-up?'

She pointed a knife at him. 'He's about to walk in that door any minute. Turn it in.' Cooney was too attractive in his rough kind of way and Catherine knew that her man would have noted it. The fact that she had sometimes slept with him for a free bed was something she knew he'd keep secret. Cooney was quite aware of her man's jealous temper.

'He pawned 'is boots for half a crown. Only just bought the bloody fings as well. Out of the hop-picking money.'

Just as the landlord was about to offer another quip, John Kelly came into the communal kitchen. Knowing a silence would be dangerous, Catherine picked up on their previous conversation.

'Hop-picking's the best though. Not that we came back wiv our pockets lined, we didn't get on too well this year, did we, cock?' She glanced at her man and smiled.

'Lousy 'arvest. The 'ops were like peas,' growled Kelly.

'Walked all the way from Hunton we did. We 'ad a bit of company fer a short while mind. Another couple who was just as broke gave me a pawn ticket for a flannel shirt. We'll claim it for John soon as we've got ninepence to spare. I'm off to me daughter's this afternoon. She might—'

'Don't you go scrounging for my sake,' her man cut in. 'Shirt or no shirt. You'll feel the back of my 'and if you do.'

Sitting down to their breakfast while Cooney brewed tea for the three of them, Catherine looked miles away. Talking about fruit-picking had drawn her into the past – to when she was a girl.

'Dad was a tinplate worker,' she said, not bothered whether the two men were listening. 'Mum was only sixteen when they married. Grandmother lived wiv us for a while, it was 'er who nicknamed me Chic.' She eyed Cooney, daring him to use her pet name again.

'They moved down to London in forty-four, when my next brother was born, moved to Bermondsey, they did. My sister still lives there. Loves the place, she does. I might well be living in that part meself if I 'adn't bin shipped off to Wolver'ampton when Mum died.'

'You're getting a bit morbid, Catherine gal,' said John Kelly, dipping his fried bread into the yolk of his egg. 'Don't wanna go brooding over the past. Ain't worth it.'

'Me daughter, Annie, lives in Bermondsey as well, she's good to me.' Wiping a piece of bread around her empty plate, soaking up the grease, she smiled. 'Yes, I shall pop in and see 'er today an' all.'

'Make sure you're back before dark if you don't stop over. That bastard's too close for comfort.'

'I should fink they've got 'im be now,' said Cooney. 'He ain't struck for a few weeks, and they've arrested enough suspects, one of 'em must be 'im.' He topped up their cups with fresh tea.

'I wouldn't be so sure. The insane bastard might be biding 'is time.' Kelly pointed his knife at Catherine. 'Home early or stop over. Right?'

'Don't you fear for me, sweet'eart, I'll take care. I shan't fall into 'is 'ands.'

'*And* stay sober.'

'Course I will. Don't you fret about that.'

But, untrue to her word, Catherine Eddowes, by eight thirty that evening, was hopelessly drunk on the pavement in Aldgate High Street. Instead of going straight back to her lodgings after visiting her sister, she had stopped at more than one public house on her way home.

A local police officer on his beat pushed his way through the small crowd which had gathered around Catherine. 'Clear the way, please, clear the way!' When he saw the crumpled body lying there in a state of unconsciousness, he called for assistance believing there had been another murder. The shrill sound of his police whistle pierced through her eardrums. Slowly lifting her eyelids, she tried to focus on the peering faces of the assembled crowd.

It took two police officers to get her to Bishopsgate police station, the pavements were especially crowded for a Saturday night. The area had become quite a notorious tourist attraction thanks to the recent gruesome murders. 'What's your name?' said one of the officers, shouting for the third time.

Slowly raising her arms, Catherine smiled at him. 'Nuffing. That's me name – Nuffing.' By ten thirty she was in a cell, comatose. She slept until midnight and by 1.00 a.m. the officers at the station had had enough of her yelling and singing. They all but threw her out of the station, knowing it was too late for her to buy any more drink.

Things certainly looked different at that time in the morning nowadays. The fear of the Ripper had swept through the lives of the streetgirls. They weren't out much after midnight and the sightseers who had poured in from other parts of London had departed, leaving the dark streets almost silent. A dog barking in the distance was acknowledged by another and apart from the distant echo of a woman yelling for the dogs to be quiet, the place was deserted. 'So much for the guardians of the law,' mumbled Catherine, slurring her words, 'never in sight when you might need them.'

Shivering against the cold night air, she pulled her coat collar close to her neck and quickened her pace, treading as softly as she could. Her own reverberating footsteps were sending shivers down her spine. She simply wasn't used to being in these streets when they were empty. Those girls who hadn't managed to do a trick would be taking refuge at the Mile End instead of curling up in makeshift bedding, in some sheltered dark corner, as they had done so many times before. Catherine prayed that Cooney had been right and that the Ripper was locked away in a police cell.

Approaching Church Passage, the sound of approaching footsteps stopped her dead. She stood as still as a statue and tried to work out which direction they were coming from. Willing herself not to move or run for her life, she backed into the shadows of the synagogue and waited as the footsteps came closer, praying that whoever it was would pass by – but he didn't.

'At least one of you isn't afraid of the dark,' came the soft, quiet American voice.

'I'm waiting for my 'usband. He should be 'ere any second now.' Her words tumbled out.

'That's a shame. I was hoping for a rub. I would be happy to pay sixpence.'

'He'd go berserk. He's known to be a violent man, wouldn't take lightly to you propositioning me.' She relaxed a little as she heard more footsteps approaching. She looked past the stranger to see two men walking away from the Imperial Club. 'This is 'im now,' she said. 'This'll be 'im and 'is pal.'

'Another time then,' said the stranger, leering into her face. He then continued on his way, leaving Catherine very frightened. She had never been so pleased to see a couple of men strolling along in the dark. Leaning on the synagogue wall, she took a long deep breath as they passed her by. With the gentlemen between her and the stranger, she felt a little safer. But that small comfort was short lived.

'You're taking a risk, aren't you?' came another voice from the entrance into Church Passage. The tone made the hair on the back of her neck stand up as she spun round to see who was there. Stepping out, the midwife stood in front of her.

'You shouldn't be out alone like this. It's asking for trouble.'

'Midwife!' She clasped her chest and her loud sigh was more akin to the howl of a terrified child. 'It's a wonder me 'eart didn't give out.' She shook her head and leaned back against the wall, thankful for the support. 'I wish I *was* tucked up in bed, I don't mind telling yer. This soddin' Ripper's driving us all inside.'

'Which way are you going? I'll walk with you. I don't

imagine the murderer will come anywhere near, my outfit seems to scare the men off.'

'I was gonna cut through the passage to Mitre Square, Midwife,' she said linking arms with her. 'I s'pose I've bin foolish. I've 'ad a drop over the top, you see, but then, so 'ave you, eh?' She could smell the gin on Jacqueline's breath.

'I was going through the passage myself when I heard footsteps and then I saw the man approach you. You were wise to refuse him.'

'He scared the bleedin' life out of me.'

Jacqueline patted Catherine's hand as if she was comforting her. 'We'll walk through together. Better to be safe than sorry.'

'Ah you're a good woman. I shall tell me 'usband. He'll be that pleased.'

Entering the dark alleyway, Jacqueline reeled off her lie. She said how she had delivered one baby and was on her way to another woman in labour. In fact, she had been waiting and hoping that Catherine Eddowes would take this route back to her lodgings. She had been watching out for her earlier on when she overheard the gossip that Eddowes had been dragged away in a drunken state to the police station. Jacqueline had banked on the police not keeping her in the cells for the night and her gamble had paid off. Yes, the long wait had been worth it.

'You must have known poor Annie Chapman,' she said, keeping in with the whore, as they arrived at the darkest and most private part of the small enclosed Mitre Square. 'Tragic what happened, poor woman.'

'Yes, I knew her well. She was a good friend of mine.'

'I'm sure she must have been, Catherine. It must have—'

'How comes you know my name, Midwife?' said Catherine, stopping in her tracks.

'Because, Annie told me.' The midwife's strong right hand was at the woman's throat in a flash. Tightening her grip she pushed her hard against the dank wall. 'She said you had someone's initials inked into your arm. And now I hear, from a war superintendent at the Mile End, that you came back from hop-picking to earn a reward. That you know who the Whitechapel murderer is.' Dropping her black bag to the floor she brought her other hand up and pushed both thumbs firmly into Catherine Eddowes' throat.

'You came all the way home just to see to it that my nephew would be hanged, did you?' Jacqueline's wild eyes glared at her terrified victim.

Fighting for breath, Catherine shook her head. Her bulging eyes stared into the midwife's face. Beyond the terror in her eyes, the midwife saw the expression of shocked revelation. 'That's right, Eddowes. You are about to get the same treatment as your best friend, Annie Chapman.' She smiled as she dug her thumbs in deeper and deeper, gritting her teeth. 'Burn in hell with all the whores,' she hissed, squeezing tighter and tighter until the head flopped forward and the spindly body went limp. Working quickly, she executed her rehearsed plan, carrying out the surgery to the letter, remembering in detail, all she had read. This must look like the work of a Free-mason.

Her task done, she wiped first her hands and then her knife on a piece of muslin and dropped both into her black medicine bag and snapped it shut. The adrenaline was pumping through her veins. Suddenly, from her dark place, she saw the glow from a police-man's lantern. To her relief the constable did little more than take a brief glance about himself before he retraced his steps and left. Her heart pounding, she walked through the square into Mitre Street, and thanked the Lord for His assistance. The constable had by the grace of God been slack in his duties.

It wasn't until she had reached the junction of Commercial Street and Commercial Road that she remembered Thomas's initials on the dead woman's body. But with her nephew shut up in an asylum it really made no difference and the initials TC could after all stand for many things. Homeward bound she began to feel calmer as a feeling of conquest swept through her. She had for certain exonerated Thomas from all guilt. The onus was no longer on him.

Meanwhile, just off Commercial Road, another murder had been committed and this one had nothing to do with the midwife. At 1.00 a.m. a Russian Jew, Louis Diemschutz, had pulled into Dutfield's Yard adjacent to the International Working Men's Educational Club in Berner Street when his pony shied to the left to avoid a dark object slumped close by the wall. It was the body of yet another woman. Striking a match the man noticed a pool of thick blood which was trickling down the yard. The corpse had a wide gash across the throat but no other signs of injury – this was not the mark of the Ripper. There was no sign of a struggle and the woman's clothes had not been disturbed. Only the soles of her boots were visible from beneath her full skirts.

Onlookers had been gathering outside the gates of the yard, silently watching and listening. Their panic and dread would have turned to hysteria had they known that just fifteen minutes' walk away, in a yard just off Aldgate High Street, another, more grisly, murder had taken place during the same hour as this one.

PC Watkins who had been the one to patrol Mitre Square had taken to his bed, swearing he would never police the streets again. The light from his bull's-eye lantern had illuminated Catherine Eddowes' body lying face up in a pool of blood. The smell of blood had been so fresh that he could feel the presence of death on that foggy night. Cursing the City police for not issuing their officers with whistles, he had had no choice but to turn and face whatever might be lurking in the shadows. Knowing that the night watchman on duty in the tea warehouse was a former constable had given him little comfort. Unable to remain calm he had strode to the entrance door of the warehouse and hammered continuously on the iron knocker. Arriving at the door, the watchman had cautiously peered at the officer, wondering if he had gone mad. 'You'll wake the entire neighbourhood carrying on like that,' he said, himself jittery.

'Come quick, there's been another murder,' was all the petrified man could manage to say. Staring down at Kate's mutilated face, he too went into shock. 'This is not the work of a human being,' he'd murmured. 'It can't be.' Turning away and retching in the gutter, PC Watkins begged the man to fetch help.

'I cannot fathom it,' was all he had managed to say in reply to Watkins who was by then begging him to get help. He himself was too shocked to walk. His legs had gone to jelly.

'It's the work of the devil,' said the watchman before turning on his heels and running away into the gloom, leaving the mortified police constable alone with the nightmare.

It didn't take long for the news to spread through the local markets where life went on twenty-four hours a day and Mitre Square soon became another macabre attraction.

Meanwhile, Sir Robert Anderson and Charles Cutbush sat in his office and could think of nothing to say. Two murders in one night was dreadful enough – the fact that they had happened while Thomas had been locked away *and* as it was most likely the killings had *not* been the work of the same evil man, made matters worse.

'It's simply not possible,' said Cutbush, 'everything points against it. We now have three killers on our hands.'

'Hell and damnation!' said Anderson, pushing a hand through his hair. 'There *must* be a connection.'

'Well . . . both women were known to be prostitutes, working the same patch.'

'Yes . . . ?'

'And yet . . . Elizabeth Pride only had her throat slit . . . and no more. No sign of a struggle; no evidence of rape. A crime of passion *or* revenge. How many more men will use this dreadful time to carry out their spitefulness under the cloak of the so-called Ripper?' Trying to induce some reaction from his colleague, Cutbush said, 'Do *you* think this could be a crime of passion?'

'Possibly.'

'So you're not convinced either.'

Lifting his head he gazed at Cutbush. 'You also have doubts then?'

'I do, Robert, I do.' He looked baffled. 'Whenever we take a step forward we seem to take six steps backwards.'

'Indeed. But we must come up with something, Charles – and soon. If we can prove to the public that Elizabeth Stride was not the work of the Ripper, that might help. What do we know of Stride?'

Charles let out a tired sigh. 'Not much. She spent the last three years with a waterside labourer – Michael Kidney. She was a heavy drinker but a good-looking Swedish woman. Her and Kidney seem to have lived harmoniously, most of the time.'

'Mmm.' Sir Robert shook his head. 'Well, I shall make my way over there now. I don't want them arresting him . . . yet.' Snapping himself out of the doldrums, Anderson stood up to leave. 'I would sooner we left your nephew where he is for the time being, Charles. Until we've learned more about these murders. What do you say?'

'I couldn't agree more. At least it's a relief knowing he's out of the way.'

Shaking hands, the men agreed to meet later at their club to reappraise the situation. 'I'll have a word with Swanson later today,' said Cutbush. 'I expect he'll be just as shocked as we are, I believe he was truly convinced that my nephew was the Ripper.'

When his cab arrived at the top end of Devonshire Street, Anderson cursed. The street was blocked with hundreds of sightseers, all greedy for the gruesome details.

Pushing his way through the crowd he approached one of the policemen and asked why they hadn't cordoned off the street. 'No time, sir,' was the reply. 'It's been like this since the morning papers went out. God knows how they managed to print the news so fast. I hear it's worse in Mitre Square than in Berner Street.'

'Damn nuisances! Grab a couple of constables and get them to clear a way through.'

'I'll do my best, sir.' The officer looked about him and shrugged. 'None of this lot can move an inch.'

'Well then why aren't your men clearing the streets, for God's sake?'

'We've been doing so all morning, sir. They just go around the block and come in at the opposite end to which they've been turned away.'

'Do what you can, sergeant. We must bring an end

to this fiasco soon. Keep up the men's spirits – it's going to be a very long day to which there is unlikely to be a break between this time and the same hour tomorrow.' With that Anderson walked away, heading for number thirty-six.

'*Evening Star*, sir! May we report that Mr Kidney is a suspect?'

'Keep them out of here,' growled Sir Robert to the officers on duty and all but barring the entrance.

'Do you expect to make an arrest today, sir!' called another reporter.

Ignoring them, he pushed his way through the other lodgers who had gathered in the passage and went directly into the deceased woman's lodging room. A man, with his back to the door, was staring out of a small window, into the backyard.

'Mr Kidney?' Anderson spoke in a quiet voice.

'Yes, sir, I'm Michael Kidney. And before you ask . . . no I did not murder my Liz.' He drew on a thin cigarette and shook his head, grief-stricken. 'I loved her.'

'So I gather.'

Kidney turned slowly to face Sir Robert with a stony-faced expression. It was obvious that the man was bottling grief and anger. 'From who did you gather it?'

'Oh come on, Kidney. You know how loose the tongue becomes where there's been a murder. Mention Long Liz and you hear Michael Kidney.'

'We were very close,' he said, turning away.

'Yes. But then you *are* known to be a jealous man,

Mr Kidney, and not long in temper. Was Elizabeth seeing someone else? Someone who threatened to take her from you?'

'She never went wiv anyone else. Never. She liked me better than any other man. She was a good girl. A bloody hard worker. Did a bit of charring an' a bit of sewin' too.'

'And occasionally ... went on the streets?' Sir Robert sat down on the one and only armchair.

'If she did, she kept that from me.'

'Well, if she did not, Mr Kidney, it seems unlikely that the Whitechapel murderer was responsible for her death. So far, he has directed his attention exclusively towards prostitutes, as you probably already know.'

'Well ... yes ... I s'pose she was known for earnin' 'er livin' like that, but only when she couldn't find other work.'

'And that made you angry?'

'I ignored it. Made out it wasn't 'appening.'

'But you had been quarrelling, Mr Kidney. So much so, that Elizabeth moved back into her old lodging rooms in Flower and Dean Street.'

'She was drinking too much, I told 'er not to. She left to teach me a lesson, that was all and it wasn't the first time. In all our three years, she's only bin away from me for five months altogether. It was always the drink that made 'er go.' A short silence followed.

'Didn't that annoy you, Mr Kidney? Her living a life quite separate from your own and you loving her the way you did.' Another silence followed. 'Mr Kidney? I asked you a question.'

'Yes!' He spun round to face his tormentor. 'Yes, it bloody annoyed me! Wouldn't it you?'

'It would, sir. I should be most upset if my wife were to behave so badly. And if I actually saw her with another man, someone she seemed fond of, well, who knows, maybe *I* would feel like cutting her throat. His too.'

Kidney pointed a trembling finger at the officer's face. 'Look, I've already told you – it wasn't me!'

As far as Sir Robert was concerned, there was no need for any more questions. He was convinced that this had been a crime of passion and that the poor bastard in front of him had been driven by jealousy to kill the woman he loved. Proving it, of course, was going to be impossible since Kidney would have secured an alibi to cover himself. To arrest him and then have to let him go was not an option in this sorry state of affairs. The people of the East End were hungry for the blood of *any* murderer they could lay their hands on. They would lynch him, no question of that . . . but the real maniac would still be on the loose and wallowing in his notoriety. Then, when he struck again, all hell would be let loose.

No, thought Anderson, Michael Kidney was not a psychotic killer. He could see that. There was a forlorn grief in his face and sorrow in his eyes. The Ripper would have no room for such sentiment.

Chapter Ten

Making her way to the tearooms where she hoped Sir Walter would be waiting, Mary tried to ignore the butterflies in her stomach. She had been awake on and off for most of the night wondering if he *had* been looking for her or if their meeting the day before was pure chance. Walking along the Waste towards the tearooms she could not help but hear the chatter going on all round her. The news placard outside a tobacconist's confirmed all that the newspaper boy was shouting as he wove his way through the packed pavements. The oglers were back. There had been a double murder in the wee hours of that very day. Shocked by this, Mary stopped dead in her tracks. Suddenly strange thoughts were flashing through her mind. How well did she know Sir Walter? Well enough to trust him implicitly? Well enough to know *for certain* that he wasn't the man the police were trying to track down? She glanced around her at the men standing in small groups, discussing the latest event. Any one of *them* could be the Ripper. Pushing fear aside she went into the tearooms only to find it chock-full with excitable customers who were chattering frantically as to who the serial killer might be and which of the accused written about in the papers was the most likely suspect.

Finding it impossible to see through the packed room, Mary pulled the door to and paused for a moment in the doorway. Deciding to give up on her meeting she wove her way rapidly through the crowds and hadn't gone far when a hand gripped her arm and stopped her short.

'Mary . . .'

It was Walter. She was confused. 'I can't see you, I must get home . . . I've left my little brother on his own . . .'

'Mary, listen to me! Please, please don't run off, I must speak with you.' He released his grip and apologised. 'I had to stop you, I couldn't lose you again. Please, let's talk, we could take a cab to a quieter part of town.'

'I don't know . . .' she said, avoiding those smouldering eyes of his. 'This news . . . this shocking news 'as put me all at sixes and sevens! All I want to do is run home and lock the door!'

'I know and I can understand why you feel frightened, you should be. Every woman must be on her guard. Especially—'

'Prostitutes?' she said, sharply.

'No, no, I didn't mean that.' He cupped her face and spoke very quietly. 'You might have been forced by tragic events to start on that road but thank God I met you before you were in the devil's claw.'

Disturbed by his choice of words, she found herself easing away from him. Again the question flew through her mind. Did she really know him well enough to put her trust in him? 'I must get back home to Arthur,' she said, 'maybe we can meet up some other time . . .'

'No, I can't let you slip away again. My life's been miserable thinking I might not see you again. Let me at least have the chance to explain *my* circumstances. I give my word not to bother you again once you've heard me out. I promise.'

'All right, but I mustn't be gone too long . . .'

'You have my word on it. A cab to Moorgate, fifteen minutes in a quiet coffee house and then a cab back home.' Unable to take his eyes from her face, he waited for her answer.

'Yes, Walter. I'll come with you.'

Once they were in a cab and on their way, Mary felt herself relax in his company. She did feel at ease with him and there was no denying the way she was feeling inside. No denying it and no way of describing it. Her heart simply felt different in his company. All pain and worry slipped away and the feeling of warmth was very welcome. If this was love and if he felt it too, it was everything that the poets said it was.

Settled at a small table for two in the quiet tasteful tearooms in Moorgate, Walter placed his hand on hers. 'You are pleased to see me?' he said, speaking with almost a broken voice.

'Of course I am.' She lowered her eyes, embarrassed. 'I've missed you. I didn't think I'd see you agen.'

'Wild horses could not keep me away. I'm going to

have to come to the point if I'm to keep my promise of just fifteen minutes.'

'Well we don't 'ave to be that strict. You can 'ave twenty minutes of my precious time,' she smiled.

Cupping both her hands in his, he leaned forward, creating the smallest of space between them. 'I meant all I said when we shared that special time at Lillian's house. And I believe you felt the same, but, if you have had a change of heart, I must know. I've not been able to sleep for thinking about you. We mustn't let it drag on.'

'Why would I 'ave had a change of heart? I wanted to see you but Lizzie said that my address wouldn't be given out and I never knew where you lived so . . .'

'I know,' he said, 'I know. And that's what I want to talk to you about.'

'How did you know where to find me?'

'Lizzie of course. She made me promise not to go to your house but I came very close to it, my sweet. Very close. You've not been out of my thoughts since we first met. You must have guessed that I'm married—'

'I'm not—'

'No! Please hear me out, then you may say your piece. Will you agree to that?'

'Go on then.' She looked at him, patiently.

'I'm not in a position to ask for your hand, otherwise I would do so without hesitation. I do have a wife already and I have two children. One is away at boarding school and the other is at home, she has a governess. My wife and I no longer share the same bed. Suffice to say that she herself instigated our separate rooms. She also suggested that I might take a lover. My immediate reaction was to reject the idea out of hand. There's no bad feeling between us though I will say ours was more of a drifting into marriage than anything else. Our families are close and we've known each other since we were children.'

'So, she's got someone else, is that what you're saying?'

'No. Well, in a way I suppose you could say that. She has many friends, but, a lover? No. Something happened when she gave birth to our second child and since then she's not in the least bit interested in that side of things. So, no . . . she doesn't have the desire for a lover. Her time is filled with arts and crafts and . . .'

Mary went quiet, trying to take all of this in. 'And she wouldn't mind if we became sweethearts? She *really* wouldn't mind?'

'No, she'd welcome it. It would take my attention away from her and her other favourite pastime: laudanum. Drugs mean more to her than any man could. I dare say she does flirt with those she mixes with from time to time but, frankly, I don't care any more. I stopped caring a long time ago. We stay together for the sake of the children. If you are agreeable I would like to keep our meetings secret. I don't want my wife or any of her friends finding out, and I wouldn't want my children to know. It would be just the two of us, darling. Then we can see how it develops, and take it from there . . .'

'Oh, Walter . . .'

'I don't presume that someone like yourself, sweet and innocent, would accept the offer I'm making but I had to at least ask.'

'Why wouldn't I want to see you in secret? The few meetings we've 'ad so far 'aven't exactly been public, 'ave they?'

He looked surprised. 'Am I to take that as a yes?'

She moved her face closer to his, their lips almost touching, and whispered, 'Yes.'

'And you won't mind the secret meetings?'

'No.' She was smiling at him now. Smiling from inside. 'Shall I tell you why? Why I'm happy to save myself for you and only for you?'

'Please do. I've been honest with you so . . .'

'You don't know?'

'I can hazard a guess but I daren't.'

'Well, you daft thing, it's because I love you, that's why.'

Touched, he could hardly speak. Clearing his throat, he began to put his proposition to her: 'I realise that the lovely little house you live in must have many happy memories—'

'Walter?' said Mary, cutting in. 'Did you hear what I said?'

'Yes, I heard. And I love you too. I love you more than I thought I could love anyone.' He turned away from her soft, beautiful eyes. He had to deliver the next bit of news and he had no idea how she would take it. He didn't want to lose her but could see no other way of making this work.

'I've been to look at a house in Bow. It's a ter-raced property and the owners are happy to leave it unfurnished. Their business has moved to another part of the country and they have no further need of a townhouse. It isn't spacious but it does have more rooms than you'll have been used to and the people are leaving all the curtains and . . .'

Mary placed a hand on his and spoke quietly. 'Walter . . . what are you telling me this for?'

'My dear Mary . . . would you agree to my renting the house for you and your brother to live in?'

'What . . . you mean . . . ? What's made you even think of such a thing? It's so generous of you, Walter, but it's not as if we're out on the streets. If I carry on seeing you at Lillian's once she opens up again and I keep on my work at the match-box factory, I can manage to keep me and Arthur out of the poorhouse.'

'But that's the whole point, darling, I don't want you to go to Lillian's house any more, even if it is only to see me. And I don't want you to slave away at that factory. You deserve more, you deserve better. It wasn't your fault that your father and mother died so unexpectedly leaving you to bring up Arthur on your own. And in any case, I *want* you to live in a house where I can come and go freely and stay the night from time to time . . . if that appeals to you.'

'Sounds very cosy, sounds like we'd be nearly mar-ried,' said Mary, grinning. 'Nearly a married couple.'

'But would "nearly" be enough?'

'I reckon it would, Walter . . . I reckon it would.'

Unable to contain his joy, he went on rapidly, 'It would be like starting anew. If you don't like the curtains they have left you can change them. Go shopping with Lizzie, pick whatever you want. Arthur would have his own rooms if he wanted, at the top of the house. He could invite his friends to stay whenever he wanted. And there's a bachelor room where I could sleep when I stay—'

'Oh . . . so you wouldn't wanna stay in my bedroom then? Gone off me before I've even moved in?'

'You can be a tease, you know. Of course I would love to share your bed but you might not want that all the time.'

'I'd be very, very happy to be your kept woman,' she said, unable to resist teasing him even more.

'You would be my *mistress*,' he said, correcting her. 'And if I wasn't already married you would be my wife.'

'"Mistress",' said Mary. 'I like the sound of that. Explaining it to Arthur might be difficult though. We'd 'ave to change his school as well, if we move out to Bow. It might not be so—'

'We could easily get him into a good school, or he could have a private tutor. Whichever you prefer.'

'No private tutor. No. He should go to school and mix with children of 'is own age and type. Bow's all right, I should know, it's where I work. So I would save on fares and even walk to work when the weather's fine.'

'I don't think you quite understand. My financial resources are such that you wouldn't have to go to work. I intend to give you a monthly allowance which should be more than adequate for your upkeep.'

She studied his face. Did he really expect her to give up her job? Her independence? 'I could never agree to that,' she said, 'I love my work at the match factory. I'm learning Pitman's shorthand soon, and I would miss all my workmates.'

'As you wish, sweetheart, but you must accept an allowance to meet all the overheads.'

'When can I see the house then?'

Charmed as ever by her straightforward manner, he couldn't help smiling. 'As soon as you like, it's vacant now, you could move in tomorrow if you wanted.'

'No, that's far too soon. I've got to get Arthur used to the idea; maybe in a couple of weeks? Would that be all right; say in two weeks' time?'

'All right, two weeks.' He sighed contentedly and leaned back.

'I don't think I should tell Arthur that you're married already. I'll tell 'im you're my sweetheart and you work out of town for most of the time. If that's all right?'

'Whatever you think best. I just wish I could introduce you into my life properly, but I can't at the present. We must be discreet.'

'The tearoom in Whitechapel after work'll suit me fine until we're settled in Bow.'

'The tearoom it is, then.'

Later that day having given in to Arthur's pestering, Mary allowed him to go with Harriet to visit her family across the river. She then busied herself with her Saturday chores of washing and cleaning the house.

When the midwife left her house to visit Thomas, Mary was using red polish on her doorstep.

'What a sight for sore eyes you are, Mary,' said Jacqueline, 'and what a lovely front door you keep.'

'Oh, Miss Turner,' said Mary, heaving herself up from her knees. 'I'm making the most of the lovely weather. Fancy us having a bit of sunshine at this time of year.'

'The last of the autumn sun is always the best, Mary. Cold air to kill off the germs and sunshine to provide the vitamin we'll need in store for winter.'

Seeing the midwife in the daylight shifted any doubts of menace from her mind. The midwife looked perfectly familiar in her smart uniform. It was only the black bag she carried which now looked sinister – and all because of the newspaper reports. Her long dark cape and hat looked quite natural during the daylight hours.

'I was wondering about Thomas, Miss Turner. We invited 'im to join us for a night out at the music hall but he never turned up? I trust he's not ill?'

'No, no, Thomas is quite well. He's found himself proper work and that seems to keep him occupied for most of the time.' Jacqueline took this opportunity to test Mary. 'When he's not working as a freelance journalist or canvassing the encyclopaedia, he's out in the streets, training.'

'Training? What for?' said Mary, already disturbed at the news of his new occupation as a snoop.

'I doubt it will come to anything but it occupies his inquisitive mind. He's taken it upon himself to be a sleuth. His new mission is to identify and report to the police all the brothels in the area. So we should be relieved, he'll have less time to harass the public with the Bible.'

Immediately on her guard, she shrugged and said, 'He'll 'ave his work cut out, Miss Turner, 'specially if he wants to list all the bad places in Shoreditch and Bethnal Green. Never mind down by the river.' Best to make light of it, she thought.

'Oh, he's not bothering himself with the obvious, you know Thomas, he's after the whore-houses that operate in secret. But there . . . what would someone as well brought up as yourself know about those kind of places.'

'Nothing at all, really, Miss Turner, and thank goodness for that. Do you think that Jack the Ripper haunts the brothels now, then?'

'We can't be sure of anything he does now,' said the midwife, walking away slowly. 'We can no longer be sure of any one thing or any one person, Mary.'

Mary felt uneasy. It sounded like Miss Turner was making a veiled accusation; a threat even. Whatever it was, it mattered not – soon she would be moving away. Screwing the lid on to her jar of polish she glanced along the turning and had a vision of herself and Arthur playing in the street as children. Here were her roots but here no longer were her parents. It *was* time for her to move away and make a new start. Even if Walter were to change his mind she knew now that she could no longer live in this street. She would have to find another small house or rooms to rent for her and Arthur. Especially now, in these dangerous times.

Chapter Eleven

Ducking and diving through the stalls, carts and milling crowds of shoppers in Middlesex Market, Arthur found it increasingly difficult to keep up with Harriet. 'You're gonna 'ave to learn 'ow ta dodge, Arfer,' she said, pulling at his sleeve. 'Come on, I can see a click, an' bloomin' well run when I says so!'

Filled with a mixture of fear and vexation at her bossiness, he pulled his arm away. 'Where? Where's there a click?'

'Her in red, all done up like a Christmas cracker. She's a posh cock, all right. I bet 'er and the other tart's bin blacking their noses round where the murders 'appened.'

'I thought we was gonna go and 'ave a look *before* we did a click,' said Arthur, hoping to delay the snatching of a purse.

'Well we ain't. It'll be jammed with nosy parkers be now.' Harriet kept her sights fixed on the woman. 'I'll touch 'er an' then pass her pogue to you, right? Then you're off in a click, stop for nuffin'. I'll meet yer outside the railway station.' She peered into Arthur's face. 'Don't look so bleedin' worried! You'll give us away, and shut yer mouth before a fly gets in.

She slipped between the two well-dressed women, knocking the taller one's shopping basket flying. 'Oh, Lord luv us, I'm really sorry! Don't beat me, lady, please don't whip me!' She cowered back, convincingly. 'I'm just a cockney. I never meant no 'arm.'

Retrieving her basket and picking up the scattered fruits she had just purchased, the woman smiled benignly. 'Silly thing. No harm will come to you, it was an accident, but you really must be more careful in the future.'

Backing up close to Arthur, Harriet pushed the purse into his hands and gave a back-heel to his shin. Spinning round to face him, she begged him most theatrically not to strike her for bumping into him too. She then mouthed one word to him – Click!

Wide-eyed, Arthur froze and then, seized by panic, dodged his way through the crowd. 'I never meant to 'urt yer!' Harriet yelled, once he had made his escape.

'Poor nervous wretch,' murmured the woman.

Harriet was quick to respond. 'I never meant you no 'arm eiver, lady, I wasn't looking, that's all.'

'And we wish you no harm, my dear. Here . . .' she offered an orange.

'Cor, fanks, missus.' She flashed a smile, grabbed the orange and darted away. 'Gawd bless yer!' she called back, mimicking the women from the Old Jago in Bethnal Green.

'We really must do more for these street children,' Sophia Barclay-Smith, a banker's wife, murmured. 'I feel so ashamed in their company.'

★   ★   ★

Clutching their small paper parcels of hot faggots and peasepudding, purchased with their ill-gotten gains, Harriet and Arthur boarded an omnibus towards Camberwell to visit Harriet's mother and sister. As Arthur wolfed into his surprise feast, he glanced around at the other passengers, hoping that Harriet wouldn't gloat over their adventure in her usual 'couldn't give a toss' manner. Slipping a greasy hand into his breeches pocket he caressed the half-crown he had earned. There had been two of them in the purse, together with a sixpence and a couple of pennies. Harriet had kept the small change saying it was her who had set it up.

The buzz of conversation on board caught both their imaginations. The adults were, in turn, giving their opinions as to the cause of so many dreadful murders in Whitechapel. They were talking about the East End as if it were a different place to the one Harriet and Arthur knew.

'I'm surprised anyone dare go out during the day, never mind after dusk,' said a rotund woman wearing a large black and red feathered hat.

'Most of the men look as if they should be in gaol,' said another. 'I pity the children. I should think they would all be better off in a children's home.'

Harriet dug her elbow into Arthur's side to get his attention. Grinning, she winked at him. 'When's your old man getting out then?'

Arthur turned his head and looked out of the window, his cheeks burning. He knew what she was up to.

'My old gel said if I don't git out there on the game soon, she's gonna put me in the cellar wiv me baby bruvver. He's bin locked down there since he was born. If I never took 'im a crust of bread now an' then, he'd 'ave starved to death. Ain't got no flesh on 'im to speak of.'

The omnibus went very quiet. 'I keep telling me muvver that one of these days farver'll find out and she'll get 'er froat slit. He was in prison when little George was born. He's the rent man's be all accounts. But the rent man says it's the coalman's. And the coalman pointed the finger at the milkman.'

Unable to stop himself, Arthur began to laugh. He nudged her with his knee, but she wasn't easily stopped.

'Still, once gran comes out of the nut'ouse, she'll soon sort 'im out. She poisoned 'im y'know? Rat poison it was. Didn't put enough of it in though. I told 'er but she never listened. He drank all of the tea though. I'll get 'er to show you 'er witches box when we go an' visit 'er. Got all sorts of fings in there. A lump of someone's hair tied wiv wool, a fingernail, a chicken's claw wot's bin dipped in 'uman blood—'

'Look!' Sitting bolt upright, Arthur dug her in the ribs. 'Over there. Just goin' into the Lambeth Asylum. It's the midwife, Miss Turner!'

Leaning across him, she dropped the remains of her faggot on to the floor and gasped. 'Stone me dead, you're right!'

Turning in their seats they peered out of the back

window of the bus as the horses galloped on and the figure of Jacqueline diminished.

'I told yer! You wouldn't listen though, would yer?' Harriet said. 'He's bleeding well bonkers. They've locked 'im up at last, thank gawd!'

'How d'yer know who she's visiting? Might be 'er sister.'

'Both of 'em more like. We 'aven't seen Daft Thomas all week, 'ave we, and now we knows why.' She slumped back in her seat. 'I'm gonna 'ave to find out wot's goin' on in that 'ouse.'

Aware that the rest of the passengers were looking at her, appalled, she poked out her tongue just as the horses drew up to let some of them off.

'Is this Camberwell, mister?' hollered Harriet to the driver.

'No, I told yer twice, I'll let you know when we're there; soddin' kids!'

'Miserable bleeder,' she murmured, turning to Arthur who was looking away from her again and staring out of the window. She turned her attention to the other passengers, and focused on a snotty-nosed nine-year-old dressed in her Sunday best.

'I fancy summink nice,' she said, peering at the girl's bag of sweets.

'Manners, Rachel. Pass the bag,' said her mother, fearful of what might happen if she didn't. A look of disdain on her face, the girl stretched an arm across to Harriet, offering a humbug.

'No, darling! Give . . . give her the bag,' she added impatiently.

Again the girl looked disbelievingly at her mother. 'All of them?'

'Of course.' The woman wiggled the tips of her fingers at her daughter and then cast a look at Harriet's grubby hands.

'Oh, yes, Mummy, of course,' she smiled and handed over the bag, careful not to touch Harriet.

'Fanks. Very generous. Gawd bless yer 'eart.' Harriet shoved a piece in her mouth and passed the bag to Arthur. 'You know what,' she said, her mouth full, 'a bit of dirt is good for yer!' Then, putting her mouth to Arthur's ear whispered, 'It got us this bag of humbugs.' Their rising laughter filled the otherwise silent carriage.

'We won't be stopping long at your aunt's 'ouse, will we?' said Arthur, once he'd settled down and had time to think. He didn't like the sound of Harriet's family and he didn't want to see her gran.

'Nar. Jus' wanna see me mum's all right and that. We'll 'ave a cup of tea and then get out. I never like me aunt and uncle 'cos they never took to me. Do you know wot he used to say, my uncle? He used to say I'd bin 'ere before.' She curled her top lip, 'You'd fink he'd show me a bit of respect if he fawt that. Silly old sod. I fink I frightened 'im. Dunno why.'

'So we won't be stopping long then?'

'No, Arfer, we defnit'ly won't be stoppin' long!'

'D'yer reckon the midwife was going in to see Thomas to fetch 'im 'ome?'

'I never said I was a mind-reader, I said I was born wiv knowledge. Fetch 'im 'ome, I reckon. Soon as we're back I'm gonna make plans to get into that place of 'ers and 'ave a butcher's round. Summink ain't right there . . . Bodies in the walls, I reckon.'

A few days later, while Arthur was at school and Mary at work, Harriet lay on her bed, thinking. Thinking about her mother and small sister. They had looked happier than she had seen them for a long time and her aunt and uncle were more relaxed than before. But it had been clear to Harriet from the moment she stepped inside the house, that one more living there would be a burden, especially if it was her. She had gone overboard to tell them how happy she was, living with Arthur and Mary so long as she could come back and visit them now and then. That seemed to ease the mood straight away.

'You'll be ten soon Harriet and leaving school,' her uncle had said. 'I expect you'll find work in a small shop or café. Save your pennies and your pounds will take care of themselves. You'll soon make your way in the world.'

She had smiled at him and made promises that she had no intention of keeping. She could earn more money in the markets fetching and carrying for the vendor and would make even more on picking pockets and doing a click now and then.

'Mary pays me well for being 'er 'ousemaid,' she had fibbed. 'So I'll be able to come and see you more often.'

'Good girl,' her uncle had said while pressing a silver threepenny-bit into her hand.

Staring up at the ceiling, Harriet's thoughts turned to Jacqueline Turner and the asylum. She felt sure she had been visiting Thomas. Everything pointed to it. But why had he suddenly been taken in there? was the question on her mind. Leaping off her bed she made a snap decision to go along to Miss Turner's and ask if she could do a bit of cleaning or run errands for her. She could have a little snoop round while the midwife was out. She wouldn't steal anything. If her father had taught her anything it was to never take from those who looked after your welfare. 'Don't bite the 'and that bleedin' well feeds yer,' was what he had said *and* more than once.

Locking Mary's front door, Harriet made her way up to Jacqueline's house and knocked three times. This was something else she had remembered from her dad. 'One knock and someone wants summink; two and it'll be the boys in blue; three is friendly.'

Waiting for Jacqueline to answer the door, Harriet peered up at the bedroom window. That was the room she wanted to get into. Downstairs had secrets but upstairs beckoned mysteriously. Upstairs where Harriet had not yet been – upstairs where no one had yet been except the midwife.

'Harriet?' There was no sign of a smile. 'Shouldn't you be at school?'

'I did go. They chucked me out,' she said, convincingly. 'Said I've gotta go to the school near the Old Jago where I used to go.'

'Well, then, you should have gone there.' Not pleased, she stood aside and waved her in. 'Your

278

brains will go dull if you do nothing. The idle mind turns dark with time.'

'I know. I was lonely by meself an' I've come to ask if I could maybe do a bit of 'ousework for yer, like polish the brass and black the irons or summink. You don't 'ave to pay me, I jus' wanna keep meself busy.'

'I would sooner you were at a desk, Harriet, truly I would.' She peered down at the skinny waif. 'Are you hungry?'

'Nar. I 'ad some bread and drippin' before I come out.'

'Came out. Your grammar needs attention, no mistake.' She looked round the room. 'I suppose you could polish the brass . . .'

'I'm gonna read them books you borrowed me . . . once I've used up a bit of energy. I've got too much of it, that's the trouble.'

'Is that what your mother used to say?' said Jacqueline, warming yet again to her.

'Nar. Me dad used to, jes before he sent me out on an errand or got me to dig up some veg'tables from the backyard an' that.' She peered at an ornate brass kettle by the fireside. 'I know you don't use that no more, Midwife, but it could'n arf do with a polish. Should be able to see yer face in brass, you know.' She looked appealingly at Jacqueline. 'I will do a bit of writing an' all. I'll show it to yer once you get back.'

'Who said I was going out?'

'You're always on the bleedin' move, ain't yer? Always having to go somewhere. I dunno 'ow you get time to make yer 'ouse nice like it is – as well as work all the hours Gawd sends yer.'

Pouring them both some lemon fizz, Jacqueline found herself smiling. 'The windows are a bit grubby as a matter of fact. You could clean those for me.'

'Course. I'm good at that, I fink glass should shine so it looks like a mirror.' She slumped down into an armchair. 'An' I'll keep the fire in, so it'll be nice for when you come back. You work too bleedin' 'ard, that's the trouble.' She sounded more like an old woman than a child.

'All right, Harriet, you've twisted my arm. But don't go cooking anything. I don't want to have to come home and find you with a blister or two. I prefer to leave nursing people at my door, if you don't mind.'

'You've gotta eat, Miss Turner, and I've bin cooking for years.'

'No. And that's my final word on it. I shall warm up a drop of mutton stew from yesterday once I'm finished with work.' She unhooked her long cape from the hat stand and fastened it around her neck. 'You'll find a bucket next to the boiler in the scullery and some old newspaper under the cushion of that chair your sitting on. Wet that to clean the windows. The ink from the print is a good cleaner.'

'Well I ain't ever 'eard of that before, I normally use an old rag. Where's your Thomas, by the way? I ain't seen 'im lately.'

Jacqueline studied her face in the mirror and then fixed her dark hat. 'He's in full-time employment now and too tired to come and visit me in the evenings.'

'Ah. That'll be it then. D'yer wanna cup o' tea before you go out?'

'No. But one when I come back would be appreciated. Don't bother with the upstairs windows. Just this room and the back scullery. It may be too cold to do the outsides. I'll leave that to you to decide.' She placed a hand on the doorknob. 'Don't let any strangers in. In fact, don't let *anyone* in. Is that clear?'

'No fear of that, I would never dream of it, speshully wiv all these murders an' that.'

Jacqueline left the house smiling to herself. The child had a woman's head on her shoulders, no mistake. A harsh life had forced her to grow up far too soon.

Alone and warming her hands by the fire, Harriet reckoned it would be safe to go upstairs for a look round after five minutes or so. Give the midwife time in case she got so far in the turning and remembered that she'd forgotten something and returned. She pulled the old newspapers from under the cushion and began to fold the pages into small pads. She would clean the windows after she had satisfied her curiosity as to what there was about this house that caused there to be a certain look on the outside and even on the pavement in front of it. A certain feeling and a certain appearance.

Sure that the midwife was well and truly on her way to see her patient, Harriet approached the dark narrow staircase with trepidation. Her heart began to beat faster as she stepped cautiously up the wooden stairs. With her good ear to the fore, she listened for any unusual sounds. Apart from the wind rattling the window panes, there was nothing much else.

'If anyone's bleedin' well up there, they'd best call out now!' she said, her voice quieter than she wanted it to be. She didn't want anyone who might be hiding to think she was afraid of them. Satisfied, she stomped upwards banging the heels of her boots as she went. 'I don't care if there is anyone upstairs!' she said. 'I've got a blooming job to do and do it I must. I'm gonna clean all the windows for Miss Turner!'

Arriving on the dark and cramped landing, she felt the hairs on the back of her neck prickling. Being braver than she had ever been before, to her mind, slowly she pushed open the door which was slightly ajar, and crept inside. It was Jacqueline's bedroom. She stood nervously in the middle of the room and drank it all in, mesmerised by the many books, pictures and ornaments. There wasn't a space which hadn't been filled. Old framed photos covered the wall above the tiny black iron fireplace while old calendars and paintings decorated every other wall. Ornaments were crammed on to the mantelshelf and two mahogany whatnot stands. Next to the bed which was pushed against a wall, there was a narrow dark oak cupboard. On it was a Bible, another book, a pair of glasses and a candle in a pewter holder.

The small bureau under the window attracted Harriet and she felt a wave of excitement fill her bones as she tiptoed towards it. The top, covered in red leather was worn and faded and there were three small Waterman's Ideal Ink bottles in a row, violet, red, and black. Jacqueline's long, tapered quill lay in a wooden container. Heaving the heavy desk chair back, Harriet sat down. She opened the desk drawer which was full of all kinds of stationery, spare candles, safety pins, and – a diary. Carefully lifting it out and marking exactly where she must replace it, so as not to be found out, she opened the book at random and tried to read a word here and there. All that she had bragged to Arthur about had been a white lie. She could read, but mostly those words off the advertisement boards which had a picture of the product, or small easy words. The first line that she tried to make out, read: *I did not give the abortion but I shall murder the whore. Chapman must die or all else will fall about us.*

Too absorbed in her effort of trying to make sense of what she saw, she could have no idea of the perilous situation in which she was placing herself. Harriet turned the pages, trying to read bits here and there, skipping words which had more than three letters. It wasn't until she thought she heard the sound of the street door opening that she realised she was trembling with mixed emotions. Quickly closing the journal she listened but the house was quiet. Opening the drawer, which was stiff and jerked with each pull, she was sure she heard the staircase creaking. Petrified, she froze, and as the bedroom door creaked and slowly opened she stared into the hardened face of the midwife.

'I did tell you *not* to come up here, child.' Her voice low and forbidding. Harriet opened her mouth to say something but the severe expression on Jacqueline's face made her think twice.

'I left my notebook and pen behind and cursed all the way back. Now I can see it was a blessing in disguise. I've caught you red-handed, young lady, and I can't say I'm best pleased. How dare you come up here when I had told you not to. And you dare to sit at my bureau and rifle through my private papers?'

Close to crying, Harriet swallowed and just managed to say, 'I was dusting.'

'You were reading my journal, my private journal. How dare you do such a thing!'

Quaking in her shoes, Harriet eased the diary back into the drawer. 'I wanted to make it nice up 'ere for yer. I never read any of it. I swear to God.'

'Are you a liar as well as a sneak, Harriet?'

'No, Miss Turner, I was dusting it, that's all. The page fell open but I never looked at it. Anyway, I can't read, not properly anyway, just a few simple words. I just said I could read to get at Arfer.'

'Where is your duster?' The grim expression on the midwife's face was fixed.

'I never use a cloth to polish, just me 'and. The sweat from the palm's good for levver. Ask anyone who chars.'

Jacqueline stepped into the room and removed her hat. 'You know what I despise more than thieving, Harriet, or snooping, for that matter? Lies, Harriet . . . lies. I cannot bear it when someone stands in front of me and tells a bare-faced lie.' She dropped her hat on to the bed. 'You have read some of the novel I am writing and you're frightened by it, I'm pleased about that. But don't lie to me in the future. One day, it might be published and I shall be famous. Then you can tell people that you saw it before anyone else; then and only then. Do you understand me, Harriet?'

'Course I do. I said this 'ouse 'ad secrets and it 'as. You're a secret writer and much better'n Charles Dickens. I couldn't put it dahn once I started. Mind you, I never got the big words but I could see it was a good story.' Suddenly and without any doubt, Harriet knew that she had been caught in a trap.

'So . . .' said Jacqueline, smiling at her as she unhooked her cloak '. . . what do you think, young Harriet, would people ever buy it?'

'I bet they would and you'd get paid 'undreds of pounds for it.'

'Now, wouldn't that be something,' she said. 'I would be a wealthy lady sailing off to America.' The midwife walked slowly towards the window and stood so close to Harriet that they were almost touching. She gazed down on to the street. 'But I would miss living here, of course.'

'No you wouldn't,' said Harriet, on her feet and backing away towards the door.

'It may not be much of a turning,' said the midwife, going to the door and closing it, 'but I was born in this street, in the big house at the end. I moved in here when my father passed away. I didn't care for all that space, with no one to share it.' She sat on the edge of the bed and patted the space beside her. 'Come and sit down and I'll tell you all about it, the way life was then, different to now of course. Much nicer in those days.'

'Oh well, everyfing changes, don't it? Ne'mind, eh? So . . . I'd best go down there and make that cuppa tea . . . I meant to put the kettle on to boil but—'

'But you came up here instead.' She patted the space again and the expression on her face told Harriet that she had best do as she was asked. She did. 'There is another room, you know, next to this one. It's very small, but it would have made a nice bedroom for you. I was thinking about that at one time. I was going to take you in and look after you.' She stroked Harriet's pale face. 'I'm very upset and feel let down by all of this, Harriet.'

'I wasn't gonna pinch anyfing, Miss Turner.' She wiped away an escaping tear. 'I just got carried away when I saw them stairs. I wanted to know wot it was like up 'ere, that's all. I was only looking . . .'

'Looking? Harriet,' she said, reading her face, 'looking for what? What stories have you been listening to out there? Has young Arthur or his sister Mary been filling your head with nonsense?'

'Nar. They don't even know I'm 'ere. Mary wouldn't be best pleased.' Harriet was beginning to feel safe again. The midwife was talking properly now and her face was relaxed. 'Mary's at the match factory and Arfer's at—'

'Good,' said the midwife, nodding at Harriet. 'That's good.' Then with not the slightest warning or hint of malice, Jacqueline lunged a hand forward and clamped it across Harriet's mouth, her other hand gripping her head. 'Silly girl,' she said, 'causing me to do such a thing.'

With Harriet's back pulled in tight to Jacqueline's fleshy body, the midwife was seething. 'I should have known not to trust someone from the Jago. Too soft, that's my trouble. Well no more of it, we shall see a change. Why does everyone seek to take advantage of me? Thomas; Mary Dean; most of my mothers, when they can; and now a child of ten tries to trick me . . . trick me into trusting her in my house.'

Harriet was trembling. She could hardly breathe let alone speak, with the strong fingers clamped over her mouth. But she could listen *and* she could think. She had been right in her first appraisal of Miss Turner and her daft nephew, Thomas. She had been right about the house having secrets, and now her sixth sense was screaming at her to hold still and stay calm.

After wrapping a small linen hand towel around Harriet's mouth and tying it at the back, Jacqueline reached out a hand for the cord of her dressing gown and pulled it from the loops then she wrapped this around Harriet's thin body, pinning her arms. Even if the girl couldn't read that well, and even though the midwife's own handwriting was not the clearest, this child had gone too far. Who knows what she might have learned from the journal? She needed time to plan her next move. Until then she would have to keep Harriet here; no way could she set her free.

Once she had tied Harriet's ankles together with twine, she dragged her into the boxroom. 'There isn't a bed in here so you must lie on the floor for now,' said Jacqueline, her voice strangely remote. 'I'll fetch a pillow and blanket before I go out. One of my mothers is expecting me.' She threw Harriet to the floor and towering above her, said, 'I've never let a soul down yet and I don't intend to start now. I shall fully deserve my trip when I sail away from England.'

She stood in the doorway, glaring down at Harriet's frightened face. 'I shan't be gone long and when I come back, if I find you have tried to do anything else to annoy me – I shall be *really* cross.' She left the room but soon returned with some bedding.

'The best thing you can do is try to sleep, Harriet. I shall be gone for an hour and no more, probably less.' With that she closed and locked the door behind her.

Once alone in the house, Harriet, in that small room which had a tiny window, began to cry. The more she pulled at the twine binding her wrists the more it cut into her skin. She had no choice other than to lie still and hope that the midwife, once she returned, would relent and let her go. She would plead for forgiveness. Say how bad it was that she had gone into the bedroom and looked at her things. She would promise to go away and never set foot in Whitehead Street again, nor would she. All she wanted now was to be back in the Jago, in the stable, with the horses, and the kind coalman who fed her on oats in hot tea. Without realising, Harriet was really crying for her mother. She was whimpering and whining like a dying kitten and she was saying the same word over and over, through her tears, *Mummy*.

Returning home from school, Arthur was surprised to find the house dark and cold. The fire had gone out and there was no sign of Harriet. Calling out to her, he checked both bedrooms upstairs, and went out into the backyard and to the lavatory in case the outside bolt had slipped, locking her inside. When he was fully convinced that she was not there, he twisted some old newspapers and built a fire with a little kindling and coal. That done he went upstairs and pulled a cover from his bed and took it back downstairs. Drawing the armchair as close to the fire as possible, he wrapped the cover round himself and waited until he had warmed enough to go into the kitchen and make a pot of tea.

Staring into the pathetic flames of the fire which seemed as if it would never burn up, he wondered where Harriet could be. He imagined she must have gone out to do a click and had been caught and taken to the police station. Or maybe she *had* done a click and gone to see her mother and sister and decided not to come back. He glanced at the clock on the mantelshelf. Mary wouldn't be home from the match factory for another two hours and he was hungry. Going into the scullery he cut a wedge of bread and spread some lemon curd on to it. He told himself that once the house was warm he would set about preparing dinner the way he had seen Harriet do it. She had never peeled the vegetables but had given them a good scrub with Mary's nail-brush and he reckoned he could manage that, if nothing else.

Back in his chair by the fire, he wolfed into the bread, believing that Harriet would be back soon. But as the clock ticked in the silent room he began to think about days gone by, when his mother was *always* there for him and his dad coming in from work, smiling and rubbing his hands together, pleased to be home. In those days there was always a fire burning in the grate and the smell of something stewing in the big pot over the copper boiler. Boiled bacon, carrots, parsnips and herbs filled his mind.

'Why does everything keep changing, God?' he murmured. 'Why did Daddy and Mummy 'ave to die and then our new baby sister? Did we do something wrong, God? Was you angry wiv me or Mary for something?' Seconds later the tears were rolling down his cheeks. He was lonely. Lonely and frightened, worried that something might have happened to Harriet and that something might happen to Mary on her way home from work in the dark or when she went out typewriting again. They still hadn't caught Jack the Ripper.

By the time Mary came in from work, Arthur had cried himself to sleep on the armchair under his blanket, and the fire had gone out – it had never really got started properly. Lighting the gas mantels, Mary peered at her little brother and smiled. She could see that he had made an attempt at lighting a fire.

Moaning and turning in his sleep, Arthur's sleepy eyes soon opened to the face of his beloved sister who was gently stroking his hair. 'Trust bloomin' Harriet to let the fire go out. Where is she, upstairs reading old comics she got off the rag-and-bone man?'

'No . . .' said Arthur, yawning. 'She wasn't in when I came 'ome from school. I fink she's run away.'

'Don't be silly, course she's not. She's probably up

at Miss Turner's earning a couple of coppers. Didn't she say she was gonna go up and ask for work?'

'Yeah, but not today. She never said anyfing this morning about it.'

'Well you know Harriet,' she said smiling. 'Now then, how about if I go out an' get us all some chips to go wiv a nice bit of meat I bought on the way 'ome?'

'No. Jack the Ripper's out there, you stay here, an' I'll go an' get 'em. Wot about Harriet though?' Arthur sat up and folded his blanket.

'Well,' said Mary, remaking the fire, 'how about if we 'ave a nice cup of tea by ourselves and cuddle up by the fire once it gets goin', and then I'll go up the midwife's and see if she's there. How about that?' She tousled his mop of hair. 'Sound all right to you?'

'Yeah. Could I 'ave a biscuit wiv me tea?'

'Oh, I reckon we can manage that,' she said, going into the kitchen. In truth, she had been putting on a brave face. All the signs pointed to Harriet having not been in the house for best part of the day. She hadn't carried out any of her chores from what Mary could tell, and that wasn't like her. For all her faults and her swearing, the girl was hardworking and very reliable. It simply wasn't like her not to be there for Arthur when he came home from school and for her to be out on Mary's arrival was totally out of character.

'I said I'd go over to Billy's after tea to play draughts!' called Arthur, more settled now that Mary was home. 'His mum always asks if I want a boiled egg wiv 'im. What shall I say this time?'

Mary came back into the room. 'Say yes, Arthur. If you've said no all the other times we're not taking liberties. You might as well eat there if she *really* don't mind.'

'She never minds. It's 'cos Billy's an only child. She sees me as 'is adopted brother. That's wot she says anyway.'

'Well,' said Mary, 'I think that's really nice. I expect they're a bit lonely as well, what with 'is dad going off. In any case, Lizzie's coming round soon, so I can sit with my mate while you sit with yours.'

'And when Harriet comes in you can send 'er over as well. They fink she's a loada laughs.'

'I think I'll just pop along to Miss Turner's to see if she's there,' said Mary, worried. 'I don't want 'er to overstay 'er welcome. I'll pour the water into the teapot and you can let it brew for a minute or two. Be careful when you pour yours out though.'

'I've done it before, Mary. Stop mollycoddlin' me.'

Arriving at Jacqueline's door, Mary had, for some inexplicable reason, a strong feeling that she was going to be disappointed and not find Harriet there. Mary knocked and when the midwife came to the door, she looked slighted. 'Yes, Mary, what is it?'

'I . . . er I'm sorry to disturb you, Miss Turner, but I wondered if Harriet might be with you?' She smiled at her neighbour. 'Arthur thinks she's run away.'

'Well if she has gone, I should check that nothing's missing. I found her in the gutter, remember, and she's more used to people from the Old Jago.'

'Oh *I* don't think she's gone off. It was Arthur who—'

'Well she's not here and I *am* rather busy, I've not been long in from a full day.' She waited and then said, 'Was there anything else, Mary?'

'No, no . . . sorry, I was drifting. I expect she'll be back soon. She won't be missing for long. She loves living with us so she'd 'ardly run away, would she?'

'Don't bank on it. Your way of life may seem cleaner and healthier, but there isn't much excitement for a girl like her. She might well have been missing the coarse jokes and the thieving.'

'Let's 'ope not, eh? I don't suppose Thomas has seen her?'

'Thomas isn't here.'

'Ah. He's . . . all right, is he . . . Thomas? Only we've not seen 'im for a while and he never turned up at the music hall that night . . .'

'Thomas is fine, he's in full-time employment now. Well if that's all then, Mary . . .'

'Yes, thanks. If you see Harriet when you're out on your rounds you might tell her we're worried. Could you do that for me?'

'If I see her I shall let you know.' With that the midwife closed her door and left Mary puzzled as to why she was so curt with her.

Walking back to her house she saw the familiar figure of her friend Lizzie strolling along. This brought a smile to her face.

'What's up with you?' said Lizzie, meeting her on the doorstep.

'Harriet's gone missing. She's been gone since this morning.'

'Tch. Missing? It's not even one day. She'll be back soon with 'er booty.'

Later, once Arthur had gone to his friend's house and the girls were sitting by the fireside, Mary filled Lizzie in on all that Walter had offered. Instead of surprise and joy over the news, Lizzie looked a touch concerned. Sir Walter was, after all said and done, a comparative stranger to Lillian and the House of Assignation. They knew little about him and he had seemed to come in out of the blue and with no personal recommendation. It was his obvious wealth, appearance and accent that had impressed her mother so much. She had given Mary's address to him too easily and afterwards had wondered why. He simply charmed her into it and this had been on her mind ever since.

'I thought you'd be pleased for me,' said Mary. 'A chance of a lifetime is what I thought you'd say. Not jealous are yer?'

'Course I'm not jealous. Well, I might be if we knew a bit more about 'im. I mean, what's good for you is bound to be good for me. I'd soon be round there enjoying meself if I 'ad 'alf the chance. I know the place he's talking about in Bow. Lovely Georgian terraced 'ouses they are and not as small as you make out. Bloomin' elegant an' all.'

'So what's the problem then?'

Lizzie cast her eyes down. 'I don't really know. I can't quite put me finger on it. We don't know much about 'im, do we? He could be Jack the Ripper for all we know.'

'Lizzie, don't say that, that's awful! I gave myself to 'im' don't forget!'

'Oh don't come the old madam with me, Mary. "Gave yerself to 'im." Anyone'd think your virginity was sacred. I'm more concerned that you don't know enough about 'im!'

'I can't make you out at times. Fancy even thinking that someone as lovely as 'im could be a murderer?'

'Murderers don't 'ave to 'ave scars on their faces and dress in black, you know. There are bogey men and murderers. Two different fings entirely, they even suspect the Prince of Wales, for Gawd's sake.'

Mary went cold at the thought of it. 'You've got a point, Lizzie, I will say that. But no . . . you're wrong. He's too kind and loving and sincere to be—'

'Be careful is all I'm saying, find out a bit more about 'im before you jump in. Where's he live, for instance?'

'Maida Vale.'

'Yeah, but where exactly? Wot's 'is address?'

'Well he's 'ardly likely to give me that, is he? The shoe can be on the other foot, you know. 'Ow can he trust I won't go knocking on 'is door or blackmail 'im even?'

'True,' sniffed Lizzie. 'I s'pose you know where he works or what he does?'

'No. But I do know they're rich.'

''Cos he told yer?'

'Yeah, and the way he dresses and that. Paid for my

services when I 'adn't even given 'em – that must prove something.'

'Well, it could mean he's trying to prove 'imself.' She glanced sideways at her friend. 'He nearly fits one of the descriptions, you know.'

'Stop it this minute, Lizzie Redmond! Thousands of men fit one or other of the descriptions. Few of 'em are ordinary, I notice, most of 'em are either famous or mad, you know them that get the finger pointed. It could just as easily be an ordinary looking bloke. Could even be one of the blokes from down this turning who hates prostitutes – could be Daft Thomas! Look 'ow he's always reading aloud from the Bible. It's always prostitutes he's damning.'

Lizzie laughed out loud at the thought of it. 'That skinny sod ain't got the strength of a rabbit, never mind a lunatic. Mind you, he does study medicine so he'd know where all the bits are that the Ripper cuts out.'

'Oh *stop* it! We're gettin' as bad as everyone else. It's not funny.'

'Never said it was.'

'Well, I'm doomed and so are you if Thomas is the one. I'm sure the midwife knows what we get up to. She's changed towards me, gone real cold. Drops hints about where my money's comin' from . . .'

'She's too old-fashioned,' said Lizzie, 'you're better off without 'er as a friendly neighbour. She's a bit of an oddball, if you ask me.'

'I think you're right. Arthur and Harriet told me they saw her going into the Lambeth Infirmary. I s'pose she was visiting 'er sister or 'er mother. She's mental as well, if she's still alive, that is. She could be, I suppose – old and mad in a madhouse. I don't think 'er sister's bin locked away.'

Lizzie placed her cup of tea on to the floor and raised her face slowly to look into Mary's eyes.

'Mary, Mother of Jesus,' she said, a shiver going down her spine. 'Let's 'ope Sir Walter *is* genuine. Sooner you get out of this street the better, if you ask me.'

'Mmm. I wonder where Harriet could be?' sighed Mary. 'It's not like 'er to just go off like this. Is anyfing missing?'

'No. What 'ave *we* got to pinch? She wouldn't do that anyway.'

'I'm not so—'

'Stop it, Lizzie,' Mary cut in, 'don't put 'er down, she's one of us now; part of our family – whether you like 'er or not!'

'Never said I didn't like 'er, Mary. I do, as it 'appens. I just think you're worrying over nuffin', that's all.'

'I'm not. Something's wrong. I can feel it.'

Pouring a glass of milk to take up to Harriet, Jacqueline Turner was not happy. Mary Dean's intrusion had angered her. She rued the day she had weakened her resolve not to get involved with her neighbours. Perhaps her mother had not been such a fool after all? She had drummed it into both Jacqueline and her sister, Celestine, that no good came from getting overly friendly with outsiders.

She climbed the stairs and walked towards the

boxroom. Opening the door into the small, darkened space where Harriet was now held prisoner, she drew the curtains with one hand, balancing the milk in the other. 'Your presence here is proving to be a problem, Harriet – a burden.' She looked down at the browbeaten and very scared ten-year-old on the floor. 'What am I to do with you?' She placed the glass of milk on an old cabin trunk under the window then knelt beside Harriet and checked that her wrists were still bound. 'And now with all your pulling the twine's cut into your wrists. I can't say I cherish the thought of looking after you for much longer.' She then left the room to fetch her medicine box. When she returned she failed to notice Harriet's tears which were streaming down her cheeks and soaking into the linen towel gagging her mouth.

'It could well be that Thomas will be coming here to live with me,' she said, more to herself than to Harriet. 'I can't have you both under my roof, that much I do know.' No longer thinking of her as the poor Harriet who had been left to fend for herself, she was now nothing more than a girl from the worst streets who would no doubt soon add to the long list of prostitutes in and around Whitechapel. 'I should have known better,' the midwife said, 'all the Jago girls end up in the gutter – drunk and filthy, earning fourpence a trick whichever way they feel fit.'

Lowering herself to the floor again, she cut the binding away from Harriet's wrists. 'I shall have to apply surgical spirit. If you cry out when it stings I shall have to gag you again. Maybe this will teach you not to be wicked to those who show you charity.'

The moment the lotion touched Harriet's skin, she flinched with pain and felt as if her whole body was burning but she did not utter a sound. 'This needs some antiseptic ointment,' said the midwife, shaking her head, 'and some lint. As if I haven't got enough to do as it is. Nursing you was far from my mind when I woke up this morning, Harriet.' She looked into Harriet's red-rimmed, frightened eyes and felt no remorse whatsoever. This girl was to blame for her having to consider rearranging her plans. First she had to see Thomas out of the institution and, then, herself on to a ship bound for America – soon. Sooner than she had planned. Whether or not she would have to silence the girl for good remained to be seen. It was, after all, the midwife's word against a thieving orphan. Once the diary was burned, there would be no evidence to substantiate anything that Harriet might choose to tell the authorities.

Once she had fed Harriet some bread and milk and made good use of her own mother's commode, Jaqueline locked her in the room and went out again. She favoured the idea of leaving England as soon as possible and decided to go and book her passage at the Royal Exchange Shipping Lines in Fenchurch Avenue. Her plans for spending this coming Christmas in England had been ruined by Harriet. Ever since the night when she had been compelled to kill the whore, Catherine Eddowes, her loyalty to this country had drained away. She wanted no more of London or its people. Once she had secured the papers for Thomas's release, there would be nothing left to keep her here.

On the omnibus to Fenchurch Street, she closed her eyes and focused on her immediate future: Two weeks, Jacqueline. Two weeks and you will be sailing away from this depressing country. Your passport to freedom is close at hand.

In a good mood, Jacqueline decided to make an impromptu visit on Charles Cutbush at Scotland Yard. Her visit to the shipping line had been somewhat exciting and successful – her passage was now confirmed.

When her in-law first opened his office door to Jacqueline, she detected a look of irritation. His abrupt manner and dour expression soon changed however when she told him that she was shortly to emigrate. 'Would that I could follow your example, Miss Turner,' he said, settling himself behind his desk. 'It's been a treacherous time for all of us. A double murder in one night. It doesn't bear thinking about.'

'Indeed. Which is why I am here, Charles.' She looked him in the eye. 'Our nephew, Thomas . . . when can I expect his release?' Her mood and air of confidence were gaining momentum. She could almost smell the fresh sea air and freedom.

Cutbush gazed pensively at the ceiling, rapping his fingertips on his desk top. 'Don't you think it best that we leave him where he is for a while longer? Let's not forget he is in need of medical treatment for the syphilis.'

'Ointment will be enough. I have already given him

some and it's my opinion that he exaggerated grossly. We've caught it at the very early stages.'

'Well, yes, you know more on that matter than I. All the same—'

'I have kept my appointment book clear for tomorrow,' said Jacqueline, cutting in. 'I shouldn't think that one day more than necessary in that place would be good for the lad.'

'You exaggerate, madam, surely? Infirmaries are better conditioned these days, are they not?' He smiled patronisingly at her.

'When may I expect him home, then?'

Irritated by her direct manner, his smile evaporated. 'Home? I had no idea that he had been living with you.'

'He has not, Mr Cutbush, as you well know. But he shall be from the day he is released until the day I depart.'

'You have no plans to take the lad with you to America, I take it?'

'You take it correctly, sir. Thomas is a grown man and independent. I believe it is in his best interest that he does not go on such a voyage with an ageing maiden aunt. Again, I ask, when may I expect him to be released?' Like a dog with a bone, she was not going to let go.

'These things take time and may not be rushed. I imagine by the time the papers are signed and passed from one to another, I should say . . . a month, perhaps?'

Laughing at him, Jacqueline said, 'You take me for

a fool, sir. In one month's time I shall be out of your life and you may do as you wish. What is to stop you from leaving him in there to rot?'

'Madam, we are talking about my brother's son. I would not wish such a thing. Your manner today is quite impertinent and my patience is far stretched.' Cutbush stood up. 'If I can manage to secure his discharge before you leave for America, of course I shall do so, and happily. If not, then you must have more faith in me as a person. Good day, Miss Turner.'

She remained seated and softened her tone. 'I should sit down if I were you, Charles,' she said. 'I fear you may need support when I say what I have to.'

He looked at his pocket watch, begrudgingly. 'I can spare you only one minute more, then I must insist you leave. I have a pressing matter to attend to.' He sat down again and waited.

'I see from the newspapers that you have arrested another imbecile: Aaron Kosminski. Whatever happened to the other main suspect, the poor man whose life has been ruined after the torment he has had to suffer? I wonder. John Pizer, or should I say Leather Apron?'

'He was the victim of a press campaign. It was none of our doing.'

'But if my memory serves me correctly a Sergeant Thick made an arrest which the Yard was most pleased with. Every policeman in the metropolis had been on the lookout for him, according to a statement from one of your officers.'

'Which you read in the newspaper.'

Ignoring that comment, she continued. 'He was a Polish Jew, I believe. A man of so little consequence. You had the East End in a furore – they were out for his blood. The poor man had to hide away in his brother's house for fear of being ripped apart.'

'The "poor man" Miss Turner, had a criminal record. Not one year previous he was convicted of stabbing a boot finisher. He served six months' hard labour in prison. Now I really must—'

'But that stabbing was the result of a fight between two men in the same trade. Even *you* must agree there is a world of difference?'

'I take it this is leading somewhere,' said Cutbush, locking his fingers.

'Indeed. Would that I had time to waste on pleasantries.' She relaxed again and chose her words carefully. 'The arrest of Thomas bears some similarity, wouldn't you agree?'

'Thomas was *not* arrested.'

'Well we shall beg to differ on that, Mr Cutbush, but you can see how my mind is working? Should a tragedy befall your good self, and I sincerely hope it does not, then is it not possible that your colleagues might turn their attention back to our nephew? And if he were still in the asylum, would that not enhance their case against him? We already know that more than one of your colleagues is aware of the Betty Millwood attack, at least.'

'Supposition slows forward action, Miss Turner. I

give it no credence and I do not intend to discuss police matters with you.'

'Well, then, I must come directly to the point of my visit. If Thomas is not released before I leave and is still imprisoned when I embark, then it is my belief that the lad has nothing more to lose. I shall therefore take it upon myself to speak with the press and tell them everything.'

Furious with her, Charles Cutbush rose to his feet. 'This has gone far enough, I insist you leave this instant.'

Jacqueline mirrored his action and stood face to face with him. 'Very well, if that's what you want. But I warn you, and please mark my word, I *shall* go to the national newspapers. I shall tell them in detail about the cover-up at Scotland Yard and I shall name *all* names. You must trust me on this, I am deadly serious.'

'Damn you, woman.' He banged his fist on his desk. 'What do you want of me? I do not run the entire police establishment. I do not make the rules, therefore I cannot break them.'

'Then you must speak with your superiors: Thomas's release for my silence. If we strike a bargain you have my word that I shall keep my side of it no matter what. You shall not see or hear from me again.'

Cutbush's pinched face paled. He lowered his head and hunched his shoulders, almost as if he were wracked with pain. She waited for his answer. They had reached the end of their discussion and she was fully aware that his answer would be the final word on the matter.

'I shall see to it,' he murmured, looking very much a broken man. 'And I would thank you not to cross my path again.'

Taking her leave she placed her hand on the doorknob. 'You must surely see that I have only our nephew's welfare at heart. We must do everything in our power to keep him from wasting away in an asylum and remove the threat of the gallows.'

They exchanged a knowing look as she nodded her farewell and left. It had not been an easy battle, she may have given Charles Cutbush the impression that she was in control, but her shaking hands gave her away.

Her main goal seemingly achieved, and with the imminent release of her nephew, Jacqueline could now turn her thoughts to the final episode of her life in England. Seeing no other way out now she would have to add something to Harriet's cocoa that night. The midwife was now convinced that Harriet would be better off dead. Her destiny was the backstreets of Whitechapel where she would walk at night looking to give fourpenny-sex to men from all filthy walks of life. Yes, Jacqueline told herself, I shall be doing the girl a great favour. She would bury the body in her back garden and sprinkle forget-me-nots on the earth as she had done to the wretched unborn child of Annie Chapman.

While Jacqueline strolled homeward bound, planning her moves, step by step, Harriet was slowly inching her way towards a tea chest in the corner of the tiny boxroom. Leaning on it, her thin arms close to one corner where the tin ends were rough, she began to rub her bindings slowly against the sharp edge of the metal rim.

When the bandage shredded apart, her bleeding hands fumbled with the tight knot behind her head until she managed to undo it. She then freed her ankles and stretched, rubbing her aching back and legs before crawling to the door. Believing the key to be in the keyhole on the other side of the door, she tore off a piece of cardboard from a box by the wall and slipped it under the gap beneath the door. That done she used the end of a teaspoon to push and poke until she heard the key drop on the cardboard on the other side of the door. Then, slowly and very carefully she pulled the cardboard through until she saw the tip of the door key and then teased it under the gap. When she snatched the key into her hand she all but cried. But there was no time for tears now, no time for anything other than to get out of that house. She must escape and do it now.

Once outside that room which had been her prison, she resisted the urge to run for her life. The door of the midwife's bedroom was ajar and it was inviting her to go inside. The diary was on her mind. If she could make her escape with that she could show it to someone later in life once she'd learned how to read properly. Fervour now replaced fear. She wasted no more seconds thinking on it. This would impress Arthur as nothing else could.

Moving at speed, she went into the bedroom and to the bureau, only to find that the drawer had been locked. Taking a brass letter opener from a tray, she pushed it above the drawer and used every bit of force to break the lock. With the journal in her shaking hands, she ran out of the room, down the stairs and towards the street door. But, what if the midwife was coming along the turning? Harriet would be trapped because Whitehead Street was a dead-end. Going to the back door instead, she unbolted it and went into the yard. Before she had closed it behind her she heard the street door being unlocked. Silent as a mouse she closed the door and stood with her back to the wall of the house. From the window the gate at the back of the yard could be clearly seen. Her heart thumping, she turned her head slightly and looked slyly into the house. Jacqueline was at the foot of the stairs and calling out.

'I'm back, Harriet, I'm going to warm some milk for your cocoa.'

The midwife's voice sent a shiver down her spine. Wasting no more time and now in a state of panic, she took flight towards the green gate in the back wall which led into the alley. Pulling at the rusty bolt she almost froze as she heard the midwife opening the back door of the house. With no other thought than to escape she began to kick at the gate, knowing the midwife would see and hear her. It was too late to think sensibly. She was too petrified to even look back and see how close her tormentor might be. A final and powerful kick knocked the gate off its rusty hinges. A mighty leap and she was out of danger but in fearsome pain. A sharp piece of splintered wood had pierced the flesh of her calf and remained there. Running for all she was worth along the cobbled alleyway, her wild ginger hair blowing in the cold wind, she felt nothing but desperation to get as far away from that place as possible.

Taking the corner of Cleveland Way and speeding along she saw Arthur and his friend playing kickball on the pavement. To avoid crashing into one of them she would have to run into the roadway and the hansom cabs were busy. Slowing her pace she wove between the boys and caught a glimpse of Arthur's look of shock at seeing her looking so wild and so terrified.

'Harriet, where you been! Mary's worried sick!' yelled Arthur.

'Out the way,' said Harriet flying through. 'Get out the way!' The other boys were laughing at the crazy ginger-haired girl, but Arthur wasn't giving up that easily. He outran her and grabbed her arm until she had to stop. Her leg was now red, swollen and throbbing.

'What 'appened to yer? Where you bin? Look at yer leg!'

'Get out my way, Arfer Dean, and keep away from the midwife and don't tell 'er you've seen me!' Shoving him aside, she sped off, leaving him to stare after her. Losing no time he flew home to Mary, banging and kicking the front door, screaming for her to open it.

'Harriet,' he said, breathlessly, 'I've seen Harriet.' He stopped talking and gazed into her face. 'She's got a bit of wood sticking out of 'er leg.' He looked about him, as frightened as a rabbit.

'What do you mean, Arthur, a piece of wood? Calm down now and go slowly. What's happened?'

His eyes widened suddenly as if he had seen the devil himself. 'Take me inside Mary, the midwife's coming.'

Stomping towards them in full uniform, the expression on her flushed face demonic, Miss Turner looked a different woman.

'Mary, take me inside, now.' Arthur was trembling. 'Please, Mary . . .' he wailed, beginning to cry. But Miss Turner was closing in and looking directly in Mary's face. The crashing of her boots on the pavement made her shudder. She had picked up on her small brother's terror. Placing a hand on his shoulder, she said, 'It's all right, Arthur, be a brave soldier.'

Stopping at Mary's door, the midwife looked down at Arthur and feigned concern. She was in no mood for compassion but her intuition was to the fore and she showed a sympathetic face as she looked at Arthur. 'Oh dear, someone's upset.'

'It's nothing,' said Mary, 'he was playing kickball with the boys and . . .'

'Omnibus . . .' stammered Arthur, backing her story. 'Nearly went under it . . .'

'Well, that'll teach you not to play kickball in the streets. Give him a hot drink with lots of sugar, Mary, and put him to bed.' With that, Jacqueline walked briskly away and Arthur was in the house like a shot.

'Shut the d-door, Mary,' he said, still trembling. 'Lock it.'

Pulling him close to her, she stroked his hair and kissed the top of his head. 'It's all right, sweetheart. No one's gonna 'urt you. No one.'

'I saw Harriet,' he said, sobbing into her breast. 'She was running for 'er life. She never 'ad no shoes or coat on an' was freezin' cold. She looked terrible, her eyes were strange, all puffy and red and staring. And there was that bit of jagged wood sticking out of her leg.' A look of horror swept across his face. 'It couldn't 'ave bin 'er bone, could it?'

'No, of course not. You're being silly.' Mary eased him away from her and looked him in the eye. 'Did she say anything to yer?'

'"Keep away from the midwife," she said, then she ran away again. We've gotta find 'er, Mary, or she'll die from that leg injury and from freezing cold.'

'We will, don't you worry. We'll get to the bottom of it. But why keep away from the midwife? Do you think that's who she was running away from?'

'She was, Mary. I know it. I fink she came out of the back alley, so she must 'ave come from Miss Turner's backyard. She was running away from 'er, Mary. I know she was,' he whimpered, wiping away tears with his sleeve.

'Well, if she was running away I should fink she's gone straight to the Old Jago, to the stable.'

'Can we go now,' said Arthur, drying his eyes on the sleeve of his coat, 'go and find 'er? Can we, Mary? *Please?*'

'Of course we can,' she said, thinking of Walter, whom she had arranged to meet that day. She was going to have to let him down and hoped that he'd understand. Hoped that he wouldn't go away and out of her life again. 'If you're really up to it, we'll go, now. Unless you wanna wait half an hour or so?'

'No, I don't wanna wait, I'm all right now. It was seeing the midwife that frightened me. She must be out there as well, looking for 'er.'

'No, I'm sure that's not true, Arthur. She's a very busy midwife with a big area to cover. She wouldn't waste time chasing after Harriet.'

'But wot if she was keeping 'er a prisoner. The back gate down the alley was smashed down. I saw it, Mary. The midwife's gone out to get Harriet back!'

'All right, Arthur, that's enough. We'll wrap up warm and go to Bethnal Green. To the Old Jago. We'll find her an' she can tell us what this is all about.'

'I'm not fibbing, Mary, I did see 'er,' said Arthur, his face earnest; worry taking over from fear.

'I believe you, silly. Now go and wash yer face and wrap up warm, and stop fretting. It'll all come out in the wash, you'll see.'

With Arthur at her side and clutching her hand, Mary walked a little more quickly than usual. Her thoughts not on Harriet, whom she felt sure they would find, but on Walter. To her way of thinking, it was a terrible insult for an ordinary working-class person like herself to let down a man of his standing. She couldn't imagine him taking it any other way than rude and thoughtless, to say the least. This would surely be the end of the new beginning she was looking forward to. She would have to try and push him from her mind and forget they had ever met. But this was not going to be easy. He was in her every waking thoughts as well as her dreams. He had become part of her world and she couldn't imagine it without him now. But the sacrifice was not coming out of selfishness but from reason, good reason. Harriet's welfare was more important than Mary's right then. At least this would be a good test for Walter. If she never heard from him again then surely he could not feel as strongly about her as she did about him? All of these thoughts were flying through her brain until she realised that she and her brother had arrived in the Old Jago.

The rank oppression in the air brought her sharply from her heady heights and any thoughts of Sir Walter and a fine life. People were curled up on the pavements, bedding down for the night, even though it was only late afternoon. Each of the covered bodies were securing the best sheltered spots.

Averting her eyes from the pale haunted faces which showed desperation and defeat she wondered if all that was left to these people was a dull acceptance of their lot. 'Spare a few coppers, miss?' said a ragged young woman with a small child clinging to her. 'For a night's shelter. They say it's gonna get foggier.'

Without giving it another thought, Mary unclasped her handbag and offered a silver threepenny bit. 'That's all I can spare, I'm sorry for you,' she said, grabbing Arthur's hand and pulling him onwards.

'I shouldn't go that way, miss!' the woman called after her. 'That leads to the back and beyond of Old Jago. I shouldn't go in there, it's not safe, not for no one. And 'specially not for a lady like yerself! They'll take everyfing – even yer boots.'

'Jago Court, that's where she lived.'

Mary turned to the woman with the baby. 'Is it really that bad?'

'Oh, you don't wanna go near it, miss, not the courtyard any'ow. Worse than anywhere, that is. A lot worse than this pavement. Only them that live in the yard dare go in, it's full of great big rats an' all.'

'You lookin' for someone, gal?' A bundle of clothing lodged in a corner moved and Mary could just see a face in the midst of it. 'Lost someone, 'ave yer?'

'I'm looking for a relative, a ten-year-old girl called Harriet. She's got ginger hair and used to live in the Old Jago.'

The bundle moved again and the shape changed as a short, round woman eased herself up. 'If yer fink one of the Jago's 'ave kidnapped 'er, yer must 'ave lost yer marbles. One less mouth to feed is a godsend to any of that lot. They'd sell a kid rather than feed it. I take it she ran off, an' if she did, best leave 'er to it. You don't wanna go meddling, she's best wiv 'er own kind.' The woman lowered herself to the ground, resuming her earlier form, her face disappearing under the filthy bedding.

'She was sleeping rough in a stable before she turned up on my doorstep,' said Mary, 'a stable round this way where a coalman kept 'is horse.'

Muffled laughter came from beneath another bundle. 'Well 'e wouldn't keep anyfing else in there, would 'e now? You best get back to where yer came from, ducks.'

Arthur pulled at Mary's hand. 'Come on, we'll look for 'er tomorrow, when it's light.'

'No, there must be a policeman manning the Jago if it's that bad.'

Another burst of laughter came from beneath the bundle and then from others who were dossing down close by. 'The coppers won't go near the place if they don't 'ave to, gel. Anyway, they're all out lookin' for Jack an' they won't find *him* in the Jago, he wouldn't dare try 'is luck there!'

'What's the name of this street?' said Mary.

'Luck Row!' laughed someone close by.

'Luck Row, that must be an omen, Arthur. We'll find her, you'll see if we don't. Come on.' She clasped his hand tight and urged him on. She hadn't taken many steps when the same voice called out.

'Oi, you! Silly drawers!' The woman stood up again and kicked at two bundles curled close to an old wall. 'Get up, you idle gits, 'ere's a chance for yer to earn a tanner between yer.' The woman turned to Mary, sighing. 'You're obstinate, I'll give you that, brave wiv it though. Don't know which's worse. My boys'll go wiv yer, but you must pay 'em sixpence for their trouble. They'll be better 'n' no one. Talk their way out of a paper bag, they could, but you do as they say or they'll leave you to fend fer yerselves. I'm not 'aving my boys coshed for no one.'

The boys turned out to be two young lads of thirteen and fourteen, both scruffy and unwashed; both with wizened faces and unruly hair. One was short like his mother and the other tall and skinny with a broken nose.

'We ain't goin' in the court, mind,' said the lanky brother, hitching up the collar of his ragged, coarse jacket.

Mary agreed to that and promised to pay them after they had taken her to where she needed to go and brought them back to the safety of the Bethnal Green Road. The lads nodded reluctantly, keeping an eye on their mother's huge heavy boots. Pushing their hands into their trouser pockets, they trudged up the street.

Following them, Mary squeezed her brother's hand. 'We'll be all right, don't you worry.'

The short journey through the backstreets frightened her but she held her tongue. She had not seen so many homeless people cramped together like this. Apart from those sitting or lying in doorways, there were several who were just milling around, talking and laughing or yelling abuse. A fight was taking place as they passed an alleyway. A fight between men and women.

'That'll be the Learys and the Ranns,' the short brother jerked a thumb in the direction of the brawl.

'Or the Dawsons and the Browns,' said the lanky one. 'Families are big round 'ere. Bruvvers, sisters, aunts, uncles, muvvers, farvers, kids an' all. If there's a fight they all join in.'

Looking from the vagrants to small clusters of bois-terous prostitutes, she thought about turning back. This was indeed another world. A very scary world at that, and all but twenty minutes' walk from where she and Arthur enjoyed a comparatively quiet, decent, existence.

'There's four stables up Edge Lane and a few more in Honey Lane. After that we'll make our way back down Jago Row, froo to the Befnal Green Road. Then you can pay us our shillin'.'

'Sixpence,' said Mary, half expecting this.

'A tanner each is wot Muvver said.'

'Sixpence between you is what I heard,' said Mary, 'I was born and bred in Stepney, you know. I'm not exactly wet behind the ears.'

'A tanner then,' said the lanky one, looking slyly at his brother.

'Do you think it might be a good idea if we explained Harriet's looks to the men in the stables, instead of just saying her name.' Mary was quite aware that her accent had changed in the present company. They were treating her as if she were a lady and she was rising to it; somehow it seemed right under the circumstances.

'Nar, no point. They'll know who ya mean. Ain't many 'Arriets round this part. Not kids anyway. Wot colour's 'er 'air then?'

'Ginger. Long and wavy.'

'Awright,' sniffed one brother, 'we'll add that bit, but that's all. We're chancing our luck as it is an' all for a few coppers.'

After tramping from one backstreet stable to another, Mary was beginning to feel that she was wasting her time. Harriet could, at that very moment, be with her family across the river.

'We'll find 'er, Mary,' said Arthur, looking up at her, sensing she was about to give up.

'Not wiv us you won't,' said the lanky brother. 'Our work's done now. Sorry we couldn't find 'er but weren't our fault.' He held out his hand for payment.

'Where are we?' said Mary, worried.

'Main street's jes dahn there.' The lad pushed his hand under Mary's nose and wiggled his fingers for his money.

Giving them the sixpence, Mary thanked them. 'You've done well,' she said, 'tell your mother I said so.'

Laughing and showing his gappy stained teeth, the short fat one clicked his finger and thumb. 'She'd drop dead jes like that if we said such a fing.'

'Or kick the 'ell out of us fer lying,' said the tall skinny one, placing a hand on either side of his nose and clicking it.

'We can come back agen, can't we?' said Arthur, smiling at their antics. The brothers were walking away and looked even funnier from the back view. They were walking in step and swinging their arms in perfect time as if they'd been practising for donkey's years.

'Wot funny lads,' said Arthur, loving every second of it. 'No wonder Harriet's a bit peculiar.'

Holding his hand tightly, Mary pulled him along

to the High Street. 'How does pease-pudding and a savaloy sound?'

'Sounds great. Can we eat it goin' along, Mary, I'm starving?'

'Don't see why not, Arthur.' She was craning her neck now, to see beyond an oncoming coalman driving his horse harder than necessary. 'We'll cross after this cart.' She grabbed Arthur's hand ready to march him smartly across the busy road. 'Now!'

Wrenching his hand from hers, Arthur suddenly called out, 'Harriet!' but the noisy clatter of the hoofs and surrounding traffic drowned his voice as the cart flew by. 'It *was* Harriet! Sitting next to the driver, she 'ad a blanket wrapped round 'er. It was 'er, Mary.'

'All right, Arthur,' said Mary, worried. 'Stop yelling, people are looking at us.'

'I don't care, it was her!' His face crumpled into a sorry sight as he began to sob. 'It was. She never saw us though, she looked as if she was asleep wiv 'er eyes open.' But Mary had seen her too, she had seen that frightened empty look on her face.

'Wot we gonna do, Mary?'

'We're gonna buy our supper and go 'ome. We'll just 'ave to think about what to do next. There's nothing else we can do.'

Chapter Twelve

Now that Harriet had got away from her and taken the journal, the midwife could see no way out, other than to leave her house as soon as possible, take a lodging room close to the docks and board the ship directly she could. She would leave all of her furniture for her nephew who could, with help from his Uncle Charles, afford to pay the rent on the house. She felt easier at the thought of him being released. If Harriet handed the journal to the authorities, once she had left for America, the midwife reasoned, the dratted girl would be dismissed as another hoaxer chasing a reward. No doubt it would go in the furnace at police headquarters, along with all the other so-called evidence that people had handed in. Her savings even after her passage had been paid for would be more than adequate to provide food and a roof above her head for a few months; then she could find work.

Picking up the telegram which had arrived earlier she read it again: *Thomas to be discharged. Sat 3rd inst. C Cutbush.* The very next day.

All things considered, the midwife was strangely calm as she collected her notepad, envelopes, and earlier journals. She would then burn all of it, every bit of scribbling, so as not to leave anything that might incriminate her, should her house ever be searched.

Later, relaxing in her armchair, a large gin in her hand, she watched as her life's writings turned to ashes in the fire. The boxroom had been cleaned up to show no sign or trace of Harriet ever having been there. If she were to go to the police with her wild story, who would they believe? A streetgirl who thieved to make her way or an upstanding citizen, a midwife, no less? And what had Harriet to gain by it? There would be no reward for a midwife's journal. A journal which she was writing out of pure fiction in order to one day write a novel on the Whitechapel murders. No, she did not have much to fear from that quarter. But still, the sooner she was away the better.

Switching her thoughts to Thomas and all she had done for him, Jacqueline found herself smiling as she recalled the newspaper report on the whore Catherine Eddowes. The initials TC which had been inked on her body had been linked to one of the streetgirl's ex-boyfriends, by chance and pure luck. Satisfied that she was on top of things, Jacqueline emptied her glass and sank her head into a cushion ready to drift off into a light doze in front of her fire.

Happy though Thomas was to be at last out of the infirmary, away from all those wretched people with wrecked brains, he now had to accept the fact that his aunt had brought forward her departure overseas. Having stayed with her for almost a week he was now resigned to the fact that nothing would change her mind. She was resolute and his constant attempts to persuade her otherwise had proved futile, she was too headstrong for her own good. He was convinced of that.

In his favourite chair by the fire, he watched his aunt pack her neatly pressed clothes into a trunk. Why was she doing this? He reasoned that she would not last a month so far away from England; a stranger in a foreign land. Yes, he was sure she would return home soon.

'I presume you did purchase a return passage, Aunt?' he said, drawing on his pipe.

'No, Thomas, I did not. I have no intention of returning. The sooner you accept that the better for the both of us.' She brushed some fluff from a grey skirt and began to fold it. 'You will always be welcome should you decide to visit me. If you work hard and save some of your earnings you will afford the fare without difficulty.'

'Anyone who works hard and saves well could afford the fare, Aunt. Providing, like you, they work and save for most of their lives.' He half smiled at her. 'It's not a dream I have, I'm afraid, even for a visit. When you see me from the ship as you sail away, you will be seeing me for the last time. Unless of course I am right and you do find it is not quite as you expect. The grass is not always greener . . .'

'Very true, Thomas.' She continued to pack, her mind on the packing.

'You're a good hard-working woman with a good degree of intelligence. I'm sure you'll do well wherever you go. But Britain is not so small, Aunt. Why do you have to go abroad—?'

'Have you seen my clothes brush?' she interrupted, preoccupied.

'Many times,' facetious, as always, 'but if you are asking if I know where it is at this precise moment, the answer is no. Did you remember to collect your passport?'

'Yes, Thomas, I did remember. It's safely tucked away in my handbag, thank you.'

'And will there be someone at the other end to welcome you when the ship docks?' He narrowed his eyes when there was no immediate response. 'Aunt Jacqueline, I asked you a question.'

'Why don't you see if the kettle has boiled, Thomas? My throat's that dry . . .' She kept her back to him, continuing to pack. It was upsetting her the way he was trying so hard to bring about a change of heart. On the surface his attitude was extremely irritating but underneath, she knew he was very upset at the thought of her going. She had to watch what she said as he might easily burst into tears despite himself. His tears were the only weapon he had, if he but knew it. Once upon a time his misery would have her do anything for him, but those days were over. She no longer had a choice. Jacqueline *had* to leave England, two prostitutes lay dead by her hand. Unworthy of this world, it was true, but nevertheless, the law was the law.

In so far as Harriet was concerned, Jacqueline convinced herself that the girl, despite her bravado, was more than a little frightened of authority. If she went to the police she might well find herself placed in the workhouse. The midwife did not think she had too much to worry about on that score.

'So . . .' said Thomas, sighing loudly, 'you will be travelling in cramped conditions for weeks on end, with no lodgings secured and no one to meet you. No one to accompany you—'

'Thomas!' she broke in, 'I have already told you, and more than once, there *will* be someone to greet me; my distant cousin, Renee. Now will you make yourself useful or go out for an evening stroll?' She pushed the lid of the trunk down with one finger, knowing it would crash as it shut. The only response from her nephew was a low tormenting chuckle.

'Be honest with *yourself* if not for my sake. Ask yourself one question: Who is going to employ an old lady as a midwife or even as a private nurse?'

'I may seem old to you, Thomas. Yes, you have youth on your side, but I assure you, in my early fifties, I am still very capable of nursing. Now, before I lose my temper,' she said, speaking fondly, 'brew a nice pot of tea, there's a good lad.'

'Please, Aunt Jacqueline, try to remember that I am the son of an intelligent man, that I am . . .'

She turned sharply to glare at him. 'I spend most of my time these days trying to forget what you are, Thomas: A murderer by your own admission.' She turned away from his cold stare. 'If you had any idea what lengths I have gone to, to prevent people from finding out . . .'

'What are you talking about now? Prevent people from finding out about what exactly?'

'I don't wish to discuss it any more. I am too stretched by the whole sordid business.' She heaved her frame up from her kneeling position and stretched. 'I shall make the tea myself.'

'You aren't truly asking me to believe that . . . that you really took my antics seriously?' The smile was back. 'All that prancing about I did, waving a knife at imaginary people? I was merely being *theatrical*, Aunt.'

'Whatever you say, Thomas. Whatever you say.'

'You truly believed I was responsible for butchering those women? Aunt Jacqueline, I was simply embroidering your dull life for you. How could you have believed I would do those terrible things?' He stood up and slowly shook his head. 'You have made me very angry. I shall abate my temper by taking a brisk walk. It's a pity you've had to spend so much time packing clothes. It would have been good for the both of us to have gone out for the evening.'

Leaving the midwife deflated and confused, he shut the street door quietly behind him. His objective was to give her time to think. Alone in that room he could only hope that she would reconsider and come to the same conclusion as himself: That each of them only had the other to draw comfort from. That neither of them should desert the other if they were to survive in this iniquitous world. She *must* come to her senses before she boarded the ship.

Approaching number thirteen, where Mary and

her brother lived, Thomas was concerned to see a gentleman at her door. Someone he did not know. A gentleman, sporting a tall hat and dark cloak. A gentleman who fitted one of the few descriptions of the murderer which held credence. On passing, he threw the man a deliberate inquisitive look.

The sound of Mary's door opening, stopped him in his tracks. He glanced back to see that the stranger was whispering to her with his face threateningly close. He retraced his steps and looked from the stranger to Mary.

'Do you know this gentleman, Miss Dean?'

'Yes, Thomas, I do. You need not concern yourself.' She had no intention of introducing Sir Walter to him.

'May I ask what your business is here, sir?' said Thomas, chin raised and head tilted to one side.

'You may not, sir,' said Walter, believing that would be the end of it.

'I see,' said Thomas, moving a little closer. 'It does look a little odd, you will agree, that someone of your status should be knocking on the door of a young lady in this part of London. A respectable young lady, I grant you, but one of a different class to your good self.'

'I'm sure your concern for Miss Dean is sincere, but I assure you, I am *not* the notorious Whitechapel murderer.' He smiled and nodded. 'Now, if you will excuse me . . .' He removed his hat and stepped inside, closing the door on Thomas.

'A jealous admirer, my sweet?'

'No, he's just an inquisitive fool; harmless enough.' Still surprised at his unexpected first visit to her house, she felt embarrassed. The room was tidy enough but his very presence made it all look a touch humble which emphasised the fact that in reality she and Sir Walter were from very different worlds.

'I feel a bit of a fool, turning up like this out of the blue but' – he looked into her lovely eyes which had captured him from the first moment they met – 'but I miss you. A day doesn't go by when you're not in my thoughts. I had to come. I had to know why you weren't at the tearooms. I have to know if you've changed your mind.'

'I'm glad you did come, Walter. I'm sorry I couldn't keep our arrangement that day. If you'll sit down for a few minutes I'll explain.'

'You don't have to, my darling,' he said, taking her into his arms. 'I love you. I love you and I don't want to lose you. One day, we *will* be man and wife. I swear it.'

On his brisk walk, Thomas found himself deep in the backstreets of Whitechapel, ignoring those prostitutes who were touting for work. Walking through Miller's Court, a stone-flagged passage no more than three feet wide, he arrived at a small paved courtyard where some six or seven decrepit houses stood. From one of the houses came the lovely soft Irish voice of a woman, as she sang, 'A Violet I Plucked From My Mother's Grave'. The lovely sound echoed in and around the courtyard and Thomas could do no more than stand still and silent, deeply moved by her voice and by the lyrics. It was as if an angel had come to him to ease the pain of losing his aunt. Staying in the shadows, he watched as Mary Jane Kelly came out of the house, still singing.

The young Irishwoman had already had her fill of drink, for she had spent the afternoon with a friend, drinking and talking in the women's lodging rooms just a few yards from where she lived. Then, earlier that same evening she had spent some time in the Horn of Plenty, a public house where she enjoyed some cheap gin and the company of her friends. Getting ready to go out on to the streets to ply her trade, knowing that business would be good since most of the other girls had moved elsewhere fearing that Jack the Ripper might strike again. She was in a good mood. So much so that she changed her mind and decided to put pleasure before business first and go in search of the man she loved but had broken up with: Joe Barnet. She was in need of a little genuine romance and he was the only man who had ever made her feel truly wanted.

With extra layers of clothes on and her thick rough maroon shawl about her shoulders and her best flower-decked bonnet pinned to her hair, she came out into the courtyard and face to face with Thomas.

'Ah, now, would it be comfort ye're after, sweet boy?' she said.

'No. I was merely taking the air and have found myself in strange parts,' he said, smelling the gin on her breath which reminded him of his Aunt Jacqueline.

'Ah, well, you know where to find me, to be sure . . .

327

should you need a little comforting. Me name is . . . Kelly.' She winked at him.

Leaving the courtyard she went in search of her man, singing as she went. Keeping to the narrow streets in which the lamps were lit, she made her way towards Buller's Lodging House in New Street, where she expected to find her Joe playing cards.

Arriving at Buller's Lodgings, she crept to the window, which had a sixpenny paraffin lamp hanging inside the window, and peeped in. As expected, her Joe and his cronies were in the smoke-filled room, drinking ale and enjoying their game. 'Ah, sure now,' she murmured, 'so happy without me.' She then turned away, deciding that her man would not be too pleased if she tried to break up their game. He didn't like it when she had too much gin inside her.

Wending her way back towards Miller's Court, she vowed to find Joe the next day and make up. She would promise faithfully, for the hundredth time, to give up her heavy drinking.

As she arrived in Dorset Street a familiar figure stepped out from the shadows. 'Ah . . . if it isn't the little sweetheart waiting for me. An' so serious he is, to be sure.' She smiled flirtatiously at him.

'You should not be out at this time, dear woman. Why do you tempt providence?'

'Well, you see, sir, it's like this . . .' she leaned forward and smiled into his face, '. . . I 'ave to earn a crust, an' besides, I felt lonely in my room. I was after some company. Sure we all need some company now, do we not?'

'I'll walk you safely home, to your lodgings,' said Thomas, 'you've been drinking too much and I fear for your safety.'

'Ah, now, if that's not the kindest thing,' she said, slipping her arm in his. 'It's not a palace, you understand, but it's me home an' I do love it so. It's a touch neglected at the moment, so it is, but if you have a small bottle of something in your pocket, an' if you can turn a blind eye to the mess, sure you would be more than welcome.'

'I notice that most of your friends are not out on the streets tonight. You should take a leaf from their book.'

'My friends, sweet boy, are either on the blanket with a client or six feet under. Our Jack the Lad has claimed them, so he has. It's a sad world for some of us, is it not?'

'And that doesn't worry you?'

'What does it matter? I shall die on these streets one way or another.' Pulling her arm from his, she began to hum her favourite tune and dance, in a fashion, through the dark passage to Miller's Court. From the corner of his eye, Thomas caught sight of a large rat hunched in a corner, watching them. As they passed, the rodent moved a fraction but gave no signs of being afraid. It was hungry.

'One of these days,' said Kelly, light-heartedly, 'I shall cut meself on this bloody thing.' She carefully guided her hand through the broken pane and pulled the latch on the inside of her street door.

'You should insist that the landlord fix it. That, to a thief, is an open invitation.'

'Indeed, but then, me lodgin' room is an open invitation, is it not? It's the way I earn me keep. Do you have a flask of somethin' then, to warm the blood?'

'No, but I have a bar of chocolate if you are hungry. You are most welcome to it.'

'A bar of chocolate, is it?' she said, laughing and offering him the open doorway. 'Well that would go down very nicely with a cup of hot tea, will it not? I have a little milk. We'll have ourselves a tea party.'

Closing the door behind them, Thomas viewed the room with disgust. A bedside cupboard was close to the ancient wooden bedstead and there was an old table, a chair draped with dirty clothes, another cupboard, a disused washstand and a fireplace, the grate of which contained burnt-out ashes. The bare floorboards were filthy as were the peeling papered walls. A ragged piece of sackcloth hung on the window to act as a curtain.

Sighing at the futility of it all, Thomas asked if she would like him to light a fire for her.

'That would be grand but I have no coal. Just some old newspapers an' a broken chair, under the bed.'

'And the chair is waiting to be repaired?'

Kelly laughed, quietly. 'The chair is like everythin' in me life. Everythin' will be repaired – one fine day.'

Thomas got down on to his knees and lifted the hem of the grimy bed cover which dangled in the thick curling dust on the floor and pulled out the old newspapers and the bits of wood, which, should they ever be glued together, might resemble a kind of chair.

'Why don't you brew the tea, Kelly, while I light a fire?'

'Oh, what a lovely polite boy you are. Would that everyone was like yerself. An' to think you don't mind me company. I'm flattered, indeed I am, but I cannot boil a kettle until you have built the fire.'

'Very well. Once we have warmed this room,' he said, breaking the splintered wood into small pieces, 'we shall talk . . . are you a Catholic?'

'That I am.' She poured water from a chipped enamel jug into a black kettle.

Twisting the sheets of newspaper, Thomas placed them in the grate and was pleased to have his small Bible in his inside pocket. He considered which proverbs he should read to her. Considering their contents as he worked on the fire, he decided to start at the beginning and work his way through to Proverbs 31. If necessary, he would read to her all through the night, until he had convinced her of the errors of her ways. To his mind, unlike the other whores, with this one, there was a glimmer of hope.

'This room will be like an oven in no time,' he said striking a match and setting fire to the twists of paper beneath the wood. Turning to see why she had gone quiet, he was disappointed to observe that she was spread-eagled on the filthy bed, out to the world. Sitting himself down on the only chair, he stared into the flames of his fire, watching as the scant remains of varnish on the broken chair legs blistered in the heat. It no longer bothered him that this prostitute was sleeping off the effects of her evening's debauchery.

She would be in a clearer frame of mind when he woke her. He pulled his Bible from his pocket and settled himself to read the holy book. Briefly, his thoughts returned to his aunt, what a foolish woman she was. If she would only stay, then he could share this sense of well-being that had moved into his soul from the moment he walked out of the asylum. With his past behind him, he was ready to move on to a better life. The dreadful experience imposed on him inside that crazy place had been for a higher reason; he knew that now. It had been a test and he had not and would not fail the Lord. His aunt had laughed at him when he told her that he had something to thank God for.

Opening the Bible at random, his eyes fell upon the words, *When anyone wants to give a thanksgiving to the Lord* . . . Startled by the coincidence of the repetition between his very last thought and that of the first line he had read, he glanced at Kelly, who was snoring softly. The sound had a rhythmic quality all of its own. He listened intently and allowed the beat to run through his brain as he focused on the page and the words . . . 'sacrificial lamb'. Was it possible that God was revealing another message to him? Watching Kelly's face and listening more intently, he saw her take in a long, deep breath, then exhale slowly and lie there without apparently breathing at all. This opportunity *had* to be a message from above. God was instructing him to expel the last intoxicated breath from her young, though far from innocent body. Yes, she was to be his offering of thanksgiving – his sacrificial lamb.

Closing his Bible, Thomas slid one hand inside his coat and touched his knife. He felt the outside of his pocket for the shape of his bone-handled penknife, yes, that too was there. He remembered his mother and the many times she had sat him down by the fire and read to him from the Bible. It was for his own good, she had said. Her words had filled him with terror, then. But now he could see the wisdom of her teaching and realised how wrong he had been to scorn her. She had been instructed by God to inculcate the Bible's teachings into his young, impressionable mind. She was the instrument through whom God would prepare Thomas for the great avenging work which lay ahead. Clasping his head, heavy with the burden of his holy mission, he knew for certain that he *was* one of the chosen ones after all.

This was why he had had to suffer. This was why Sir Robert Anderson had stopped him in his work tracking down *all* whores and not just the cheap streetgirls. This was why he had been locked away. But God had intervened, it was his appointed time. Without any explanation, they had released him from the asylum, and on this seventh day after his release he had been led to Kelly.

He gazed at the sleeping woman laid out before him. He had not made God's work easy. His mind had been restless and he had not fully listened; but now that he had at last seen the light, he would do his work and do it well. The lamb would be sacrificed. He would study the writings of Moses in the book of Exodus, chapter 29. Word for word, this very night, he would carefully examine the procedures he must follow. As he read, he fed the flames with pieces of broken chair and when he was ready, he rose, removed his long-bladed knife and trod towards the bed purposefully.

Standing over Kelly, he placed the open Bible beside her head and acknowledged her silently for offering herself to Him like this. He then placed the long sharp knife at her throat and whispered, 'Kelly, *the time has come . . .*'

Slowing lifting her heavy eyelids, she mumbled drowsily, 'Have you got the fire going, sweet man?'

'Yes . . . and it's time, Kelly . . . your time . . .'

'Time?' She looked from his strangely twisted face to his arm and then to his hand. Terrified, she flinched at the sight and in that instant she realised. '*Oh Mary, Mother of Jesus . . .*' she croaked, her throat dry. '*It's you!*'

'Yes, it is I, come to heal you,' he said, offering a faint smile. Then, with his hand clasped firmly on her mouth, he once again quoted from the Bible, in hushed tones: '"*Hear the word of the Lord. Because you poured out your lust and exposed your nakedness in your promiscuity with your lovers, therefore I am going to gather all your lovers, with whom you found pleasure, those you loved as well as those you hated. I will gather them against you from all around and will strip you in front of them and they will see your nakedness.*"'

He brought his other hand to her throat and gently squeezed it. '"*I will direct my jealous anger against you, and deal with you in a fury. I will cut off your nose and ears – you will fall by my sword . . .*"'

The rumble of distant thunder was soon followed quickly by a deluge of rain as if from Heaven itself.

By morning, the storm had passed and a light drizzle saw the end of the night's downpour. John McCarthy the landlord was in his office checking his ledger when he came to Mary Kelly's name. Removing his spectacles and rubbing his tired eyes, he said, 'You'd best make number thirteen, Miller's Court, your first call, Mr Bowyer. I fear Kelly will do a runner now that Joe Barnet has moved out. If we allow her arrears to go on much longer we may well be left high and dry. Get some of the money at least, the best way you can.'

'I'll get round there straight away, guvnor,' the rent collector replied.

'Good man.' He replaced his spectacles and continued with his bookkeeping.

When Bowyer arrived at Kelly's door he was surprised not to hear any sounds of activity. At this time of day, the girl could usually be heard singing or at least moving about. He could understand her door being closed against the damp November morning, but why didn't she answer his loud knocking? Cursing his bad luck at having missed her, he stepped round the corner and spotted the broken window pane, he reached inside and pulled the makeshift curtain aside. In the gloom he could make out her mutilated corpse lying on the bed – blood everywhere – it was horrible. He panicked. His stomach heaved. 'Oh my God!' He ran as fast as he could back to the landlord's office. Gasping for breath he started to babble 'Another one . . . it's . . . Kelly . . . the Ripper . . . horrible it is . . . !'

Not wanting to believe that the worst had happened, Mr McCarthy sat his employee down and told him to take his time and be sure of what he was saying. 'I knocked at the door . . . no answer. Then I looked . . . looked through the . . . window. Blood . . . so much blood . . . even on the walls! We've gotta get back there, guv . . . please . . . come back wiv me now.'

McCarthy helped his man to his feet and once he had regathered his senses they rushed to Kelly's lodging rooms. The landlord did not have the stomach for the harrowing sight any more than Bowyer. Kelly's body, grotesquely mutilated, lay on the blood-saturated bed. Her face and body had been butchered. The two men were close to collapse as they raised the alarm.

It was the day of the Lord Mayor's Show and the city was a heaving mass. News of the murder swept through the courts and alleys. Men and women ran through the streets venting their anger, screaming with rage and indignation. And as the Mayoral procession moved into Fleet Street from Ludgate Circus the news reached the crowds lining the route. Spectators rushed from the show in their thousands heading for Dorset Street. A solid wall of police at either end denied them access but the entrance from Bell Land and Commercial Street soon became choked by groups of frenzied people. This was a scene of panic and terror as never seen before. There was a crazed, wild satanic beast in human form loose on the streets of London.

With his long dark coat covering his blood-soaked clothes, Thomas had attracted no undue attention from the folk he had passed before reaching the High Street and hailing a cab. He had been surprisingly calm as he journeyed through Holborn heading for Red Lion Square and his Uncle Charles's place of residence. On arrival he rang the doorbell calmly until the lights came on in the house and the housekeeper opened the door.

The look on Cutbush's face when he found his nephew awaiting him in the library had been a rewarding sight for Thomas. His uncle had been very angry at being disturbed at four-thirty in the morning. After instructing the housemaid to return to her rooms, he had closed the door quietly and then demanded to know what Thomas had been up to. Opening his topcoat, Thomas had given his answer to his uncle with the ghastly spectacle of his bloody clothes.

'*What have you done?*'

'I have put a prostitute out of her misery and out of the reach of simple-minded young men who may contract syphilis from her. But I am not here to boast, Uncle. I need to bathe and some fresh clothing would be most welcome.' His manner had been so matter-of-fact that Charles Cutbush had been rendered speechless.

Staggering to a chair he had covered his face muttering, 'Tell me you are fantasising, Thomas. Assure me that this is but another of your cruel, heartless stories of fiction. Please tell me it isn't true.'

'"*A good man hates lies; wicked men lie constantly and come to shame.*"'

'Please do not quote from the Bible, Thomas, I can't bear it.' His drawn ashen face was aghast. 'Would that you had sought solace from your Aunt Jacqueline instead of coming here.'

His reply had been short, to the point, and lacking any emotion whatsoever. 'I am not seeking solace, Uncle Charles. I am seeking clean clothes and a good alibi. And what could be better than here, with you, a superintendent of police? My aunt sails away to America on the tide, it is just you and I now. We must look out for each other's interests.'

With the remains of Mary Kelly in the Shoreditch mortuary, the windows of number thirteen were boarded up and the door padlocked. But, despite the police presence, droves of people still roamed through Dorset Street and along Miller's Court hoping for a glimpse of the macabre.

As soon as news of the gruesome murder was received at Scotland Yard, plans were made to have the main suspect, who was still behind bars, to be released as soon as possible. Kosminski was the second Jew to be arrested in connection with the Whitechapel murders and the Jewish community were outraged. There was great unrest in the East End of London; neighbour was turning against neighbour and the situation was turning uglier by the minute.

It was a terrifying thought: a devil in the shape of a man was walking the streets of the East End *and going unnoticed*, even though he would surely have been covered in blood. Did the police authorities know more than they were telling? Rumours were rife: were they shielding someone important? A Royal personage or a Member of Parliament? Or was the killer the innocent-looking man next door? The public were demanding action.

As soon as word reached him of this the latest and most gruesome murder, the Commissioner of the Metropolitan Police was quick off the mark. He dispatched this brief note to the Home Office for the attention of the Secretary of State: *Sir, I have to acquaint you that information has just been received that the dead body of a mutilated woman is reported to have been found this morning inside a room in a house in Dorset Street, Spitalfields. I have appointed Sir Robert Anderson to investigate this most heinous crime without delay. I can assure you that the entire resources at my disposal will be utilised forthwith to apprehend the murderer.*

The newspaper accounts of the murder once again drew much needed attention to the appalling, cramped conditions in this poorer section of London. There were approximately 80,000 people in Whitechapel alone; the whole of the East End totalling almost a million. The living conditions for the lowest class of all – the dossers and the homeless outcasts, who slept under market stalls, on staircases, in doorways and even in dustbins and lavatories for warmth – was beyond imagination.

Almost half the children of the *very* poor were not surviving beyond five years of age, and those more fortunate to survive were ragged and often separated from their parents, attending pauper schools or in Dr Barnardo's homes. The workhouse also took hundreds of them.

Children who were going to school, sometimes went crying with hunger pains and would collapse at their desks from exhaustion. Surviving *not* learning was the priority.

The injustices were overwhelming as the rich got richer and the poor got sick and died. And Jack the Ripper was playing his part to the best of his demonic activity.

Sir Robert Anderson was at Miller's Court within an hour of receiving the news of Kelly's murder and he watched with dismay as the police inspector explored the smouldering ashes in the fire grate of her room. It had been such a fierce blaze that it had melted the spout of the kettle but the only clues discovered in the search were a few badly charred remnants of women's clothing: A piece of burnt velvet; the remains of Kelly's jacket; the rim and wirework of a felt hat, and what was left of a skirt. How such a fierce fire broke out was as much a mystery to them as *any* of the sordid business. The guessing games had begun all over again.

By now, the entire populace of the capital city was screaming for the resignation of the Commissioner of the Metropolitan Police. There had to be a scape-goat if the minimum of calm was to be restored. It was the worst of all embarrassments for both the Metropolitan Police and for Scotland Yard. Having been summoned urgently, by telegram, to the home of Charles Cutbush, Chief Inspector Swanson and Sir Robert Anderson had no idea of the shock that awaited them. But they knew that Charles's nephew would be involved in it somewhere. However, when he told them what had actually happened, they were thunderstruck. Sir Robert was furious. 'Had you not gone against my wishes and secured your damned nephew's release from the asylum, the press wouldn't be having a field day. They are completely against us, and who can blame them!' He turned his back on both Cutbush and Swanson, and looked out of the window across the well-stocked flowerbeds.

'We are in a very tight spot and I could see no way out of it,' said Charles Cutbush. 'We were victims of the worst kind of blackmail and my sister-in-law is a most formidable woman. Had we not secured his release, I feel sure that she *would* have gone to the newspapers and spilt the beans on the Millwood case *and* our part in perverting the course of justice.' Cutbush kept his head down, clenching his fists tightly, his knuckles white. 'I assure you, gentlemen, my desire was also to see my nephew kept under lock and key. We may take solace from the fact that at least his aunt is on her way to the other side of the world. We shall hear no more of the Millwood case from that dreadful woman.'

'And where is Thomas now, Charles?' Swanson asked. His mood at that moment was not to let this crisis become a drama. They all must remain calm; they could not afford to lose their heads now. 'You say he was here earlier . . .'

'I have an idea where he may be, where he spends as much time as possible. I shouldn't have let him go but he left while my back was turned. I was totally appalled by what he said, as you would be too, gentleman, had you seen him at that time. And his clothes were covered in that Kelly woman's blood. To be honest I will admit I was glad when he left. My family know nothing of this, gentlemen. My children are not even aware that the strange young man who occasionally calls is their cousin.

'I have told them that he is an aspiring police student whom I have been trying to encourage. I am not proud of that side of my family. If only my brother were alive, things would be different where Thomas is concerned, I am sure of it.'

'Really? Well I cannot say that I am best pleased to have been sucked into your devious web of deceit, Cutbush!' Anderson still would not look at either man.

'I have apologised until I can apologise no more. What else can I do?'

'An apology – what good is that now! I would not like to suggest what is on my mind. I am sure you may work it out for yourself.'

'If resignation is on your mind, sir, you may put it aside. It would not improve matters one iota. I am sure you will deduce that for yourself, once your temper is down and you have had time to think sensibly.'

'Damn and blast you, man!' Anderson spun around and glared at Charles. 'Your audacity is despicable!'

'And, if I may say so, so is your reaction and behaviour, sir.'

'Where *might* your nephew have gone, Charles?' said Swanson who was strangely calm.

'Why? What is on your mind?'

'Well . . . he must be arrested immediately. Not so?'

Both men stared at him. 'Are you mad, Swanson? We shall all three be ripped apart by the public if this comes out.'

'No, Sir Robert. My reasoning is quite sound. He must be stopped. And *we* must face the consequences.' He leaned back in his chair and drew on his pipe. 'I do have a plan in which we can see him locked away *and* we retain our reputation unblemished.'

'Let's hear it!' snapped Anderson, impatiently.

'It's true we should have been more aware of his devious cunning.' He looked at Cutbush. 'You have made it clear to us in the past that he is a familiar figure, not only among the patrolling officers but also within the world of the prostitutes. It is not just us three who have been fooled. Now, with the worrisome aunt out of the way, we should expect no further interference from that quarter. We will receive public acclaim for catching the Ripper, and you may well be the unsung hero, Charles. For turning in your own nephew.'

'If it were that bloody easy why have we let it go this

far?' retorted Anderson, the tone of his voice indicating that he was warming to Swanson's reasoning.

'Because Thomas knows too much,' said Cutbush. 'Mark my words, he will sing like a canary and take pleasure from it. His cockiness is unbelievable and he fears no one.'

'Well if he wants to sing, let him. We are discussing a homicidal maniac, not a choirboy. Neither the public nor press will be in the mood to listen to a young man, who by his own uncle's hand, has been ensnared' – Swanson looked into Cutbush's face – 'who by his own uncle's hand, shall face the gallows. Face facts, Charles, you cannot protect him any longer.'

'And what of us, Swanson? How do we get out of this unscathed?' said Anderson.

'What can they do? We were called here today to be informed by Charles, that he has learned, only this very morning, that his nephew is Jack the Ripper and that he must be brought to justice.'

'And when the whores of Whitechapel hear this news? Do you think they will remain silent? Let us not forget that between some of them, a small group, I grant you, it is common knowledge that this young devil was involved with Betty Millwood. How long do you think it will take before the press reach the obvious conclusion? Namely, that we investigated the first killing, and should have incarcerated Thomas at the time. The ramifications are too serious to contemplate.'

'But Millwood is *not* and has *never* been in the picture, Sir Robert. She died of septic wounds—'

'Tell that to her relatives! Have you forgotten that

they demanded justice and insisted we investigate further? We got away with that by the skin of our teeth!'

A blanket of silence descended until Sir Robert spoke in a grave voice. 'Even if we were to render your nephew incapable of coherent speech, a course which I for one would fully endorse, others would reach the same conclusion in short time.'

'Well then, what *do* you suggest, Robert?' Swanson's optimism and confidence were waning. 'What *are* we to do?'

'For a start let's not release Kosminski. He and John Pizer are known to each other. We could suggest they were working as a team. Pizer is not under detention so we could lay the blame at his feet for this recent attack. Spread the word that they're both mad, so it won't be the gallows but the lunatic asylum.'

'We could suggest it, but could we make it stick?' said Swanson.

'It would at least give us breathing space,' Anderson raised an eyebrow. 'I take it your nephew showed no interest in accompanying his aunt to America, Charles? It could be worth our while to pay his passage.'

Cutbush broke into a wry smile. 'None could have tried harder than I. I tried eveything. I would have given half my life savings to see the back of him.' He shook his head, his lips pursed. 'My nephew believes that London *needs* him. England, for that matter. He sees himself as a crusader. I cannot begin to describe his mentality, it's beyond anything in my experience. If only I had watched over him more, spent more time with him; I would have seen the flaws in his personality. Wouldn't I?'

'Anyone could be forgiven for not taking him seriously, Charles, he seemed such a fool. Who would have thought he could be so unbelievably evil. The graphic details of this latest killing are—'

'Please, Chief Inspector,' said Cutbush, raising a hand to stop him, 'leave aside the details. I can hardly bear it.' He shook his head slowly. 'A nephew of mine capable of such evil . . . thank God my brother is not alive . . .'

'We must be decisive and find a solution,' snapped Anderson. 'Not look over our shoulders at past mistakes.' He looked at Cutbush, a new thought forming in his mind, 'I don't suppose your nephew could have come here directly *after* he'd heard from the streets what had happened and then carried out some kind of wild fantasy to shock you – could that be at all possible?'

'Would you care to look at his bloodstained clothing before I see it burned to ashes?'

Lowering himself into an armchair, Cutbush looked despairingly at his two colleagues, his eyes moist. 'How can something like this happen? He related the precise details to me as if he were reporting a bit of trifling news.' Lowering his head, he continued, his voice low. 'My God! He cut out the wretched woman's heart and cast it to a rat in the courtyard.'

There was a stunned silence. Here were three men of Scotland Yard who thought they were beyond the realms of shock. 'We *must* have him sectioned as

346

soon as possible,' Sir Robert was adamant, 'once the publicity of this killing has eased. But, it must be done in secret. If the press catch a whiff of it we are done for.'

'What do you suggest . . .' said Cutbush, a broken man '. . . how long should we wait?'

'Several days, but mark my word . . . if he is let out of your sight for one second . . .'

'No, that won't happen. I've two or three men I can trust, between them they will maintain close surveillance whenever he leaves the house, day and night. He will never get another opportunity to harm anyone.'

'And which house might that be?' said Anderson, not wishing to leave anything to chance.

'The midwife's house, the former home of his dear Aunt Jacqueline. That's where he will be hiding out – Whitehead Street.'

In that very street, at that very moment, Mary Dean was busy with her ironing, her thoughts focused on Arthur and herself living in their new home in Bow. She felt happy and carefree for the first time since her mother had passed away. Without Walter coming into her life, it was anyone's guess as to what might become of her and her little brother. She shuddered at the thought. Explaining it to her brother had been easier than she had imagined. Arthur had listened to what she had to say and instead of reacting against it, as she thought he might, he had been excited at the prospect of going to a new school in a new area where he would meet new friends. When she explained about Walter and how he would visit sometimes and stay overnight, he showed little reaction. His mind was on someone else – Harriet. His sister had promised him that she would never give up on her and they would go searching again. When she tried to suggest that Harriet might well prefer to be back in her familiar surroundings, he would have none of it.

The sudden, quiet tapping on the door brought her from her thoughts. Setting the iron down on to the stand, she hoped that Walter hadn't decided to call again unexpectedly. She was dressed in her plainest clothes and her hair hadn't been brushed out. Opening the door she was perturbed to see that Thomas had had the nerve to return so soon after he had insulted Walter. He was looking as calm and confident as ever.

'May I come in, Miss Dean? I have something I should like to discuss with you, in private.'

'Sorry, Thomas, I'm very busy with my housework,' said Mary.

'It won't take more than a few minutes, it's about Aunt Jacqueline. Did you know that she has already left and is staying overnight in Southampton, until her ship sails for America? Did she say anything to you about going to Southampton a day earlier than scheduled?'

With a mixture of relief and puzzlement at his questions, she stood aside and allowed him inside. She wanted to know more. Maybe he could throw some light on Arthur's version of Harriet's disappearance

– that she was escaping from the midwife. 'I hadn't realised your aunt was going so soon, Thomas, to be perfectly honest. Never mind a day earlier than you expected. I've not seen much of her this past week. I expect that's because she's been busy tying up loose ends. I'm sorry for you. It must 'ave been a shock.' She closed the door behind them and decided to coax more from him. 'I expect she left like that to make it easier. Easier for both of you. Saying goodbye's not easy, is it now? Harriet went off in the same way. I don't suppose you've seen anything of her, have you?'

'No, Miss Dean, I have not. And nor do I want to. My first impressions of the girl are still with me. She looks directly into my eyes – searching – and thinks I don't know it. What is she looking for, I wonder, does she hope to see my very soul?'

'No, she's partially deaf, Thomas. So she lipreads a little.'

'I said that she looks into my eyes, Miss Dean, not at my lips.'

'I can offer you a cup of tea if you'd like?' she said, getting off the subject.

'No, thank you. I shan't stay long. I intend to make my way to Southampton and try just once more to make aunt see the error of her ways. She is too old to settle in another country.'

'Well she can always come back, can't she? I'll miss her too. She was a good neighbour. Mind you . . . she seemed to put the wind up Harriet. Why do you think that might be?'

'Mary . . .' he hesitated and narrowed his eyes

349

'. . . you don't mind if I call you Mary? Miss Dean seems a trifle formal.'

'Course I don't mind, we've known each other for a long time, ever since we were kids. Not that we played together—'

'I didn't play with *any* of the children, if you remember rightly, and do you know why?'

'I can't say I ever took much notice; too busy playing hopscotch.'

'Children, especially boys, have a habit of cheating no matter what the game is. I know this because I stood back and watched from a very young age, that's why I never joined in, and they were rowdy. Do you mind if I sit down, I shan't stay long?'

'Course not. Would you like a glass of lemon water?'

'No, but thank you for asking. There is something I should like to discuss, if you can spare me a few minutes.' He was now taking on the pose of someone in authority and reminded her of a schoolteacher. 'I expect you've heard about this latest murder, in Miller's Court? They say it's the worst so far.'

'So I gather. But to tell you the honest truth, Thomas, I don't want to. It's all too horrible.'

'Which is why I'm here. It *is* horrible and I have to say that the face of your gentleman visitor still haunts me. You do realise he fits the description of the man associated with the Chapman murder?'

'Thomas, please, that gentleman had a foreign accent. I trust my friend implicitly and would thank you not to make any more accusations.'

He smiled condescendingly. 'To assume a foreign accent, Miss Dean, is not difficult.'

'Thomas, I'm very sorry that your aunt left without saying goodbye but I really don't want to get into this kind of discussion. I've got my ironing to do and I've an appointment this afternoon and—'

'With your gentleman friend,' he said, confidently.

'I don't think that's any of your business, I think you should leave now. I'm sorry but I'm not used to being alone in the house with a gentleman.'

'I'm sorry, but of course you're right. What was I thinking? It's just that now aunt isn't here to look over you I feel responsible, I apologise.' He laid a hand on her shoulder. 'I'm sorry if I offended you.' He then sat down in the chair by the fire.

'Thomas, I thought you was leaving?' By now, Mary was beginning to feel edgy and a touch afraid of him.

'Yes, but before that you asked me to sit down. I shall take each request in *turn*.' He raised his chin and adopted a posture befitting a magistrate and Mary felt *she* was on trial. 'Now, about this friend. You need not pretend or feel you have to hide anything from me. I do know where you met him and I know why he calls. I wish only to read you a small piece from the Bible. It won't take long and all will become clear. Trust me, Mary. I don't blame you for the road into which you had to turn. You have suffered a great deal this past year, but you did not allow yourself time enough to mourn. I believe this is why you strayed from the path of righteousness.'

He pulled his Bible from his coat pocket. 'Please join me by the fire, Mary. I promise this will take no more than a few minutes of your time. I know my aunt would approve, were she here.'

Frightened now, Mary glanced at the street door and this did not go unnoticed. He stood up casually, the Bible open in one hand, and positioned himself in front of the door, making her feel like his captive. He began to read. '*Stay far from men of his like, for crime is their way of life, and murder is their speciality. When a bird sees a trap being set, it stays away.*' He slowly raised his eyes to meet Mary's.

'Thomas please open the door or the window. I've been ironing and the air in this room's stuffy, and I feel slightly giddy with all this talk of murder.'

'You do look pale, Miss Dean. Or may I call you Mary?'

'Yes, Thomas, I *said* you could, Mary's fine. Now just open the door, there's a kind chap.'

'You would pass out as soon as the fresh air hit you, Mary. I am an authority on this because I read my medical books daily, as you know. I think you should lie down . . .' He spoke in a soft, caring voice. 'Go to your room and I shall fetch you a cup of weak, sweet tea. This is what any doctor would recommend.' He moved closer to her. 'If you still insist on fresh air we can open the bedroom window. That way, you will be lying on the bed when the air hits you.' Raising a hand he gestured towards the narrow staircase in the corner of the room. 'Come, now, Mary, you know I am right.'

Her heart was thumping and she felt trapped. But, he *was* being kind and so considerate ... however, something about him wasn't right. His eyes seemed glazed. She could feel herself perspiring, her armpits were soaking wet. 'I don't want to lie down, Thomas, I want to open the door, I need fresh air. As a matter of fact I think I'll go outside.'

'I wouldn't recommend it but if you must.' He stood up and moved closer to her. 'It's my opinion that you're unwell. It could be influenza. I think you should go upstairs to your room and rest.' He lifted his hand, showing the Bible to her. 'It is hard to stop a quarrel once it starts, so don't let it begin. It says so in the good book.'

He tucked the Bible under his arm and guided her gently towards the stairs. 'You are feverish, Mary, I can feel you trembling. I will go and fetch a doctor if it makes you feel easier.'

Frightened, she decided to go to her room and turn the key behind her. Upstairs she would be safe even if Thomas stayed downstairs longer than he should. She would wait for Arthur to come home from school before she ventured down. 'I *am* feverish, Thomas, you're right. Thank goodness you're a medical man, I'll take to my bed straight away, but I would prefer that you leave first.'

'As you wish, Mary. I shall place your tea in the doorway of your bedroom, will that be acceptable to you?'

Her legs about to buckle under her, she gripped the stair rail, telling herself not to be silly and that

Thomas was just a harmless fool. But still she was placing herself in jeopardy. 'Let me help you upstairs, Mary, you look as if you might faint.'

'No, I'll be fine. Just leave me be.' She climbed the stairs slowly and knew he was following her. She could sense him right behind her. When his hand touched her elbow she jerked away and pushed herself against the wall and stared into his face – a face which had a strange, distant expression.

He looked quite mad. 'I'm not going to hurt you, Mary,' he said, smiling. 'I'm only doing what my aunt would do in my place.'

'Stay away from me, Thomas. Please leave my house now.'

'But you're in no fit state to realise what's best for you. I shan't enter your chamber. I shall merely see you into it. Then I shall bring you a warm drink. Maybe I should add a little something to it, something that would help you sleep.'

'Don't you dare put anything in my drink! Don't even bring me a drink.'

He put up a hand to stop her talking. 'Very well, nothing in your drink. And if I find you are sleeping when I come up with the tray I shall fetch it back down again and leave the house.'

Seeing a way out of this, she nodded. 'I *am* tired, you're right, I should sleep. And I would be obliged if you didn't wake me if I do doze off.'

'I won't come into the room and you won't hear me leave. I shall give your best wishes to my aunt once I reach Southampton.'

Going upstairs, Mary wished she had never opened the door to him. 'Thank you, Thomas.' She went into her room, very much aware of how quiet the house had become.

Lying on her bed, with Thomas coming up the stairs, she remembered that she hadn't turned the key in the lock. Closing her eyes she feigned sleep and trusted that he would go away. She heard the creaking of the door and began to breathe as if she was in a deep sleep.

'Mary,' whispered Thomas, 'are you awake?' He came into the bedroom, placed the tea on a side table and sat on the low bedroom chair, watching her. Then, taking his Bible from his jacket pocket he began to read in silence.

His presence in the room was more than she could bear, but if only to see the back of him, she would keep up the pretence. Beads of sweat were on her brow. Hearing a shuffle as he moved round the room, pangs of terror swept through her. When she felt him unlace her boots she instantly sat up. 'What are you *doing*?'

'Taking off your boots, Mary. You were asleep and you shouldn't sleep in boots, it's not good for the circulation.' He placed her footwear under the bed and sat down on the chair again. He began to read, his voice no more than a whisper.

'*Hear the word of the Lord. Because you poured out your lust and exposed your nakedness in your promiscuity with your lovers . . . therefore I am going to gather all your lovers, with whom you found pleasure, those you loved as well as those you hated. I will gather them against you*

355

from all around and will strip you in front of them and they will see your nakedness . . .'

The sudden banging on the front door startled them both. Mary, thankful for the intrusion, caught the strange look in Thomas's eyes. 'Let whoever it is go away, Mary?' The loud banging continued and then the high-pitched voice yelled through the letter-box and was music to Mary's ears.

'Open this bloomin' door, Mary, I know yer in there! 'Urry up!'

'Harriet!' Mary jumped off the bed and was out of the room and down the stairs in a flash. When she opened the door to see the dirty unkempt face of her charge she swept her up as if she were a rag doll and hugged her tight, kissing the top of her head. 'Thank God you're safe.' Thomas was close behind her.

'What's *he* doin' 'ere?' Harriet could see Thomas standing at the foot of the stairwell.

'I shall leave you now, Mary. I'm happier now that you have someone with you, should you feel faint.' He turned to Harriet. 'You may call at my door if Miss Dean needs someone to go for the doctor. The door to the house in which my Aunt Jacqueline once lived. For that shall be my residence from now on.' He collected his hat and bade them both farewell.

'As if I'd go dahn there! You should never 'ave let 'im in 'ere, Mary.' She slammed the door shut behind him. 'You look bloomin' terrible. Wot'd he do to yer?'

'No more than read something dreadful from his Bible. He's just a lonely soul, Harriet, even more so now. His Aunt Jacqueline's left for America.'

'Bleedin' good riddance as well. Pity he never went wiv 'er.'

Mary peered at Harriet, remembering what Arthur had reported. She had told him to keep away from the midwife. 'Why, Harriet? Why's it good that the midwife's gone?'

'I don't wanna talk about it. I'll never talk about it, Mary, so don't bovver tryin'. I'm bleedin'-well glad she's gone that's all. I don't ever wanna mention 'er name agen.' She plonked herself down into the chair by the fire. 'Where's Arfer?' Rubbing her hands together by the flames, she shivered. 'Bloomin' freezin' out there, it is.'

'Harriet, where 'ave you bin? Why did you run away? We've been looking for yer. We went to the Old Jago and—'

'Fank Gawd you never got yer froat slit for yer pogue,' she said. 'Arfer should 'ave known better'n that. I went to see me muvver and sister 'cos I was missin' 'em and then I went to stop wiv the coalman 'cos he was lonely. Then when I 'eard about this uvver bleedin' murder I came straight back 'ere. Ain't safe in a stable now, is it?'

Smiling through her tears, Mary pulled a handkerchief from her skirt pocket. 'Stop swearing, Harriet. It's not clever.'

'Never said it was. So can I stop wiv yer or wot?'

'Course you can . . . Now, wash your hair and give it a good brushing, and give your body a good scrub. I've some clothes in a trunk in the loft from when I was a girl. There must be something to fit you.'

'Bleedin' 'ell! We goin' to Buckingham Palace to see the Queen?'

'Stop swearing, I said. There doesn't 'ave to be a special reason to wash and feel fresh and clean, Harriet . . .' Mary's voice trailed off and a frown appeared on her brow.

'Now wot?' said Harriet, her nose screwed up and her face pushed forward. 'Wotsa matter now?'

'Thomas,' she murmured. 'I'm glad he's gone, I'm so glad you knocked on the door when you did. He's not right, Harriet . . .' Gradually, it was sinking in. His behaviour was odd and downright impertinent, and yet to him it all seemed so natural.

'You don't 'ave to tell me! Wot 'ave I said from the first time I saw 'im? He's bonkers, and scary. I wouldn't 'ave let 'im in my 'ouse. You took a long time opening the door an' all. Wot was goin' on?'

'I'm not sure.' She suddenly felt an urgency to get away from the street – the sooner the better. 'Harriet, we're gonna be movin' house.'

'Bleedin' soddin' 'ell. Wot's come over yer, Mary? Movin'? Movin' where?'

'Go and get cleaned up Harriet. You've had your instructions. And don't waste time. I'm gonna pop down to the removal man. See if he'll move some of our furniture out today and store it in 'is yard.'

'Wot's bin goin' on?' said Harriet, dumbfounded.

'Don't ask questions. Just do as you're told or go back to the stable.'

'Awright. No need to get yer arse in a snit. Where is this 'ouse then?'

'Bow. Now then – scullery, now! You look filthy *and* you smell.'

Harriet stayed right where she was. She wiped her runny nose on the sleeve of her ragged coat. 'Wot will I be, yer 'ousemaid or yer sister?'

'That depends on how you behave. No more *swearing*; no more *clicks*; no more rude noises in public. Do all of that and you'll be my sister. And you must take a bath by the fire every five days.'

'Sounds awright. So long as I don't 'ave to share the tin barf wiv Arfer.'

'Have I ever asked you to take a bath with 'im before? Come on, get movin'.

'Nar. But you ain't told me to take a load of baths, neiver. I don't know wot's come over yer, Mary, but I'll go along wiv it. If I must.'

In Jacqueline's silent front room, Thomas read the note she had left for him. She wished him well. Said it was best that there had been no sad parting. Hoped he would work hard and save enough to visit her one fine day.

Walking slowly into the scullery, feeling a deep sense of loss, he looked out of the window into the backyard. His Aunt Jacqueline's flowerbeds had been sadly neglected and he reasoned that she had probably lost all interest in the house and garden since the day her thoughts had turned to emigrating. Going from the scullery to her bedroom he was pleased at least to see that she had left the furniture behind. Furniture that was familiar to him. On the oak linen cupboard was a

359

neat pile of bed linen and two sparkling white towels, freshly aired. Her family photographs had gone from the wall except the one of himself as a boy holding his aunt's hand. On the white line surrounding the picture she had written. *Thomas, if you are sad remember the good times gone by and the good times to come when you join me.* She signed with three kisses.

As the winter sun beamed in through a gap in the curtain, Thomas knew what he was meant to do. It was ordained that he live in his aunt's house until she returned. Thinking of Mary Dean and his original thought he realised that he had been wrong. He was not meant to do unto her as he had done by Kelly the prostitute. The young girl by the name of Harriet, with the flame-coloured hair, had been a divine intervention.

Lying on his aunt's bed, hands behind his head, legs crossed, he contemplated his future. He would arrange things with the landlord and take over the rent book. He would call upon his Uncle Charles and let him know that he was now truly ready to be independent and responsible for himself. That he would find regular and respectable work in the offices of one of the buildings around the Bank, in the City of London. To his mind, his work in Whitechapel was over. The last sacrifice had been tiring and had, in truth, drained him. Besides which, he felt sure that the prostitutes would now flee the neighbourhood and go across the river, to where his mother lived. Things were becoming clearer by the minute. His entire life had been mapped out and he had been following instructions to the letter. He, and he alone, had made Whitechapel and the surrounding east London hamlets, a safer and more respectable place to live in. For wasn't it him who began the cleansing?

Relaxed and feeling tired, he closed his eyes, comfortable and content to be in this house – where he was destined to be. Soon he would introduce himself properly to each and every neighbour and no longer preach unless he was asked. On Sundays, he would knock on doors and offer his thoughts and his Bible readings. *Seek and ye shall find. Knock and the door shall open.* No more would they call him Daft Thomas Cutbush. The boy had at last become a man. For hadn't his aunt trusted her home and contents to him? Had she not sailed away across the world knowing he was now mature enough to live a responsible and contented life? 'Well done, Aunt Jacqueline, and thank you,' he said, quietly and sincerely. 'I did not credit you with the wisdom you kept hidden away. Soon you will write to me and in my reply I shall congratulate you.'

Thomas's sense of well-being was brought on by his new-found freedom. Freedom from his mother who made his life a misery and freedom from his aunt whom he thought he could never live without. He was now independent – free! *And* he had done God's work. Almost all the world had by now heard of the slaying of whores in the back and beyond of Whitechapel. He had brought about the ruin of those women who lured away good men from their homes.

361

And he had a disciple. Three of the killings were not by his hand, he had an accomplice or two even, whom he would dearly like to meet. To talk to, to exchange views on how to make this England a better and safer place for everyone. Whores were fleeing the streets of Whitechapel and he had every reason to celebrate. He would miss his aunt, naturally, she had a good heart, and for all her faults, she did listen to him when he needed to get things off his chest.

Lighting his pipe he allowed his thoughts to drift back, to his first love, Betty Millwood. He was sorry now that he had killed the poor wretch, for although his self-diagnosis of syphilis had not been wrong, it had not worsened and the ointment was working well. But then, considering all that had happened since, he saw his Betty as being, not the cause of him cleansing the streets of whores, but the catalyst. Therefore her premature end was not for nothing. Yes, thought Thomas Cutbush, I am satisfied.

Thomas's freedom, however, was to be short-lived. Unknown to him matters had been taken out of his hands. He did not know it, but Thomas Cutbush was no longer in control of his destiny. During his time with Mary Dean, conclusions had been reached at the meeting between his uncle, Chief Inspector Swanson, and Sir Robert Anderson. It had been decided that to appease the Jewish fraternity, Kosminski would be released immediately and wheels set in motion for him and John Pizer, nicknamed Leather Apron, to soon be placed in a lunatic asylum, probably within a few weeks. Thomas Cutbush would not be named as the killer but returned to the Lambeth Infirmary until he could be arraigned at the London County Sessions and found insane, and sentenced to be detained indefinitely. In the past, Thomas had written to Lord Grimthorpe and others, including the Treasury, complaining of a Dr Brooks of Westminster, whom he had once threatened to kill for having supplied him with 'bad medicines', so, to have Thomas sectioned, would not be a problem. Having knowledge of his nephew's insane letter-writing to these men of importance, together with the fact that his mother was known to be of unsound mind, Charles Cutbush felt sure the plan was foolproof. The other two men were convinced of it. Neither would it be a problem to have John Pizer detained in an asylum. He had been ill-treating prostitutes for some time and a search of his house revealed long-bladed knives, which Pizer claimed he used in his work as a slipper-maker. There was no evidence however to link him with the murders. As for the Polish Jew, Kosminski, also residing in Whitechapel, it was also reputed that he had made public his hatred of *all* women, especially prostitutes, and had homicidal tendencies.

The detainment at Her Majesty's pleasure of Kosminski and Pizer would, all three men felt certain, calm the frenzied public. There would be no evidence of murder to convict any of them to the gallows but they would be locked up and out of the way.

Sir Robert Anderson had left Cutbush's house a calmer man than when he had arrived. They had at last come up with a solution: Kosminski and Pizer would be certified insane and locked away. And Thomas Cutbush would be watched every minute of every day, until he could be detained. Jack the Ripper's bloody crusade was at an end.

On moving day, a wave of panic rushed through Mary as she saw the last of her possessions lifted on to the removal cart. For a blinding moment she was set on instructing the man to take everything back into the house. Her parents' house, where she had lived all her life and been so very happy. Harriet, ever astute, had seen the expression on her face and placed a reassuring hand on Mary's arm. 'You didn't wanna live dahn this turnin' no more, Mary. Not now yer mum and dad 'ave gawn. Can't stop 'ere for ever, can yer? We all 'avta move abaht a bit, don't we?'

Lost for words, Mary gazed down at the skinny waif who was trying to smile. Touched by her affectionate face, she swallowed against a lump in her throat. 'I'll be all right. Where's Arthur?'

'In the backyard. We've bin pulling your dad's roses up. Got all the roots an' all. Wot d'yer want us to do abaht the other bushes?'

'Leave 'em where they are. Our childhood pets are buried there. Blackie under the hydrangea bushes and Ginger close to the lilac. We mustn't disturb them.' Her thoughts back on practicalities, she looked at the overloaded wagon. 'I don't think there's room for rose bushes, Harriet.'

'Course there is.' She narrowed her eyes and looked round for the driver. He was watering his carthorse.

'Oi, mister! Got a bit of room for Mary's dad's prize roses?'

'Chuck 'em on top, ginger nut!'

'We don't wanna chuck 'em anywhere, fank you, wot abaht next to you up front?'

Roaring with laughter, a cigarette tucked in the corner of his mouth, the driver waved a hand at her. 'Go on then, saucy mare!'

'See,' said Harriet, hands on her hips. 'Anyfing's possible, Mary, anyfing. Now then, wot abaht the cupboard under the stairs. Anyfing in there worf taking?'

'No, just some old boots and some gardening tools. The driver's coming back and keeping whatever I leave so it won't go wasted.'

'I 'ope he's paying yer for it.'

'Yes, Harriet. He knocked a bit off the removal price. It's not worth anything to me but him clearing the house cheap is.'

'Yeah?' she said, scratching her neck. 'I'll 'ava word wiv 'im anyhow.'

'No you won't, young lady, don't interfere in my business. Now go and fetch the rose bushes and Arthur, so the driver can be on 'is way.'

'No need to get aerated,' said Harriet, pleased that she'd diverted Mary from becoming sad at leaving her family home. 'Anyone'd fink I was a bleedin' slave,' she grumbled, going into the house for the last time.

With just her own handbag to carry, Mary went to the driver and gave him the address in Bow and paid him his fee. She then gave him a key to her parents' home so he could return and carry out his work. 'You've been very 'elpful, Mr Baptist, thank you,' she said. He tipped his cap and climbed up into his seat, satisfied to please. Taking the reins, he said, 'Tell ginger nut to move 'erself.'

'Don't 'ave to!' came the shrill voice from just inside the street door. 'We've got 'em now. Come on, Arfer, move yer arse!'

'She's a right cough drop, ain't she?'

'No, I ain't,' said Harriet, arriving and dragging two big rose bushes behind her. 'Get yerself dahn 'ere an' give us an 'and wiv these two, lazy sod. You should be doin' this, not me!'

Mary rolled her eyes and a certain look passed between her and the driver. 'Got your work cut out there, Mary. If you're thinking of adopting 'er, that is. Bit of a wild one, ain't she?'

'Just very spirited, Mr Baptist, that's all.'

With the rose bushes safely up front with him, the man cracked his whip and clicked his teeth, and his obedient carthorse sallied forth.

Locking the door behind her for the last time, Mary glanced at her brother and then tousled his hair. 'New beginnings, eh, Arthur?'

'Yeah, I s'pose so,' he said, choked. 'Who's gonna live in our 'ouse now, though?'

'A family who needs it as much as we did, I expect. If you like, we can come back and give 'em a sixpenny gift from the corner shop as an 'ouse warming present. That way you'd get to see 'em. What d'yer reckon?'

He looked from the door of the house to the upstairs

window of the front bedroom where his mum and dad used to sleep. 'Nar, I might not like 'em.'

'Fair enough,' she said, 'but if you 'ave a change of 'eart the house'll always be 'ere. You'll probably wanna come and visit Billy over the road. You can make your mind up then. You might fancy going in and seeing your bedroom again.'

'Dunno. Might do.'

'Oh take no notice of 'im, Mary, sulkin' sod. Come on, let's go and 'ave a butchers at this 'ouse in Bow, I 'ope there's some grub there, I'm starvin'.'

'I bet *you'd* wanna come back,' he said, glowering at Harriet.

'No I bleedin' wouldn't, this turnin's got secrets. That midwife was a witch, I reckon, and Daft Thomas is bonkers. Went in the loony bin, he did. Nah, you wouldn't catch me comin' 'ere no more, no fear. I dunno 'ow you put up wiv it this long, Mary. It's posher than Old Jago but not as safe, if you asks me.'

'The midwife's gone away, ain't she?' said Arthur, defending his birthplace. 'So it's all right now.'

'Wot if she comes back though? *You* don't know wot I know.'

'Yes, I do.'

'No, you don't.'

'Yes, I do.'

'No, you bleedin' don't. I've got her diary hidden away and there's fings in there that I reckon ain't right. Once I can read prop'ly, I'll find out, won't I?'

'I thought you *could* read properly.' He grinned at her, pleased to have caught her out.

'Well you don't know everyfing then, do yer?'

'Come on, you two. Let's go and catch the omnibus or Mr Baptist'll get there too soon before us. See if you can keep quiet for five minutes while we walk away from this turning. Have a bit of respect. I spent my whole life 'ere, don't forget.'

Harriet glanced at Arthur who rolled his eyes. Mary was getting sentimental again. 'I can't favom you at times, Mary Dean.'

'Well, that's all right, Harriet, 'cos I can't fathom you neither.'

Arriving in front of number 41 Bow Villas, Harriet let out a low whistle. 'Bleedin' 'ell, Mary, it's a bit posh, innit?' Harriet was staring up at the tall, narrow terraced house in Bow. 'There ain't no paint peeling off!'

Amused by her honesty, Walter, who had arrived by hansom cab a few minutes earlier, smiled broadly at Mary. 'We may assume she likes it then?'

'Course I bleedin' like it. What about you, Arfer? You've gone a bit quiet.'

'I'm finkin'. I'm finkin' that it'll be good not 'avin' to share a bedroom with *you*.'

'You will the first night. I ain't sleeping on me own till I know there ain't no ghosts. Like it or lump it.'

There was no more to be said. Handing Mary the keys, Walter's expression said it all. He was making a commitment and a vow to look after her every need and to spend as much time with her as he possibly could. Pushing the key into the lock, she eased the heavy door open and stepped inside her new home and into her new life. Lost for words she was mesmerised by her surroundings. It was a far cry from what she had been used to. On the polished oak floor lay a richly patterned carpet and on the walls, red and green flower motif wallpaper highlighted by the milky glass wall lights and on the far wall, leading into the small old garden, was a beautiful stained-glass window through which the sun shone, casting dappled rays of light.

'Stone me blind,' murmured Harriet. 'We can't live 'ere. It's too bleedin' posh. An' it don't smell of anyfing but . . .' she sniffed the air and pulled a face, 'polish?'

'It's beautiful,' whispered Mary to Walter as she caught his eyes. 'I love it.'

'Mind you,' said Harriet, pushing the carpet back with her toe. 'This floor'll be good for dancing on. Better'n the pavements. I could never get the 'ang on doing a spin on the pavement.'

'Now she's gonna say she's a dancer,' said Arthur, mindful of her boasting.

'Course I am. Watch this.' She pulled the carpet back and gracefully bowed to her audience of three. Walter was both amused and touched by the skinny ginger waif.

'She'll be saying she can play the piana next . . .' said Arthur, begrudgingly. All he wanted to do was explore the rest of the house. 'Can't we . . . go . . . ?' his voice trailed off as he watched in astonishment as

Harriet danced . . . springing and leaping through the air as if she were a leaf blowing in a warm breeze. Her feet hardly ever seeming to touch the ground she began to hum a tune as she quickened her pace and danced towards the staircase. Before she arrived there, she began to sing, surprising them all.

'*Yes, Jesus loves me. Yes, Jesus loves me. Yes, Jesus loves me,*
The Bi-ble tells me so!
So . . . come now, and join us, come now, and join us,
Come now, and join our happy band.
Jesus loves me, Jesus loves me, Jesus loves me,
To him the little children go!'

'She's gone bonkers,' murmured Arthur, 'that's a religious song.'

'Shush. It's all she knows,' whispered Mary. 'It's what the Salvation Army band sing.'

Still in her own world, Harriet continued to dance and sing as she made her way upstairs and out of view. 'Well,' said Mary, 'I never knew she could dance like that.'

'She most likely danced for her supper, my love,' said Walter. 'Outside the music halls. Plenty of children do . . . but I've never seen one who could pass so lightly through the air.' He glanced at Mary who had gone quiet. 'Maybe I should leave you to settle in, my sweet,' he said, feeling like an intruder in this touching scene.

'Yeah . . .' said Mary. 'If that's all right with you. It's gonna take a while for us to get our things inside and packed away. Without saying another word, he kissed her lightly on the cheek and left.

'D'yer fink we'll be all right in this 'ouse, Mary?' said Arthur, looking around him.

'We'll soon find out, won't we? If not, we'll move somewhere else. Nothing's forever, sweetheart – as we both full know.'

'Arfer! Git up 'ere and 'ave a look at this then! I've chose my bedroom! Bleedin' 'ansome it is!'

Chuckling, Mary said, 'I think we'll be happy wherever we are . . . while she's around.'

'Yeah,' he said, grinning. 'I fink so as well.' With that he was away, bounding up the stairs eager to explore.

By herself in her lovely surroundings, Mary looked at the key in her hand and shed a private tear. 'Thank you, Lord Jesus,' she whispered. 'Thank you.'

Postscript

Jacqueline the Midwife sailed away to America and was not heard of again. Her nephew, Thomas Cutbush, was eventually placed in the Lambeth Infirmary but escaped twice. He was finally arrested in March 1891 and charged with the malicious wounding of Florence Grace Johnson and attempting to wound Isabella Fraser Anderson in Kennington. He was sentenced to be detained during Her Majesty's pleasure and died in Broadmoor prison. Thomas's uncle, Charles Cutbush of Scotland Yard, ended his life by shooting himself in the head while in his own kitchen and in front of his own daughter.

Sir Arthur Conan Doyle, best known as the creator of Sherlock Holmes and a searcher for political and theological truth, gave his opinion on the infamous Jack the Ripper. He thought it quite possible that the murderer could be someone dressed as a midwife which would allow whoever it was to move around the East End of London at night, rushing from one place to another, carrying a black surgical bag and covered in blood. This caused him to be the butt of mockery and embarrassment at the time, but fortunately, mockery and embarrassment was something that did not bring down Conan Doyle.